THE HAG

THE BLOODLETTER COLLECTIONS

II

ERIK HENRY VICK

RATATOSKR PUBLISHING

NEW YORK

RATATOSKR PUBLISHING
769 BROADWAY #1060
MANHATTAN, NY 10003

THE HAG/ ERIK HENRY VICK. -- 1ST ED.
ISBN 978-0-9990795-8-4

Table of Contents

For Jackson W. Barnett, with my thanks, and
for the residents of Lake Lida, Minnesota.

It doesn't matter what you pretend, she'll wreck it
It doesn't matter what you defend, she'll wreck it
It doesn't matter how you live your life
Doesn't matter anymore to your wife
Doesn't matter even how you die,
she'll wreck that too

—Dave Mustaine

My angel's left me, sorrows are my own
Now I'm here, with the Devil on my own
Just like a churchyard shadow, craving after me
It's only there to terrify my mind,
a black swan keeps haunting me.

—Dave Mustaine

I hope you enjoy *THE HAG.* If so, please consider joining my Readers Group—details can be found at the end of the last chapter.

BOOK ONE:
WRECKER

Chapter 1

1986

I

As the placid surface of Genosgwa Lake began to chop, Greg glanced over his shoulder to judge how far he was from his grandparents' dock. He was almost halfway across the lake, and the mild gray sky had turned dark and ugly.

Greg didn't like bad storms, even though the storms in Western New York were nothing compared to the ones in his Florida hometown. He gazed toward the shore opposite his grandparents' lake house and tried to guess how far he'd have to travel to get there.

A small convenience store stood on that bank. Well, it wasn't right on the shore or anything, but it was a short walk from where the waves lapped at the small beach. It was close enough that in the evenings, he could read the neon sign for the store as if it were next door.

He dithered, trying to decide whether to turn back or risk being caught out in the storm. On the one hand, he was already damp as a result of horsing around in the kayak before he set out, but storms could be freezing on the lake. Regardless of the rain, his grandfather had given him five dollars for candy.

Five *whole* dollars.

His parents had gone shopping for the afternoon, and they would make him give the five dollars back on their return. No question there, not without serious pleading. Not only would they want him to return the money, but they wouldn't want him to have five dollars' worth of candy even if they allowed him to keep the Franklin. Not in one afternoon, not in one week.

He glanced up at the sky, trying to judge whether the ugly, purple-black clouds meant business or not. In Florida, there would have been no question. In Florida, dark clouds indicated a sky-shattering thunderstorm—usually within the next fifteen minutes. But at the lake, a dark, ugly sky could mean nothing at all.

Again, he glanced over his shoulder at the yellow and white dock his grandfather maintained with precision. Some docks on the lake had faded paint or missing slats, but not his grandpa's dock. His dock was pristine, year after year.

Greg twisted back around and looked at the far shore over the bow of his red kayak. He couldn't tell for sure—he wasn't good with distance—but he thought he was halfway. He glanced down at the pocket of his bathing suit, where the five-dollar bill lay nestled inside a Ziploc bag.

"What do I do?" he asked no one.

As if in answer, a cold wind gusted at him from behind, and he shivered. He couldn't remember the last time he'd gone swimming in Florida and had gotten cold. It was hard to understand why people would want to have a lake house in a state where you could only swim two-and-a-half months out of the year—and freeze while you did it part of that short time—but there was no figuring out adults.

If he were still in Florida, that same cold wind would mean that the coming thunderstorm would be a bad one. But up on Genosgwa Lake, the same cold wind might mean nothing at all.

The five-dollar bill seemed heavy, hot.

It's now or never, kiddo. If you don't go, your daddy will make you give it back, and if you have to give it back, no candy.

"Yeah, but…those clouds look like they mean business," he muttered. The kids back home would make fun of him for talking to himself, but it was just something he did. His mom called the voice his invisible friend. Greg didn't know about that, he seemed real—even if Greg hadn't ever learned his name.

Do you want the candy or not?

"Of course I want the candy! Don't be an idiot."

Do it, Greg. Do it, do it, do it.

"But what about the storm?"

Good grief, kid. I'm telling you if you don't go now, no candy. I'll ask you once more: do you want the candy or not?

His imaginary friend seemed…different somehow since they'd arrived in New York. A little less understanding, a little more insistent. A little meaner. *Why is that*? he wondered.

He shifted his position and dipped the paddle into the water but withdrew it without taking a stroke. "I don't even know what types of candy they have." That sounded whiny, even to his own ears.

Come on, Greggy. Get it together. If you want candy, put that paddle in the water and get moving. Even if the storm comes, you're halfway there already. How wet could you get?

"But it will be cold."

Candy. Candy. Candy, candy, candy.

"Yeah, yeah. Candy."

Look, boyo, if you turn back now, you will lose that five-dollar bill. You know it, I know it. Your mom and dad will never let you buy five dollars' worth of candy, even if they let you keep the bill—which they won't. Your dad will say five dollars is too much for a boy of eleven and make you give it back to your grandpa.

"I know. Trust me, I know that all too well." Greg scratched his ear. He didn't like his friend's new habit of calling him things such as "boyo" or "sport" either.

So what are you waiting for? *Why are you sitting here talking to me*?

With a shrug, Greg dug at the water with the kayak's paddle. He dug hard, making long strokes through the water, leaning back as he pulled. The kayak skimmed across the surface of the water like a sleek torpedo running at the surface.

He made it a game, pretending he was racing in the Olympics, and he was out front in the gold-medal race. Greg could almost hear the crowd cheering.

He kept his eyes on the far shore, which grew nearer and nearer with each pull of his arms. He wasn't looking at the convenience store, he was looking at the line where the shore turned into someone's lawn. That was his finish line.

The only problem was, Greg was a horrible judge of distance, and when the rain fell, he had just reached the actual center of the lake. Fat, cold raindrops slapped and splattered all over his body and made the temperature out on the lake feel colder in an instant.

Greg stopped paddling and peered over his shoulder at his grandparents' lake house. The yellow and white building stood out as if bathed with Batman's spotlight—as if it were the only safe place left in the world. Despite not paddling, the kayak continued to glide through the choppy water, carrying him farther and farther away from warmth and his grandmother's cookies. *Cookies aren't candy, but they're almost as good.*

Greg glanced in the direction he was traveling, sure he must be almost there, but he wasn't. It appeared each shore was the same distance away, and the rain seemed colder, wetter.

"Great idea," he muttered. "Try to race the storm to get candy. Well, tell me something, smarty-pants. How much candy can I enjoy if I'm at the bottom of this lake?"

Aw, is little Greggy scared? Does the storm terrify you?

"Shut up! Why do I ever listen to you? You think you're so smart, but you're not. You're dumb."

Yes, I'm the dumb one... So, besides calling me names, what are you going to do, sport?

Greg rested the kayak's paddle across his lap and lifted his shoulders. Again, he glanced over his shoulder at the yellow and white lake house, and again, he pivoted his head back toward the other shore.

Is looking back and forth helping? Because I can stop making suggestions here... You know, because I'm dumb.

Greg dithered, unsure of which direction to go. He was tired of talking to his invisible, nameless friend, but when it came right down to it, who else was he going to ask for help? The lake?

With a shake of his head, Greg sighed. "Okay, okay. I'm sorry, okay? I'm sorry I called you dumb. Now, will you tell me which way to go?"

You remember why you listen to me? It's okay for me to make suggestions?

"I said I was sorry. What more do you want?"

Hmmm. Let's see…should we start with you telling me how smart I am? It seems only fair and right since you felt justified in telling me how dumb I was.

"I know you're smart, I was frustrated."

Hmmm. I suppose that will have to do, but we must work on your ability to apologize.

"For an invisible friend, you sure do enjoy busting a guy's balls."

You know this from your extensive experience with other invisible friends?

Greg sighed. The wind at his back seemed to have dropped ten degrees in temperature, and the raindrops were falling harder. He thought the sting that came with the drops was ice falling with it. "Come on! It's summer!" he shouted.

Was that directed at me?

"You know it wasn't! Tell me what to do, I'm cold."

Say please.

"Please!" Greg snapped.

Say pretty please.

Greg stuck his paddle in the water again but withdrew it without taking a stroke. "Pretty please," he grated.

That's better.

Greg suppressed a sigh. *Of all the invisible friends in the world, I had to get one who's a smartass.*

You know I can hear your thoughts, right?

A sigh gusted out of Greg despite his best efforts.

Relax, Maddie McMadhead. You're halfway across, you might as well go to the other side and get your candy because the same amount of rain will fall on you no matter which way you go.

"But—"

Just do it, Greg. Do it, do it, do it.

Greg dipped his paddle into the water and pulled for the far shore. The rain lashed at his back, so cold and coming so hard that it felt like hail. "At least this way, the wind is helping me, right?"

You're not as dumb as you look, kiddo.

"If you're my imaginary friend, why aren't you nicer to me?"

Imaginary? Who said I was imaginary? *I am invisible… I suppose that much is obvious even to someone of your determined lack of smarts.*

"Imaginary, invisible. What's the difference?"

From my point of view, the difference is enormous.

"Whatever. Why can't you be nice? You were nicer back in Florida."

You think I'm being mean? Kids these days… You're so soft. We need to toughen you up, chump.

Greg shook his head but kept his mouth shut. He had to tilt his face down toward the front deck of the kayak because of the stinging rain. He no longer pretended at being in the Olympics, but he pulled just as hard.

Greg Canton hated the rain, and in his effort to minimize its impact, he never saw the slimy, greenish-gray hand rising from the water in front of him.

2

Elizabet Canton looked out the large bay window as the storm broke. Greg's red kayak shuttled up and down on the chop building out in the center of the lake. "Joe, I wish you hadn't given the boy five dollars and told him he could row across the lake. You know his parents wouldn't like him taking that much money from you, and, now he's trapped out in the middle of the lake during a storm that promises to be ugly."

Joe Canton grunted and glanced out the bay window himself. "He'll be fine. Boys his age are always fine, and it's only a little rain." But as soon as he said it, a purple bolt of lightning crackled across the sky, briefly illuminating the bruise-colored clouds.

"Only a little rain? Look at that sky, Joe. Can't you see how rough the lake is getting, and there he is, our grandson, out in the middle of it in a plastic kayak!"

Joe grunted again but knew better than to keep arguing. At any rate, there was the off chance that she might be right.

"You go out there, Joe Canton. Take the fishing boat and go get him."

"Now, Elizabet, let's wait a moment. You know how the storms come and go during the summer. Hell, half the time the storms blow themselves out in the first two minutes."

She whirled to face him, and her face was all scrunched up in that way that meant he'd already lost. "Joe Canton!"

With a sigh and yet another grunt, Joe pushed himself out of his comfortable chair. Holding up a hand to forestall any other comments, Joe headed toward the door to the back porch. "Yes, dear. Just let me get on my shoes and get the boat out of the boathouse. Won't take a moment."

"You'd already be on the water if you had listened to me in the first place."

"Yes, dear."

"Can't understand why he doesn't start with that," Elizabet muttered—but loud enough for Joe to hear. As he went through the door into the porch, she smiled lovingly at his back.

3

Mason Harper stood at his grandmother's big bay window, watching the storm roll in. A grin spread across his face—the dope from next door was out on the lake in his stupid little red kayak.

He knew what came next. *She* came next.

"Mason, come away from that window. That storm looks to be a doozy," called his grandmother from the kitchen.

He rolled his eyes but raised a hand to wave—indicating that he heard her, though he didn't move a single step away from the window. His gaze tracked the Canton kid's progress, and his grin stretched. The little red kayak would be close to the middle of the lake when the storm hit. Mason was almost sure of it.

It was all part of the trap—all arranged to give her the best opportunity to…make introductions.

"Mason Harper! Thirteen is not too old for me to take you over my knee. You listen to me now!"

"Coming, Grandma." His gaze lingered on the red kayak cutting through the water. He wanted to watch the start of it all.

More than anything else, though, Mason wanted to see *her* again.

4

His little red kayak stopped dead in the water, and Greg's momentum carried him forward, slamming him into the lip of the kayak's cockpit. His breath exploded out of him, and he almost lost the paddle into the depths of the lake.

Tears filled his eyes, but through them, he saw something gray and slimy on the point of the kayak. He tried to draw air into his lungs, tried to gasp for breath, but he couldn't. His stomach hurt.

I don't know, champ. Might be that your stomach hurts now, but if you don't get it together soon, I'll bet a lot more of you will hurt.

With his free hand, Greg grabbed his belly, and with the other, he held onto the paddle. His lungs burned, but he still couldn't force air into them.

The kayak lurched as if the bow were being pulled under, and Greg threw his weight back, which only forced him to slide farther forward into the cockpit of the kayak until he could no longer sit up. He thrashed with the arm holding the paddle, and the other end of it clunked into the hull of the little red boat again and again. The bow continued to slant into the water, and panic gripped him.

He pressed hard with his legs, forcing himself back into a seated position, and pawed the tears out of his eyes. The kayak tilted at a stomach-wrenching angle, and the dark water of the lake lapped over the bow.

He grabbed the paddle with both hands and shoved at the water, trying to propel the boat backward—away from whatever had snagged the bow and was pulling it under the water. *Fishing line, maybe, or an old boat anchor and its rope, kicked up by the storm.*

I don't think so, captain.

He didn't have time to reply—or perhaps the will to argue with his invisible friend. He continued to chop at the water in long, panic-driven sweeps of the paddle.

The bow of the kayak continued to slide into the dark depths of the lake, and with the chop brought on by the storm, cold lake water was already pouring into the cockpit. *Help me*!

I'm not sure what you expect me to do, kiddo, but I will tell you that what you are doing isn't working. You aren't snagged on fishing line or an old abandoned anchor. Whatever is pulling you down, it has a will of its own. The harder you slap at the water with that oar, the harder it's dragging you down.

Greg didn't stop, though. He couldn't, his panic would not let him. *I'm getting out of this boat*!

Hmmm. I wouldn't do that. I would do something else—anything but get into the water. Trust me, kiddo.

Do what? Don't paddle, don't dive in the water, then do what? Greg's eyes scanned the surrounding water, his brain supplying the image of sharks lurking under the surface, even though he knew there were no sharks in Grandma and Grandpa's lake. *Sharks don't even live in freshwater.*

Sharks? Who said anything about sharks? I don't want to be a nag, but you're still flailing at the water with that paddle as if it's an ax, and the lake is a woodpile. Do you imagine it's helping?

Greg's heart was in his throat, making it difficult to swallow. "Tell me what to do!" he shouted.

I wouldn't do that, either, Greg. I wouldn't speak out loud, were I you.

Greg's head swiveled back and forth, searching for something—anything—that might help him, or he could use, but there was nothing. He was in the middle of the lake, after all.

If you keep on as you are, the kayak will fill with water, and if that happens, you'll be in the water with her.

Who? I'll be in the water with who?

The Woman in White. The Lady in the Lake, if you'd rather.

Greg finally convinced his arms to stop, to rest the kayak's paddle across his lap, but kept both hands on it, his knuckles shining white in the dim light. *Either help me or shut up!*

I'll overlook that because of how scared you are, but my patience does have bounds, kid. All I do is help you. Such as right now…I told you not to get in the water, didn't I?

Yes! And I listened! Tell me what to do next!

Above his head, the sky split, and purple lightning danced across it. Thunder rumbled, sounding far away—almost an afterthought—nothing close to the brutal growl of thunder in Florida.

His friend had been right, though. As soon as he stopped paddling, the boat leveled out. It made little sense. *If something is pulling the bow down and I paddle backward, that should make the boat stop bucking, right?*

Not if that something pulls harder when you paddle. Never thought of that, did you?

Tell me what to do! Tell me…tell me how to get away!

Ah, finally, a good question. Let's see…how to get away…okay, I can do this… Oh, it's so easy! Give her whatever she wants.

What does she want? The bow of the boat broke the rough surface of the lake. A hand wrapped around the point—a gray, dead-looking hand with long cracked fingernails.

Want? How would I know?

How do I give her what she wants, if you don't know what she wants? The fingers on the hand relaxed but then clenched the pointed bow of the little red kayak and shook it back and forth with more violence than it had before.

Look, kiddo, I'm not omnipotent here—or is it omniscient? I always get those two mixed up.

Frustration boiled in Greg's throat. His imaginary friend was getting to be a pain.

Back to that? I told you—

Shut up! Just shut up so I can think! He slammed back and forth in the cockpit of the red plastic boat. Without conscious thought, he shifted his hands on the paddle until he held it as he would a baseball bat, and then he swung for the fences.

5

Joe sat in the right rear corner of his twelve-foot Alumacraft fishing boat. He had onc arm on the starboard gunnel and the other steady hand on the throttle of his Mercury outboard. His gaze was riveted to the little red kayak in the center of the lake.

The kayak was shaking side to side and pitching forward and back at the same time—much more than the chop of the water indicated. Greg still held the paddle but wasn't using it. "What's he doing?" Joe muttered.

As Joe watched, the boy took the kayak paddle in a two-handed grip as if he were holding a baseball bat and swung it hard at the bow of the kayak. The wide blade on the end of the paddle hit the point of the bow with a solid-sounding *thunk*. For a moment, the kayak stopped thrashing on the surface of the lake, but then it began again, same as before, but with greater violence.

Joe twisted the throttle, and the Mercury responded with a roar. He didn't know what was going on out there, but any fool could see that Greg was in trouble.

6

Greg slammed the paddle into the disgusting hand holding onto the bow, and the hand disappeared under the waves. His eyes danced around the kayak, peering into the black depths of the lake.

After a moment, the hand slapped across the deck of the kayak halfway between the bow and the cockpit where Greg sat, and along with it came a long forearm the color of moldy, decaying cabbage. Once the creature got a grip on the opposite edge of the boat, the boat rocked from side to side and pitched forward and back like a bucking bronco.

Greg's teeth slammed together on his tongue, and red splotches flashed before his eyes. He kept his grip on the paddle, however, and this time raised it straight above his head before bringing it down like a samurai swinging his sword.

The blade hit edge-on, square in the middle of the forearm, making the sound of an ax chopping into a wet log. The blade sank into the spongy flesh about a quarter of an inch, releasing a noxious odor. A strange noise came from underneath the boat—part scream of rage, part shriek of pain—but the arm didn't let go.

"Leave me alone!" Greg shrieked. He jerked the paddle high into the air and brought it down again, the blade whistling through the wind. His blow struck above the wrist with enough force to send a shockwave coursing up his arms.

The thing in the water shrieked a second time, but this time it was much louder—as though it were right up next to the boat.

Greg jerked the paddle out of the spongy gray flesh, and it made the same squelching sound as when he pulled his foot from thick mud. "Get off!" He brought the paddle down, again and again, putting as much force behind each blow as he could. With each strike, the thing in the water made the shrieking noise, and each time it did, it sounded louder and angrier.

Peering into the water to his right, he could see stringy, greenish-black strands of something—maybe hair—moving in a sinuous manner, though knotted and snarled. Beneath it, he thought he could see the gray outline of a person's shoulders.

He shifted to his right and brought the paddle down, blade flat to the water, onto the mass of black strands. The paddle made a loud slapping noise, but he hit nothing but water.

The thing in the water tilted her head back and glared at him with hate-filled eyes. Her irises were the color of dank graveyard earth, and the sickly yellow sclera of her eyes glowed in the water. The skin of her face bore a greenish tint over the mottled gray and black of decaying flesh. Her nose fluttered to the side as though it had been broken one too many times. Below her nose was a lipless slit that must have served as her mouth. She opened her mouth and shrieked, exposing ugly, crooked fangs—fangs that looked sharp enough to puncture steel.

Greg screamed in mindless terror, lifted the paddle above his head, and rained a frenzy of blows down on her forearm. He struck her again and again and again, each strike sending a numbing jolt racing up both of his arms, and each blow eliciting another shriek from the monster in the water.

Her forearm looked as if it had lost a battle with the propeller of a boat—deep cuts and gouges appeared at random intervals, and out of them a viscous ichor dribbled and mixed with the water from the rain and the lake.

Greg continued to chop at her arm, bringing the paddle down on her forearm faster and faster, harder and harder. He was screaming the same phrase over and over, "Go away!"

She let go of the kayak and jerked her arm back into the black water, but she continued to float there, staring daggers of hate up at Greg. He changed his grip on the paddle and pulled for the other shore as hard as he could. Tears streamed down his face, and he continued to scream "go away" like it was a mantra of redemption.

He felt the impact the first time he dipped the paddle into the water on the right side of his kayak, but he kept going, kept pulling. Greg dug deep into the water on the left side and hauled back with all of his strength. He switched sides and dug deep into the water of the right side, but the paddle stopped dead in the water.

7

John Morton slid into the booth across from Tom Walton. He glanced around Jenny's Diner, a small smile creasing his face. "Never changes, does it?"

Tom cocked his head to the side and treated him to a wry grin. "Some things change, John. You for instance…I'm not sure you've ever been on time for one of these things, let alone early."

John chuckled. "A man can't get too predictable."

"How is Izzy? Your son?"

A tremor twitched across John's face—his flesh-and-blood son had died in Vietnam in 1972, though the fourteen years hadn't dulled his pain in the least. He glanced away. "Isabel is doing great—especially since we took in our foster-son, Eddie. How's Janet? The kids?"

"All good." Tom cleared his throat. "Sorry about—"

"So, what do you think of this new Sherriff?"

"Well, going strictly by the election results he's the right man for the job, but other than that…" Tom said in a dry tone. "What about you?"

John shrugged and put his thick hands on the table on either side of his plate. "He's no Bobby Jefferson."

"That he ain't."

Jenny strolled over and put her hand on her hip. "I guess I better go check."

Tom cocked an eyebrow at her. "Check what, Jenny?"

She threw a wink at Tom and turned a stoic gaze on John. "I better go check and see if Hell's frozen over. I don't think you've ever been on time to anything in your life, John Morton."

John chuckled and shook his head.

"I guess it is possible to teach an old dog new tricks," said Jenny, pulling an order pad out of her apron. "Anyone else coming today, or do you two want to order?"

"I guess it's only the two of us."

"That Dave Wallace has never once stepped in here. Not once."

John shook his head.

"They broke the mold after Bobby," said Tom.

"That they did. Matt, too."

It had been seven years since the murders in Oneka Falls, but some days it felt much more recent to John. He cleared his throat. "Good men are hard to find."

"Present company excepted," said Jenny. "Although, why you'd want a man, John Morton, I'll never understand. Me on the other hand…"

"Jenny, I bet you have them lined up from here to Buffalo," said Tom with a grin.

Jenny almost blushed. *Almost.* "Yeah, yeah. What do you two bastions of the law want to eat?"

"Almost got her, Tom," said John with a grin.

"Liver and pig ears for John, then. How about you Tom?"

With a grin, Tom winked at John. "I'll have what he's having."

"You've been coming here too long, boys. You know all my pranks." Jenny jotted their orders down. The whole business of taking their orders was ninety percent joke, and ten percent a chance for them to order something new.

They never did.

"Give me the usual few minutes."

"I'll tell you, Jenny, ninety-minute waits for two cheeseburgers seems extravagant."

Jenny had half-turned to walk away but stopped, pulled out her pad, and wrote something on it. "Extra pig ears for Tom." Without another word, she turned and walked through the swinging doors into the kitchen.

John's gaze lingered on the swinging doors. "I miss Bobby's weekly meetings."

Tom nodded. "Wallace doesn't even seem aware we exist."

"Or care. He ain't no Bobby Jefferson."

"Nope, but you already said that." Tom leaned back and heaved a sigh. "Anything on your missing persons?"

"You mean the boy and girl that disappeared back in 1979?"

Tom arched an eyebrow. "You have others?"

"Well, now that you mention it, no. And to answer your question, I've got nothing. Never had nothing, don't expect to ever have nothing." John twitched his shoulders in a shrug. "You?"

"Not a thing. I don't much like it, but at the same time, I don't know what to do about it. At least those families over in Oneka Falls either got their kids back or found out what happened. Well, sort of, anyway."

"Ayup. Not that the family of my two care, but the community sure would appreciate knowing what happened to them."

"Yeah. Everything points to Ferguson—I mean Gray—but until we have proof…" Tom shook his head.

"Exactly. I'm not sure we ever will. Have you heard anything about the search for Gray's girlfriend?"

"No." Tom cleared his throat and leaned forward as though to whisper a secret. "I'll tell you, John, since Jonas Gregory left the NYSP, it appears the case is dead."

"Ayup. He drove things for a while, but… I still don't understand how all that went down up at the hospital."

"Neither do I. Matt Greshin was a big man. Armed, experienced." Tom shook his head again. "And by all accounts, Gray's girlfriend wasn't very big. I can see how she might've gotten Jim Cartwright—sneak in there while he's asleep and do the deed, him being already hurt—but Matt was wide awake and already amped up from the fight with Gray."

"We've got to be missing something."

Tom spread his hands. "Unless we find her, I doubt we'll ever understand what happened."

"Ayup. And too much from that timeframe fits in that category. At least that Ferguson bastard got locked up and won't ever get out."

"You mean Gray." A slow smile broke across his face, and Tom chuckled. "Want to hear what I heard about his stay in Sing Sing? He's playing crazy to stay out of general population."

John shrugged and smiled. "It doesn't surprise me a tremendous amount, Tom. I don't expect a man who hides up in the trees to shoot women and children would be much other than a coward."

Jenny came bustling through the swinging door with their lunches.

Neither one of them had to eat pig ears.

8

Fear surged in Joe's mind, and adrenaline dumped into his bloodstream in copious amounts. His grandson swung the paddle up and down, up and down, as fast as he could. He kept striking at the front of the kayak, and Joe saw something thin and gray wrapped around the bow of the little red boat. *Can't be a snake,* Joe thought. *No snakes here. Innertube*? He twisted the throttle to wide open, and the light aluminum fishing boat leaped forward.

As he got closer, Greg's screams reached him over the whine of the outboard. The boy started paddling hard, reaching deep into the water and pulling. On his second stroke on the right side, however, the paddle stopped dead in the water. Greg pulled and pulled, but he couldn't budge the plastic thing.

"What the hell?" Joe murmured.

9

Greg jerked at the paddle but that didn't help. He wiggled it side to side and then pulled straight up, but that only sent the kayak skittering sideways across the choppy lake.

Let go of it, boyo.

"Are you crazy?" Greg shouted.

It's the only way.

No way! Greg tried to twist the paddle, but the woman in the water held the blade, and he only had the part in the middle—plus his hands were wet, and so was the plastic paddle. He pulled the kayak sideways through the water and jerked the oar straight up. He couldn't move the thing in any direction.

"Let go!" he screamed. Panic clawed at him, and he thrashed the paddle back and forth, up and down, left to right. Nothing made any difference.

The thing in the water pulled the paddle straight down, and Greg's only choice was to either let go or follow it into the water. He slackened his grip and the paddle slid through his hands. He watched it sink beneath the waves, and his stomach with it. *Now what*?

See? *Now she's gone away. Now's your chance to escape.*

Greg scoffed and slapped his hand flat on the surface of the red kayak. *That's your big plan*? *Tell me, genius, how am I supposed to get away without the paddle*?

Well, I'll tell you, sport: I'm not here to solve all of your problems for you.

"Stop helping me! Stop talking to me!" Greg's panic seemed distant, replaced by fury. He considered dipping his hands into the water and paddling, but he didn't want that gross hand wrapped around his wrist. He didn't want that…that…*dead* woman pulling him into the water with her.

Then he heard it or rather *paid attention to it*. The sound of an outboard motor.

10

Joe's mouth dropped open as the paddle slid through Greg's hands. He already had the little Mercury outboard wide open—there was nothing more he could do to get there faster.

Over the sound of the motor, and the waves slapping against the bow of the aluminum hull, Greg's screams were thin, barely audible, but Joe heard them. He glanced at the Mercury. "Come on, you bastard! Faster!"

He snapped his gaze back to Greg and the red kayak. Something broke the surface of the water behind Greg and to his left, something dark gray with a hint of green. "What in the hell? Is that an *arm*?"

His heart skipped a beat, and his breath came in ragged gasps. He no longer saw anything but his grandson and the red kayak…and the arm coming up out of the water to grab him.

II

Greg stared into the water to the right of the kayak, willing his eyes to see into the depths, to discern her form from the blackness of the water. All he could think about was the hate in the woman's eyes. He didn't understand why she would hate him, but she did.

He'd forgotten about the cold wind, the icy rain. Greg had forgotten about the candy, the five-dollar bill, his parents—even the yellow and white cabin. He no longer felt the chill, but he was freezing.

Her hand was colder.

The hand slapped down on his left shoulder like a wet snowball, and Greg shrieked at the top of his lungs. He swept his hand over hers, trying to dislodge her grip, trying to shove her away, but he might as well have tried to dislodge gravity's grip, to shove the planet away.

She pulled him back, toward the water, toward the black depths. Greg slammed his hands down into the cockpit of the kayak and wedged them underneath the deck of the boat. His head swiveled back and forth like a dog with a chew toy, looking for his grandfather. He could still hear the whine of the outboard motor, and now the sound of the hull slicing through the choppy water was audible as well.

But she continued to pull him back, back, back—as inexorable as the sun rising in the morning. His ploy of holding onto the kayak was doing nothing. She pulled and pulled, and the bow of the kayak lifted out of the water.

He jerked his hands up and pried at her fingers, wincing at the cold, dead feel of her flesh. Her fingernails dug into his shoulder as though they were knives. Her grip was as strong as iron, and no matter how hard he pulled, no matter how hard he tried to twist her fingers away, it was no use.

He shot a terrified glance at his grandfather, who was now close enough that Greg could make out his expression. "Grandpa! She's got me! She's got me, Grandpa! Help me!"

"Stay in that boat! Do you hear me, Greg? You stay in that boat!" his grandfather called.

Tears streamed down Greg's face, hot where the rain was cold. He made fists and beat at the woman's hand, but that helped no more than prying at her fingers had. He was halfway out of the kayak already, going into the water backward, going into her embrace blind.

As suddenly as she had gripped him, the woman let go. The kayak slapped down onto the surface, and Greg, who had been pulling against the force of her grip, slammed to the right and almost went into the black water. Greg's hand scrabbled at the red, pebbly plastic of the kayak, shoving and pushing, lifting his face away from the lake.

His grandfather's boat cut a tight circle around him, pitching to the side at a forty-five-degree angle, the starboard gunnel almost touching the water. His grandfather's gaze tracked across the surface of the lake between them and then snapped up to meet Greg's eyes.

He slowed the aluminum boat, still circling, his prop adding to the chop, and Greg held tightly to the kayak. His searched the water, but of the dead woman in the lake, there was no sign.

"Grandpa!" Greg stretched his arms toward the aluminum fishing boat, as a little child asking to be picked up might.

Joe Canton's face softened, and he nodded reassuringly. He slowed his fishing boat to a stop and drifted close to the kayak. "Shhh, now. You've had a scare, Greg, that's all. Grandpa's here."

Greg sobbed, still holding his arms out. His grandfather grabbed his hands and lifted him out of the kayak, setting him on the bench seat of the fishing boat right in front of him. He whipped off his windbreaker and wrapped it around Greg.

Greg lunged across the space between them and wrapped his arms around his grandpa's middle.

Joe Canton returned the hug. "It's okay, Greg. Everything's okay now." But his eyes scanned the surface of the lake, alert, watching.

12

Standing well away from the big bay window, Mason couldn't keep his eyes off the scene as it unfolded. The old man from next door pulled his boat up to the dock, his expression one of worry tinged with confusion. He paused for a moment, glancing over his shoulder at the lake behind them. The brat was bawling, sitting hunched on one of the benches in the aluminum fishing boat. Mr. Canton turned his gaze back to his grandson, and his expression softened.

"I'm going outside to help Mr. Canton, Grandma." He took five quick steps and pushed through the door leading to the porch.

"Mason, the storm—"

"It's okay. It's already dying off, and anyway, Mr. Canton needs help." Mason banged through the screen door and out onto the strip of anemic grass separating his grandmother's cottage from the lake's shore. "Mr. Canton!" In the house behind him, his grandmother went on speaking, but Mason paid her no mind.

Mr. Canton glanced at him but couldn't wave. He held the brat with one hand while struggling to loop the boat's bow rope over one of the dock's stanchions with the other.

Plastering a smile on his face, Mason trotted over and took the rope. He squatted and tied it off before standing up straight. "Got trapped out on the lake, did you?" he asked the little kid.

The brat turned his teary face away and said nothing.

"It's okay now," said Mr. Canton. "Only a little rain."

Mason fought to keep his expression pleasant, helpful, fought to keep the glee out of his eyes. He longed to ask the kid about *her*.

But that wouldn't be smart, not with Mr. Canton standing right there.

Besides, as Mason understood it, the brat and his family were staying for another couple of weeks, and he had a few tasks to carry out in that time—one of which was an afternoon alone with the brat.

He reached over and patted the kid on the back, watching Old Man Canton's face the whole time. "Don't you worry, little guy," Mason said. "You'll feel better in a bit. The lake can be scary in the middle of the storm."

Mr. Canton flashed an appreciative smile at him and then turned toward the house. "Thanks for your help, Mason. Appreciate it."

"Anytime, Mr. Canton."

Mason stood on the Canton dock, watching as the old man carried his grandson up and into the house. When the door closed, he turned toward the lake, his eyes zipping around that surface, a wolflike smile plastered on his face.

13

Greg sat on his grandpa's lap, wrapped in warm blankets, sipping cocoa with the little marshmallows. His skin bore the rosy glow of warmth and love. His grandmother sat next to them on the couch and smoothed his still-damp hair. No one said a word, content to sit and hold each other.

They were still sitting there twenty-two minutes later when Mary and Stephen Canton came home.

Mary took one look at her son, dropped the brown paper sack she carried, and sprinted toward him. "What happened?" she asked.

"He's okay, Mary. He took a fright, that's all," said Elizabet.

"Dad?" asked Stephen.

Joe glanced at his son and treated him to a stern nod. "It's as Mother said."

Mary squatted in front of her son. "What happened, baby?"

Greg shrank back against his grandpa's chest and shook his head. Even though he'd quit sucking his thumb three years before, he brought his hand up and stuck his thumb in his mouth.

"Now, now," said Joe, squeezing Greg tight. "Everything's okay."

Elizabet motioned toward the bedroom with her head, then stood and walked through the door. With a glance at Stephen, Mary followed.

Once inside, Elizabet reached past her and closed the door. She lay her hand on Mary's forearm and patted it.

"He took fright," she said. "But he's okay. His imagination ran away with him, that's all."

Mary shook her head. "What..." Her eyes darted around the room.

"No, no. Greg was out on the lake, in the kayak, and the storm broke. He decided continuing toward the other side was better than turning back. Joe gave him a bit of money for candy, and I think he didn't want to risk missing out by coming home."

"But he knows better! He knows better than to be out on the lake during a storm."

Elizabet patted Mary's arm again. "Yes, dear, but up here dark skies don't mean what they do down there—at least not always. He knows that, too. And even *this* storm was more of a bluster than a buster. A little rain, a little wind, a lightning bolt or two."

"The storm scared him? Paddling back in the storm?"

Elizabet shook her head. "Like I said, his imagination ran away with him."

"His imagination?" The low rumble of Stephen and Joe talking in the other room came through the door behind her, and Mary tilted her head but couldn't make out any of the words.

"Yes. Greg saw—his words, mind you—a 'dead lady' under the water. He dropped his paddle in his panic and now imagines that this dead lady took it from him and tried to pull him into the water."

"But if he lost his paddle, how did he get back to shore?"

For the third time, Elizabet patted her forearm. "I sent Joe for him the moment the storm broke, dear. Joe picked him up in the fishing boat."

"I see." Without another word, Mary turned and went back out into the family room. As she stepped closer, the two men stopped speaking and turned her way. Stephen flashed a reassuring smile at her. "Did Joe tell you?"

Stephen cut his gaze toward Greg and returned it to hers. He inclined his head. "Dad told me about Greg getting caught out in the storm and about going to get him with the fishing boat." He ruffled his son's hair. "Everything's okay, right, Greg?"

Without looking at either parent, Greg snuggled closer to his grandfather but nodded.

Mary fixed Joe with a stern gaze. "We can talk about the rest of it later," she said.

Joe's ice-blue eyes met hers candidly for a moment, and he nodded. "Ayup."

Chapter 2

2007

I

"So LaBouche is still around," said Scott Lewis. Lee LaBouche—his so-called partner with the NYSP—the demon who killed his daughter and his wife was still out there, unpunished, free to murder again and again and again.

"Oh, yes," said Benny. "He's still around somewhere. So is Brigitta. We need to be careful for a while."

"What do we do about Oneka Falls?"

"I've got an idea about that," said Benny. "Here's what we need to do…"

Dusk fell as they spoke, and high in a tree at the edge of the woods, a lone, yellow magpie looked down on them, watching.

"Well? What's this great idea?" asked Mike. He nudged Toby with his elbow and grinned, but Toby didn't smile back. His attention had strayed toward the trees at the edge of the parking lot. Mike followed his gaze, and his grin died stillborn. "Is that—"

"So, Benny, what's your big idea? It's not something like a letter-writing campaign, is it?" asked Toby in a too-loud voice. He turned away from the woods and walked toward the back of the Jeep.

Benny smiled and hugged Shannon closer. “Couldn’t we start a—”

“Mike, can you help me with this?” asked Toby, fiddling with the spare tire on the back door of the Jeep.

Mike started and tore his gaze away from the little yellow bird that was now hopping from foot to foot on a branch overhanging the edge of the parking lot. He glanced at Scott. “Sure thing, Toby. Scott help us.”

Scott seemed lost in his thoughts, leaning against the front fender of Toby’s BMW. At the sound of his name, he lifted his head and glanced toward the woods.

“Hey,” said Benny. “I thought you wanted to talk about my idea?” He glanced at Shannon, an expression of hurt and bewilderment on his face. She shrugged and gave his hand a squeeze. “You asked me, and I was about to explain that—”

“What’s the matter? The guy with all the graduate degrees can’t change a tire?” asked Mike. He turned and strode toward Toby. “Don’t say anything else,” he whispered as he passed Benny and Shannon.”

“It’s stuck,” said Toby. He reached in through the back window of the Jeep and moved things around with a clatter.

Benny shook his head. “Guys…” he said.

“One minute, Benny,” said Toby. “Let us handle this first. Afterward, you can tell us all about your idea.”

"Can't you change the tire while I explain? It's not complicated. I think I can—"

"*LaBouche*!" Scott yelled. His Glock 37 appeared in his hand as he came away from the BMW and sank into a shooting stance. He raised the pistol and snapped off two quick shots, the .45's report thundering into the stillness of the coming dusk.

"Dammit!" yelled Toby. He stepped away from the Jeep carrying the Remington 870 tactical they had carried against Herlequin. He tossed the shotgun to Mike as he rounded the Jeep, going toward the passenger door.

"Benny! Shannon! Clear out!" shouted Mike. He caught the shotgun and racked the slide one-handed like a trick shot artist.

Scott fired, again and again, the big caliber gunshots echoing across the parking lot. He walked forward toward the trees, firing as he moved, his face set in a rictus of lividity and loathing.

The yellow magpie had taken wing and darted deeper into the trees, jinking left and right at random intervals.

"*LaBouche*!" Scott screamed again.

Mike jogged forward, carrying the Remington at port arms. "Let me have point, Scott!" he called. Scott didn't respond, just stood pumping round after round at the yellow bird until the slide of his Glock locked back. Mike passed him as Scott ejected the empty magazine and slapped his hand on his belt where his spare magazine pouch should have been but wasn't.

Raising the shotgun to his shoulder, Mike stopped and spread his feet. He aimed and squeezed the trigger in the space between his heartbeats, and banana-yellow feathers flew from the little bird. Though the bird squawked and lost altitude for a moment, it didn't fall from the sky, and he didn't stop flapping his wings, even for an instant.

"*LaBouche*!" Scott screamed for the third time, but this time, his voice cracked and broke. He turned and sprinted to the BMW and leaned in through the open driver's window.

Mike worked the slide, ejecting the spent shell and slamming a new one into the chamber. He drew a bead on the dodging yellow spot in the fading light and fired again. Another squawk sounded, but still, the bird didn't slow, let alone fall from the sky.

"*God damn you, Lee*!" Scott straightened from the car and slammed a fresh magazine into his weapon and darted forward, fouling Mike's sightline before he could fire another round.

"Scott!" shouted Shannon.

He paid her no mind. Scott sprinted between the trees, his Glock pointed toward the sky.

"Stop him!" said Toby.

Mike ran after the trooper, cursing under his breath. "Scott!" he cried.

As the sun descended below the horizon, the yellow magpie darted below the treetops, angling into the murk of the coming night. He dodged around a thick trunk and disappeared. Scott raced after him, circling the tree and peering into the shadows, but the little bird had ducked away, the same as the sun. Mike reached him as Scott shoved his pistol into the holster tucked into his waistband.

"God damn it!" Scott snapped. "I'm going to get that evil son of a bitch if it's the last thing I ever do!"

"And we'll help you, Scott," said Mike in a calm voice.

Scott glanced at him but couldn't meet his gaze for long. "Total rooky bullshit back there," he said. "Sorry. I lost my head."

Mike waved it away. "Come on. Let's get back. No telling what that bastard is up to." He eyed the darkening woods with easy-to-read nervousness. "No telling what else is in these woods, and I've fought enough demons for one day." He lay his hand on Scott's shoulder and gave it a gentle tug, but Scott resisted a moment, his gaze crawling from shadow to shadow, still searching for the little yellow bird. "Come on, Scott."

With a nod, Scott turned and strode back toward the parking lot, head down, walking in silence.

Toby, Shannon, and Benny stood in a tight knot between their two vehicles. Toby held his fancy tranquilizer rifle, but the other two were unarmed. "Get him?" asked Shannon.

Scott couldn't meet anyone's gaze. "No. He got away."

"Our firearms won't stop him," said Toby with an air of gentleness. "We don't have enough firepower."

"Yeah," muttered Scott.

"We *will* get him, Scott. Even if he's the only one we get, we'll get him."

Scott crossed his arms and leaned against the front of the Jeep, his face turned away from them.

"That was LaBouche? Really?" asked Benny. "That *bird* was LaBouche?"

Toby nodded. "Yes. What's more, what you all saw was no illusion. He is, in fact, a banana-colored magpie."

"I thought you said they only appear to change shapes? That it's all illusion?" asked Shannon. "How could he fly? Does LaBouche have wings?"

"He does now," Toby said with a wry curl to his lips. "I don't understand it, but however it happened, LaBouche is a little yellow bird in fact as well as appearance."

"Good thing, too," said Benny. "Otherwise he'd have probably killed us."

"Yeah," said Scott. "I lost my head."

"Oh, I didn't mean—" Benny bit off whatever he was going to say as Shannon lay a hand on his arm and shook her head.

"It won't happen again," Scott murmured.

But chances were, he would lose his head where LaBouche was concerned, and they all knew it. No one could blame him, either.

"So, Benny..." said Mike into the uncomfortable silence.

"Yeah?"

"What's this big idea?"

Benny's gaze scanned the darkening forest. "Maybe we shouldn't discuss it here."

"Whisper," said Mike. "The suspense is killing me." He winked at Shannon.

"Well...okay, if you think it's safe." Benny smiled, and his eyes danced like an eleven-year-old's at the prospect of an extra dessert. "Politics!" he crowed. "We take the town away from them through elections!"

Toby rolled his eyes. "Too slow."

"No, listen for a second. This guy, this town manager—"

"Chaz Welsh," said Mike.

"Yeah. His position is by *appointment by the town council*, right? Isn't that how it works when there's no mayor? All we have to do is stack the council!"

"Yeah, but this is Oneka Falls we're talking about," said Mike.

"So?"

"So, Chaz is king. The town council does whatever he wants. No questions, no arguments. We call them the rubber-stamp brigade."

"But not if we put our people on the council! Don't you see? We can get Chaz out, then we can get an independent law enforcement agency in there and clean up the town once and for all! The State Troopers, for instance!"

Scott grunted. "Know any troopers?" he asked sourly.

"We do," said Mike. "And a good one."

"It'll never work," said Toby. "Besides, it's too slow."

Benny's face fell. "Think about it, okay?"

Toby shrugged. "No promises, but we can talk about it later."

"Let's get out of here," said Scott in a monotone voice. "I want to go home. I want to get away from this fucking town."

2

LaBouche raced away from the confrontation in the park as fast as his little yellow wings could carry him. He grunted little birdy grunts as his body pushed each pellet of birdshot out…one at a time. The pain was inconsequential, but even so, it was still *pain*.

His fury mounted with each expelled pellet, and his rage thrummed in time to each wingbeat in the thinning air. In the distance, a giant column of black smoke marked the place where Herlequin had died.

Looking at it gave LaBouche a perverse sense of satisfaction but at the same time a profound sense of loss. Herlequin had been…not quite a father-figure, not quite a friend, but someone to look up to. A *standard*.

Brigitta, though… LaBouche forgot and shook his tiny yellow head and tumbled for a moment in the onrushing wind. *I hate being a damn bird! I'm going to add Brigitta's name to Scotty's' and whoever that punk with the shotgun was.*

LaBouche rarely held a grudge, but when he did…he really *held* a grudge. As he flew, not knowing exactly where to go, only knowing he had to get away from those idiots and the damn shotgun, he considered what he might do to them—to the people on his list.

I've already cleaned out Scotty's immediate family, so not much to do there. Cripple him? Leave him able to think, to plan, to remember, but unable to act? It was something to consider. *The idiot with the shotgun will be much easier.* All *I need do is track down his family, and I can inflict my revenge for these goddamn pellets!*

Brigitta though…he'd have to be careful taking his revenge on her. She was *powerful* in a way that eclipsed even Herlequin—though she lacked the old demon's style. He could not ignore the indignity of changing him into a little yellow magpie, though. *No, I'll need something special for the first daughter of Herlequin. Something that will send a message to every other old demon on the planet. Something that says, 'Don't fuck with LaBouche.'* He tried to grin at the thought, momentarily forgetting that a stupid little beak had replaced his mouth.

LaBouche needed a safe place to hide until he convinced Brigitta to change him back, to give him the power to create illusions again. He was helpless—a tiny little yellow thing with no strength and no way to hide his nature. At the same time, he still needed nourishment. *Perhaps…if I can stay out of sight…*

He angled his wings and banked toward Oneka Falls.

3

Benny, Shannon, and Toby climbed into the red BMW, planning to retrieve Toby's Odin Desperado from its hiding place on the other side of Oneka Falls. Mike and Scott took the Jeep and headed straight back to Rochester. Both vehicles took the long way around Oneka Falls, not willing to risk an encounter with the town's demons.

They needed time and space to plan, to rest, and to gather their resources. The fight to clean up Oneka Falls was going to be a long one. A hard one.

"Penny," said Shannon from the backseat.

Toby glanced at Benny in the passenger seat, but Benny, too, was staring at Toby. "What?"

"She means she wants—"

"I understand what 'penny for your thoughts' means, Benny. I meant why are you both staring at me."

"Your thoughts—" said Shannon.

"—are so dark—" said Benny.

"—so bitter, so—"

"—ugly and angry—"

"—full of pain…"

Toby shook his head, a sour grin on his lips. "That's cute. And when I say cute, what I really mean is that it makes me want to deafen myself with a pencil. Can we expect more of this 'gee-we're-so-cute-don't-you-just-want-to-die' nonsense from you two?"

At least Benny had the good grace to blush, Shannon only laughed. "We can't help it," she said.

"Are you going to play the twins card now? You're not, you know."

"Twins card? Toby, you know Shannon is not my sister, let alone my twin—"

Shannon's hand snaked over Benny's shoulder and squeezed it lightly. "He knows that, Benny. It's that twins often finish each—"

"—other's sentences. Oh, I see. Another one of his jokes." Benny held up one hand on each side of his face and made the quote gesture with his fingers.

"Yes, my—" Shannon's teeth snapped together with an audible click. "Benny, slap me every time I say that."

Benny turned a startled glance on Toby.

"Figure of speech, Ben."

"It's 'Benny.'"

"I don't want to say that anymore. I don't want to imitate…*her*." Thunder clouds rippled across Shannon's expression. "I absolutely *detest* that I spent so many years mimicking Gray and that…that zombie-faced bitch! It's bad enough…it's bad enough saying the words, let alone the fact that I'm repeating the words because *she* said them all the time to *him*. How did I get so screwed up?"

"Shannon, you're not—"

"We all were, Shan. Hell, I couldn't even *remember* any of it. I ran around killing demons like some kind of…some kind of serial killer without even knowing why—"

"Except you did. You chased them because they were *hurting* people, *killing* people," said Benny.

"—I was doing it! And at the same time, feeling it was…it was *wrong*."

"But at least you did something, Toby. I sat around and pined after a man I knew was a homosexual but pretended was straight. I thought about cleaning all the time. Fantasized about it, even. Anything to keep my mind busy, to keep from thinking, to keep from…"

"Remembering." Benny shifted position so that his back was against the door, and he could see both of them with a small turn of his head. "Was I any better? Hiding out in a locked psychiatric facility, pretending I was *Toby*? All so I didn't have to be out here in the world facing the things that you two were?" Benny shook his head and followed it with a sweeping motion of his hand as if pushing all the arguments to the side. "No, we did what we had to do. None of us was ready to confront Herlequin. He would've *eaten* us if we had. You both know that as well as I do. We needed—"

"But, we could—"

"No! We needed time to…to let *this*—" Benny drew a triangle in the air, connecting each of them together. "—develop. And, we needed Mike. We—"

"Scott, too. Without him, Owen Gray would still be out there. And if he hadn't scared Brigitta away, she'd have seen through my…my…my whatever-you-call-it, my illusion, and she would have scratched my eyes out for real."

Benny shrugged. "Okay, we needed Mike *and* Scott. The point—"

"Still do," muttered Toby.

"Granted. We need them. They complete us in a way that may not be apparent yet. But my point was none of us—not at eleven, not at fifteen, not at twenty-one—could have gone against Herlequin and the demons in Oneka Falls. We wouldn't have stood a chance." Benny shrugged and ran his hand through his now-neatly trimmed hair. For a moment, he looked confused, but then he flashed a smile at Shannon. "We're better together."

"No question about it," she said.

"I'm just tired," said Toby. "Don't mind my mister-grumpy-britches routine. I'm not used to being around people for so long."

"You'll get used to us," said Benny brightly.

"I suppose I'll have to."

He pulled the red BMW into the barn behind his motorhome. "Why don't the two of you drive this car back, and I'll bring the motorhome?"

Benny looked stricken. "I never learned to drive."

With a wide grin, Shannon stuck her head between the two bucket seats in the front. "I did!"

Chuckling, Toby popped open the driver side door and got out. He turned and bent over so he could look Benny in the eye. "Here's some food for thought, Benny.

What if *others* are out there that we need? Others like Scott and Mike? How do we find them?"

Benny opened his mouth to speak, but Toby held up his hand to stop him. "Food for thought, remember?"

4

The demon who called himself Chaz Welsh raged through the town hall building. The demons who worked there took one look at him and ducked for cover—at least the ones with enough awareness to sense trouble coming.

Sally McBride stood chatting with one of the human secretaries. She was smiling and laughing as if nothing were happening outside.

Acting the fool again! *I should send her back—let the Four deal with her*! *It would serve her right after she screwed up so badly at Play Time.*

The human Sally was talking to glanced over Sally's shoulder and retreated into the depths of the planning department. Sally's spine went rigid, and she quivered. It started in the tips of her fingers, then extended to her hands, wrists, and elbows. Her whole torso shook, and soon after that, her knees were knocking. "Ch-Ch-Chaz?"

"In my office, Sally," he growled. "And stop calling me Chaz! We aren't friends. I'm your—" He glanced around and lowered his voice. "I'm your *superior.*"

"I…uh…I…have to get back to the phones! I can't leave them unattended, Mr. Welsh. We could speak after—"

"Alternately, I could send you home now, Sally," he said with quiet menace. "*All the way home.*"

"No! Please don't say that. Your office is fine." She scurried toward the town manager's office, her fat legs pumping.

"Goddamn right!" Chaz snapped under his breath, but he kept a pleasant expression on the face of his visage. No doubt Sally was broadcasting her fear to half the world, but he was starting to think he couldn't expect much from Fuck-it-up McBride.

He followed her into his office, pausing only long enough to put the do not disturb sign on the outside of his doorknob. The door closed with a metallic snick. Chaz always thought it sounded like a giant pair of snippers slicing through a human finger. He turned slowly, enjoying McBride's palpable fear, *feeding* off it.

His laconic gaze scanned the doodads—the *junk*—with which he decorated his office. He delayed the moment of eye contact, enjoying how the delay heightened Sally's fear. He heaved a sigh and muttered, "What am I to do with you?" As soon as the last word left his mouth, he snapped his gaze to hers and bored into her eyes with the not insignificant totality of his will.

Sally whimpered and took a step back, her hands coming up as if to defend herself—though there was nothing she could do to protect herself from Chaz. "*What*?" she screeched.

Chaz made a chopping motion through the air. "Keep it down, Fuck-it-up," he hissed. "If anyone hears you…" He poured as much vitriol and menace into his voice as he could muster.

Sally's eyes darted toward the closed door to the hall, and Chaz almost hoped she would make a run for it. He was in the mood to chase something—to chase something down and kill it with his teeth. When Sally's gaze returned to his face, she must've seen his thoughts, seen how much he wanted to run her down. She sank to the floor on her knees and whimpered, "What have I *done*?"

Chaz brought his thick, scaled fists up in front of him, shaking them in rage. "*Do you really not know*?" His voice sounded similar to a cross between an industrial boiler about to blow and metal grinding against metal at very high speed.

Sally whimpered and dropped her gaze to a point halfway between them. "No, my lord! I'm stupid. You *know* that. If I've done something—"

“Shut…your…*fucking*…mouth!” Chaz leaned his bulk against the desk he’d modified to support such a maneuver. He held up an index finger, which any demon could see ended in a massive, gleaming claw. “If you speak again—no, scratch that. If you make another noise, I’m going to *really* hurt you, Sally. Once I’m finished, I’ll send you somewhere where you will truly learn what pain is. I’ll send you to *them*, gift wrapped and sporting a ribbon.”

She opened her mouth but snapped it shut and nodded instead.

“Since your idiocy knows no bounds, let me tell you what has happened. But you know what? You should work on your situational awareness, McBride! It’s not as if anything that happened isn’t right there in the ether for any of us to sense!”

Sally gazed up at him, tears glimmering in her eyes. She lifted her hands and let them drop listlessly.

“*Herlequin is dead*, you ridiculous sack of pus! *Dead*!” he raged, springing to his feet without meaning to. He towered over her, his hands clenching into fists and releasing—clenching and releasing, clenching and releasing. His breath cycled in and out of his massive chest, sounding for all the world like a bellows driven by a motor. “They have *sent him back*!”

McBride shook her head, eyes wide, terror written on her face.

Chaz extended his hand, putting his claws in her face, almost touching her left eye with his claw-tipped right index finger. "What's more, they scared Brigitta off with a…a *trick*! They arrested Brigitta's pet—a *useless* human piece of trash that one is! He never even fired a shot! All that talk…all that boasting…"

With a start, Chaz realized he had punctured Sally's left eye, and a viscous pale-green ooze dripped down her cheek. Her face blazed with pain, but her lips remained sealed.

"You might not be as stupid as I first thought, McBride."

5

From his stoop on a branch in the maple tree outside the town hall, LaBouche watched as Chaz assaulted Sally McBride. It was sweet—not as sweet as torturing Lewis' daughter, but satisfying, nonetheless. He felt almost sated as McBride crawled out of the office on her knees. The emotions of demons did not taste as good as the emotions of humans, but they would do in a pinch.

He could feel her shame, her pain, and her indignation wafting off her like perfume. Chaz slumped behind his large desk, not *doing* anything, only sitting and staring at his hands.

Approaching him is suicidal in my current form. Unless… His tiny black eyes flew to the door of Welsh's office as it slid quietly shut. *Unless I had an in-between…someone I could cow. Someone such as that idiot who just crawled away like a slave.*

LaBouche took wing, angling around the building to roost on the overhang above the door to the parking lot. He waited there, shifting from foot to foot with impatience, and resisting the urge to go root for insects in the dirt. *I will get you for this, Brigitta*!

He hadn't long to wait. McBride pushed her way through the door, crying quietly. She was a hideous thing—almost porcine in body structure, with sickly pink skin practically identical to that of the humans, large oval-shaped eyes—well, *eye* thanks to Chaz's most recent alteration—over a full mouth surrounded by thick, sausage-like lips that always seemed too moist as if coated with a natural oil. She walked with a distinctive gait—as if she usually ran on all fours, but out in public put on airs and walked on her hind legs. Tiny stubs—malformed wings—adorned her upper back, and a short nub of a tail finished off the look.

McBride sickened him, and the thought of spending time near her made him want to gouge his own eyes out with a dull piece of metal. He watched her sink into her beat-up, old green Chevy. *This could be a terrible idea.*

The green heap shuddered and clattered to life, belching a mixture of blue and black smoke mixed with wisps of white steam into the parking lot. McBride sat for a moment as if waiting for the car to warm up, but no amount of warming up could still that shivering beast.

She rolled down the driver's side window and leaned across the long bench seat to open the passenger side as well. With Sally otherwise occupied, LaBouche dove off the overhang and angled his wings to flit right through the open driver's side window and land on the floor in the backseat.

The scent was atrocious: a mixture of rotting skin, defecation, and—strangely—potpourri. To his tiny olfactory apparatus, the odor was overpowering, almost incapacitating. He breathed through his open beak.

Brigitta chose this. She made me into this idiotic parody. I will need something exceptional for her.

The ride to McBride's home seemed to take a year. The stench of the car was horrible, but what was genuinely intolerable was McBride's penchant of singing show tunes at the top of her sour voice.

When the tires finally thumped up over the curb and rolled through gravel, LaBouche readied himself. Chances were that McBride would leave the windows open—she didn't strike him as one who cared much about material possessions—but if she didn't, he needed to be ready to dart through a closing door.

McBride killed the clattering engine, and it was a relief to LaBouche's tiny ears. He hopped up on the seat cushion in the back and waited. She sat there a moment, muttering to herself.

He didn't catch much of it, but what he caught of it proved that McBride wasn't devoid of a strong sense of vengeance, but she *was* devoid of any kind of backbone. She opened the driver's side door and got out, leaving both the driver's side and the passenger window open.

As she walked away from the car, LaBouche took wing and flew out the window. He approached her from behind, his little black eyes scanning their surroundings. He swooped down and landed on her shoulder, and she stifled a scream.

"Oh, look at the pretty little bird!" she crooned.

Are you as stupid as you look? he thought at her. *It's not an act you put on for Welsh*?

Oh.

Is that all? *A demon in the shape of a tiny yellow bird lands on your shoulder and speaks into your mind, and that's the best you can do*? *I see why Chaz treats you as a servant.*

McBride turned her face away, but not before LaBouche saw the sneer form. *What do you want*? she asked in as toneless a mental voice as LaBouche had ever heard.

Want? What does it matter what I want? LaBouche cocked his tiny yellow head to the side. *Has he bound you?*

What? Who?

Chaz. Who else might have bound you?

Herlequin.

Yes, but he's dead, isn't he? Any binding Herlequin had over you died with him. LaBouche sensed an utter, black depression inside her at the thought of Herlequin's death. *They broke the mold after they made him*, he thought at her.

He was one of the best.

No doubt, no doubt. He rode on her shoulder in silence for a moment, pretending to be as caught up in his sadness as she appeared to be in her own. *But Chaz...well, I'm sure I don't need to tell you this, but he's no Herlequin.*

She glanced at him sharply, lips drawn into a moue of disapproval mixed with fear, then she scanned the surrounding area—eyes scouring every shadow, every nook, every cranny. *No, he isn't.*

Why do you continue to serve him?

McBride shrugged, dislodging his perch, and LaBouche had to flap his wings furiously to arrest his fall toward the gravel. He rolled his eyes and hovered near her. *Don't do that again, idiot.*

Oh! I'm sorry.

He alit on her shoulder, shaking his head. She was so strange, more human than demon. He could see why Chaz abused her so. It would be so easy to fall into that pattern with her—hurting her, feeding off her pain and degradation. LaBouche would have sneered if his features had allowed it. *Damn Brigitta!*

Brigitta?

He'd let that last thought go through. He would have to watch himself, being in such close contact with a demon. The years he'd spent with Scott had allowed him to grow sloppy. *It's nothing, just wondering where she is. She is Herlequin's heir, after all, isn't she? Shouldn't she be here? Taking charge of things?*

I don't... McBride's whole body tensed. *I don't know about such things.*

You don't have to watch what you say with me. I'm not the same as the other older ones; I still have a sense of humor.

I...I see. Her mental tone was not one of confidence and belief. She'd no doubt heard something similar from Chaz—a trick used to allow him to punish her.

You'll see. My word is my bond. Besides, I'd much rather dine on humans than on demons. Wouldn't you?

Of course!

She walked toward the door of the rundown colonial she lived in. Her hands wrestled with one another. *What... Why...*

What do I want? Why have I come to you?

Well... She took two full steps before she nodded.

Brigitta punished me hours before they killed her father. She cast me into this ridiculous form, and she blocked my ability to project facades. Had she not been so petty, I would have been there...I would have been able to fight by Herlequin's side. I could've turned the tide of that battle, and Herlequin would still be alive.

I'm sure I don't know about such things.

Standing on her shoulder, LaBouche rolled his eyes. He had a lot of work to do to get McBride where he needed her. *I only mention these things so I can explain what I want and why I've chosen you. That is what you want, isn't it? An explanation?*

McBride nodded.

Simply put, I need your help. I can't approach Chaz or any of the other older demons in my present form. Let's say it wouldn't be wise. You, however, can go where you please, do as you please. So you see, I've come to recruit you to act as my intermediary. We cannot go without a leader...we can't afford to, not with those human hunters free to do as they please. Someone must take command.

And that someone is you?

Ire sparkled in his heart, but it was too soon to let that show. Not after he had spent several minutes assuring her that he was not like everyone else, but she could speak her mind without fear of retribution.

Even so, he added her name to his list.

Not necessarily. I can't lead them in this form, can I? Chaz is a likely candidate—at least to be the face we show to the others.

The face we show to the others?

Exactly. What I want to suggest to Chaz is that we form a limited partnership. He and I make the decisions, yet he gives all the commands to the others. He will appear to be in charge. Chaz will get all the credit.

She stopped dead in her tracks but said nothing, thought nothing he could hear. She stood there, as still as if carved from marble for several minutes.

He will like that, she finally thought to him.

Had his physiology allowed it, LaBouche would have grinned.

6

"What did he mean?" Chaz demanded.

Sally knelt before him, her head down, but her one usable eye flitted around the room. "He said he believes the two of you should take command, but that the others wouldn't be able to understand how two demons of power could cooperate…that…that he would let you take all the credit, that you could appear to be the leader."

Chaz swatted her across the back of her head. "Yes, I got that from the first time you said it." His tone was wry yet tinged with anger. "I asked you: 'what did he mean?' That's your opportunity to tell me what he *meant.* Are you capable of that, Fuck-it-up?"

A mewling whine escaped her before she could stop it. "I don't know what you want me to tell you, Lord."

Chaz sighed, and the promise of pain filled his expression. "I don't know how to make it any plainer. I'm speaking English, aren't I? Do you speak the language?"

"I believe…" McBride bowed her head further toward the floor.

"Yes?"

"I believe he would take command himself but for Brigitta. He wants to set you up if Brigitta ever returns—to make it seem as though you are the usurper. And in the meantime, he still has his say in the running of things." It was what LaBouche had told her to say, but it was also what she *believed.*

"Hmm," hummed Chaz. "A plan with merit. And what do you think, Fuck-it-up? Will Brigitta ever return?"

She looked up at him helplessly. "Such things are beyond me, Lord."

The slap seemed to come from nowhere and knocked her sideways off of her knees and onto her side. "Now, that was beyond you. But, never mind. Your opinion is worthless anyway. She's gone—probably dead. She should know better than to go rushing headlong to die by Herlequin's side."

She lay where she'd fallen, not even raising a hand to her burning cheek. "Yes, Lord. What shall I tell him?" Her eyes danced to the long window behind Chaz's desk, up into the boughs of the maple tree where the bright yellow magpie sat.

"LaBouche? You tell him 'yes,' of course. His fears aren't my own. Brigitta's *gone*. I will partner with him for now, but I will need a valid excuse to kill him later. You watch him, Sally, and you report back to me. His every move, mind! I don't want him taking a nap without you letting me know." He came to stand over her, one foot on either side. "Tell me, Sally, can you do this simple task? Can you serve me in this way? Can you do this simple task without screwing everything up?"

She drew her eyes away from the picture window and fixed them on Chaz's kneecaps. "Yes, Lord," she said in a husky whisper.

"You understand that this is your chance to redeem yourself? Your *only* chance to redeem yourself?"

"Yes, Lord, and I thank you for the opportunity."

Chaz walked away from her and stood gazing out the picture window. Butterflies performed feats of acrobatics in her guts. *Should he see that little yellow bird…*

"You're not entirely without merit, Sally. Keep that in mind."

"Yes, Lord."

He turned to face her, gazing down like a benevolent uncle. "On your feet, Sally. Your days of groveling before me are over."

"Yes, Lord."

"And no more of that. We have our facades to maintain."

Sally stood and shrugged. "Okay, Chaz."

He narrowed his eyelids, and his eyes burned at her from behind them for a moment. "Very well. Go be about your work."

"Yes, sir, Mr. Welsh."

The fire burning in his eyes lessened, and he nodded. "I will have a statement for you to deliver to our co-

conspirator for his approval within the hour. See that you are here when I am ready for you."

Sally nodded and backed out of the town manager's office. She pulled the door closed behind her and turned away. When she was ten steps from the office door, a sigh of relief exploded out of her. She couldn't wait to see what LaBouche thought.

She couldn't wait to see Chaz writhing in pain at the end of their conspiracy. *Brigitta isn't far away,* she thought. *She's in mourning, that's all. Both of these posturing idiots are too dimwitted see it. They will both burn in the fire of her wrath. I'll see to it.*

7

Kelly-Ann made a face as she piloted her beat up Civic to the side of the road. It had been cruising right along before it coughed twice and died dead. "Perfect," she muttered. She switched off the ignition and slumped back in her seat. The car wasn't in good shape—she couldn't afford to maintain the car nor to pay a mechanic to fix the Civic after it broke.

She rubbed her eyes with her thumb and index finger, already feeling the headache blossoming behind them. First, her boss had kept her over—mostly to ogle her legs—and afterward, the car hadn't wanted to start. After twenty minutes of trying, it *had* started, only to give up its mechanical ghost way out in the middle of nowhere—halfway between Oneka Falls and Genosgwa.

She let her arms fall to her sides, limp and nerveless, and sighed, fighting back tears of frustration. "Fuck," she whispered. "This damn car… Fuck!" Hot tears splashed down her cheeks as she slapped the steering wheel twice with her palm. She twisted the key in the ignition, but the car didn't even crank, let alone start.

Kelly-Ann fished her purse from the back seat and dug through it, looking for her phone. "Where is it?" she murmured when she couldn't lay hands on it. She ruffled through the purse again, with a touch more energy.

Still, no phone.

She dumped the contents of her purse into the passenger seat and fished through them in the dying light. The last thing she wanted was to be walking down the side of a deserted county road after sunset, but if she couldn't find her phone, she suspected that was *exactly* what the night held in store for her.

"Where did I put it?" She looked on the passenger-side floorboard, squinting to see past its shadows. Kelly-Ann checked the console again and again. She even went as far as opening the glovebox and rooting around inside it—though she'd never put a cell phone in any glovebox in her life. She patted her pockets at least thirty times.

It was no use. Her phone had disappeared into the ether.

She slumped in the seat, cocking her head on one palm, her elbow wedged against the window. She squeezed her eyes shut and pressed her lips into a thin, white line. It was the perfect end of a shitty day, the perfect end of a shitty week, a shitty month, a shitty year. It was the perfect capstone on her entire fucked-up life.

Someone tapped on her window.

Kelly-Ann shrieked and bolted up in her seat. Her eyes snapped open.

A man stood next to her door. He was average in almost every way—height, weight, brown haired, dressed well, but without much expense. But his eyes…his eyes were exceptional. They were bright hazel and seemed to spin in the low light of the coming dusk.

He flashed a smile at her and held both palms toward her. "Sorry. I didn't mean to scare you."

One hand covered her mouth and one pressed between her breasts, right over her racing heart. She stared at him through her window, her mind trying to come up with something to say. *How long has he been standing there*? she wondered.

"Car trouble?" he asked, spinning one hand in a circle—the international hand signal for "roll down the window."

She blinked and blew out a breath, smiling. She cranked the window down and laughed. "Holy crow, man. You about scared me to death!"

He smiled back, his eyes glinting in the dying of the sun. "Sorry," he said. "Car trouble?"

"It just quit on me. Doesn't even crank now."

He nodded, and his eyes danced away. "Pop the hood. I'll give her a look."

"You don't have to do that. I can—"

"Don't be silly. Unless you've got a cell phone in there somewhere, you'll be walking all night." He peered into the car. "I take it you don't have one?"

She shook her head. "I have one, but I have no idea where I left it."

His eyes found hers, glinting with amusement. "Dadgum things hide, I swear it." His laugh was warm, gentle, and she chuckled along with him.

"Yeah," she said. "Kind of like cops—they're never around when you need one."

He nodded, expression sobering. He tapped the hood. "Pop it."

With a quick smile of thanks, Kelly-Ann leaned forward to grab the release. That's when he hit her.

8

When the group reassembled, they did it at Toby's "professor apartment" near the campus where he worked. They hadn't needed phone calls to arrange the meeting time, they all just decided to visit the apartment at about the same time.

Two days had passed. Toby had stayed in the Desperado, once again parked on the shores of Lake Ontario, though this time in a different RV park. Scott had checked into a hotel a few hours after they made it to Rochester—the cleaners needed a few days at his house to remove the gore. Mike got the room next to his. Shannon and Benny had spent the time together, and no one asked them where or what they did.

It seemed obvious.

"Toby, you seem much more relaxed," said Benny. "What did you do out there, alone?"

"Who said he was alone?" said Mike.

"What?" asked Benny. "You have a…"

Toby rolled his eyes.

Scott cleared his throat. "Has anyone given any more thought to how we'll deal with our friends down south?"

"We should try to outfox them politically," said Benny in an excited tone of voice.

"We could do that," said Mike. "Oneka Falls isn't such a complicated place. There's a lot of nepotism, and we won't get far if we picked the wrong people, but it's doable if we can figure out what safeguards they have in place to keep from losing."

"Yeah…" Toby scuffed the worn sole of his tennis shoe against the linoleum in the apartment's foyer. "I spent the last couple of days thinking."

"That's always dangerous," said Mike with a grin.

"I… Look, guys, I've been doing this for a while. I'm good at what I do, and my talent led me to do things the way I do. What am I going to do in a political fight?"

"We can each do something that suits our particular—"

"No, Benny. You aren't hearing me."

"Oh, I heard you, Toby. I mean, I'm right across the room. But hear me out a minute. We can each fill a role in a political machine that—"

"No," said Toby. "You hear me out a minute, Benny. I'm set up for *this.*" He swept his hands outward, encompassing the apartment, the campus, and everything that went with it. "I've been doing this for years—long enough to get over sixty of them. I know how to track them, I know how to take them out, and I know how to get rid of them and make sure they stay gotten rid of. Switching gears won't do any of us any good."

Scott watched him as he spoke, tilting his head to the side and appraising him. "Yeah, I don't know what I could contribute to this political thing, either. I'm not wound that way."

Benny looked from one to the other, his expression growing grimmer and grimmer. He glanced at Shannon as if lost, and she came to stand next to them and stroked his forearm. "I don't understand. This is the best way."

Toby shook his head again. "Not for me, Benny. I'm not sure it would work, anyway. I mean, surely these guys have faced political fights in the past twenty-something years, right? They've held power the entire time. Right, Mike?"

Mike nodded and stroked his chin with his thumb.

"So what are those safeguards? Strong-arm tactics? Ballot box stuffing?"

Mike chuckled. "Nothing as Tom Clancy as all that. I mean, think about it, they've got more demons in the town limits than people, right? That's quite a voting bloc. It could be they command everyone to come out and vote a certain way in a referendum or something."

"No matter what they do, wouldn't we face the same resistance if we tried to mount a challenge?"

Benny's grimace deepened. "But back at the park, we all agreed—"

"We were all full of adrenaline, and we were all worried about having to face every single one of those demons at once. But we don't have to do that. Even if we don't do the political challenge thing, there are other ways. I've been doing one of those ways for years now."

"But going at them one at a time, Toby… That'll take years," said Shannon. "And from what I've seen, every single one we take out that way represents a significant threat and a significant risk to each one of us."

Toby shrugged but shook his head at the same time. "The ones we faced—Red Bortha, Brigitta, Herlequin—they're the cream of the crop. They were the oldest demons, some of the first to arrive in this world. I'm sure at least a few others of their caliber exist, but we don't have to go after them until we've dealt with all the others."

"Even so, this can't become a battle of attrition," said Mike. "I mean, Shannon's right. That will take forever. No matter how weak or strong any given demon is, each one can kill any one of us with ease."

"That's true, of course, but it doesn't change the fact that if we're careful, if we go in prepared, we can win. As I told you in the car that night, I've done this sixty-one—well, sixty-three times now if we count Herlequin and Red Bortha—and every one of those sixty-three demons could have killed me. But they didn't. To the point, *I killed them.*"

Benny shook his head and looked at the carpet.

"Working together, Benny, you, me, and Mike killed *Herlequin.* Despite his tricks, despite his dog-things, despite a deck that was stacked against us from the very beginning. And in a way, we beat Herlequin when we were eleven. What makes you think any of these demons will be harder to kill than him?"

When Benny looked up, his eyes blazed with passion, and his gaze locked on Toby's. "Herlequin couldn't move—not really. Sure, over time he could move to another forest, but the tree itself? That took a long time to move. He couldn't run from us, and once I realized that, the solution presented itself."

"You're making my point, Benny."

Benny shook his head hard enough to make his hair fly around his face. "No, Toby, you misunderstand me. We didn't beat Herlequin by working together—well, we did, but that's not why we won. No, we won because he was arrogant, and he assumed there was nothing we could do to him—that we'd never understand his nature. He assumed that even if we caught him, we would focus on killing his puppet and leave as soon as that was accomplished, assuming we'd won, while he packed up and moved to a different forest, free to start his trick-show all over again." Benny slapped his hands together. "Don't you realize how lucky we are? Lucky that you brought those canisters full of that incendiary? Lucky that Herlequin didn't bring everything he had against us? He could've had *hundreds* of demons in the Thousand Acre Wood. He could've had his daughters in better forms—the dog-things might be great for chasing little kids, but they didn't seem very effective against us."

Scott cleared his throat. "You're making good points, Benny. But aren't all of these demons as arrogant? Don't they all think we're puny humans ripe for harvesting? I mean, are you scared of a cow?"

Shannon giggled.

"No, I'm not scared of a cow," said Benny. "But if a group of cows got together, cornered one of you in a pasture, and figured out how to kill you despite your best efforts, I might *become* scared of cows."

"I don't feel right sitting around letting demons feed on people," said Toby in an enervated voice. "I can't sit by. I've been given this ability to see them for a reason. I have to use it."

Benny nodded. "I agree, but using it doesn't mean that you have to be out there killing them, Rambo-style."

"Give the devil his due, Benny. It was more Dexter-style," said Mike with a smile.

Scott looked from Benny to Toby to Mike, and finally, to Shannon. "The political thing's a bust because they are already good at combating that kind of thing. We *know* they are because they are still in power all these years later. Hunting them one at a time is no good, because it's too slow, and even if we killed one of them a day that would leave them plenty of time to hunt us down or to bring more of them from wherever they're from—"

"Hell," said Mike.

Benny shook his head. "Fire and brimstone? No."

"Well, they're not from Derry."

"You got me there, Mike."

"So what do we do?" asked Scott in a voice laced with iron. "How can we deal with them *en masse*? Or at least in greater numbers than one at a time?"

Toby smacked his hand against his forehead. "We've been looking at this all wrong. We need to plan strategically. Once we are, then, and only then, can we think tactically."

"The political campaign *was* thinking strategically," said Benny.

"As a feint, perhaps." Mike glanced at Benny and shrugged.

"How can we pull them out of Oneka Falls? How can we make the town so uncomfortable for them that they leave on their own? How can we break their stranglehold on the area?" Shannon looked at Benny askance and blushed.

Toby nodded with each point. "All good questions, Shan. And those are some of the questions we need to start with. But also, why Oneka Falls? What draws them there? And given the small population of food animals—

humans living in Oneka Falls—for them, why stay there?"

"Strength in numbers?" asked Scott.

"They don't seem to be pack hunters. The opposite, really," said Benny.

"So why are they all bunched up together in a herd?"

Toby pointed at Mike. "That's question number one. If we can answer that, the answers to those other questions we listed should become obvious."

Mike chuckled and shifted his weight from one foot to the other. "Too bad there isn't an Internet guide. Or a walk-through."

"A walk-through?" asked Benny.

"Yeah, like in an RPG or an MMO where somebody amasses all the information about a dungeon or a boss fight or something and posts the steps you have to follow to win."

The expression on Benny's face transitioned from one of utter bewilderment to suspicion and back to confusion. "An RPG? MMO? What the hell are you talking about?"

Toby chopped his hand through the air. "Videogames, Benny. I'll show you later. But for right now, I've got an idea how we can get answers to those questions." He cocked his head to the side. "At least, some of them."

Scott tilted his head. "How?"

"You're not going to like it."

"The sinking feeling in my gut already let me in on that." Scott laughed, shaking his head. "Then again, I don't like the idea of LaBouche running around doing whatever he wants while both Jenny and Becky—" His voice broke.

Both Mike and Shannon put a hand on his shoulder at the same time.

Toby took a step toward him, an earnest expression on his face. "We will get him, Scott. If we do nothing else, *we will get him.*"

Scott nodded, his face suffused with blood, his eyes down.

"So," said Benny with too much enthusiasm. "What's this big idea, Toby?"

Toby glanced at him over his shoulder. "Simple. We're going to interrogate one of the weaker demons."

9

Scott Lewis closed the front door behind him. He stood for a moment, listening to the silence of the house. The professional cleaners he had hired had done their work well, but he could still detect a faint whiff of disinfectant and some other harsh chemical.

He spent a moment thinking about going upstairs, about getting undressed and crawling into bed. He glanced to his left, into the living room, his eyes skimming over the familiar furniture, the pictures on the wall, the decorations Jenny had put up. Scott shook his head, overcome with grief. He lifted his foot to step farther into the house, but after a moment, he returned it to where it was to start with.

He no longer felt as though he belonged there. It was as if he were a visitor in someone else's home, as if he were peeking behind the curtain into someone else's private life. He shook his head. *This is* my *house. It's where we raised Becky. Where Jenny and I raised her.*

But those thoughts—*facts*—did nothing to change the way he felt inside the house. Shaking his head, he took a deep breath and let it leak out with a sound akin to a balloon deflating. *I* belong *here*! The air in the house smelled flat as if a necessary, vital force had departed.

He lifted his foot again, and again he put it back down in its original position. *This is stupid. Get a grip, Scotty.*

He dithered there, in the foyer, lifting his foot, putting it down, turning his head to the left, peering down the hall toward the den, and all the while he berated himself and tried to convince himself that the home which was no longer there still existed.

After fifteen minutes, Scott Lewis turned and exited the house for the last time. He locked the front door behind him and walked back to his car, head down.

I no longer have a place in this world, he thought. *LaBouche took everything from me.*

10

LaBouche settled into the heart of the hydrangea, his breast muscles aching from the effort of flying over ninety miles. *This form…so, so stupid. My revenge on Brigitta will be…*must be…*epic. It will be spoken of for centuries.*

He watched Scott Lewis climb out of his car as if he were too weary to contemplate going on with life. He would have grinned, if not for the stupid beak. Lewis dragged his feet to the door, unlocked it, and slouched inside.

I wish I could be in there with you, Scotty. LaBouche imagined the emotions raging through his former partner—the loss, the grief, and the anger. It was almost enough to draw sustenance from.

But there was no time for concerns about things such as nourishment and delight. He hopped out of the hydrangea next to Scotty's driveway and shuffled his way toward the car. He walked right underneath it and found a nice spot to ride nestled within the rear suspension.

A quarter of an hour later, Scott left his house—as LaBouche had predicted he would. He got back in the car, started the engine, and backed out of the driveway.

No ordinary bird would have ridden where LaBouche chose to ride—but then again, LaBouche was no ordinary bird.

At least I'll know where their Honeycomb Hideout is. We can set an ambush there, maybe pick them off one by one when they think they're safe.

His reptilian heart warmed at the prospect.

II

Kelly-Ann awoke with a pounding head and a stiff neck. For a moment, she thought she was in her own bed, but as the aches and pains in her back began to sing, she remembered her "Good Samaritan." She forced her eyes open, but it didn't help much. There wasn't enough light to see by.

She shivered, goose-flesh rippling along her arms and legs. With a shudder, she checked her clothing—wondering if the man had taken liberties, but it seemed he hadn't.

Not yet, said a jaded voice in her head.

She lay on a slick, cold surface—something like porcelain. Her fingers found the edge of the table, and she swung her legs over the side.

"No, no," said the man who'd "helped" her. "Lie back. I'm not done looking at you yet."

See? I told you, said the jaded voice.

"Listen, I don't remember your face. You can just let me go. I promise I won't—"

"*LIE THE FUCK DOWN*!" he screamed.

She flopped back on the table, her body obeying before she had a chance to think. "I promise I won't say anything. I don't know where I am, and, more importantly, I don't know who you are." Silence was her only answer. "I can't identify you! You can let me go."

"No," he said without emotion.

"Please listen a minute. Whatever you want; you can't get it from me. I'm broke, and I have no one to pay any ransom."

Harsh, mocking laughter echoed in the darkness.

Fear sank its icy talons into her guts, and she started to push herself up. He took two quick steps out of the shadows—her green-eyed Samaritan—and slammed her back onto the table hard enough to knock the wind out of her.

"Rule one," he said. "You do what I say. Rule two: refer to rule one." His voice was curiously flat, unemotional.

"What do you want?"

"Rule three: keep your trap shut. When I want to hear from you, I'll make you scream."

She sucked in a breath, as if to speak, but held it, staring up into his face, and kept silent.

"Good," he crooned. "If you keep this up, I won't have to kill you." He approached her left side and leaned down until his face loomed large before her, his magnetic green eyes seeming to spin and spin and spin. "At least not tonight."

12

The others had taken his idea a lot better than Toby had imagined they would. He checked his gear for the fifth time and then turned his gaze back to the small house on the outskirts of Webster, New York.

He'd known about this demon for months. Toby had been planning his elimination when Scott and LaBouche had first approached him.

This one had chosen the name of Bill Hartman, and he had an office job, but one with flexible hours. He fed on anger and despair, especially that of children. He spent a lot of time watching inner-city school playgrounds. At one time, Toby had considered framing him as a pedophile, but at the end of the day, that would've left one more demon alive in the world, and his usual methods would not have.

Hartman lived on a large plot of land on the southern shore of Lake Ontario. Apple orchards surrounded his lot, which were free of people for most of the year. Hartman's house sat well back from the lake, with the copse of trees blocking the view of the shore. A single rutted track wound its way through trees and through the orchard itself, leading to Lake Road.

It was a perfect place for an ambush.

The house itself was large, built from stone quarried nearby—almost a castle. The front doors were made of thick oak and hung on iron hinges. Hartman lived alone, of course, and when he was away, the house stood empty.

Toby crouched in the flowerbed at the side of the house. Scott was somewhere out there in the orchard, covering him with a high-powered rifle. Sitting in Scott's cruiser out at the edge of the road, Mike doubled as both look-out and backup.

After making sure the rutted track was clear, Toby stood and approached the front door. Locked with a modern lock as it was, gaining entry through the front door wouldn't be much of an impediment. He crouched to get a better look at the lock and fished out his lock picks. A few seconds later, the bolt sprang open, and Toby stepped inside.

The living room of the house held only a large television, a single recliner, and a scarred wooden side table. The recliner appeared well-worn and on its last legs. He walked through the room into the back of the house, which was remarkable only because of its complete lack of furnishings. A layer of dust coated the kitchen counters and the sink.

Can he live in that front room only? Toby climbed the stairs to the upper floors, but it was more of the same—empty rooms and dust. *He must have something here. Even if it's a paltry list of phone numbers to call. Then again, he doesn't even have phone service out here, so…*

Toby descended into the basement and found a row of cages built into the basement wall. Each cell was roughly three feet square—just enough for a human to stand wedged against the wall. Another well-worn recliner sat in the center of the floor facing the cages.

"Car coming," said Mike into the receiver nestled in Toby's ear canal. "It's got its turn signal on."

"Ten-four," said Scott. "Get ready, Toby."

Toby raced up the stairs, taking them two or three at a time. He slipped out into the backyard by way of the kitchen door and skidded to a halt at the corner of the house. He pressed his shoulder blades into the cold stone and waited.

"I think it's him," said Mike. "He gave me the stink-eye until I flashed Scott's badge at him. He's headed up the drive now. You should have him any second, Scott."

Scott keyed the mic twice but said nothing.

Toby's muscles tensed, and he felt the familiar excitement rumbling around his belly. He unslung his custom-made tranquilizer gun and slapped in a loaded magazine. *We need more of these guns.* He had loaded the darts with M99—an extra-large dose for sureties' sake. He chambered a dart and held the gun in one hand, barrel-down.

"Danger close," hissed Scott in his ear.

Toby dropped into a crouch as he heard tires crunching over the gravel in front of the house. He slunk around the corner, staying low and tight to the wall. The engine of Hartman's car died, and a car door opened and slammed.

Toby advanced to the end of the wall and grabbed a quick glance around the corner. Hartman was a traditional demon—dark red leathery wings, bright red flesh, and cloven hooves. He was small for a demon and thin almost to the point of emaciation.

Hartman stood for a moment, his gaze scanning the apple orchard. His shoulders twitched, and Toby ducked back.

"Looking your way," whispered Scott. "Just looking, but maybe you should fall back."

Toby waddled backward two steps and brought the tranquilizer gun to his shoulder, aiming an inch or two in front of the corner. He kept the gun leveled at about where he expected Hartman's head would appear if he peeked around the corner.

"Hold," said Scott. "Mike, be ready."

What's he doing? Come on, Scott, tell me what he's doing, Toby thought. Without Benny around, thinking things at people was useless, but that little fact didn't stop him from trying.

"Okay…okay, everything's okay. He's sniffing the air, but maybe he's just looking at the upstairs windows. He's glancing at your corner, Toby, but not staring at it."

Moving silently, Toby shuffled back several yards.

"Freeze! He may have heard you, Toby. He's staring at the corner, now."

In the distance, a car horn blared.

"Good, Mike! Get back on him, Toby!"

Toby duck walked to the corner and peered around it. Hartman stood staring up the rutted track, his back to the house—and Toby.

The tranquilizer gun was still tight against his shoulder, and all Toby had to do was lean around the corner. He squeezed the trigger three times, and the weapon spat darts at the demon's back. He pulled back, turning his back to the corner and moving in a running crouch toward the rear of the house.

"That's got his attention," said Scott. "He looks a little woozy."

He should—that's enough M99 to kill ten men! Toby slid around the back corner of the house and took the same position squatting against the wall.

"In the side yard now, Toby. He's looking around, looking for you." Scott's voice was calm—almost too serene for Toby's tastes. It was hard to judge how close the demon was with all that calm. Scott laughed. "He's down. Damn that M99 works well."

Toby didn't move. The demons sometimes played dead when they couldn't find their attacker.

"All right, I'm coming down," said Scott.

No! Where was Benny when he was needed? Toby didn't dare speak in his own throat mic—Hartman would hear him for sure—and if Benny were around, he could've relayed his thoughts to Scott.

Staying as close to the wall as possible, Toby peered around the corner, exposing only one eye. Hartman lay on the ground, eyes open, staring up at the sky, but one of his large pointed ears twitched and oriented toward the orchard.

Dammit, Scott! Toby brought the gun up and sprinted around the corner, firing as he moved, sending two more darts into the demon. He ejected the spent magazine and slapped a full one in its place.

Hartman's other ear twitched, twisting toward Toby as he rounded the corner. He snap-fired the tranquilizer rifle twice from his hip as he ran, zigzagging toward the tree line on the side of the house. One dart drifted wide, but the other hit the demon in the side of the neck—right where a human's jugular would be.

The demon's ears swiveled independently to track both threats at the same time. After a moment more of playing dead, Hartman sprang to his feet like a martial artist in an old '80s Kung Fu movie and squalled at the sky. He sank into a crouch, arms extended to either side as if offering a hug, claws bared, and hissed at Toby.

Toby continued to circle, trying to clear Scott's line of fire, hoping Scott still had a sightline. The demon turned—too quickly—and staggered to the side, his leathery wings flapped for balance, and he swept the tranquilizer darts out of his skin with one hand.

A round from Scott's rifle buzzed by Toby, sounding similar to a wasp buzzing nearby, and slammed into Hartman's shoulder, half spinning the demon away from Toby. A deep purple ichor splashed across the grass, and the rifle's report echoed in from the apple orchard. Toby dropped to one knee, raised his tranquilizer gun, and slammed three more darts into the demon's back.

Ten darts... Either the M99 is getting weaker, or all of the demons are somehow building a tolerance to it. Toby rolled to the side, ejecting the empty magazine and sliding his last loaded magazine into the gun. *One more question to ask this bozo.*

Hartman staggered toward him, like a drunken maniac, wheeling his arms and flapping his wings for balance. His eyelids drooped, and he leaned forward, then stumbled back. Another rifle round buzzed by—this time slamming into Hartman's middle and hurling him to the ground. The demon tried to stand, tried to push up on his elbows, and gave up consciousness.

Toby stayed where he was, covering Hartman with his tranquilizer gun.

"Mike, bring in the car," Scott said over the radio. "He's down."

"Who's down? Toby?" Panic danced around the edges of Mike's voice.

"No, no. Sorry, Mike. *Hartman's* down."

Nice to know Mike still cares, thought Toby. Hartman's wings twitched, and his fingers trembled, but other than that he didn't move. Toby straightened, keeping the tranquilizer gun on the demon's center of mass.

He heard Scott jogging in from his hiding place in the apple orchard, and out on Lake Road, the NYSP car rumbled to life and crunched gravel down the two-rut track.

"Hartman," said Toby. "You're an ugly son of a bitch, aren't you?"

The demon didn't move, not even a twitch of his wings.

Toby stepped closer, keeping the rifle pointed at the thing's middle, and kicked his foot, but the demon didn't react.

"Is he out?" asked Scott over the radio.

Toby held his left fist over his head. *And that's how you kidnap a demon*, he thought.

Chapter 3

1986

I

"Hello, Mrs. Canton. Can your grandson come out and play?"

"Well, hello, Mason. Joe told me how you helped him the other day. That was very nice of you."

Mason returned the old lady's smile. He'd learned a while before that a bright smile went a long way—especially with grandmothers. "It was the neighborly thing to do."

"My oh my! Listen to you, getting all grown up." She half turned and glanced inside her house. "Greg, dear!" she called.

Greg! I have to remember that this time. Mason waited, the smile plastered on his face in case the old woman turned back to him. From deeper inside the Canton house, the kid answered, but Mason couldn't hear what he said.

"Mason from next-door is here, Greg. He wants you to come out and play."

Again, the boy answered, and this time he sounded closer, but the response was still too low for Mason to discern. "I thought we might play in the woods since he had the...*trouble*...out on the lake the other day."

"I'm sure that he would enjoy that, dear," said the old woman absently. "Greg enjoys the woods."

"What boy doesn't?"

Mrs. Canton's gaze snapped back to his face, her expression unreadable. "I forget how fast boys grow up," she murmured. "How old are you now, dear?"

Mason smiled and nodded. "I just turned thirteen."

"My oh my," murmured the old woman. "Getting all grown up."

"Yes, ma'am." He looked down quickly, so she wouldn't see his sneer. He hated it when people said things like that to him.

"Ah, here's Greggy. Dear, you remember Mason."

Mason lifted his gaze to the younger boy's. "Hi, Greg. Do you want to come out? We can play explorers in the woods…"

"I…"

Mrs. Canton put her hand on Greg's shoulder and exerted a little pressure toward the door. "Go on out, dear. Have fun with someone your own age for a few hours."

Again, Mason dropped his gaze to the concrete path beneath his Reebok sneakers. *His own age*? *That twerp is way younger than me*!

"Okay. For a little bit, then." The brat put his hand on the screen door and pushed it open a crack.

Don't do me any favors, jerkwad. Mason stepped back, giving the door room to swing open all the way. "Yeah, it can't be too long, anyway. I've got other stuff to do this afternoon."

"You two boys have fun," said Mrs. Canton, already turning away.

Greg stepped outside and let the screen door close behind him. He glanced at Mason, then looked away. "What do you want to play?" he asked in a quiet tone.

"Come on, kid. I've got a game we can play in the woods." Mason turned and walked away before the boy had a chance to answer, hiding a smile.

"In the woods?"

Mason didn't answer. Instead, he ducked his head and sprinted across the gravel lane and between the trees beyond the lane's edge. "Keep up!" After a moment, the boy's running footsteps crunched in the gravel behind him.

"Hey! Wait up!"

Without pausing, Mason called, "Come on!" He zigged behind a tree before circling around another. "Keep up! Follow in my footsteps…"

"Why do we have to run!"

"It's part of the game." Mason leaped over the trunk of the fallen tree, kicking at the leaves on the other side. "Do what I do." He put his head down and ran as fast as he could. He sprinted in a straight line, leaving the younger boy behind.

Mason threw out his hand, skidded around the trunk of a sapling, a predatory grin on his face. Greg ran toward him, but before he could get close, Mason laughed, spun on his heels, and sprinted away.

"Is this it? Is this the whole game?" asked Greg.

Mason laughed louder and kept running. He wanted to get the boy farther into the woods—farther away from the lane and the row of houses on the opposite side. "Come on! I've got something to show you," he said over his shoulder. "It's really cool. All the thirteen-year-olds around here think so."

"What is it?"

"Keep up to find out!" Mason feinted to the right but sprinted left, ducking behind a thick tree trunk dotted with knurls. He slowed, listening for the younger boy's footsteps. As Greg approached, Mason moved around the tree, keeping it between them.

"Hey!"

Mason wanted to laugh at the discomfort in the brat's voice. He moved as quietly as he knew how, circling the tree. Greg stood, facing away from him and staring into the deeper woods.

"Where'd you go? Mason?"

Mason allowed a nasty grin to break across his face as he crept up behind the boy.

"Mason?"

"Got you!" he screamed as he grabbed Greg by the shoulders and flung him to the ground. He laughed at the expression on the brat's face, pointing at him. "You should see your face!"

"That's not funny!"

Mason squatted next to Greg, still laughing. "Oh, don't be that way. Don't be a brat! I was *teasing*."

"Yeah? Well, I don't like your kind of teasing."

Drawing his eyelids into a squint, Mason frowned. "I knew you'd act this way. My grandma said you'd be more grown up this year." He shook his head, tsking. "I guess she was wrong, huh? You're still a bratty little kid, huh?"

"Maybe I am, but you're just a jerk! You got me all dirty!"

Mason rocked back on his heels. "Well, *excuse* me!" He shook his head, putting as much disgust into his facial expression as he knew how. "I just thought you might want to do something other than hanging out with your parents and grandparents. I just thought you might want to play with a kid close to your own age." He stood, dusting his hands on his jeans. "My mistake, brat. I won't make it again."

Greg drew his legs up, wrapped his arms around his knees and shrugged. "I don't like rough horseplay, is all."

He ducked his head but peeked up at Mason from the corner of his eye. "Sorry I called you a jerk."

Mason stared at him for the space of a few breaths, his face wrapped in a rictus of wrath that he didn't feel. He gazed off into the woods, scratching the side of his head, before allowing his face to relax. "Yeah. Sorry about the stuff I said, too."

Greg got to his feet. "So what is this thing you wanted to show me?"

With a friendly smile, Mason rested his hand on the younger boy's shoulder. "Come on. It's over this way." They walked in silence for few minutes, Mason's hand still on Greg's shoulder.

"So…"

"You live down in Florida, right?" Mason asked.

"Yeah."

"It's pretty hot down there, yeah? Not like here."

Greg nodded his head. "Yeah, it's a lot hotter. Plus, the humidity is real high, so you sweat all the time."

"And Disneyland? Have you ever been there?"

Greg chuckled. "Disneyland is in California, silly. Disney *World* is the one in Florida."

Mason lifted his hand from the boy's shoulder and slapped him on the back of the head, but without much force. "Excuse the fuck right out of me. I guess you're a big man of the world, and all, and I'm just some rube from Western New York." He hawked and spat into the woods. "But I'll tell you something, sport. You'd better learn a bit of fucking respect." He pushed the younger boy hard to the side, and Greg stumbled away, fighting for balance. Mason kept right on walking, ignoring his squawk.

Greg regained his balance, and hesitated a moment, staring after Mason. Then he ran to catch up. "Sorry. I didn't mean anything by it."

Mason wagged his head back and forth. "Respect, kid. It's important. The lack of it can get your ass kicked, but the use of it can get you what you want in life."

"Yeah, sorry."

Mason looked at him askance. "What had your panties in a wad on the lake the other day? During the storm."

Greg looked at his sneakers. "Nothing," he muttered.

Mason smiled crookedly. "Nah, I'm not buying that. You were all crying and sniveling when your gramps brought you back. Like a little baby."

Greg shook his head.

"Come on, kid. Tell me what it was."

Greg kept his head down and didn't answer.

Mason stopped walking. "Either tell me, or I won't show you this thing."

"You'll make fun of me."

"Nah."

A sullen expression darkened Greg's face. "You will."

Mason laughed, but it was far from an amused sound. "Listen, kid, I know all about *her*. I've been coming here for a long time, and I spend *all* summer here, not just a few weeks." He turned and faced Greg. "What you saw was *real*."

"What…" Greg shook his head and crossed his arms over his chest. "How do you know what I saw?"

Mason smirked and spread his arms wide. "That's an easy one, *Greggy*. She asked me who she should pay *special* attention to. She asked me for a list." He leaned forward, tilting his head toward the ground so he could look at Greg from beneath his brows. "Guess whose name I put right on top?"

"It's not funny!" shouted Greg.

"It is to me." Mason shrugged and wrinkled his nose at Greg. "What's more, it is to *her*."

Greg took two steps back, shaking his head. "It was just a…"

"What? It was just a what? A trick of the light? A blip of your imagination? A bad dream?" Mason sneered at the younger boy. "She's none of those things, Greggy. She's *magnificent*."

Greg turned away, hanging his head and dropping his hands to his sides. "I told you you'd tease me."

Mason sighed and glanced around. When he returned his gaze to Greg, a smile of genuine pleasure was on his face. "You ain't seen nothing yet, kid." He took two quick steps forward and shoved Greg to the ground. Then, without another word, he leaped over him and sprinted away through the woods.

"I'm not following you! I don't want to play with you anymore, Mason!"

Mason sniggered to himself as he ran. *Some kids are dense. She's right—some kids are cattle, waiting for the wolves of the world to gobble them up.* He'd done everything she'd told him to, and she'd been right about how Greg would react. He thought about how pleased she would be with him, about how she might reward him, and his smile stretched from ear to ear.

2

A few hours later, all five of the Cantons piled into Stephen's rented Bonneville and headed into town. One of the local tourist spots made fresh fried chicken and homemade ice cream. It also contained a gift shop of sorts, with a few products made in the area, but junk from China for the most part.

As with kids everywhere, Greg loved the gift shop. Every time they ate at the Chicken Shack, he clamored to visit the little shop. And every time, trying to hide smiles, his parents allowed him to go inside—mostly holding Grandma's hand, and she'd buy him a little toy before they all strolled over to the restaurant side and ate as a family.

That day, things didn't go as they usually did.

Stephen, Mary, and Joe stood by the door, just inside the gift shop, watching Greg lead Elizabet through the aisles of stuff. A heavyset woman called out to Elizabet and trundled over, all smiles. She bent and fussed over Greg for a minute or two before asking him something. Greg turned a panicked expression toward his mother as a dark stain spread across the crotch of his jeans. He reddened and ran to Mary, tears streaming down his face.

"What's wrong, Greggy?" she asked.

His response was lost in his sobs.

Mary cast a worried glance at her husband. "Let's go in the bathroom and get you cleaned up. What do you say, Greggy?"

Joe ordered their food to go. No one said anything to Greg as they piled back into the car, but as soon as the car door shut, he turned his face to the door and sucked his thumb.

Mason Harper was outside when they came home. He took one look at Greg's wet jeans and burst into laughter.

3

After Greg was asleep, his parents and grandparents filed out onto the screened porch to enjoy the night air—and to discuss the events of the day.

"I'm wondering if he'll need to see a doctor," said Mary.

"Whatever for? He's fine, dear."

"Physically, sure. I'm concerned about… This business about the dead lady concerns me, Elizabet."

Joe packed and lit his pipe, and its orange glow cast warm tones across his face. "It's the light."

"The light?" asked Mary.

"Ayup. Overcast as it was, and the lake as deep and dark as it is…" Joe shook his head. "A fella can trick himself into seeing all sorts of things."

Mary glanced at Stephen and treated him to a minute shake of her head.

"Honey," he said. "He's fine. He's a little shaken up, is all."

"I don't know. He was sucking his thumb all the way home, Stephen."

"He's still a boy, dear," said Elizabet.

Mary nodded but didn't look convinced. "Why would a grown woman ask a boy his age something like that?"

Joe nodded and drew on his pipe and released a cloud of sickly-sweet smoke. "Folks around here…well, we've got our superstitions, same as anywhere else. Around these parts, the story's viewed as about a quarter serious, and three-quarters joke. She didn't mean anything, and she didn't know about his scare the other day."

"I'm sure she thought he knew all about the legends." Stephen put his arm around his wife.

"Maybe. But why would anyone ask a boy his age…"

"It's akin to a campfire story. A—what do you call'em—a ghost story, but a local one. The locals always tell their families these stories and consider it nothing untoward."

"And he would've loved it before his experience the other day," said Stephen.

"Well, what is this 'Woman in White?'"

"Joe will tell it," said Elizabet. "He enjoys the telling."

Joe turned in his chair and treated Elizabet to a look. "It goes back to a couple hundred years or more. The story says a widow lived on the other shore of the lake, almost right across from this house. She had a teenage daughter, follow? One day during a bad thunderstorm, the daughter says she wants to go down to the lake. She likes the rain, you see? She likes to watch the lightning reflecting in the water." Joe drew on his pipe and released another cloud of smoke. "Well, you can guess what happens next. That girl never came home. No trace of her. Just gone."

"And she's the Woman in White?" asked Mary.

"Nope, guessed wrong there. No, the girl never came home—was never seen again, living or dead. Well, that widow, she set about looking. Every day, she traipsed out and scoured the countryside looking for signs of her daughter. Never found a thing. Sad. She's supposed to be the creature in the story. Some folks call her the Lady in the Lake, but most around here call her the Woman in White because after her daughter disappeared, she took on religious airs that extended to wearing white anytime she graced the public with her presence."

"Most claim to see her on misty days," said Elizabet. "Out walking in the mist, calling for her long-lost baby."

Joe sat back and nodded. "And that's it."

"How... I don't understand how that story connects with Greg's dead lady."

"Remember we said it was about a quarter serious and three-quarters fun? That story was the three-quarters fun version." Elizabet swatted Joe's leg with the back of her hand. "Go on. Tell her the other version."

Joe arched an eyebrow at his wife. "It's not near as nice."

"Tell me anyway, Joe." The flicker of unease in her eyes belied Mary's firm tone.

"Well, okay. This version is no doubt stretched all the hell over the place, but it might be closer to the truth. In this version, the widow was crazy. She had a teenage daughter, as with the 'Woman in White' version, but this widow locked her daughter up good and tight. Chained her right to the wall of their cabin. Never let her out. Let no one in to visit her."

More sweet-smelling smoke filled the night air.

"One night, there was one hell of a storm. The widow's cabin was under these big trees, follow? The wind blew one of them right over. Took one wall clean off the cabin when it came down. You can probably guess which wall the widow had chained the girl to. Well, she up and ran the second she figured out she was free. The widow chased her, right down to the lake. Watching her crazy mother bearing down on her, the girl waded out into the water, chain and all." Joe leaned forward in his chair and fixed Mary with a steely glance. "That crazy old woman followed her daughter right down into the water. Drowned them both. The crazy old woman is supposed to be the ghost we call the Lady in the Lake."

He leaned back in his chair and arched his eyebrow at Elizabet. "Good enough?"

Elizabet smiled and patted him on the knee.

Mary looked at Stephen. "You knew the stories?"

"Sort of. Mom and Dad didn't buy this place until after I was away at college. I've heard the stories, sure, but I didn't know the history. Or how involved the community was in these legends."

"You see, dear? No one means anything by it."

Mary didn't answer, she only shook her head and shrugged.

4

After Mary and Elizabet headed to bed, Joe and Stephen sat out on the porch and drank beer in companionable silence. Joe lit his pipe for the umpteenth time that night, and Stephen tried to hide a smile.

"I can still see that smile," said Joe.

"You always could."

"Ayup."

"So...are you going to tell me?"

Joe turned his head and arched his eyebrow.

Stephen looked out toward the black patch that was the lake. "You know what I'm asking you."

Joe relaxed back into his chair and drew on the pipe. "Ayup."

They sat in silence for a few more minutes before Stephen cleared his throat.

Joe cast an irritated glance his way. "Well, if you're going to nag..."

Stephen raised his hand to hide his smile.

"It's the light. Gray skies, dark water. Plays tricks on a fella. Might make him think he sees something."

"Like a dead woman in the lake?"

Without looking at him, Joe nodded. "Could go that-a-way."

"But it didn't?"

Joe sighed and drew on his pipe again. "What I saw, was a little boy panicking out in the middle of the lake by himself in a red plastic kayak. Could be, I picked up a touch of that panic myself."

"I've never seen you panic, Dad."

Joe nodded slowly and examined the glowing tobacco in the bowl of his pipe. "It's hard to explain any other way." He made a vague gesture with his pipe stem. "Quarter serious or not, those are stories. Tall tales."

"What did you see?"

Joe drew a deep breath and blew his cheeks out. "As I was coming up on Greg, the first thing I saw was the kayak shimmying left and right, all while tilting bow first into the water. Next thing, everything settled down for a minute before the shaking started up again, but with more oomph. I cranked her up—the Mercury. As I got closer, I saw something stretched across the top of the kayak. Something gray, slick."

"What was it?"

Joe shrugged and looked his son in the eye. "Could have been a bike innertube. Something such as that."

"Could have been?"

"That's what I said, isn't it?" Joe snapped. "I was too far away, in a moving boat with the spray, the rain. I didn't get a good look."

"Okay, okay. What then?"

"Your boy swung the paddle like he was trying to kill something. He really went at it, whatever it was, and then he slapped the paddle against the water hard. The gray thing was off the kayak by that time." Joe set the pipe down on the metal table between them. "After that, he stopped hitting things and paddled as though his britches were on fire. He made about one or two full strokes, and..."

Stephen waited, letting his dad tell the story in his own time.

Joe shook his head. "This next part could make a guy wonder if he was getting the dementia.

"No judgments here, Dad."

"Yeah, well. There are plenty of those damn things over in this chair." Joe sat for a few moments, breathing and staring out at the lake. "Well, on that second or third stroke, the paddle stopped."

"*Stopped*? Greg just stopped paddling?"

"It was the damnedest thing, Son. Greg didn't stop the paddle, the paddle stopped Greg."

"What do you mean?"

"That paddle was sticking straight up and down out of the water, and your boy...well, he was pulling and pushing at it every which way. He couldn't budge it, not at all. He tried jerking it up, nothing happened. After a few seconds of that, it looked as if something jerked that paddle out of his hands—straight down into the water."

"Is that how it *looked* or is that *what happened*?"

"You're at the wrong house. Fortune-teller's two down."

"Okay. What happened next."

Joe hitched a deep breath and let it ease back out. "I was pretty close by that time. Greg was sitting there, slumped over in the kayak, staring into the water to his right. He saw me and yelled for help, said someone was trying to get him or some such. That's when—"

Joe snapped his mouth shut with an audible click. "If I tell you this, and you don't believe me, it's too bad. Ain't going to no nursing home."

"No judgments, remember?"

"Needed to be said, that's all. This is the part where I don't much trust my memory. Perhaps it was panic, as I said before—you know, because Greg was so scared. I think... I thought I saw an arm coming up out of the water behind him. That arm was gray, same as the thing that had been wrapped over the front of the kayak. It looked as if… Greg leaned back, far back like he was going to fall in the water backward."

"What happened next?"

"Most things in the water—most things that want to hurt somebody—they're scared of the motorboat. I circled around the kayak, spinning that Mercury as fast as it would spin. I cut a tight circle, mind, setting the water all a-roil. I saw nothing else. Greg, he—"

Joe's voice caught in his throat. "He held out his arms like a little kid, so I grabbed him and pulled him over into the Alumacraft. I wrapped my jacket around him, and away we skipped."

They sat in silence for what felt like a long time, both staring out at the impenetrable blackness that was Genosgwa Lake. Joe picked up his pipe and dug out the ash with his pinky. He glanced at Stephen out of the corner of his eye but said nothing.

Joe set the cleaned pipe back on the metal table. "Well? Am I crazy?"

Stephen turned and favored him with a penetrating gaze. "Yes. You are crazy, but you always have been."

"Hilarious."

"I don't know what you witnessed; I wasn't there. All I know, Dad, is that you saved my son."

Joe looked at his shoes. "Well…"

Stephen turned and gazed out at the lake once more. "I guess…"

Joe leaned forward and rested his elbows on his knees. "Yes?"

"I guess my only real question is this. What do *you* think you saw?"

Joe dropped his head and let it hang. "Son, I've never lied to you, and I'm not lying now—"

"Dad, I'm not—"

"No, let me finish. I've never lied to you, and I'm not lying to you now when I say I have no idea what to think." He sat still for a while, elbows on his knees, head hanging. When he spoke again, it was barely audible. "All I know is that I never want to see it—or anything remotely akin to it—ever again."

As fate would have it, Joe would not get his wish.

5

As the full moon shone down on the deep, black lake, Will Seeger pushed his fishing boat away from his dock. "Nothing better than a little midnight fishing," he said to his son-in-law, Chris.

"You get more action?"

"Could be."

"Definitely not as hot, this time of day. Or night, rather."

"True." Will didn't much care for his son-in-law. He didn't much enjoy his company, and he didn't enjoy hosting him at his lake house—his summer sanctum from a world full of assholes like Chris. He hitched a deep breath and sighed. Chris had married his daughter, and that meant he had to be pleasant. *But if he's doing what I think he's doing to my Sammy, and I catch sign of it, by God the time for being nice will have ended.*

He piloted the boat in silence for a few minutes, with nothing more than the soft slap of the tranquil lake against the bow. Chris slumped on the bench in the middle of the boat, and every now and again, Will's gaze left the water and tracked to the back of the younger man's head.

Chris was a fancy Wall Street man—a banker or some such—always making calls late at night or lording his financial knowledge over everyone—playing the big man, in other words. To Will's mind, it was yet another mark against him.

Sure, he provided Sammy with a good life…though Will believed she was paying for it. But there wasn't anything explicit he could point to, no strange bruises, no injuries from walking into doors or tripping down steps. It was only a feeling, but Will was a good judge of character, and to his mind, Chris didn't have much of that.

"What's that?" asked Chris. He pointed off the bow to port.

Will let his gaze drift away from Chris long enough to check out what he was pointing at. "A log."

"Is that… Will, that's no log."

Will squinted, cursing his old eyes in silent annoyance, and he turned the boat to bring them alongside whatever it was in the water. "We'll take a look."

As they drew closer, it became more and more apparent that the thing floating in the water wasn't a log. Not unless a log had a head, two arms, and two legs.

"Uh, Will?"

Will hated the sniveling sound of his son-in-law's voice. He kept the boat pointed toward the body floating in the lake and kept the propeller spinning.

"Will, we should head back to the house and call the authorities."

Will scoffed. "If we do that, and that body sinks again, they have to drag this lake and the depth—"

"Yes, but we shouldn't disturb the crime scene."

"Crime scene? You've been watching too much television. This isn't the crime scene, Chris."

"Maybe not, but we shouldn't disturb the body."

Will shook his head and spat over the gunnel into the black water. "Son, do you think somebody's going to be out here with crime scene tape and chalk? No. We'll deal with this and afterward, go call the police."

"It's your boat, and everything, Will, but I'm not comfortable with this."

Even though his son-in-law was facing the wrong direction to see it, Will shrugged and sneered. "You'll get over it."

Chris hunched his shoulders as if he were pouting, but he said nothing more.

Will cut the engine when they were close enough and drifted up alongside the bloated body floating in the water. The girl was swollen and shriveled at the same time, and there was a waxy substance coating her.

"Help me get her in the boat."

"Nuh-uh. No way."

"Chris," Will said with a trace of steel in his voice. "I can't get her in by myself. Get up off your ass and get over to the side and grab her legs."

"We should—"

"Do what I say! We're not leaving here without this body."

Chris swiveled at his tone and stared at Will with an ugly, strong emotion crawling around underneath the skin of his face. His eyes were blank, almost glassy, and for a moment, Will expected they might exchange a blow or six—boat or no boat. Then, without another word,

Chris turned and positioned himself along the port gunnel.

That bastard hits her. I'm almost sure of it, Will thought. *When I am sure, by God, this sniveling little coward better pack his lunch.*

Will took the young girl's body by the armpits and motioned with his head for Chris to grab her lower legs. "On the count of three."

"Oh, for Christ's sake, Will! Lift!" Chris hauled on her legs.

Shaking his head, Will lifted the girl's torso out of the water, and they lay her on the bottom of the boat.

"Now, Will, turn this goddamn boat around."

Will held his son-in-law's eyes for a heartbeat and another. The words were there, lounging on the tip of his tongue, but he didn't dare ask them now. Because if he did, Chris might answer, and if he was angry enough to let Will see the darker side of him, he might be angry enough to answer with the truth.

And, if that happened, there would be two bodies in the bottom of the boat. One way or another.

Will crawled back to the outboard and started it. He turned toward the bow, and his gaze tracked down to where the girl lay. She was young—prepubescent—and the clothes she wore…it seemed she been in the water a while. A lump formed in his throat for the little girl's father.

He whipped the boat around and opened the throttle full. They roared back to the dock, and Chris jumped out before they'd tied up. He ran up to the house and slammed the door going in.

Will watched it all, shaking his head. He tied the boat off himself and glanced toward the house. Sammy came to the screen door and looked out but said nothing. "Tell your mother to call Tom Walton," Will called up to her.

Sammy nodded and turned back into the house.

Under the dock's lights, the state of the body became visible. Before she'd gone into the lake, someone had done a number on her. She was bruised, battered, and slashed with something wicked sharp. It sickened Will, but he didn't seem to be able to turn away.

His gaze continued to crawl down her body, coming to rest on her feet. She'd lost her shoes, and her feet were shredded, but whether by a natural process in the lake or abuse before she died, Will couldn't say.

The longer he looked, the worse he felt. He glanced toward the house and imagined Chris striking Sammy, and his pulse and respiration accelerated. His hands ached as if they longed to be around his son-in-law's neck.

6

The phone jarred John Morton out of a deep sleep, but he'd been a cop for years, and when he was awake, he was *awake*. "John Morton," he said.

"Hey, John. Tom Walton. I've got a question or two for you."

John scrubbed his eyes with the heel of his hand and peered at the alarm clock on the nightstand. It was just shy of six in the morning. "Give me a second, Tom. I'll call you right back."

"Sure thing. I'm at the office."

He got out of bed and padded to the hall door, closing it with as little ruckus as he could. He shuffled out to the kitchen and dialed Tom's direct number.

Tom picked up on the first ring. "Seems that one of your missing people back in '79 was a young girl?"

"Yeah, sure." John set about making coffee.

"I may have her."

"What? Alive?"

The line hissed and popped for a moment. "No, not alive. A body floated to the surface of Lake Genosgwa last night. Fishermen found her."

"Ah. I suppose you need an ID?"

"It would help. Do you have contact information for the parents?"

"Well, that one's going to be difficult. They split up after the little girl disappeared. Her mother pointed the finger at her father. Drunk, worthless. Got himself wrapped around a telephone pole coming home from Oneka Falls one night."

"And the mother?"

"Gone. I'll ask around, find out if anyone has contact information on her."

"She didn't leave contact information? What if you found her daughter?"

John sighed. "Her mom and dad were cut from the same cloth."

"I see. You still have pictures in your files?"

"I do, and I'll bring them by later this morning. Nine o'clock sound good?"

"Yeah, it's not as if she's going anywhere."

7

Joe was sitting in the same chair he had sat in the night before when Stephen came out with a steaming mug of coffee. He was looking out at the lake, at the Sheriff's Department boat that was going back and forth along the shore on the other side.

Stephen pointed at it with his coffee mug. “Little early for fishing, isn’t it?”

Joe grunted and shifted his weight in the chair. “Dragging the lake, I imagine.”

“Why would they do that, Dad?”

They watched as the boat reached the end of its search line, and they pulled the drag out of the water. From their vantage, it looked empty. The deputies turned the boat and threw the drag out behind as they started back the way they had come.

“Evidence.”

“Evidence of what, Dad?”

Joe lifted both hands and held them out toward the lake. “Of whatever they’re looking for. A body, perhaps.”

Stephen thought of the story his father had told him about rescuing Greg. About the arm coming up out of the water and grabbing his son. “Could it… If it is a body they’re looking for, it could have been what you saw. What Greg saw. He could’ve snagged it somehow, and in his panic…”

Joe’s only answer was a shrug. He glanced at his son’s mug of coffee. “Sure, I’ll take a cup.”

Shaking his head but grinning, Stephen handed the mug to his father. “Haven’t even touched it. I’ll go get myself another.”

"You're a good son." Joe's gaze slipped away, back toward the Sheriff's boat zigzagging back and forth across the lake.

They got their answers on the noon-time local news. All the Cantons, except for Greg, watched the broadcast in silence. When the coverage ended, Joe stood and snapped the television off.

"Maybe that's our answer," said Stephen.

"Maybe so," said Joe.

Elizabet and Mary exchanged glances.

"Dad told me last night that he caught a glimpse of something out there near Greg's kayak. Something that looked gray and dead and had wrapped around the front of the kayak. I can understand it…how that would freak a boy out."

Joe nodded once. "Might've sunk as I approached in the Alumacraft. It was rough out there, whitecaps, the lot. Maybe she sank again and resurfaced later after the storm."

Mary glanced out the large bay window at the lake, and at her son who lay in the hammock reading a book. "My poor baby," she whispered.

Elizabet patted her arm. "Children are much more resilient than we give them credit for."

"That's true, honey," said Stephen. "You watch. He'll bounce back from this before the week's out."

Mary said nothing, only nodded in an absent way.

John motioned toward the kitchen with his head, and Stephen followed him. When they got there, Stephen turned, and Joe glanced over his shoulder. "I'm going to go into town and try to talk to Tom Walton. You should stay here."

"Think there might be trouble?"

Joe's eyes slipped to the bay window and his grandson beyond. "Nah. But still…the body of a young kid like that." He met his son's gaze and shrugged. "Why take chances?"

Stephen nodded, his eyes never leaving his father's. "Rifle still in the same place?"

"Ammunition, too. Do you remember the code? Not that I expect you'll need it."

"Yes, I've got it. You go talk to Tom; I'll hold down the fort."

"Good boy. Make sure somebody keeps an eye on Greg. At least until I've spoken with Tom."

Joe turned to go, but Stephen's hand on his shoulder stopped him. "Ask Tom what measures we need to take."

"Absolutely. Tom's a good man, and he'll tell me the right of it."

"Make sure he knows we have a boy about the same age here right now."

"First thing on my list."

Together, father and son nodded. Joe turned and strode out to the freestanding garage that stood behind the lake house. Inside he kept a cherry-red 1965 Pontiac GTO. He'd bought it brand new and had maintained it himself.

The car fired up with a roar, and he pulled away, big tires crunching over the gravel road. As he hit the highway, he fed it the gas, enjoying the brisk wind caused by his passage. For a twenty-one-year-old car, it was still a screaming demon.

He hit the Genosgwa town limits a short time later. The lake house was the perfect distance away from town—far enough he didn't want to go for every little thing, but close enough he could get there in a hurry when he wanted to. Especially as the owner of a 1965 Goat.

Joe wheeled into the parking lot of the Genosgwa Police Department and raised his eyebrows at the Cottonwood Vale police car parked up front. Joe took a spot far from the door, angling the car so no one parked next to him. He left the windows down—Genosgwa was that sort of a town.

They knew him there, and they greeted him with smiles and waves as he walked through the Police Department's front doors. It was just past twelve forty-five, but he didn't believe Tom would be at lunch—not with a new body sitting in his morgue.

"Ho, there, Joe."

Joe turned to find Gary Dennis striding toward him, hand already out. Gary was one of the senior police officers with the Genosgwa Police Department, and a friendly sort—especially in the Legion Hall's bar. "Hello there, Gary. You mean to tell me they haven't found you out yet?"

Gary made a show of shushing Joe, wrapping a conspiratorial arm around his shoulders. "Now, now, Joe. We promised to keep all that to ourselves."

Joe smiled, but it didn't last for long.

Gary sobered and nodded. "I know why you're here. Tom's in with John Morton from Cottonwood Vale, but I'll stick my head in and find out how long he'll be."

"I don't want to be a bother, but..." Joe sighed scratched his head. "My grandson and I may have seen this body the other day—right as that storm rolled in."

Gary looked at him somberly. "Might have?"

Joe looked him right in the eye. "Might have. I'm an old man, and my grandson is a young one. Between his fright and my eyesight, I can't do better than 'might have.'"

Gary nodded. "Hold here a minute, Joe. I'm sure Tom will want to talk to you." Gary turned on his heel and walked toward the chief's office.

A few minutes later, Gary was back with Tom in tow. "Through here, Joe," said Tom.

"Chief," Joe said with a nod.

"I've got John Morton in my office, and we'd both appreciate hearing what you and your grandson saw—er, might have seen."

Joe nodded once and followed the chief down the hall and into his office. John Morton lounged in the other chair but got to his feet as Joe came in. He held out his hand. "John Morton," he said.

"Joe Canton." He shook the big man's hand, and everyone sat down.

"John's the chief of the Cottonwood Vale Police Department," said Tom. "The body we found might belong to Cottonwood Vale."

John sighed and nodded. "Not that that information will do anybody any good."

Joe looked back and forth between the two police chiefs. "Tom, I…" Joe pursed his lips and looked Tom in the eye.

"It's okay, John's good people."

"I don't doubt it. It's only that I…" Joe let the words trail off, embarrassed.

"I can step out," said John, though he didn't stand.

"No, no. I've got something a little embarrassing to tell, and I need to ask Tom something. And, Tom, I will need a straight answer."

Tom nodded. "No worry about that, Joe. Anything you can tell me, you can tell John with absolute confidence."

Joe nodded once, as was his way. "I slid my grandson a five-dollar bill a few days ago. Told him he could row across the lake in his kayak and buy as much candy as he could get with a Franklin."

Tom nodded and twirled his fingers for Joe to go on.

"You remember the storm the other day? The one that rolled in so quick? Well, that was the day, and Greg—my grandson—set out ten minutes before that storm hit. He was right out in the middle of the lake when it got rough and—"

"Lake Genosgwa?" asked Chief Morton.

"Ayup. We got a lake house there."

Morton nodded and repeated Tom's finger twirling motion.

"Well, Elizabet let me know that I should go out and check on the boy in the fishing boat. I don't mind telling you, she was right. But by the time I got out on the water, the storm was coming in with a bit of fury." Joe held up a hand palm out. "Now, it was choppy, and there were whitecaps everywhere, but given what you folks found this morning, certain things about what happened next make more sense."

Tom's gaze zipped toward Chief Morton but came right back. "Joe, if you're about to tell us what I expect you are about to…"

"I already told Gary—I don't know anything for sure."

Tom nodded. "Go on, then."

"By the time I got close enough to see anything, little Greg was in a state. There was something across the front of the kayak. From where I sat, it could've been an innertube from a bicycle or anything like it. It was gray, and it stretched from one side to the other. But the kayak was jigging back and forth in the water and teetering up and down as if someone wanted to capsize it. Greg was hitting at the thing draped over the front with his paddle—and I mean swinging to beat all. After that, he laid into the water with the same paddle, and everything stopped for a while. As I got closer, Greg was staring into the water off to the right, but there was…" Joe closed his mouth, feeling his cheeks heat up.

"Nobody here but us men," said John Morton.

Joe nodded once and cleared his throat. "I thought I saw an arm sticking straight up out of the water, the same color gray as whatever was on the front of the kayak. It looked as if it were…reaching…for Greg. I hollered, but it was the wind and the storm and my Mercury that Greggy heard."

"Sticking straight up, you say?" asked Tom.

"Ayup. Straight up. Elbow locked, as you would if you were reaching to pull something over."

Tom nodded and twirled his fingers.

"Greg started to…slide backward as though he were going into the water. I don't… I didn't know what else to do, so I kept that old Mercury pinned and I cut a tight circle with my Alumacraft. You know how you would do to drive something off."

"Sure."

"Well, Greg was really shaken up—still is, truth to tell. His mother worries he might have suffered a breakdown, but I…"

"But you saw it, too."

"Perhaps I did. I wasn't sure, and I doubted myself until I watched the Sheriff's boat dragging the lake this morning." He cocked his eyebrow at Tom. "As deep as that lake is, I wouldn't think dragging would be productive. Must be a ton of junk down there, to boot."

Tom and John exchanged a quick glance, and both men smiled. "The new sheriff is from down south. He thinks ten feet is a deep lake."

John Morton cleared his throat and leaned forward, putting his elbows on his knees. "You believe you and your grandson saw the body?"

"Maybe, though Greg swears the thing attacked him, and I thought I saw its arm sticking straight up out of the water, as I said. Could've been an old branch or something such as that…"

"But an old branch wouldn't have scared your grandson—not after it was all over, right?" asked Tom.

"I guess that's right."

"And you, Joe?" asked Morton.

Joe turned sideways in his chair to look at the man face-to-face. "And me what?"

"After it was all over, after everything had calmed down… Did you revisit the idea that an arm reached out of the water and tried to grab your grandson?"

"Well, that's the embarrassing part, ain't it?"

Morton chuckled. "I guess so."

Joe gave his slow, single nod yet again. "I tracked back and forth on it, to tell the truth. It might've been a branch, but…Greg…he was going over backward into the water, and I've never seen a branch get scared off by a fishing boat."

Tom's office rang with silence after that. The clock that adorned the credenza behind the desk spoke to all three of the men in the room, but that was it. Joe shifted his gaze between the two police chiefs, who stared at one another. After a few moments, Morton nodded, and Tom turned to Joe.

"The body we found…we think it's a girl who disappeared in Cottonwood Vale in 1979."

Joe let his eyes slide shut. "When all those kids disappeared over to Oneka Falls? With that crazy Marine sniper?"

"Around that time, yeah."

"And didn't we lose a couple?"

Tom sighed. "Yes."

"Never found them?" asked Joe.

"Not even a clue. It was the same with all of them, even after old Reg Thorndike hiked into Thousand Acre Wood and brought that little boy and girl out. Besides the first boy who somehow escaped on his own, that little boy and girl were the only ones ever found."

John leaned forward. "And if the body in the morgue is the little girl from my town, this will be the first body, the first anything, that we've found."

Joe shook his head. "Sad."

"It is that," said John.

"If I understand what you're telling us, Joe, you think it's possible that your grandson panicked when he saw this body surface on the lake. And that—"

"Could've gotten the little girl's arm hooked over the kayak."

"It's possible. And you think the arm you saw was in rigor?"

Joe shrugged. "I turned wrenches and sold gas, Tom. What do I know about forensics?"

Tom nodded, looking weary and nearly worn through. "Appreciate you coming in to tell us, but she couldn't have been in rigor. Not if she is the girl who disappeared in 1979."

"No, I don't imagine she would be."

"But it's still possible you and your grandson both mistook our body for something…alive. It was a hectic situation—the storm, your grandson—and sometimes, the eye can play tricks on a man."

"Ayup. I considered that."

Tom's old wooden office chair creaked as he leaned back in it." You said you had something to ask me?"

"I did. And I guess I still will on the off chance that this little girl isn't the one from Cottonwood Vale. My grandson's up to my lake house, along with Elizabet and my daughter-in-law."

"And you want to know if it's safe?"

"Ayup."

Tom leaned forward to put his arms on the desk. "You're a straight shooter, Joe, so I'll give it to you straight. We don't know for a fact that that little girl is who we think she is. If she is, she's remarkably preserved. It could be, however, that her…mishap occurred more recently. If it were my grandson up there on the lake, I'd think to myself that it couldn't hurt to keep an extra sharp eye on the goings-on around the house."

"My thoughts, exactly."

"You know you can always call us, and we will get a car cranking out to you. But that may take ten minutes, plus or minus a few, given how far out you are. It wouldn't hurt to prepare yourself."

Joe nodded once. "I thank you for your directness, Tom." He turned to John Morton. "Nice to meet you, Chief Morton. I don't know if my story is any help or not, but if I can help, Tom, here, has my phone number and address."

John stood, towering over Joe. He held out a meaty hand. "As Tom said, we appreciate you coming in."

8

Greg lay in the hammock, listening to the soft, soothing sounds of the lake caressing the shore. He pretended to read, but really, his mind worked on the problem of the Lady in the Lake. He heard his grandfather's old muscle car roar to life and pull away from the lake house, its tires crunching the gravel in that way that Greg liked.

His parents and grandparents were worried about him, and in truth, he was a little concerned himself. It made little sense to him. "Zombies and junk like that aren't real," he murmured.

Oh no? Then what happened the other day?

Greg sighed and shook his head. "I just want to think."

So why are you talking?

He looked out at the lake, making sure to avoid looking toward the Harper's cottage. His gaze followed the Sheriff's skiff as it pursued its pattern back and forth across the deep water. *Maybe…maybe she will come to them.*

I doubt it, boyo. She seemed to run away when your gramps showed up. I'll bet she does that when any adult comes around.

But why? Greg thought. *Why only come after kids?*

How would I know, sport? I'm only a voice in your head, remember? A what-did-you-call-me…an imaginary *friend.*

Greg shook his head and blew out a breath. Possibly, he was misremembering, but it seemed as though his invisible friend was much friendlier back in Florida. *Why are you so mad at me all the time?*

Mad at you? Who said I'm mad at you?

You're so…so angry sounding, so bitter. My mom would say "snappish" and ground you if you talked to her as you've been talking to me.

Well, it's a good thing she can't hear me, isn't it? But all this…none of it matters, champ.

To Greg's mind, his invisible friend sounded amused at the idea of being scolded. *What is it that matters?*

Here are two questions for you to consider, boyo. What did you really *see? And if you saw what you think you did; how can you be safe lying in that hammock?*

Greg's gaze left the boat zigzagging across the lake and rapidly scanned across the shoreline. From there, his gaze tracked down the cove to where a patch of flowering rush grew off the point. *Safe*?

Sure, sport. If what you saw was real, what's stopping it from coming after you?

Her, not it. Greg shivered at the thought of that arm coming up out of the water and grabbing him by the shoulder. Where her fingers had touched his skin, he was still numb, and the skin felt odd.

Are you now an expert on things that live beneath the waves?

What? *What are you talking about*?

I said "it," you said "her, not it," so what makes you such an expert?

Greg scoffed. *I guess the same thing that makes* you *such an expert.*

A harsh cackle rang inside his mind. *You are funny, boyo. I wish we could play together in the woods, but I bet your friend in the lake might object.*

Greg shook his head, bewildered. *What are you talking about*?

Oh, nothing. Just thinking aloud.

Uh, you're not doing anything out loud. Imaginary *friend, remember*?

For a moment, the voice in his head didn't reply, but when it did, Greg had the sense of a bitter anger, barely contained behind the words. *Back to that, sport*? *Didn't we discuss the fact that I am* not imaginary? *If you could only come to play with me in the woods, I could prove it to you in ways you would never forget. Never.*

Yeah, sorry. The phrase all the adults use when they talk about you is "imaginary" friend. It kind of sticks in my brain.

Well, UNSTICK *it*!

Greg recoiled at the volume of the mental voice, setting the hammock swinging. *I said I was sorry. You don't have to yell.*

Greg's gaze continued to traverse a pattern between the shore in front of him, to the strand of rush, to the rocks on the opposite point of the cove. His stomach felt strange, almost the way he felt when he did something bad. He felt…sneaky.

The sheriff's boat throttled up, and Greg watched it race longways up the finger-shaped lake. The wake behind the boat made waves slapping against the shore with noisy violence. It almost sounded as though someone was coming up out of the water.

He snapped up in the hammock, swinging his bare feet into the rich black earth beneath it. His heart hammered in his chest, but there was nothing on the shore, nothing standing in the plants at one end of the cove, nothing crouching on the rocks at the other. Greg heaved a sigh of relief and settled back into the hammock, sitting in it as he would a swing, rocking himself with one foot in the black earth.

He stared out at the lake, his gaze following the waves back to where the sheriff's boat had left a wake. There was something oily on the water where the boat had throttled up. Something…something gray.

Once again, Greg snapped up, this time going all the way to his feet. His gaze stuck to that gray spot in the water.

As he watched, a hand rose in the exact center of the oily spot and waved at him.

Tears streaming down his face, Greg raced into the house, breaking Grandma's cardinal rule, and letting the screen door slam behind him.

9

For dinner, Elizabet fried walleye in her electric skillet, and Mary made a diced potatoes and vegetable stir-fry to go along with it. Though the two women stood almost shoulder to shoulder, they worked in silence, each lost in her own thoughts, her own worry about Greg.

Joe had returned midafternoon, and from the moment he walked through the door, Greg hadn't left him alone long enough to use the restroom. Whenever Joe took a seat, Greg crawled into his lap. But perhaps most worrying, the boy hadn't taken his thumb out of his mouth all afternoon.

Stephen looked on, perplexed, confused. He'd never seen his son act in that way, and Greg refused to say what was wrong. Stephen didn't know what to do, and as a father, that racked him, ripped at him.

Joe met his gaze, with calm eyes and a placid expression. One of his gnarled hands stroked Greg's back as they sat. His other hand lay on the arm of his chair.

Stephen shook his head, reviewing the day's events. When he first arrived, Joe had told him about the meeting with the two police chiefs, and about Tom Walton's suggestion that they be prepared to defend themselves for ten to fifteen minutes, while Mary held Greg and cooed in his ear. Afterward, the two men had checked the gun safe and the rifle within it.

That the tranquility of the little house on Genosgwa Lake should be ripped away angered Stephen. His parents hadn't owned the place when he was a child, but he and Mary—and later, he, Mary, and Greg—had spent many beautiful summer days there. It was a place of campfires, of s'mores cooked over open flames, of fishing with his father, of long walks on the gravel roads around the lake, of boating, of swimming. It shouldn't have been a place of stress, and he hated that it had become such.

When Elizabet announced that the food was ready, they tried to get Greg to sit at the table, promising he could sit next to Joe, but all Greg would do was shake his head and turn his face toward his grandfather's chest. So, they sat in the living room, resting their plates on their knees, all except for Joe who rested his on the arm of his chair as he tried to get Greg to take bites of the walleye—his favorite fresh fish.

When the phone rang, a shrill little scream escaped Mary. She glanced around, shame burning in her cheeks. "Sorry," she said in a hushed voice.

As if without thinking, Elizabet patted her on the arm. With a glance at Joe and Greg, she said, "Stephen, please answer the phone."

Stephen put his plate down on the floor and walked to the lake house's only phone. He lifted the handset and put it against his ear. "Canton residence."

"Joe, Tom Walton here. Listen I—"

"Excuse me, Chief Walton. This is Stephen, Joe's son. My dad is… Well, my son has had another scare, and Dad is the only one who seems to be able to comfort him right now. Can I take a message for him?"

"I can speak to you, Stephen. Your dad told you he came to see me earlier today, correct?"

"Yes, and he told me about the conversation."

Walton sighed, and when he spoke, his voice was grim. "Your father mentioned that the two of you were worried about whether…the situation…at the lake was from current events or those in the past."

"Yes, very."

"The body found last night results from a seven-year-old crime."

"That is a relief. I'm so glad—"

"Hold on, Stephen. There's more news, and it's bad. A family on the other side and opposite end of the lake from you reported their eleven-year-old son missing an hour or so ago."

Stephen's stomach dropped.

"Now, we have no idea what has happened to that child. Might be he's at a friend's house or something equally innocent. I have nothing concrete to pass on, but I promised your father I would call if anything developed."

Steven's pulse beat in his temples like a triphammer. "And we all thank you for calling. Are we… I mean, should we—"

"Are you safe? Without a doubt. Should you leave the lake house for a while? That might be premature. As I said, the missing child may only be a missing child, with no nefarious overtone."

"But maybe not?"

Tom Walton paused, and in the background, Stephen heard paper shuffling. "Affirmative. Listen, Stephen, things are happening over here, and I need to get off the line."

"Thanks for calling. We appreciate it."

The police chief hung up, but Stephen stood there for a moment, still holding the phone's handset against his ear. His mind was whirling, thoughts streaking by at light speed. *Should we leave? How can I explain it, if we do? Should I get Mom and Dad out of here, too? How do I explain all this to Mary?*

With the speed of thick oil in winter, Stephen cradled the handset. He stood staring out the kitchen window and into the darkness-shrouded trees across the road. Each shadow looked like a kidnapper lurking in the trees. Each shadow seemed to grin and leer at him. *My mind's playing tricks, nothing more.* He turned away from the window and returned to his dinner.

He rejoined the others in the living room, and without saying a word, retrieved his plate, sat down, and began eating again. Mary's gaze was on his face like a physical thing, and the silence seemed to harry him. He took a quick glance at his father, his gaze straying across his son's blond head. "Tom Walton."

Joe grunted, his gaze darting down to his grandson's face. "Do I need to call him back?"

Stephen took a bite of fish and shook his head. "He told me what he needed to tell you."

"And?" asked Mary.

He could hear the ire in her voice, her frustration at his tight-lipped responses. He turned to her and plastered a reassuring smile on his face. "We can discuss it later," he said with a meaningful glance at their son.

Her face screwed up in a little moue, but she let it go.

Through it all, Elizabet's gaze tracked from Stephen to Mary and back again, her expression a careful neutral. She darted a glance at her husband but put her head down and returned to her food.

They ate in silence for a while before Joe cleared his throat. "Greg?" he asked. The boy didn't move. "Greggy, can you look at me?"

Greg tilted his head back at an extreme angle and gazed up into his grandfather's face.

"Feeling better?"

Greg shook his head.

"Doesn't this fried walleye smell wonderful?" asked Elizabet.

Greg's gaze darted toward her.

"Would what I have set aside for dessert interest you, dear one?"

Greg nodded slowly, but his thumb remained entrenched in his mouth.

"Banana cream pie…" sang Elizabet. "But only for people who have eaten their dinner."

For the first time since his grandfather had returned home, Greg sat up and took his thumb out of his mouth. "Can I have two pieces?"

Elizabet glanced at Mary, who nodded, smiling at her son. "Your mother agrees. Would you like a plate, now?"

Greg leaned against his grandfather's torso and hugged him tight. "Thanks, Grandpa," he whispered.

"Any time, Greggy."

With a small smile, Greg crawled off his grandfather's lap and moved over to stand next to Elizabet. "May I have my dinner now, please?"

With a laugh and a one-armed hug, Elizabet stood, holding her plate in one hand and Greg's hand in the other. "Let's go into the kitchen. Just the two of us. You can tell me all about that book you're reading."

As soon as they are out of earshot, Mary turned to Stephen. "Tell me. *Now.*"

With a glance at his father, Stephen suppressed a sigh. "Tom Walton said another child has gone missing. Across the lake and toward the other end. They have no idea if it's related to the body they found this morning, and in that regard, Tom thinks what they told you earlier in the day is probably right."

"Another child?" whispered Mary.

"Now, don't get upset. Chief Walton stressed that this could be a missing child—no nefarious activities involved. He might be at a friend's house and forgot to call."

Mary nodded, and her gaze drifted toward the kitchen. "Is it…" She cast a sheepish glance at Joe. "No offense, Joe, but is it safe here? For Greg, I mean?"

"*Of course* it is, Mary!" snapped Stephen. He felt a pang of instant guilt at the strength of his response, given his thoughts in the kitchen, and a blush crept up from his neck to his cheeks.

"Now, now, Son. It's a fair question, and I don't begrudge Mary asking it." He looked Mary in the eye. "We are not defenseless here. So even if a roving madman *is* out there, your son is safe. I would never—*never*—let anything happen to that boy."

"I understand that, Joe. But if—"

"Mary," began Stephen in a soft, calm tone, "we don't even know for sure anyone is in danger, yet."

She nodded, her gaze leaving Joe's face and landing on Stephen's. "And if we *did*?"

"If we did, I'd be loading the car right now, Mary," said Joe. "In the meantime, take my word that we are not defenseless here."

Her gaze bounced back and forth between the two men for a moment. "I'm not sure I have an accurate understanding of what that means, but I have an idea. Is Greg safe from the thing that's defending us?"

“Yes. Absolutely.” Joe waved an empty hand at Stephen. “Only the two of us can get to it.”

“Should Elizabet and I—”

“No.” Joe shook his head. “These things…these things require practice—*training*—or they can be dangerous to the people you are trying to protect. No, it’s best we keep things as they are.”

“But if someone hurt the two of you, or you couldn’t get to it—”

“Honey, he’s right. Dad is a Marine, and you remember he taught me how to shoot. Leave it with us for now.”

“But if someone hurt the two of you,” Mary said doggedly, “say, they hurt your legs, and you can’t get to what you need. Elizabet and I should be able to at least go get it.”

“If that were to happen, we could tell you what you need to know at that time,” said Joe.

“And all of this is academic, Mary. There’s every chance we will get a call from Tom Walton later this evening saying it was a false alarm. Tomorrow morning at the latest. Everything will be fine. You’ll see.”

But it didn’t happen that way. It didn’t happen that way, and Stephen would come to regret those words.

10

Tom Walton pulled his car off to the side of the narrow road, hoping the spring rains hadn't undercut the ridge more than it looked. He opened his door and stepped out, stretching his back and peering into the dark woods across the road from the lake.

Ever since Randy Fergusson—*Owen Gray*—had shot up half the countryside, let alone stalked the kids in the Thousand Acre Wood, Tom had grown uncomfortable around any large copse of trees. Especially at night.

With a sigh and a shake of his head, Tom turned away from the gathering darkness and took the stairs down to the lake house at the bottom of the ridge. The stairs were made of sturdy wood, but they creaked under his weight. The house below was lit up as if for a party. It looked as if all the lights of the residence were on, both inside and out. Tom could understand that—all too well—after his years spent in law enforcement. After Owen Gray.

Man, I wish Bobby Jefferson was still around. Or Matt Greshin. Stand up guys, both of them. I could use their brainpower, right about now.

He walked across the light-bathed front yard, climbed the steps, and knocked on the door. One of his own men—Pete Martin—let him in.

"Where's Gary?" Tom asked.

"He's in the kitchen, Chief."

Tom grunted. "Things quiet?" Martin was new to the job and young to boot. He barely looked old enough to shave, but he'd passed his courses at the Academy, and in the past three months, had done an excellent job. Even so, Tom wondered if this detail would be too much for him.

"So far," said Martin." No phone calls, and the only visitors that came by, either Gary or I recognized by sight."

"Good enough." Tom stepped around the young officer and headed into the kitchen. He nodded to Gary and walked to the table where both Martha and Hedrick Stensgaard sat, looking lost. "Mr. and Mrs. Stensgaard, I'm sorry to meet in a manner such as this. I'm Tom Walton, Genosgwa's Chief of Police." He held out his hand, and Hedrick shook it without standing.

"Any news?" asked Martha.

"Unfortunately, no." Tom glanced at Gary and said, "Has anyone called your son's friends?"

Martha glanced at her husband and shook her head. "We purchased this place a few months ago. It's our first season here. I…I don't think he has any friends, yet."

Hedrick Stensgaard cleared his throat and lay his hand across his wife's. "He's a boy, Martha. He has friends—" He glanced up at Tom. "—but no good friends, you understand."

Tom nodded and put his hand on the back of one of the kitchen chairs.

Hedrick followed his motion and nodded his head. "Please have a seat. I don't know where our manners are tonight."

"Don't worry about it. This is a time of crisis for you." Tom sank into a chair and looked up at the distraught couple. "Mr. Stensgaard—"

"Hedy, please."

Tom nodded to indicate that he heard him. "—you mentioned that the boy has a few friends, at least. So, you've seen him playing with other kids? Perhaps houses up and down the shore?"

Hedy shrugged. "I recognized none of them, but I assume they're from nearby."

Tom swiveled in his seat and cast a glance at Gary, who nodded and left the room. "We'll get right on that. At least then we can rule out that he's not two houses away eating dinner with his new friends."

Hedy nodded, but Martha looked at her lap, and her shoulders hitched.

"My officers already asked you these questions, but if you don't mind answering them again, it will help my process. When was the last time you saw your son?"

"His name is Stellan," murmured Martha.

"He went out to play after lunch. For a while, he was out back—down by the lake."

"And when was the last time you saw Stellan down by the lake?"

The Stensgaards glanced at each other. "I looked out at around one thirty, I guess," said Hedy.

"I saw him closer to two," said Martha. "He had moved down the shore a little, toward the head of the lake."

"And what was he doing?"

"He was… It was as if he had a toy boat with him or something, that he was floating in the lake. You know, as if he were pushing it along and watching it move."

"Okay. Stellan walked or ran?"

Martha shrugged. "A little of both, I guess."

"You said it was as if he had a boat in the water. Did you see the boat?"

"Well, I don't guess I saw whatever it was, but—"

"Maybe it was a leaf or stick," said Hedy. "He's young for his age."

Tom nodded and glanced around the small kitchen. As in most lake houses, space was at a premium, and the builders did the best they could with what they had. Even so, the small kitchen wasn't cluttered, and despite the upsets of the day, it was clean. "And neither of you saw him after he ran off toward the head of the lake?"

Again, the Stensgaards looked at one another before looking at Tom and shaking their heads.

"Okay, that's that. Had you… Did Stellan get into trouble earlier today?"

Martha shook her head. "For the most part, he's a good boy."

"I'm sure he is. Hedy?"

Hedrick started and looked up from his lap. "We had words in the morning. But it was nothing serious." He shrugged almost bashfully. "Slamming the door."

Tom nodded. "I have kids of my own. Sometimes, kids get in trouble and run off for a while."

"You don't think…" Hedy's face had gone an ashen gray.

"No, I don't. I'm not here to judge, Hedy, and as I said, I have kids of my own. I've been out in the woods with darkness falling looking for a little girl who's mad at me for taking away privileges. That wasn't my fault, and this isn't yours, even if he ran away over the scolding."

"That's right, Hedy," said Martha in a quiet voice.

"But if—"

"No." That was all Martha said, one single word, but she said it as if speaking it closed any discussion that Hedy was to blame.

"And slamming the door, I imagine you weren't too stern?"

Hedy glanced at Martha but shook his head. "Words."

Tom nodded. "We talked about friends, and we've talked about reasons he could be angry. Is there anything either of you can think of—anything at all—that might have upset or depressed Stellan?"

Martha's eyes opened wide, and in them, Tom could see her terror. He held up his hands, palms out. "Upset enough to run off. That's all I meant. It's important, based on my experience with this kind of thing, that you try to keep a tight rein on both your emotions and your imaginations."

Hedy nodded and patted Martha on the shoulder. It was almost…platonic.

"Have there been… The sheriff's boat… I thought I heard something about another child on the radio during lunch. But we turned it off so Stellan wouldn't hear."

Tom shook his head. "That's unrelated to this."

"But you said you had experience in this? Outside of your own children, I mean." Hedy's gaze bored into Tom's.

Tom felt the grimace coming but couldn't stop it. "Unfortunately, yes. But we caught the man, and most of it occurred in another town."

"That… Oneka Falls?"

The scowl wrinkling his face deepened. "Yes. You've heard of it."

"I didn't know that was close to here." Hedy's gaze left Tom's face and tracked to his wife's. "We…we wouldn't have bought here had we known."

Tom waved it all away. "What happened in Oneka Falls happened seven years ago, that was a different situation. And Oneka Falls is forty minutes away, so it's not really close."

"But there were children from Genosgwa?"

"Yes."

"I will sue that real estate agent!" snapped Hedy.

"Can't we focus on our son? You can get all riled up about the real estate agent later!"

Tom made placating gestures with his hands. "Remember what I said: it's best if you can keep your emotions in check for now. There'll be time to sort all this out later."

Hedy nodded but did not seem mollified. "To answer your earlier question, no, I can think of nothing that would have upset Stellan so."

Tom tilted his head to the side and straightened. "Okay. Let's move on. Has either of you seen strangers around? People who don't seem to fit in?"

Martha laughed bitterly. "Everyone's a stranger to us here."

"But everyone seems to belong here," said Hedy.

"No deliveries? No servicemen?"

"Not that we've seen."

"Okay. My officers are already out there, looking, and I assure you that I will do everything in my power to bring Stellan home."

Outside, Tom found Gary Dennis waiting for him. By his expression, Tom expected terrible news. "Gary," he said with a nod.

"Chief. We checked the houses on both sides five lots in each direction. A couple of the kids said that they knew Stellan, but none of them admit to playing with him today. I sent Martin on, told him to keep walking until he had something good to tell us."

Tom rubbed his temples, trying to force the splitting headache back into its dark cave. "Did you pick up on any hesitation?"

Gary shook his head.

"But they have seen him here in the last couple of days?"

"By all accounts, yes." Gary glanced toward the Stensgaard house. "You suspect the parents?"

"What? Oh, no. Covering the bases."

Gary nodded.

"And the parents of Stellan's friends? Did any of them seem uneasy?"

Gary lifted his hands, palms up, and sighed. "No, Boss. Nothing I picked up on."

"Well, fuck."

"We could use him right now, couldn't we? Chief Greshin, I mean." Despite the situation, Gary smiled a little at Greshin's iconic phrase.

"Hell, yes. He always had a way of seeing things…"

"I know what you mean."

"Did you ask these other households about servicemen and deliveries and such?"

"I asked. It seems it's been quiet around here, today." Gary scratched his chin and glanced at the woods across the road. "You don't think…"

"What?"

"You don't think it's starting all over again, do you?"

"I think what happened in Oneka Falls only happens once in a lifetime, if that. And besides, Owen Gray is in Sing Sing."

"You're right on that score, but the girlfriend…"

"Girlfriend, schmerlfriend. No one ever saw her before Owen Gray, and no one's seen her since. I don't know who she was, but she headed off into the sunset, and you can bet your bottom dollar on that."

"I sure hope so," said Gary. He waved his hand toward the Stensgaards' house. "Do you think their boy is somewhere playing? Somewhere sulking?"

A grim, ugly expression distorted Tom's face as he answered. "No, Gary. I want that to be true with every ounce of my being, but there's a small voice in the back of my head that says 'no.'"

"Yeah," Gary said with a sigh. "Mine, too."

Tom cleared his throat and spat into the grass. "Better call everyone in, Gary. Overtime is in everyone's future. Double up on the patrols, I want two units near this lake at all times. You can handle the scheduling, correct?"

"Yessir."

II

Greg snuggled down under the covers, luxuriating in the bed's warmth and the softness of the sheets. It had been a hard day, of that there was no doubt. First, the argument with his invisible friend, then seeing the Lady in the Lake waving from below the surface of the water.

"Feeling better, now, Greggy?" his mother asked.

He nodded, but deep inside, something wanted to shout "No!" at the top of his lungs. His invisible friend had left him alone all afternoon—maybe because he'd cuddled in Grandpa's lap, or maybe because of their argument, but either way Greg was a little relieved.

"Well, that's good, dear. Don't you want to tell Mommy what happened? To tell me what got you so upset again?"

Greg shook his head and avoided eye contact.

"That's okay, Greggy. You can tell me when you're ready." She smoothed the hair across the top of his head. "That Grandpa you have…he sure is special, isn't he?"

"Yes. He's the best!"

"And what about Grandma?"

"Her, too."

His mother smiled her "mommy-smile" and chucked him under the chin—something she'd been doing as long as he could remember. Bedtime was "mommy-time," and that was okay with Greg. He spent plenty of time with his dad, playing games, or reading books.

Usually, he and his mother talked about all kinds of things—everything from what he did that day in school, to what he wanted for Christmas, to whatever was on her mind—but Greg didn't feel much like talking, so he kept his answers short, and his mother didn't stay long.

The little bedroom he used in his grandparents' lake house had a view of the lake, and if the night were warm enough, he would crack a window and listen to the gentle susurration of the waves lapping against the shore. That night, however, his mother had said it was too cold—even though it wasn't. After she left the room, Greg slid out from between the sheets and padded over to the window. He turned the little crank that opened the window and smiled at the soft, rhythmic sound of the waves on the shore. The sound had always relaxed him.

He crawled back into bed and snuggled into the covers yet again. His mind tried to turn back to when the Sheriff's Department boat turned for the top of the lake, but he wouldn't let it. Next, his brain tried to dredge up the argument with his invisible friend, but he stopped that, too.

He didn't want to think, didn't want to remember the Lady in the Lake, so he did what he always did when he tried to avoid something: he replayed episodes of Transformers cartoons in his mind.

His favorite was Bumblebee, although most of his friends chose Optimus Prime. Greg thought Bumblebee was spunky, and that spunk was more important than size and strength. He let his mind wander through memories of the episodes he'd watched before coming to the lake that summer, smiling a little at the scenes that flashed before his eyes.

Out in the lake, something splashed, and Greg came up on his elbows, heart beating fast. *Don't be silly, Greggy*, he told himself. *That's only a fish jumping. Grandpa says it happens all the time.* Even so, Greg stayed alert for a few minutes, straining his ears to hear extraneous sounds. But there was nothing else, and he soon turned to his Transformers once more. His mind drifted, mixing and matching scenes from various episodes, creating his own stories, his own epic battles.

He was almost asleep when the splashing sound came again.

In an instant, Greg was wide awake, all thoughts of Transformers wiped clear of his mind, and all drowsiness expunged. *Was it closer this time*? he asked himself. *Do you really believe that was a fish*? He listened to the sounds of the night, the lake lapping at the shore, insects buzzing and chirping, the wind whispering through the leaves in the trees across the road.

Greg relaxed back into the bed with a soft sigh. He pulled his arms back under the covers and pulled the covers up to his chin. *Now, where was I*?

In the lake, something splashed a third time, and there could be no doubt. *That was too big for a fish. But that doesn't mean some dead lady's on her way to get me.*

You are so amusing sometimes, sport.

"I thought you were mad at me," Greg whispered.

I will not lie to you, boyo. I was *mad at you. But sometimes that happens between friends, doesn't it? And we are friends, right?*

"I've always thought so."

That's not the same thing as a 'yes.' Is it, Greggy?

"You've been…different…since we came to New York. Did I do something?"

Now, now. Don't carry on so, sport. These things happen, and sometimes I can be a grumpy old man.

"A grumpy old man?"

Figure of speech, Greggy.

Even though his invisible friend intended the words to sound amused, and to be reassuring, Greg thought he heard annoyance in it. He wracked his brain, trying to remember any other time that his invisible friend had called himself a grumpy old man.

Don't you think going over to the window would serve you better? To see if you can see what's making that splashing noise?

The sound of splashing was coming at regular intervals. Almost…

Footsteps!

Maybe so, maybe no. You'll never know unless you go look. Go on, sport. Do it, do it, do it. Looking is always free, right?

Icy terror descended Greg's spine, and the last thing he wanted to do was go to the window and look out. He pulled the covers up, over his head, and shook his head from side to side.

Boring. You're acting like a little kid, Greg. I don't enjoy your company when you carry on this way.

"Sorry," whispered Greg. "The Lady in the Lake scares me."

Oh, kiddo. What's there to fear? An old woman who lives down at the bottom of the lake? I bet she's never even seen a Transformers cartoon.

Outside, the splashing stopped, but a low squelching noise took its place. Greg drew in a deep breath and held it.

Oh, Greggy, I don't think that will help you. If the Lady in the Lake is out there making that noise, you can bet your last nickel she knows where you are with minute precision.

"What do I do? What do I do?"

First thing you need to do, sport, is get out of bed and go over to that window. You need to see who's coming up from the shore. How can you make any kind of plan without knowing who the enemy is?

It sounded so reasonable, but, at the same time, so dreadful, that Greg found the thought of going to the window abhorrent. His bladder felt full, even though he had gone to the bathroom before getting into bed.

The air temperature in his room took a sudden dip and Greg shivered—though whether from fear or cold, he couldn't say. He moved the covers minutely—just enough so that he could peek into the darkened room. Strange shadows danced on the wall opposite the window. "Trees! It's only the trees blowing in the wind!" But no matter how much he said it, he couldn't dispel the image of something lurching up the gentle slope from the lake.

I don't know, kiddo. If you're going to lie there and cower, you're not doing anyone any good. Now, get up and get over to that window. Do it, Greg. Do it, do it, do it.

With trembling limbs, Greg pushed the covers away and swung his legs down to the floor. He stood, but his knees felt so weak he almost fell back onto the bed. He couldn't rip his gaze away from the window long enough to recheck the shadows. The window…the window looked as if it were icing over…in the middle of July.

Greg shook his head and tried to steel his nerves. "I don't want to," he hissed. "I don't want to see her."

Sometimes life sucks, kid. We all have to do things we don't enjoy. My lot in this life seems to be dealing with whining brats who won't do as they're told.

Greg hesitated and even looked to the side where he always imagined his invisible friend stood. Of course, there was no one there—or if he was, Greg couldn't see him. Which made sense, once he thought about it, since his friend was invisible and all.

When he brought his gaze back to the window, a dark form stood right outside. Three colors mottled the Lady in the Lake's skin: charcoal gray, black, and a sickly green—the colors Greg's mind associated with zombies, with decomposition and death. Her eyes were closed, as was her mouth. Her hair streamed water down the rest of her body, and when she breathed out, the window grew even foggier.

Run! *Just run*! He shouted it again and again inside his mind, but his feet weren't listening. He tried to close his eyes, to pretend she wasn't there, but not even his eyelids would obey him.

When she opened her eyes, warm liquid exploded down his leg, and it felt as if his heart had stopped dead in his chest. She held up her arms, and the rips and tears he'd inflicted on her with the kayak's paddle gaped like hungry mouths. She emitted an angry hiss, and when she opened her mouth, Greg saw hundreds and hundreds of gleaming bone-colored, hook-shaped teeth.

He opened his mouth to scream, or he tried to, but hysteria locked his jaw. All he could do was stand there and stare at the Lady in the Lake—who was no longer in the lake.

The thing outside his window cocked her head to the side, sniffed and made a face. She reached forward and touched the glass but jerked her hand away as if scalded by the glass. She frowned at him through the window.

"Go away," he croaked through a dry mouth and an even more parched throat.

She smiled, and it was enough to drive someone insane. She raised her index finger and shook it back and forth, as a mother scolding an errant child might. With the same finger, she tapped the glass again, then pressed harder—hard enough that the glass bowed a little. Her smile changed, becoming predatory, and she licked her lips. She grasped the outside edge of the window Greg had opened and pulled it open wider.

Greg's paralysis broke, and he turned and ran from the room. Behind him, the windowpane cracked, and a ragged scream erupted from his throat.

The Lady in the Lake laughed.

12

Joe Canton bolted up out of his comfortable chair as Greg came screeching into the room. Mary was on her feet in a second and already running toward the boy. Joe's gaze locked on his son, Stephen's, and he saw understanding reflected there. He nodded and turned on his heel, hustling toward the kitchen. Joe turned the corner around the large refrigerator and trotted into the deep, walk-in pantry. He worked the hidden switch that exposed a gun safe tucked behind the built-in shelving at the back of the pantry.

He typed in the code as fast as his fingers could move, but with a calm precision that at any other time would have made Joe proud. The thick steel door popped open, and he reached in, grabbing his customized M1 carbine. He slid a magazine into the waiting orifice and slapped his palm against the bottom. He racked the slide and flicked on the safety.

As he turned on his heel, he heard Greg wailing in the other room, and an unreasoning, unfettered fury sang in his veins. His ragged respiration rasped in his throat for the moment it took for his training—decades-old, but valuable still—to kick in.

Joe raised the butt of the carbine to his shoulder, holding it there with one hand, set himself, and opened the back door, making as little noise as possible, and slid out into the night. He circled around the house on the side of the road, his eyes darting from the shadows behind the house to the gloom that shrouded the forest across the way.

He moved far quicker than a man his age should be able to and as quiet as any man could. Along the back of the house, he saw nothing but darkness. He came to the corner where the back wall of the house and the wall that enclosed Greg's bedroom window intersected, and pressed his shoulder blades against the house, gathering his strength and his breath.

When he was ready, he darted his head around the corner—as quick as a striking snake—before pulling his head back. He thought for a moment, processing the brief glance, trying to identify danger spots. Joe stepped away from the house to make a wide turn into the side yard, in case anyone had set up in the side yard, expecting him to come right around the corner.

He took a deep breath and sprinted in a wide arc around the side of the house. He angled his run so it would end near the big stump at the edge of the yard. When he reached the stump, he slid on his knees behind it, listening with everything he had. He thumbed off the rifle's safety and drew a deep breath. He came up on one knee in the classic kneeling position, then leaned to the right, supporting the barrel against the stump and with an elbow on his knee.

Using the M1's iron sights, Joe scanned the space alongside his house, his right index finger resting on the trigger like a feather. There were shadows, but none of them were deep enough to hide a person.

Joe came up into a crouch and swept the rifle from the side yard down toward the lake. He hadn't expected to find anything—not after Greg's screams—and he didn't. He brought the gun back around, circling around the stump, and repeated his sweep of the forest across the road.

Nothing moved. He saw no one and nothing. There were no sounds of someone sprinting through the underbrush, no harsh breathing, nothing.

With slow precision, Joe reestablished his trigger discipline and thumbed on the safety—as they'd drilled into him in boot camp many years before. Still holding the gun up, he left the cover of the large stump and walked toward Greg's bedroom.

Stephen was doing his job inside, keeping everyone quiet, and keeping everyone out of Greg's room. Joe approached the window with care, his eyes flicking from the cracked windowpane in the bent frame of the pop-out window. Something dark and nasty was smeared across the glass in the broken pane…something that might be mud or maybe blood.

Joe stood outside the window, his M1 carbine held at high port. He peered inside, but the room was dark compared to the moon-bathed side yard. He stood for a moment, staring at dark spots in the room, straining his ears to hear movement or breath sounds.

Nothing.

Joe turned, and still holding the M1 at high port, scanned the side yard again. A column of muddy footprints led from the lake to where he stood. With a quiet curse, Joe stepped out of the flower bed, and peered down, hoping he hadn't disturbed any evidence. He looked for footprints leading away from the house, but there were none.

His pulse rate tripled as he sprinted around the house, eschewing silence in favor of raw speed. He banged in through the kitchen door, barely slowing, and raced to Greg's bedroom door. In his hyper-aware state, Joe took in everything and everyone in the living room in one glance. Stephen had things under control, though Mary made a strange sound in the back of her throat. To her credit, she kept still.

Joe set up on his grandson's bedroom door, standing to the side of the hinges so that as the door arced open, he could follow it with the barrel of his carbine, ready to shoot any targets that presented themselves. With the M1 in one hand, he opened the door with his left hand and pushed it inward.

The room was empty.

Joe searched every square inch anyway.

13

Tom was still outside the Stensgaard house when the radio call came in. His dispatcher relayed the information from Joe Canton, and with a glance toward Gary, Tom sprinted toward his car. As he slammed the driver's side door of his cruiser, Gary Dennis slid into the passenger seat.

Gary saw Tom watching him and held his hand up, palm angled up at a forty-five-degree angle, extended toward the road in front of them. "You'll need backup, Chief, and Joe is my friend. Haul ass."

Walton grunted and put his right foot to the floor, sending gravel spinning through the night air for hundreds of yards behind the fishtailing police cruiser. He drove fast with the lights and siren doing their things, but he stuck to his training and didn't take risks. Joe was competent enough—hell, more than competent enough—to protect his family.

Tom circled the lake on the aptly named asphalt road—Lake Circle. He braked hard as Thomas Hill Road appeared on his left. The cruiser slewed around the corner drunkenly, but Tom kept it on the gravel by miracle alone. He slowed to a stop behind the Canton's lake house, flung the door open, slammed the cruiser into park, and sprinted toward the door bathed in the red and blue lights spinning from atop his car. Dennis was half a step behind him, his service weapon drawn, his gaze ping-ponging from shadow to shadow.

"Gary, stand post," snapped Tom. Gary grunted and took a position catty-corner to the corner of the house where he had a good view of both the side yard and the back of the house. Tom rapped on the door that led into the Canton's kitchen but opened it and stepped inside without waiting for an answer. His hand rested on the butt of his pistol. He'd unsnapped it, but he didn't draw it. "Joe? Elizabet?"

"Living room," called Joe in a gruff voice. A boy sobbed from deeper in the house.

Tom strode through the kitchen, glancing into the open pantry, and nodding to himself when he saw the hidden door was open. He knew all about the secret gun safe—he had recommended the contractor when Joe had asked.

Joe stood near the hall that led toward the back of the house, his M1 carbine held at high port. He nodded once and set the rifle in the closet, closed the door, and stepped away from it.

"Appreciate it. See anything?" Tom asked Joe. "I've got Gary on post outside."

Joe nodded, but his expression was grim. He motioned with his head toward the kitchen, and Tom nodded. Together they stepped to the kitchen and out the back door.

Once outside, Joe leaned toward the chief and whispered, "I found footprints between the house and the lake. Greg's bedroom window has a cracked pane, with something on it—maybe blood, maybe mud—and the opposite window's frame is bent. I…"

"Go on, Joe," said the chief.

Joe nodded once, then looked at the ground. "It's the damnedest thing, Tom."

Walton nodded but said nothing.

"I found footprints from the lake to the boy's window. Muddy prints, mind."

"You said."

Joe shook his head. "Nothing else."

Tom shook his head. "I'm not following you, Joe."

"I didn't find any other footprints. Nothing."

"So there was only one of them?"

"No, Tom. I only found footprints leading to the window. I didn't find any leading *away*. I assumed the bastard had gotten in through the window, despite how small the opening is."

"But you searched." Tom held his face still as he said the words, his tone flat.

"I did. No one inside." Joe peered at Tom in the darkness. "If I didn't know better, I'd say this was all a dream."

"Damn. To tell the truth, I was hoping it was a nightmare."

"It is," said Joe in funereal tones. "It is."

14

As the sun's rays crept through the leaves of the forest surrounding Lake Genosgwa, Tom and Gary sat in the front seat of his cruiser, drinking acidic gas station coffee and grimacing with each swallow. They watched as Leland Chambers pulled dog after dog out of the back of his modified pickup and clipped them to a long lead.

Leland had the best bloodhounds in Kanowa County and was often used by law enforcement. He didn't come cheap, but Tom had insisted they use him over the new K-9 unit Dave Wallace had established at the Sheriff's Department. It hadn't won him any points with Wallace, but Tom didn't much care.

"Old Leland," mused Gary Dennis. "Old" wasn't only a sign of affection—Leland was at least seventy-five years old but still spry and strong. He handled his dogs as if born to it.

"You can say that again. I hope…"

"Yeah," said Gary. "Hope it twice, once for me."

Leland clipped his last dog to the lead and glanced Tom's way.

"That's our signal," said Tom, and both men exited the vehicle. He held Stellan's favorite teddy bear in one hand and a single dirty sock in the other. He approached the pack of yapping hounds and nodded to Leland. "Morning."

"Ayup, that she is. No offense, Tom, but I wish I wasn't seeing you this morning."

The chief nodded. "No offense taken, Leland. I'd much rather wait until Saturday night and have a beer." Tom shrugged. "Duty calls."

Leland shook his head, a bleak look in his eyes. "I don't much enjoy these kinds of cases, Tom. Tracking fugitives, sure, I'm there with bells on. But I don't want to be the one to find a dead child."

"I can't blame you. But this boy may not be dead. There's nothing to indicate that. He may only be lost."

Leland nodded but averted his gaze, as if to say, "sure, sure." He held out his hand. "Let's start with that sock. Probably has more of the boy's scent."

Tom nodded and passed it over. Leland took the grimy sock and held it out for all his dogs to sniff. "Ayup," said Leland after a moment and handed the sock back. "Down to the lake, you said?"

Tom glanced down toward the Stensgaard house and motioned for Martha and Hedy to go back inside. Then he held out his hand as if inviting Leland to go on down.

The dogs created quite a ruckus going down the steep steps. Tom and Gary followed a suitable distance behind, watching the dogs.

The dogs dropped their noses to the ground, each seeming to want to go in a different direction, but Leland called them to heel, and from then on, they functioned as a pack.

The dogs raced back and forth along the shore, pulling Leland to a jog. They circled what seemed like thousands of times in the Stensgaards' backyard, charging up toward the back door, down toward the dock, toward both edges of the yard, and back up to the door. After a short time, the dogs pulled Leland up toward the head of the lake, following the boy's scent at the edge of the shore. The trail veered through the yard of the last house, across the road, and headed into the woods.

At the edge of the road, Leland stopped and pointed to a jumble of tracks. "Did you have the Sheriff's Department out here before me?"

Tom shook his head. "Why?"

"Mess of dog tracks here. Strange." Leland shook his head and let the dogs run, his head down scanning the ground.

As he followed the dogs into the forest, Tom's heart sank. *He still may be lost. Not every kid that goes into the forest ends up dead.* Tom tried to dispel his anxiety by sheer force of will but failed. *Yeah, some of them just disappear forever*, said a grim, disgruntled voice in the back of his mind. He glanced at Gary's sour expression and assumed the man suffered similar thoughts.

They hadn't found so much as a hair at the Canton residence, though the Sheriff's crime scene team was still there. The footprints had turned out to be mud, but with no discernible tread marks—and none leading away from the house. The spot Joe had seen on the window had also been mud.

Tom shook his head and spat into the forest.

The dogs led them deep into the woods, leaping across small gorges, sniffing at every tree, every bush.

After an hour of trotting around with their noses down, the dogs seemed to become confused.

"Leland?" Tom asked.

"Damnedest thing, Chief," said Leland watching his dogs circle and yap at one another. "The way they act, I'd bet my bottom dollar that the boy walked to this point and disappeared into thin air." The handler glanced at Tom and Gary in turn before looking at his feet. "That's not all, either."

"More dog tracks?"

"Ayup. Pretty easy trail. But that's not the weirdest part."

"What is?" asked Gary.

"The woman's footprints."

"What woman?" asked Tom.

Leland shook his head slowly. "Weird shit, here, Tom. Every now and again, there are tracks of a barefoot woman mixed in with the dog tracks. After a bit, they're gone—just like the boy's tracks disappear right here."

"A woman's tracks?"

Leland nodded but wouldn't meet his or Gary's gaze. "I know it sounds crazy, Tom," he said in a quiet voice.

Tom released a sigh. "I've heard it before, Leland, so don't worry. Just last night, in fact. Joe Canton had an intruder or a peeper. Tracks led up from the lake to Joe's grandson's window, but no tracks led away." Tom shook his head. *Not again*! *I don't want to do this again*!

His thoughts must've shown on his face because Leland treated him to a sharp nod. "I'll spiral them out. Someone might've picked the boy up to fool with his trail."

Tom nodded and gestured for the tracker to proceed.

Gary stood beside him, breathing a little too hard, a little too fast, grim lines distorting his face.

Tom glanced at him, not much liking the color high in his cheeks. "You feeling okay, Gary?" he asked.

"Hell, no! This…" His shoulders slumped. "Tom, tell me this ain't going to be another…"

Tom nodded, his face donning an expression to match Gary's. "I've been thinking the same thing, trust me. But so far, it's only one boy."

The sigh exploded from Gary. "Yeah, but someone was messing around out at the Canton's house. Someone was trying to get in that window at that little boy."

"Yeah." Without another word, Tom started after the braying dogs, and Gary fell in step.

15

Greg had refused to sleep in the bedroom set aside for him on their visits to the lake. Instead, he and his father had slept on couches in the living room, and Greg awoke as the sun painted beautiful colors on the surface of the lake.

He lay still for a moment, taking in the morning's beauty and enjoying the crisp air on his cheeks. What had happened the night before was already taking on the dressings of a nightmare. *What* did *I see last night*? he asked himself. *Was it a person*? *A bad person*?

He stared at the oranges and pinks dancing on the waves near the end of the dock. He loved coming to the lake house. It had always created such a deep sense of relaxation, such a feeling of…belonging, love, warmth. But now…

But now you're having second thoughts? *What kind of grandson are you, boyo*?

Greg tried to suppress it, but a considerable sigh whistled through his lips. *Leave me alone.*

Aw, what kind of greeting is that? *Aren't we friends anymore, sport*?

Were you ever my friend?

Now you've gone and hurt my feelings. Mayhap I'll go pout. Mayhap I'll go hide under a rock at the bottom of the lake. Mayhap I'll go tell the Lady in the Lake how to get at you.

The words seemed to scald the inside of Greg's mind as if someone had cracked his skull and dumped in a quart of Mr. Clean. *You wouldn't do that.*

Well, I certainly wouldn't do that to one of my friends. *But you haven't been treating me as a friend should, have you, sport?*

Why are you calling me those things?

What things?

Kiddo. Boyo. Sport. Those things.

Oh, that's nothing. It's only the way I talk, nothing to be offended by.

A thoughtful expression stole over Greg's face. *You never talked that way back in Florid*a.

Didn't I? I'm sure I did. Maybe you never noticed. Could be you were too busy taking advantage of my good graces.

The voice inside his head sounded enraged, the way a thwarted bully would. Greg was growing to dislike his invisible friend—maybe even to hate him a little. His mother had told him he could get rid of this invisible friend when he was ready. Of course, she hadn't said how.

You're thinking of getting rid of me, aren't you? Is that a thing friends do? What's to stop me thinking of ways of getting rid of you, champ? Like talking to that dead lady in the lake.

Well, is threatening to tell the Lady in the Lake how to attack me something friends do?

There was no answer. Nothing except an acidic burp that brought a foul taste into Greg's mouth. He swung his legs off the couch, wrapping the blanket around him and pulling it over his head like a hood. He shuffled to the porch door and stepped through it as quiet as a church mouse. Greg left it ajar to avoid waking anyone in the house.

He stood there, breathing the sweet, cold air that wafted across the lake, admiring the continually changing painting the sun and the waves created on the water.

"It's a beaut, ain't it?" said Joe.

Greg jumped with a little cry that squeaked out between his lips. He whirled, ends of the blanket flapping.

Joe sat in his accustomed chair, his pipe smoking in the ashtray next to him, and the neat rifle that Greg hadn't known he owned leaning in the corner. "Sorry, Greggy. I didn't mean to frighten you."

"Grandpa!" Greg laughed, half relief, half pent-up anxiety. "I thought I was the first one up."

Joe smiled at his grandson with fondness. "I never got to bed, so you *are* the first one up." He ruffled Greg's hair.

Greg gave his grandfather a hug and stepped back, his gaze glued to the wood and metal death machine leaning in the corner.

Joe followed his gaze and clucked his tongue. "That's not something for you to think about, Greg. Not yet. Not until you're older, and not before your parents approve."

Greg nodded and switched his gaze to his grandfather's craggy features, but he couldn't stop himself from darting glances at the thing. "You didn't go to bed?"

"No, I didn't. With everything that happened last night, I thought it might be best to sit up and take in the dregs of the night."

"Did…did you…" Greg raised his arms and let them drop in a frustrated shrug.

Joe licked his lips. "Those county boys rolled out of here around four thirty this morning. After that, everything was quiet—only me and the lake were awake." Joe leaned forward and rested his elbows on his knees, peering into his grandson's face. "I'd never let anything happen to you, Greggy. Not if I was close by, and not if I could do anything to stop it. You know that, right?"

Strong emotion swirled inside of Greg—love for his grandfather, comfort at his grandfather's words, fear that his grandfather felt compelled to say them. "I know, Grandpa."

Joe nodded gravely, not breaking eye contact. "Anytime you're scared here, Greg, you just sing out. I'll come running, and whoever's scaring you had better damn-well be scared himself."

Rather than taking comfort from the assurance, the words aroused fear in Greg. Fear for his grandfather.

16

Stellan Stensgaard ran. He didn't understand what was behind him, or who, but that didn't matter, because he understood all too well what would happen if he stopped running. In the distance, he thought he could hear dogs, but then again, he thought dogs were chasing him.

Dogs, or something *like* dogs. Even while he ran, he shuddered at the thought of the four-legged things with eyeless faces and weird, human-like paws.

His chest burned, and his breath grated through his throat. He had no idea how long he'd been running, but he thought it had been through the whole of the night. He was lost and getting more lost with each random turn he made.

Where are you going, sport? Are you having fun? Didn't I say this game would be fun?

"It's not fun!" Stellan screamed.

Now, what did I say about that attitude?

Behind him, Stellan heard one of the dog-things sprinting toward him. The thing slammed into him from behind, knocking one of his legs out from under him. His arms pinwheeled through the air as he fought for a dancing, hopping, one-footed balance.

It wasn't until he was sure he would not fall that Stellan realized blood was pouring down the back of his right leg. There was no pain—not yet—but the sight of the blood pouring down into his shoe was enough to make him want to vomit.

Not for the first time since the Lady in the Lake had chased him from the shore into the seeming safety of the woods, Stellan burst into tears.

Chapter 4

2007

I

Toby, Scott, and Mike dragged the unconscious creature down into his own basement dungeon. According to Toby's experience with M99, the demon calling himself Bill Hartman wouldn't be under for long. They locked him inside a three-by-three cell he'd had built against the cement block walls of the basement, chaining his hands and feet using the cuffs already attached to the wall. To supplement that, they wrapped thick stainless-steel chain around the demon's arms and chest, then looped them down around his hips and legs.

"His wings will be a problem," said Mike, running a critical eye over the chains.

"Not much of one," said Toby. "He can't even open them in that tiny space."

Mike wobbled his head from side to side, making a face as he did so. "Still… I'd feel more comfortable if we could secure those wings somehow."

"If wishes were fishes," said Scott. "He looks secure enough. How long until he is awake, Toby?"

"I'd say ten or fifteen minutes."

Scott whistled. "Even with ten darts full of M99?"

"Yeah, the effectiveness seems to be dropping fast. That dose would kill a couple of elephants." Toby chuckled, shaking his head. "This guy stinks like an elephant, so there's that."

Mike turned toward the stairs that ascended to the kitchen. "Let's go see what we can find out by pawing through his underwear drawer," he said.

Toby shook his head. "There's not much up there. One television, a chair the same as this one, and a lot of dust bunnies."

"There's got to be something. Even if it's only part of his disguise."

"You're welcome to go look, Mike, but I checked most of the rooms, and it's as I said—empty."

With a shrug, Mike climbed the stairs but paused halfway up. "Scott? Want to look around?"

The trooper shook his head. "No, you go ahead. I want to be here when this guy wakes up."

"Fair enough." Mike turned and resumed his climb.

"Sing out if you need us."

At the top of the steps, Mike rapped his knuckles against the doorframe. "Don't start without me."

Scott glanced up the stairs before turning to Toby. "What can I expect?" he said in a restrained voice.

"Expect?"

Scott nodded and jerked his thumb at Hartman.

"Oh." Toby fidgeted a moment and took a deep breath. "I've never interrogated one of the demons before. But they have an incredible tolerance for pain."

Scott frowned and shook his head. "So, what are we talking about?"

"No matter what we do, it's unlikely to kill him. I learned that fact the hard way. It may cause him pain, but nothing we can do to him has more consequence than that."

Scott's frown grew into a deep scowl, and he scratched his head. "I didn't take Torture 101, so I'd appreciate a few specifics."

"Look, Scott, I'm making this up as I go along, same as you. But we have firearms, and they won't kill him. Alternately, there's fire."

Scott closed his eyes and let his breath whistle through his teeth. "I don't think I'll get off on this afternoon's activities."

"No," said Toby. "I don't think any of us will."

They stood in silence for a while, each lost in his own thoughts while Mike tromped around upstairs. The television in the front room came on, an excited sportscaster screaming "Goal!" over and over. Mike let it run for a few seconds before turning it off again.

"Why do you think we haven't seen LaBouche?"

Toby shivered at the bleakness in Scott's voice. "To be honest, I'm surprised we haven't seen him. After the fight in the parking lot, I'd think he wants revenge."

Scott nodded, a flinty, forbidding expression settling on his features. "I partnered with LaBouche for a long time, and if there's one thing about him I can say with certainty, he *will* want revenge." His eyes opened wide. "Do you think..."

"I doubt he considers the things he's done to you as revenge for anything you could have done as his partner. He did it..." Toby dropped his gaze to his own feet. "He fed on your pain, Scott."

Scott nodded and slid down the wall opposite the cells. He rested his forearms on his knees, letting his hands droop toward the floor. "How could he pretend to be my friend and still do that?"

"Scott, don't take this the wrong way, but from what I've witnessed, what LaBouche did to you wasn't—"

"All that bad?"

Toby shook his head. "No, I wasn't going to say that. What I was going to say was: what LaBouche did to you wasn't that far out of the norm for *them*. Keep in mind that they get off on torturing children, for the most part."

Scott dropped his gaze to the floor between his feet and heaved a sigh. "I suppose. It seems..."

"Personal? Yeah, I'm willing to bet that for LaBouche, a personal touch makes it better. The taste, or whatever they get out of it. It heightens it."

"Not far from serial killers, are they?"

Toby sank into the recliner and yawned. "You'd know more about serial killers than I would. I've never met one that wasn't a demon."

"You're not saying that *all* of them—"

"No, no. Not at all. I imagine the ones that get caught are all human. The ones I've met..." Toby shook his head as if trying to rid himself of distasteful memories.

"Ah." Scott fell silent and stretched his legs out in front of him. "At least the guy could have more than one chair."

"I do," Hartman grated. "I have one here and one upstairs. I am the only one who sits in this house."

"Not after today," said Toby. "Going forward, you're the only one who will stand in one of your little cages."

Hartman thrashed back and forth in the tight confines of the cell. The chain rattled and clanked but held.

"Mike!" Scott yelled.

They heard Mike's pounding feet on the floorboards above them, and Hartman glanced up. "Who else is in my house?"

Toby turned lazy eyes on the demon. "I'm not quite sure you've grasped the situation here."

The demon threw back his head and laughed. "Is that so, mister? Let me see if I can recap today's events. First, you assaulted me in the yard of my own house, shooting me with tranquilizer darts. I'm not sure those are illegal, but I'm willing to bet shooting a person with one is. Second, having tranquilized me, you broke into my house and dragged me into my basement, where you chained me to a wall." He laughed again, and its sound grated at the air like grinding gears in a tractor-trailer. "How did I do? Does that sound as if I grasp the situation?"

Toby leaned forward in the chair, putting his hands on his knees. "What you've failed to grasp, Hartman, is that we *know* about you."

Hartman narrowed his eyelids and cocked his head to the side. "And what is it you think you know?" He glanced down the line of cells. "What do you imagine I do with these? I'm not a serial killer. I built these for research purposes. You see, I'm—"

A slow smile spread across Toby's face. He lifted a hand and pointed at different parts of Hartman's anatomy. "Wings. Red scales. Hooves. Fangs."

"What is that supposed to mean?" Hartman put on a good front, but there was a quaver in his voice.

"It means I can see you, demon. I can see past your illusion. *I can see you.*"

Hartman's gaze flicked over Toby's shoulder, seeking Scott. "Your friend here is nuts, isn't he?" His gaze returned to Toby's face. "More than a little, too."

The door to the kitchen rattled open, and Mike came down the stairs, boots drumming a staccato rhythm on the treads of the stairs. He came to stand next to the recliner Toby sat in. "He's awake."

Hartman's gaze snapped to Mike's face. "Do you understand what your friends have done? Assault, battery—"

"Kidnapping," added Mike. "Maybe it's not obvious to you, Hartman, but we don't give a shit. Besides, Scott and I are cops. Who do you think people will believe? A guy with a dungeon in his basement or two fine, upstanding cops?"

That revelation seemed to knock Hartman off kilter. He stood still, all except his eyes. His gaze bounced from Mike to Scott to Toby and back again as if a complex logic problem related to them captivated his attention.

"Why are you here?" asked Toby in a deceptively mild voice.

The demon stared at him. "That should be obvious. I'm here because you knocked me out with tranquilizers and locked me in this cage. Why not let me out? We can have a civilized conversation."

Mike chuckled and nudged Toby's shoulder. "He wants us to let him out..."

"Did you let the humans you imprisoned down here out of their cages just because they asked, Hartman? I doubt you did."

"You need to seek medical attention. You seem to have gone off the deep end, friend." Hartman's voice sounded confident, but something flickered in his eyes. Fear, perhaps.

"Let's cut to the chase," said Scott, springing to his feet. He drew his service weapon and eased the hammer back. "Have you heard from your friends in Oneka Falls? Have you assimilated the fact that the big tree is no more?"

Despite being chained to a wall, Hartman tried to take a step back. "Oneka Falls? I'm not familiar with anybody in Oneka Falls. And what tree are you talking about?"

Toby shot to his feet in a heartbeat and lunged across the small space between the recliner and the front of the cage. "*Herlequin*!"

Hartman's gaze returned to Toby's face, and his expression shifted from one of pretended confidence to one of abject terror. "I don't recognize that name!" His gaze left Toby's face as Scott strolled across the room toward him, rapping the pistol against his thigh with each step. "I don't!" he whined.

"Yes, you do," said Toby in a mild voice. "And if you haven't already heard, we killed him three days ago."

"No, you didn't!" sneered Hartman. "We *can't* die—any of us, let alone one as old as Herlequin."

Toby shrugged and laughed easily. "Well, perhaps our definition of killed differs from yours, but we ended his existence—at least in this plane." Toby turned as if to walk away but pivoted back and slammed his hands into the cage door. "*We burned him*!"

Hartman lurched back, his gaze dancing from Scott and his pistol to Toby.

Scott tapped Toby on the shoulder, and after looking back, Toby stepped aside. Scott stepped up to the front of the cage and tapped the metal bars with the barrel of his Glock 37. "You no doubt recognize what this is. You don't understand, yet, that we already realize it won't kill you." The trooper shrugged. "That means I can shoot you as much as I want, and I know you'll be all right." Without waiting for Hartman to reply, Scott pulled the trigger.

The .45's report rang like cannon fire in the enclosed space of the basement. Purplish-black blood splattered the back wall of the cage, and Hartman shrieked in both pain and fury. The demon glanced down at the small smoking hole that had appeared in the left side of his chest, and his expression darkened.

"So, you see, friend, it's going to be a very unpleasant afternoon for you unless you come to face facts."

Hartman glowered at Scott through slit eyelids but kept his lips together.

As if he'd expected that, Scott nodded and pulled the trigger a second time. This time the hole was lower and closer to the demon's centerline. More purplish-black blood splattered the block wall behind him, and Hartman squalled. "Stop it!" he shrieked.

"Are you done playing games?" Scott asked in a hard voice. "Because if you're not, I've got plenty of ammunition."

"We should've brought Benny," muttered Mike. "I bet he could *read* this guy."

The demon's gaze flickered toward Mike and away again.

Scott banged on the bars of the cage with his pistol. "Pay attention, hellspawn! I asked you if you've finished playing games."

"Come on, Scott," said Mike. "There's no need—"

"Mike," murmured Toby as he shook his head.

Hartman didn't say a word, he just stood there staring at them each in turn and took it all in. "What is it you expect to gain here?"

Scott smiled, and it was a sight that could have curdled milk. "All we want is a little information."

"Information? And if I give it to you? What happens if I do?"

Scott shrugged and placed his hand on the lock of the cage. "In that case, there'd be no need for these theatrics. I imagine this door will open."

The demon leaned forward, staring intently into Scott's face. "And that means I can go free?"

Again, Scott shrugged. "The door will be open."

The demon leaned back, gazing at each of them, one after another. He ran his tongue around his fangs inside his lips and sniffed the air as a bloodhound would. "What information do you need?"

"Why are you here?" asked Toby.

"Because you—"

"Why are *all of you* here?"

Hartman's gaze flicked to Scott's face and then down at his gun. "Uh, do you mean here in New York?"

"Why Oneka Falls?" asked Mike.

"It's a nice town. Why not Oneka Falls?"

"Stop playing games!" snapped Scott.

"We…" Hartman's gaze skittered around the room in the manner of a nervous schoolgirl. He swallowed convulsively. "Where we are from, it's different. It's…"

"Where are you from? Hell?" Scott's voice was devoid of emotion, tone.

The demon tried to shrug inside his chains. "As good a name as any other."

"So, it's different where you're from, and this is the reason you came here and started eating children?"

Hartman recoiled at the venom in Mike's voice. "Not all of us do that—only the coarser, the baser among us. Most of us have more refined tastes."

Mike's face blazed with anger, and he took a single, threatening step forward. "Like that bastard Herlequin? Did Herlequin have refined tastes?" He laid a hand on Toby's shoulder and gave it a gentle squeeze.

Hartman tried to shrug again, setting his chains a-clanking. "He didn't *hurt* any of them."

"Yes, he did." Toby's voice was filled with such finality, such authority, that Hartman didn't even try to argue.

"What's so bad about where you're from?"

Hartman's gaze met Scott's. "Not much to eat. Once, food was plentiful, but now…less so. Plus, there are…*others*. Older ones."

"And?"

"And they fed on *us*. They enslaved us."

Scott darted a glance at Toby over his shoulder and arched his eyebrows.

With a minute shake of his head, Toby walked a few steps away, then turned and faced Hartman again. "And that… To escape them, you found a way to come here."

Hartman nodded.

"And once here, you fed on us, enslaved us."

"Nothing could be more natural," Hartman said. "We are stronger than you. We deserve our place in this world."

"Now, there is a bit of fucked-up logic," said Mike.

"Not at all. Your kind are weak, comparable to an extinct herd animal from home."

"In Hell, right?" Toby peered at the demon through slit eyelids.

"I've already answered that, haven't I?"

"Have you?" asked Toby in a caustic tone. "You evaded the question."

Hartman's chains clanked as he made an abortive shrugging motion. "That's not our name for it."

"What is your name for it?" asked Scott.

Hartman tilted his head to the side and fixed Scott with a glare. "Your primitive vocal apparatus couldn't pronounce it."

"I don't have to pronounce it; I only have to hear it." Scott raised his pistol, not exactly pointing it at Hartman, but not pointing it in a safe direction, either.

In a fit of bravado, Hartman took the half step forward that his chains allowed him, lifted his chin, and opened his eyes wide. "You don't scare me, little man. Neither does your toy."

Scott's next round went into the beast's thigh, and Hartman squealed as an infant would. "It seems to me, that was a lie, Mr. Hartman. The new rule is every lie buys you a bullet."

For a moment, Hartman stared at Scott with hatred blazing in his eyes. Without warning, Hartman threw his weight against the chains in earnest. "When I get out of here…" he grated.

"I got to tell you, buddy… The way things are going, you getting out of there doesn't seem all that likely." Mike's tone was matter of fact, but he kept stealing strange little glances at Scott.

"Tell us the name," said Toby in a voice laced with iron. "Stop playing games."

Hartman turned his head ponderously, one eye focused on Toby, and the other staring daggers at Scott. What he uttered next sounded more akin to a series of hisses, pops, and clicks than a word.

"That's it? That yaddy-hiss-click-pop-snap-crackle-pop is the name of your world?" asked Mike. "Do you live in a box of cereal?"

Hartman jerked his head back, and both eyes tracked to Mike's face. "Cereal?"

"That's the name of your world?" asked Scott.

For a moment, Hartman ignored him. Keeping both eyes focused on Mike, he began to hum. The tune was haunting, creepy. It sounded vaguely Middle Eastern but with a haunted house twist.

"Stop that!" snapped Toby.

Without stopping the dirge-like tune, Hartman turned his gaze toward Toby. His head listed to the side a bit, and the smirk distended his lips.

Toby held his hand out to the side. "Scott."

The boom of the pistol's report echoed around the basement, followed by Hartman's shriek and the sound of more blood splattering on the wall. The demon continued to stare at Toby, but he didn't hum again.

"Answer my question, partner," said Scott in a casual drawl. "Unless you want to see if the next round is a dud."

Hartman shook his head without breaking his probing stare at Toby. "Yes, that is what we call our world."

"And the ones who enslave you?" asked Toby.

"What about them?" Hartman's gaze bored into Toby's, filled with rage and recrimination.

"What is the name of their race?"

"I'd have to hum it." Hartman shifted his gaze to Scott, and then to Scott's service weapon. "I don't want to get shot again."

"Fair enough. What is the name of your kind? Or do you have to hum that, too?" Toby paced a few steps to the left and turned and stared at Hartman.

"Does it matter? I don't understand why you want this information. It changes nothing—none of my answers change anything. We're here, and there's not a damn thing any of you can do about it."

"Is that so? I bet Herlequin thought the same thing…but, now he's dead, and we can't ask him." Toby flopped his hands back and forth. "Guess we'll never know."

"Why do you persist with this lie?" asked Hartman in a surly tone. "Why do you persist with this…this farce of an interrogation? You can't feed on my emotion, my pain, so I fail to see the point."

"Luckily for you, we don't give a shit whether you see the point or not. Unluckily for you, we are in control, and—"

"For the moment," sneered Hartman.

"—we want information from you. We don't care if you understand why we want it. We don't care if you want to give it to us. *We will have the information we want*!"

Hartman shrank away as Scott screamed the last sentence in his face, brandishing his pistol. "Then ask sensible questions. Pragmatic questions."

"Fine," said Toby, the bastion of calm. "Why are there so many of your kind living in Oneka Falls?"

"Why wouldn't we choose a town—any town—and live there together?"

Toby shrugged, and a small smile played on his lips. "I've learned a lot about your kind, Hartman. I've been *watching*, you see. I've been hunting you demons. Stopping your kind from feeding where I could."

"And what is it you think you know about us? Why wouldn't we live in a small town together?"

"For the same reason you live way out here in the middle of nowhere—no neighbors, no nothing. Your kind doesn't get along well with each other. You are apex predators, not herd animals."

"Oh, aren't you *sweet*," Hartman crooned while sneering. "Who said we don't get along? Who said we can't live with each other in proximity?"

Toby treated him to a nasty chuckle. "Oh, I'm sure weak demons such as yourself can live close to one another if they are forced to, and especially if the neighboring demons are older and stronger than ones such as yourself."

"*Weak* demons? Such as…*myself*?" Hartman growled the words and rattled his chains for good measure. "If you'd care to release me from the stupid chains, we could test how *weak* I am."

Toby laughed outright, lacing as much contempt and attitude into it as he could. "Been there, done that, Hartman, and here you sit, chained and imprisoned. A single human did that."

Hartman's eyes flicked from Scott to Mike to Toby. "The way you count is strange. I count *three* humans."

His eyes turned toward Scott. "One with a penchant for popping off irrelevant chunks of lead in my direction."

Toby shook his head, plastering a sneer on his face. "Maybe—and I mean *maybe*—we can count the two rounds Scott fired into you, but all Mike did was sit out on the road and watch for visitors." Toby shook his head again and stepped right up to the gate of Hartman's cage. He tilted his head back and glared into the demon's eyes. "But you and I both know one thing, Hartman."

"Oh? And what is that? What is it we both know?"

A ferocious grin ripped across Toby's face. "We both know that *I kicked your demon ass*, Hartman."

Laughter burst from Scott. "That he did. I saw the whole thing, and from where I was, all you did was suck up M99."

Hartman's eyelids closed until the merest fraction of his eyes were visible. He flicked his gaze between Toby and Scott as if it were a whip. "Ambush. Backup in the trees." He spat on the ground at Toby's feet. "Hardly an honorable fight."

"Honorable?" Toby sputtered, laughter leaking out around the edges. "Is anything you demons do honorable?"

Hartman drew himself up, struck a regal pose. "*Everything* we do is honorable, unlike you humans."

Mike snorted as if choking, then released deep, booming laughter. "I've lived my whole life in Oneka

Falls—among *your* kind, demon—and I've never seen a more dishonorable bunch. You bicker with one another over the pettiest of things. You kill, you maim… Your kind has sucked the life out of a good town."

"In your opinion," said Hartman.

"My opinion—"

Toby chopped his hand through the air. "This is getting us nowhere. Are you going to answer our questions or not, Hartman?"

"And if I don't?" The demon's head swiveled toward Toby, and he locked gazes with him.

"In that case, we'll test your theory."

Hartman turned his head halfway to the side. "My theory?"

"Sure. Your theory that we can't kill one of you."

A jagged smile broke across Hartman's face. "Oh, scary."

Toby shrugged and arched his eyebrow at the demon. "Mike, you want to run upstairs and grab my tranquilizer gun?" He winked at Hartman and treated him to a smile. "Don't worry, demon. You'll sleep right through your death."

For the first time, Hartman looked a little shaken. "Do you…" He shook his head from side to side as if trying to deny the truth of the thought in his mind.

"Do we what?" asked Scott.

"For the sake of argument, suppose you are successful at whatever it is you think will kill me. Do you understand what would happen to me?"

"We are familiar with the concept of death," said Mike.

Hartman shook his head, almost appearing sad as he did so. "Not our deaths."

"Educate us!" snapped Toby.

Hartman sought Toby's gaze with his own. He stood silently for the space of five breaths, peering into Toby's face, searching his eyes. "If you could make us…die and…"

"I can make you die, Hartman. What's more, I can make you stay dead."

As if he'd been waiting to hear the words, Hartman snapped his head up and down in a single, jerky nod. "Okay. You know that secret. What you don't seem to grasp is that we don't die. If you make us 'stay dead,' all you are really doing is destroying our physical form in this world."

"We know that too," said Scott.

Again, Hartman nodded as though he were a puppet on a string. "Where do you suppose the rest of us goes?"

"Back to Rice Krispies Land?" asked Mike.

As if moving in a thick, viscous fluid, Hartman turned his head toward Mike at a speed that would make glaciers jealous. He blinked twice and nodded. "Back home," he murmured.

"And that would be bad for us, how?" asked Scott in a demanding tone.

Hartman shrugged and leaned against the wall behind him as if his strength had drained out of him.

"So we send you back to the place where you are the prey animal, you are the slave. I can't see much of a downside."

Hartman shook his head, giving every appearance he was the weariest creature on Earth. "Each time…" he shook his head again, and, with the coughing sound of field artillery, he cleared his throat. "Each time you force one of us back in that way, it weakens the barrier that separates your world from mine. Each time you 'kill' one of us, you make it easier for the others…for the *older ones* to come through." He shuddered with what appeared to be genuine fear. "Trust me when I say that that is the last thing you want. As things stand, only the weakest of my kind can sneak past the—" He startled as if he realized he was saying too much.

Scott glanced at Toby and raised his eyebrows.

"No, go on, Hartman." Toby glanced at Scott and motioned at the pistol in his hand. "*He* insists."

"As things stand, only the weakest of my kind can sneak through."

"Didn't your sneaking—your passage here—do the same thing? Weaken the barrier, I mean," said Toby in a small voice. "There must be tens of thousands of your kind here."

"Hardly," scoffed Hartman. "If there were that many of us, we wouldn't need to hide from you." He leaned his head back against the wall, scrunching his wings. "No, our numbers are relatively small. Many, many more of us remain trapped at home." He drew a deep breath and released it all at once. "And we didn't force our way through the barrier…we took the Passage."

"The Passage?" asked Mike. "Is that some kind of cruise ship?"

Hartman sighed again and let his eyelids droop closed. "No. The Passage is a pathway between my world and yours. Our legends say one of the first to live on my world forged it. She came here because she could hear your kind calling her."

"What, like a wizard summoning a demon?" Mike blurted, then laughed. "This would make a cool video game."

Hartman's shoulders hitched up and dropped. He made a shooing gesture toward Mike, all without opening his eyes.

"And her name?" asked Toby. "The first to come here?"

"I have no idea what your people call her."

"Is she still here? How powerful is she?"

A crooked grin spread across Hartman's face, and he opened his eyes to peer at Toby. "The answer to that question, human, would not bring you pleasure. We consider her one of the most powerful of the older ones. Compared to the demons you've encountered, she is a goddess."

An icy touch of fear ran down Toby's spine. He turned toward Scott, gave him a short nod, and glanced at Mike.

"Wait a second," said Scott. "I thought you said only the weakest could cross this Passage thing."

Hartman's lips quivered, and a fat tear with the consistency and color of olive oil escaped from his left eye. He nodded, and as he did so, his cheeks twitched.

Scott stepped away from the cage and raised his service weapon. "Don't try anything!"

Hartman shook his head, but his shoulders had joined in the twitching and shaking.

"What I'm having a problem with," said Toby, "is that once you've escaped your torment, you became the tormentors."

Hartman dropped his head and shook it from side to side. His respiration grew strange—a rhythmic in and out interrupted with the occasional hitching gulp. He didn't speak, he didn't move—other than the twitching.

"Help us understand this. Why do to us what your tormentors did to you?"

A hissing, shrieking clangor erupted from Hartman. His twitching shoulders heaved up and down, other tears joined the first, and they plopped on the floor of the cage. He lifted his head, his expression rigid—a pained rictus.

"What the hell is wrong with him?" asked Mike.

"A reaction to the M99?" asked Scott.

Toby didn't answer. Instead, he watched Hartman with a spooky intensity. He waved Scott farther away from the cage. "You're not fooling us. Whatever you think this act will achieve, it will fail."

Hartman's blustery cacophony fell into a rhythm with the hitching of his respiration, and the harsh lines of his expression softened. He tilted his head back and brayed at the ceiling.

"He's laughing," said Toby in a mirthless, dead-sounding voice.

"Laughing? What about?"

"You…should…see…your…faces!" Hartman forced the words out between gales of spine-tingling laughter. His entire body shook with the force of his mirth.

"What's… Toby, I don't get it." Mike walked until he stood in front of the cage, though ten or twelve feet from its gate. "You! Demon! What the hell are you laughing at?"

"It's all lies," said Toby.

"All of it?" asked Mike in a small voice.

Hartman roared, his laughter filling the basement much as the sound of Scott's gunfire had. Oily tears continued to stream down his face and dripped on the chains and floor.

Toby let his eyes fall shut and drew a deep breath. He held it for a moment and let it slip out of him like a lover out a woman's window in the middle of the night. "Scott…"

"Can we trust any other?" asked Mike.

When Toby opened his eyes, Scott's gaze was locked on Hartman. "Scott."

Scott nodded and lifted his pistol. He aimed carefully, and his finger began to take up the trigger's slack. Behind him, Mike sighed and put his fingers in his ears.

Hartman's laughter wound down into a series of chuckles and guffaws, and his eyes widened at the sight of Scott's pistol pointed at him. His chains clanked as he tried to raise his arms.

"We warned you," said Scott.

Toby tapped Mike on the shoulder and pointed toward the stairs. "Would you grab my tranquilizer gun?"

With a curt nod, Mike turned on his heel and ran up the steps.

"Wait!" Hartman's eyes widened, and he shook his head from side to side. "Wait, I'll tell you!"

Scott glanced at Toby, who nodded, and he pulled the trigger as fast as he could. Hartman jerked back and forth in his cell, purplish-black blood bathing the back wall. His screams and the discharges of Scott's Glock filled the dungeon.

2

At two in the afternoon, Chaz Welsh left the Oneka Falls Town Hall with a spring in his step and a smile on his scaly lips. It was going to be an incredible afternoon—his first as leader of his people. He slid behind the wheel of his BMW, and not for the first time, admired the shade of blue that adorned its skin. He cranked the engine and pulled out of the parking lot, resisting the urge to squeal his tires as he did so.

Chaz drove toward the edge of town and turned in at the Thousand Acre Wood trailhead sign. The parking lot was full of cars of all shapes and sizes, some rotting on their tires, some brand-new. There was a gaggle of demons standing at the head of the trail, conversing amongst themselves.

Chaz got out of his car and couldn't help but puff out his chest as he walked toward the knot of waiting demons. He scanned the eyes as he approached, looking for signs of both subservience and rebellion.

"Hello, Chaz," called a demon.

Chaz shook his head and tapped his chest with two fat fingers. "No. It's 'Lord Chaz' now. Best that everyone gets accustomed to that right now."

The demon who had spoken to him nodded. "Yes, Lord Chaz."

Chaz smiled at him—his expression was a little condescending, but he was allowed that pleasure. "Let's be on our way to the meeting place."

He turned toward the trail, grimacing at the odor of smoke that still filled the woods—the scent of Herlequin's demise. He set off with a bold pace, not waiting for the others, not checking if they could keep up. It was their responsibility to meet Chaz's speed, not the other way around. He led them deep into the woods, off the trail and to the place where Herlequin had held all of his meetings.

With a single frown at the charred place at its center, Chaz strode to the glade and stood, hoping he struck a regal figure, and hoping no one guessed at his unease at being in the center of that circle.

"Welcome," Chaz said in a booming voice. "We meet here today to establish my reign, my succession from

Herlequin. I take this as my right, given I'm the strongest amongst us, and given that no one has challenged me or my rule." He scanned the assembled demons, once more looking for signs of rebellion and signs of subservience. "Are there any among you that wish to challenge?" The forest was silent, filled only by the rustle of animals and the rustle of demons turning to look at one another. "Very well. I assume that from this point on my rule will be unquestioned." His gaze darted to the edges of the glade, looking for signs of Herlequin's daughters.

Again, the glade remained silent, filled with an expectation, as if those present were waiting to see if Brigitta would appear and punish Chaz for his insolence.

Chaz smiled, and it was a nasty smile. "Very well. Here is my first set of orders." He turned a full circle, making eye contact with every demon present—in other words, every demon who lived in Oneka Falls.

3

"He should sleep for at least another hour," said Toby. "We may as well go upstairs and relax."

"And the new one? How long will she sleep?" asked Mike right on cue.

"It's hard to tell with the stronger demons. She took much more M99 than this pathetic example of the breed. I'd guess an hour or less," said Toby.

Making a show of stomping up the stairs, Toby and Mike ascended into the kitchen and slammed the door to the basement.

Slumped in her cell, several yards away from Hartman's, Shannon let out a sigh. She'd projected an image akin to one of the undead class of demons from the moment Toby and Mike had picked her up to carry her down the stairs. She chose an image similar to Brigitta's—undead flesh, blackened and loose, yet regal and aloof at the same time. "Are you awake?" she asked.

"Shhh!" said Hartman. "It may be a trick."

Shannon did her best to laugh in an imperious manner, as she might expect Brigitta to. "Do you question my judgment, youngster?"

"No. I do not question you, but these humans are tricky. They are not the same as the others."

Shannon stood, taking it slow and focusing on keeping the image she projected in sequence with her movements. "They are upstairs." Her tone was dismissive, almost derisive. "They think we will sleep for another hour yet. We must use this time to strategize. You must tell me everything you've told them, so I can tell the same lies."

Silence filled the basement for the space of several breaths, then Hartman straightened and turned toward her. "I don't recognize you."

"And why would you? You are far beneath my station."

Hartman nodded. "I told them partial truths—just enough to lead them astray. I told them we fled another race of beings when we came here. That the other race—I called them the older ones—had enslaved us and was feeding on our emotions."

Shannon arched an eyebrow at him. "Risky," she said.

"Yes, but as I said, these humans seem more capable than most. I didn't want to risk an outright lie." Hartman tilted his head to the side. "Besides, I didn't tell them we were fleeing our own gods—I said we were slaves of these 'older ones,' though."

Shannon nodded. "And how we arrived? What lie did you tell them?"

Hartman smiled, and it was a ghastly sight. "There again, I mixed truth and lie in equal measure. I told them of the Passage, but I also told them that each time they 'kill' one of us, each time they force one of us back into the other realm—that it weakens the barrier between our two domains. I told them that this practice of killing demons would eventually lead to their own doom, as it would allow the 'older ones' to make the trip once the barrier weakened enough." He grinned, showing his fangs. "To further confuse them, I laughed as if it were all a lie."

Shannon forced a bell-like laugh from her lips. "Superb. That should leave them confused and too scared to kill more of us."

"Thank you, mistress," said Hartman. "I thought it would suit."

Shannon nodded once more and casually extended her hand to push open the door to her cell. She stepped into the central part of the basement, tossing a look at Hartman over her shoulder as she did so. "Thank you," she said.

"Mistress! Open my cell, and together, we can break these humans to bits. We can storm the first floor and take them by surprise."

Shannon laughed, and this time, it was her genuine laugh, not a put-on sham. She allowed the visage she had adopted to dissolve and showed Hartman her true form. "I don't think so, bucky. I think we'll keep you where you are for now," she said with a laugh.

Hartman growled deep in his throat and thrashed against the chains which bound him.

"Come on down, boys!" called Shannon. "It worked."

Benny led the others down the stairs, a broad grin on his face and mirth dancing in his eyes. "I knew you could do it, Shan! I knew you could fool him."

In his cell, Hartman stole a glance at Benny before growling again and rattling his chains as he tried to break their stainless-steel grip.

"Is it as we thought?" asked Toby.

"Yes," said Shannon. "What he told you was a mixture of lies and half-truths, but the essential points were true."

"Who are they fleeing?"

"He said they were the gods of his kind." Shannon turned to stare at Hartman as he struggled. "He said the thing about the Passage was true, but the part about weakening the barrier between the realms every time we killed one of them was false."

"Traitor!" snapped Hartman.

Shannon laughed. "As you see me now, demon, is how I truly am. The demon skin you saw before was the disguise."

"Impossible!" screamed Hartman. "Humans cannot present visages! And even if they could, it wouldn't fool a demon."

Benny giggled, and Shannon laughed outright. "It's worked on three of you, now," said Shannon. "I'm willing to bet it will work on all of you."

"Not the more powerful amongst us," said Hartman with a sneer.

"It worked on Chaz Welsh, and it worked on Brigitta herself," said Shannon.

Hartman shook his head and turned his back to them. The clanking and clanging of the chains continued.

"And you, Benny? Get anything from him?" asked Mike.

"I can read him," said Benny. "But it is difficult, and not everything is clear. The part about the gods is especially fuzzy. He's terrified of them, though."

"Do you think you could read a demon from a distance greater than what we have here today?"

"Like reading someone in Oneka Falls? I don't know." Benny lifted his shoulders and let them drop, walked to Shannon's side, and put his arm around her shoulders. He gave her a little hug and smiled. "I'll give it a try when we're home."

"What do we do with him?" asked Scott from his place on the stairs.

"The same thing we do with any demon," said Toby in a cold voice. "We drain his blood and put his body in the digester."

Scott nodded and descended the steps. He continued walking until he stood in front of Hartman's cage. "Hartman, I have another question for you."

Hartman didn't move, didn't turn, didn't answer.

"Tell me about the one called LaBouche."

Toby nodded. "And tell me why your kind is developing a resistance to the M99."

Shannon giggled. "Maybe one of us should ask him how to close the Passage? Permanently, I mean."

"No." Hartman stopped struggling against the chains with his back to the room. "You'll send me back, anyway, why should I help you?"

"To avoid pain," said Scott in a grim voice. He tapped the bars of the cage with the barrel of his pistol. "To die while unconscious."

Hartman tilted his head back and laughed. "On the one hand you're threatening to send me back to the greatest pain I will ever experience in my life, feeding the cruel gods and goddesses of our kind—from whom I have no hope of escaping again—and on the other hand you expect your puny pistol to make me give you information." He shook his head and rustled his wings in the tight confines of his cell. "Give me something. Give me a reason to help you." He turned and took a step toward the bars.

Scott took two steps back and raised his pistol, pointing it at Hartman's face. "Don't try anything!"

"Give me a reason," asked Hartman. "Give me something for my help."

Scott glanced at Toby over his shoulder, and Toby shrugged. "Like what?" asked Scott.

"Let me go! I will leave this area. I will travel far from here. I'll go to the other side of the planet. You will never see me again."

Toby stepped up next to Scott, leaned close to him, and whispered something in his ear. Scott nodded. "What you're asking…it's not something we're prepared to deal on."

"Promise not to send me back. Keep me confined…here or elsewhere, but don't send me back."

Scott looked at Toby, who nodded. "Deal." He holstered his pistol and looked expectantly at Hartman. "Now, tell me everything you know about LaBouche. And remember the questions about the M99 and how to close this Passage of yours."

4

High in the boughs of an ash tree, LaBouche sat gazing down at the front of the weak demon's house. Scott and his little band of friends were all inside, as was the demon, no doubt. He had crouched in the suspension underneath Scott's cruiser as they had laid their trap and waited for the demon to return.

LaBouche didn't know the demon's name, only that he was young and weak. He had no doubt that the M99 Toby loaded into his tranquilizer darts would have incapacitated him. He'd worried about Scott catching sight of him, so he hadn't left his hiding place underneath the car. But he had witnessed the woman and the man from the insane asylum arrive in the red BMW.

Why would they keep him alive? Why not kill him immediately as they had Red Bortha? It made little sense...unless they were after something other than removing one more demon from the equation. *Information*, he thought. *They need information about us.*

The thought chilled LaBouche down to his tiny bird feet. He hopped out from underneath the car and took wing. He flew a tight circle around the house straining what served as his ears for any sound, any indication of what was going on inside the house.

Young demons lack fortitude, strength. No doubt they will soon stumble on a way to make him talk. But what could LaBouche do? Brigitta had trapped him in the body of a magpie.

He thought he heard a commotion in the basement and landed near one of the blacked-out windows. LaBouche hopped close to the glass and leaned forward until his stupid little beak rested against it. He could almost understand the words being said inside.

5

The five of them huddled as far from Hartman's cell as they could get. They weren't sure how good his hearing was, but as they gathered together and whispered, Hartman's large, pointed ears articulated toward them.

"Upstairs," said Toby, and they all climbed up into the kitchen. Toby closed the door to the basement and motioned for everyone to follow him outside. As they came through the front doors of the home, something caught Toby's eye. He pointed and shouted as the yellow magpie took wing.

"LaBouche!" shouted Scott. He sprinted after the banana-yellow bird, following him even as LaBouche darted into the apple grove surrounding the house.

"Scott! No!" shouted Benny.

Mike sprinted after him, yanking a pistol from the waistband of his jeans.

"Was that…" began Shannon.

"Yes, that was LaBouche. We can't let him—"

"Toby, listen!" Benny turned back toward the house. "Something is wrong!"

Toby stood in the gravel drive, halfway between the house and the edge of the grove. "Benny…"

Gunfire erupted in the orchard and something small and yellow darted above the tops of the trees. "Scott!" yelled Mike from deep in the trees.

"Toby!" hissed Benny.

Shannon stood between Toby and Benny, her gaze darting back and forth between them.

"Mike! Scott!" shouted Toby. "Something's wrong!" Toby turned toward the house, and all hell broke loose.

7

The demon known as Bill Hartman smiled as the humans raced upstairs, trying to get out of the range of his hearing. *Humans are so easy to manipulate.*

As soon as he heard the front door close, he let the chains they had put so much stock in fall to the floor. The humans had thought the stainless-steel links were strong enough to hold him, and they may have been, but Hartman knew how to pick the cheap locks that held them closed with his talons.

With a snide smile, he ripped the cage door off its hinges and flung it away from him. He never expected to be caught in one of his own cells, but he also had not built them to hold a demon—only humans.

With an angry rictus settling over his features, he unfurled his wings and ascended into the kitchen without touching a single step.

8

LaBouche darted in and out of the trees, trying to keep something substantial between himself and his old partner. Scott only had a pistol, and that made it somewhat easier to avoid taking damage, but Scott was insane with hatred.

It tasted as good as a fine wine.

Even so, LaBouche couldn't enjoy it as much as he would have liked. He cut to the left and at once dropped his right wing tip and shot around behind an apple tree. He dove toward the ground, pulling up only as rounds from Scott's pistol threw dirt into the air beneath him.

LaBouche needed a place to hide, a place to shelter until Scott tired of looking for him, but everywhere he looked, it was the same: apple trees. He gained altitude, breaking free of the grove, accompanied by more bullets from Scott's gun.

He knew the man was tenacious—years of partnering with him had taught LaBouche that. Scott wouldn't let this go. *As long as he can see me, he will chase me*. Not for the first time since Brigitta had punished him with the form of a magpie, LaBouche wished he could generate a visage—an illusion to throw Scott off his scent.

But I can't. Damn you, Brigitta!

He flew as fast as he could, dipping a wingtip and dropping a handful of feet, climbing fast, darting first one way, then the other, but still, Scott pursued him.

9

Hartman watched from the second-story window above the front door as the asshole who'd used the pistol on him chased a little yellow bird into the apple grove. A hateful smile settled on his features. He watched the one who had shot the tranquilizer darts at him step toward the apple grove, then stop. *Scott and Toby*, he thought. *They will pay for what they did here today.*

"Mike! Scott!" shouted Toby. "Something's wrong!" The man turned toward the house, his gaze going to the open front door before flitting to each of the windows on the first floor. Without warning, the human's gaze jumped to the second-floor window above the front door and locked on Hartman's.

Time to pay the bill, Toby! thought Hartman with an evil smile. He smashed through the window and dove at Toby, talons extended, fangs bared.

10

In the grove, more shots rang out. Benny was still staring in through the open front door, and Toby's gaze had locked on something on the second floor. A horrible crash accompanied the glass daggers and shards that fell from the sky around Shannon, catching the afternoon sun and winking it at her.

Above her, the demon shrieked, sounding every bit a pterodactyl. She threw her arms up out of instinct and looked up from behind splayed fingers. She knew he was a demon, but she couldn't see through their facades the way Toby could, so to her, Hartman looked like something straight out of a martial arts movie made in the 1980s. He seemed to be a normal man with a medium athletic build who could levitate in midair, arms held out, toes pointed at Toby.

"Watch out, Toby!" she yelled. The glass rain continued to fall around her, the larger chunks shattering again when they hit the gravel of the driveway, flinging more sharp daggers at her legs. Toby dove toward the door of Scott's cruiser, ignoring the glass minefield that surrounded him, and mere seconds later the demon landed where Toby had been standing, gouging furrows through the gravel and into the soil beneath. He shot a glare of pure malevolence at Shannon before he turned his attention back to Toby who jerked the handle of the cruiser's back door again and again.

Without giving herself time to think, Shannon took two giant running steps forward and threw a kick at the demon's midsection, but she might as well have kicked a stone pillar. Hartman cast a look of derision her way, then swatted her backhand, knocking her feet out from under her and sending her spinning into the gravel and glass.

"No!" Benny shouted. More shots rang out in the apple grove, and Mike shouted something unintelligible.

Hartman turned his back on both Benny and Shannon. He spun Toby around and swept his legs out from under him at the same time. He crouched, straddling Toby's torso and leaned down to bare his fangs in Toby's face. The demon lifted an arm high behind him and bared his claws.

Shannon shook her head to clear the confusion from her mind. *Hartman can kill Toby with one swipe of those claws across his neck. I have to do something*!

Benny glanced in her direction, smiling a little with a strange, sorrowful expression in his eyes, before charging at Hartman. He lowered his shoulder right before he slammed into the demon's side and pinned him against the cruiser's front door. With a roar, Hartman flung Benny aside as if he represented no threat at all. With two quick steps, he stood over Toby again, raising his hand high behind him, ready to strike.

Benny's gone! *Toby's gone*! *Where have your victims gone, Hartman*? Shannon sent the pulse with as much mental strength as she could muster and deep in her sinuses, a warm trickle of blood began.

Hartman flinched and looked around in confusion.

That's right, Toby's disappeared, you rat-faced demon. Toby is gone. Gone!

Hartman spun away from the car, twisting his head back and forth, trying to find Toby. He turned, putting his back to all three of them and took two uncertain steps toward the apple grove.

There! *Don't you see Toby running toward the road*? *He's right there on the drive*! Shannon imagined Toby sprinting down the rutted track that cut through the apple grove. Blood made its way into her nose and slid down toward her lips.

Hartman sprinted toward the road, growling as if he were an attack-trained dog going after an invader.

"Quick!" Shannon hissed. "I don't know how much longer I can fool him."

Benny crawled over to her and put his hand on her shoulder. "Let me help." Both he and Shannon adopted a dreamy expression.

Toby got to his knees and fumbled the back door of the cruiser open. Lying on the back seat was his tranquilizer rifle and backpack. He jerked them out on the ground and reloaded all three magazines as fast as he could. He moved to squat near the rear tire of the cruiser, his container of spare darts in front of him. "Bring him back, Shannon. Bring him this way."

"I don't know…" Shannon had gone pale and rocked back and forth on her knees as if exhausted.

"Do it. Benny, get Mike and Scott back here." When Benny didn't react, Toby threw a glare in his direction. "Benny!"

He inched his head around and met Toby's gaze, but it was as if he were under the influence of a powerful hallucinogen or in the middle of a dream.

"Benny!" Toby shouted.

Benny shook himself, and his eyes cleared. "What?"

"Get Mike and Scott back here!"

Benny nodded once. "Hartman's on his way back. It took some convincing."

"I'll be ready. Get Shannon inside. Give me what help you can once Hartman gets in range, but make sure Mike and Scott are on their way."

"Will do." Benny hugged Shannon under her arms and drew her to her feet. He led her inside the house and closed the door behind them.

Toby felt the familiar rush of fear and excitement as he heard Hartman's footsteps crunching on the gravel. He sprang up and rested the tranquilizer rifle on the trunk of the cruiser. He aimed with care, hesitating long enough for Hartman to close the distance to inside the gun's most effective range before firing all five darts out of the magazine.

Hartman dodged to the left and right, but despite his best efforts four of the five darts lodged between his scales. He roared with anger and frustration and leaped into the air, his wings flapping furiously.

Moving by rote, by muscle memory, Toby ejected the spent magazine and slammed a full one in its place. He brought the rifle up and fired.

With each new dart that slammed into his body, Hartman shrieked with rage. He wobbled in midair, his wings becoming uncoordinated.

Toby kept firing until the second magazine was also empty. Based on the first encounter, that was more than enough M99 to put Hartman to sleep, but Toby wanted to be sure. He loaded the third and last magazine into the tranquilizer rifle.

Hartman landed on the cruiser's trunk, talons from his feet scrabbling along the slick painted metal. His gazed burned on Toby, his mouth agape. He folded his wings behind him and extended his claws.

Toby threw himself away from the car, rolling in the gravel and glass. He hadn't had time to grab the bag holding his filled darts, but judging by how Hartman staggered, he didn't think he would need them. "Benny! Mike and Scott?"

Almost here, said Benny in his mind.

Hartman slipped and fell on the trunk's lid, then slid off the car altogether, landing in the gravel on his hip. He still glared at Toby, but his efforts to regain his footing were more comical than concerning.

Toby fired his remaining five darts into the demon and treated him to a nasty smile as Hartman quivered and thrashed. He circled wide, giving the flailing claws a wide berth.

Hartman groaned and lunged in his direction but missed, his claws sweeping through thin air.

"How did he get out?" asked Mike, stepping out of the grove behind him.

Toby shrugged and continued loading his magazines while keeping an eye on Hartman. "Where's Scott?"

Hartman flopped on his back, drool sliding out of the corner of his mouth.

Mike gestured behind him at the apple grove. "Last I saw him he was moving slow. It's hard to walk and scan the sky for a little yellow magpie at the same time, I guess."

"You didn't get him?"

"LaBouche?" asked Mike. "No. He got away again."

Toby grimaced. "That's no good."

"In more ways than one," muttered Scott, stepping out of the trees.

"We'll need chains again. I'll see if I can figure out how he slipped out of them last time." Mike turned and approached the front doors.

"Forget that," said Toby. He approached Hartman, who was staring up at the sky with bleary eyes. With a fresh magazine in his tranquilizer rifle, Toby pointed it at the demon and fired five more darts into him, point-blank.

"Shouldn't we keep him around? Think of the information we could learn from him."

"Not worth the risk." Toby shook his head. "Besides, we got answers to most of our questions. If we need more information, there's a woman living near Batavia who would suit."

11

Anger burned through LaBouche as he flew south. *They kidnapped a demon*! *Interrogated him like some…some criminal*! He had to get back to Oneka Falls, had to tell Chaz what was going on.

He had to tell Chaz that the war was starting in earnest.

12

Ice cold water splashed across Kelly-Ann, soaking her clothes and hair. She gasped and cracked her eyes open. Candles burned around the periphery of the room, casting golden light and flickering shadows on the walls of a lake cottage with the windows obscured.

"Wakey, wakey!" He stood at the foot of the table, grinning with malicious glee, an empty bucket held loosely in one hand.

"Ugh," she breathed, settling back onto the cold, hard table on which frigid water now puddled. "I'm easy to wake up—no water required."

His gleeful expression died. "What fun would that be?"

She let her eyelids sink closed, but a stinging slap opened them wide.

He leaned close, his eyes burning, lips curled in a snarl. "No," he said.

"Sorry!" she gasped, pressing a hand to her burning cheek.

"Don't mistake my letting you live through the night for weakness. Don't mistake it for cowardice."

"No," she murmured. "I wouldn't do that."

"Have you guessed who I am yet?"

She shook her head, gaze glued to his face.

He straightened, a small smile playing on his lips. "But I know who you are, Kelly-Ann Malley."

"Sure. You have my driver's license."

He shook his head, his grin blossoming into a sneer. "I knew before we met. I knew before your car broke down." He winked at her, and something in his eyes sent shivers racing down her spine. "I knew before I *rigged* your car to break down and lifted your phone out of your purse."

During the long night, she'd suspected he'd been stalking her, that he may have done something to her car, but hearing it confirmed brought her terror to the fore. "I don't want to die," she said in a very small voice.

"No, of course, you don't. Who does?" He patted her shoulder. "But, like everyone else, you can't control when Abaddon comes calling." He leaned in again, a chuckle rumbling in his throat. His breath smelled of garlic and onions and strong coffee. He stared into her face as if expecting something.

...when Abaddon will come calling, she thought, dread wrapping hot, sticky fingers around her soul. Abaddon was the name the press had given the serial killer active in New York, Pennsylvania, and Ohio. He was suspected of killing more than fifteen women, and the FBI had no clue who he was. She tried to shrink away, but he grabbed her by the hair and pulled her even closer.

"No, no, Kelly-Ann. You can't get away."

"Oh my..." Her breath ran out before she could go on. Her pulse pounded in her temples, but her face felt like a slab of ice.

"*Yesssss*," he breathed. "You see it now."

She tried to nod, but as he was still holding a fistful of her hair, she succeeded only in pulling her own hair. "You're...you're Abaddon..."

He let go of her hair and straightened up, face suffused with pride. "Yes, that's what the press calls me." He shrugged. "It's but one cross we artists must bear—nicknames in the press. Don Daba, at your service."

"Artist," she repeated numbly.

"Oh, yes. Killing can be an artform, as with almost every other human activity. I've surpassed the mundane murderer in every way." He patted her shoulder in an almost fatherly manner. "Before I turned eighteen, if you want the truth of it." He lifted his shoulders and let them fall. "But then again, I apprenticed to a master. A teacher, a tutor, if you will." He arched his eyebrows, his eyes taking on a far-away look. "More than one."

"Tutor," she murmured. She felt frozen, sluggish. Her thinking seemed stalled, and she struggled to process what he told her.

"Yes!" he snapped. "Can you do nothing more than parrot what I say?"

"Sorry," she said in a weak, tremulous voice. "Why... I mean, I'm..."

He waited to see if she could finish the thought, a malevolent grin playing on his lips, eyes whirling. When she shrugged, he chuckled. "Why you? Why *not* you? You're nobody? You're unimportant? Not to me, you're not." He turned and began to pace toward the foot of the table where he turned and came back toward the head in even steps. "Do you understand what it takes to make good art? Have you ever tried? Oils on canvas? Pencil sketches? Music? Anything?"

She shook her head.

He frowned at her, and a twitch developed in the corner of his left eye. "Such a *wasted* life." He sighed, shaking his head. "Well, I'll tell you. Good art develops at the intersection of a good subject, the artist, and a good medium—a good canvas. Do you see?"

She thought furiously, aware that his words might be the ravings of a broken mind but searching for any thread she might weave into a lifeline. "I get the part about subject and artist, but can't a good artist make art regardless of the media?"

He curled his lip. "Perhaps it's okay for a mundane artist, but a true master? No. Never. *You* are both the subject *and* the canvas."

She swallowed hard, her dry throat clicking in the silence that followed his pronouncement.

He smiled. "I'm sorry for your discomfort, but it won't last long." He reached behind him, and when he brought his hand forward, a scalpel glinted in the low, flickering light.

Kelly-Ann Malley screamed as the scalpel descended toward her face, but as with her thirst, her screams didn't last long.

Chapter 5

1986

I

Tom Walton climbed out of his cruiser in the parking lot of Jenny's Diner just in time to catch the sunset. The place was garish—full of chrome and candy apple red—but it was a great place to meet. For once, John Morton's cruiser was already in the lot.

Tom walked inside and spied the big man right away, sitting in their usual booth. He glanced at Jenny, and she gave him a wide-eyed look and a shrug. Wearing a puzzled smile, Tom slid into the booth opposite John Morton. "John," he said.

"Tom. How's it all going?" John spread his thick hands on the table in front of him.

Tom swept the hair off his forehead and rubbed his temples. "I don't want to..." He sighed and shook his head instead of finishing the sentence.

John rubbed his chin, a grave expression settling over his features. "Is it the same as the other time? You know, back then?"

"I'll tell you this for nothing, John. I keep trying to convince myself that it's nothing like what happened in 1979, but..." Tom rested his elbows on the table and rested his face in his cupped hands. "It reminds me so much of how those kids disappeared over in Oneka Falls."

John shook his head. "You know what? It's as though I've been holding my breath since we caught Gray but missed his woman. Like I've been waiting for the other shoe to drop."

Tom's chuckle was a sour one. "I understand *exactly* what you mean, John. I wish I didn't—God knows I wish I didn't—but I do. This disappearance, though, it makes me feel as hinky as back in '79." A thousand-yard stare settled in Tom's eyes. "Maybe hinkier."

"Not sure that's a word, partner," said John in a grave voice. "But I know what you mean all too well."

"Anyone…" started Tom.

"Anyone from Cottonwood Vale go missing? Thankfully, no. And I haven't gotten any calls from anyone else, either."

"So it's just me. Only Genosgwa?"

"Seems like it. Is Wallace being of any help or just getting in your way?"

Tom scoffed and made a shooing gesture with his hand. "The bastard had the gall to be pissed off that I'd rather use Leland Chambers' dogs than the new K-9 unit. Can you imagine?"

"I don't know, Tom. Attack-trained German Shepherds versus trail-trained bloodhounds?" Morton made a funny face and lifted one large hand to twirl a finger next to his temple. "Just think...those dogs could've attacked every bush between the road and the heart of the forest."

Despite his mood, Tom chuckled. "No doubt. No doubt."

"Did Leland turn anything up?"

Tom leaned back in the booth and threw one arm over the seat's back. "It's the weirdest thing. At first, his hounds were on the boy's trail like...well, if you'll excuse the bad metaphor...like ticks on a hound dog. But later... I don't know. It was as if the scent disappeared into nothing. As though the boy walked out to a certain point in the woods and got picked up by one of them UFOs."

"No, I believe you're wrong there, Tom. Leland's dogs could track a UFO."

They looked at each other for a moment, and both men chuckled.

Jenny strolled up, order pad held in her hand, her gaze directed at John Morton. She continued to stare at him even after she reached the table.

He raised an eyebrow at her. "Do I have a cowlick or something?"

Jenny shook her head. "I was trying to figure out if you're one of them pod-people or not. You know, from outer space."

Tom chuckled.

"You must be," Jenny said. "Since you were here first and all, I'm having a hard time accepting you're John Morton."

John lifted a big hand and flapped it back and forth. "Yeah, yeah." Despite the tone of his voice, she amused him, and he smiled to show it.

"Well, boys, what'll it be?" As she asked, Jenny folded her order pad and stuck it in her apron. "No, let me guess. John will have the usual, and Tom will have what John's having."

Tom made a finger gun and shot her with it.

Without another word, Jenny whirled and strode into the kitchen. Through the red vinyl padded swinging door, they heard her shout, "Two orders of cockroach stew, heavy on the cockroaches."

Both men chuckled.

After a moment, John took a deep breath and leaned back. He fixed Tom with a stern gaze. "Tell me, Tom, what can I do to help you? And none of this 'it's my problem nonsense.'"

Tom closed his eyes and pressed his thumb and forefinger against his eyelids. "I wish I had any idea what you could do to help, John. I'd welcome you by my side in a heartbeat—*if* there were anything *I* could do. It seems it's sitting-on-my-hands-time. Waiting-for-something-else-to-happen-time."

John made a face and shook his head. "That's the worst part, isn't it?"

"Sure is."

2

Greg's parents had decided to pack up and leave early. The news about the kidnapped kid had resolved the issue. Greg didn't want to go despite everything that was happening, but his mother was firm. Grandma and Grandpa Canton would come with them back to Florida and stay for a while, so at least there was that.

He lay on the couch in the living room, still too scared to sleep in the bedroom, but not so frightened that his dad had to sleep with him anymore. In a way, Greg preferred sleeping on the couch in the living room. The room was larger, and the big bay window let in a lot of moonlight. From where he lay, the shore was invisible, but starting from the middle of the dock, the lake was visible. The sounds of the lake comforted him again rather than making him feel scared, but at night, he wanted that big bay window between him and the water. It didn't open.

Everyone was so understanding. Everyone said they would feel the same way he did. He still felt like a seven-year-old. And now, they were cutting out early—because of him. Guilt edged around the corners of his mind, jeering at him and taunting.

Greg should have been sleeping already. Their flight was an early one, and the trip from Genosgwa Lake to the airport in Buffalo took two hours. Under his thick blanket, he shrugged. It was as if something inside of his mind refused to go to sleep.

It was as if something inside of his mind sat there waiting for something to happen.

He forced his eyes closed and tried to count sheep, even though it never worked. He tried to think sleepy thoughts, tried to imagine himself in a deep sleep.

Outside, the sound of the wind changed.

One of his eyes cracked open, and he glanced nervously at the plate-glass window. The window rattled in its frame as if the wind blew straight at it from across the lake. Greg opened his other eye and propped himself up with his elbows.

Sure enough, whitecaps dotted the lake and clouds covered the moon. It reminded him of the storm…the storm that had started everything. The storm that had unveiled the Lady in the Lake—that had maybe awakened her. He stared at the black water, eyes dancing from whitecap to whitecap, searching for any shape, any color that didn't belong.

Greg swung his legs off the couch and sat up, keeping the blanket wrapped around him. *Like a shroud*, said a voice in his head, but it sounded like his own voice. His little red kayak had escaped its place on the shore and was drifting against the wind toward the center of the lake. He sucked in a breath of cold air, and goosebumps erupted across his back. *Kayaks can't do that.*

Are you sure, sport? Looks as though your kayak is doing just that.

There'd been an uneasy truce the past couple of days between Greg and his invisible friend. His friend had told jokes, Greg had laughed, and they'd left it at that.

You know who it is.

Greg didn't speak, didn't think, he only shook his head.

Come off it, Greggy. You know it's her.

Greg squeezed his eyelids shut—hard enough that tears sprang to his eyes. *I don't care*, he thought. *We're leaving tomorrow. She can have the kayak.*

Sport, if you think the kayak is what she's after… And why do you believe she'll allow you—any of you—to leave tomorrow?

Greg twisted his head from side to side hard enough to make his spine crackle. *No.*

His invisible friend sounded amused when he spoke next. *No? What does that even mean? No, you don't think she's after the kayak? No, you don't think she'll allow you to leave?*

No. No. The kayak passed the end of the dock, and as it did so, a lazy hand extended toward the sky from the stern. Like a puppeteer, the hand seemed to look in one direction, then the other, before the palm turned toward Greg, and the hand waved *bye-bye.*

You know what she will do, right, kiddo?

Greg didn't, and he didn't want his invisible friend to tell him, either.

What kind of friend would I be, if I didn't tell you what you needed to do? Well, I'll say it anyway, boyo. The way she will stop you is by killing. She will kill someone in your family, so you have to stay. Who do you suppose it will be? Mommy? Daddy? Gramps?

No. No, no, no, no!

I don't know what you think you're doing there, sport. What will be will be. The Lady in the Lake will do as she pleases.

Greg shook his head and continued to shake it nonstop. *No! I won't let her!* Greg smashed his fist into his other hand. "I won't let her!"

"Greggy?" came the sleep-slurred voice of his mother from the bedroom she shared with his father.

Again, Greg had the sense of great amusement from his invisible friend. *Not too loud, kiddo. Not too loud or you'll have the whole house awake, and if that happens, there's nothing that can be done.* Nothing!

I'll stop her! I'll...I'll...

You'll what, boyo? Hmm? How do you intend to stop her? What, will you say pretty please? Will you cover your eyes and pretend she's not doing what she's doing?

Panic gripped Greg around his middle. *What can I do? You have to help me!* Really *help me this time! Tell me what to do!*

Hmmm. I'm not sure I should.

But...but...but... Greg's gaze bounced around the living room, searching for something—*anything*—that he could use as a weapon.

Okay, I approve of how your mind is working now, champ. Hitting on all eight cylinders, there. You know where it is.

Where what is? Greg fought to keep the image of the neat rifle from his mind; instead, he thought about the Transformers, He-Man, Thundercats—any cartoon that came to mind.

Oh, Greggy... Let's not be coy with one another! You know what I'm referring to, and I know you do.

Greg continued to run through cartoon characters in his head, even going as far as pretending to hear the jingle that started each show.

Oh. I see. You don't need my help after all.

No, I do! I need your help, but...

Well, if you don't want to use the obvious solution, I guess we might *find an alternative.*

Greg imagined he sensed a smug satisfaction behind his invisible friend's words. *Alternative*?

I don't know… I don't know if you want it bad enough. I don't know if you're willing to make the sacrifice to save the ones you love.

Greg's belly did flip-flops, but besides that, a strange sense of calm enveloped him. *Tell me.*

It seems to me, boyo, that if you were to lead her away from the lake, she might lose some of her power. She might…she might even become stoppable.

Hope dawned within him, and a grim resolve settled over him. *What do I have to do*?

I knew you'd see it my way, sport. That's why we get along so well. We think so much alike.

Greg tried not to feel pleasure at the words, but it burned within him, nonetheless. *Tell me what to do.*

And you're sure you don't want to use…the other thing?

I don't even know where it is. Or how to use it. Greg pulled his clothes on.

Such a shame. That way would've been such fun. Here's what you need to do…

3

Stellan ran. He ran and ran. Footfall after footfall, he ran. The things behind him trumpeted their victory as they herded him toward the deepest part of the forest. He had a sense of great amusement from somewhere around him—and great hunger.

The boy's mind was numb, but his feet weren't. His feet shrieked with each step, screamed with each slip, bled with each root he tripped on. His arms flopped uselessly at his sides—he no longer had the energy to hold them up. Stellan's eyelids drooped, his mouth hung open, and his tongue was as dry as fresh kitty litter and tasted about the same.

The Lady in the Lake... He darted a glance over his shoulder—roughly the thirty cajillionth such glance since he'd crossed the road that separated the woods from his house—to check. Sometimes she was there, chasing him, and other times she was missing. She wasn't as fast as the four-legged creatures, but she was just as relentless.

He turned his attention to the front, gaze twitching from side to side, from tree to tree, trying to find a place to hide, a safe place to rest. He saw only trees and darkness.

Stellan's eyes ached with exhaustion, and his throat burned. His lips had chapped sometime during the day's brutal marathon, and his mouth…his tongue tasted like some foreign thing, an old dead lizard that had crawled inside his mouth without him knowing.

He staggered across a knot of roots and slapped at the tree, pushing himself upright to steady himself. He darted yet another glance over his shoulder, trying to gauge how much of a lead he had over the dog-things chasing him.

Stellan gasped and lost his breath. Even looking at *her* inspired new fear in him. The Lady in the Lake was back, scowling at him. Her midnight-black form seemed off, like a bad copy of a person, and though her legs pumped as a running woman's would, her feet didn't touch the ground. She winked at him, and her feet touched down without a sound.

She opened her mouth, exposing too many sharp fangs. Her irises shifted from bright green to black to a blazing crimson as blood ran from the corners of her eyes like gory tears. Her wet, muddy skin appeared loose, and weeping pustulent sores added the greenish sheen of slime to the wetness of the mud sliding down her body.

One of the dog-like things chasing him yipped, then made a peculiar sound that Stellan thought was meant to be laughter. The Lady in the Lake grinned in hideous fashion and dropped her hand to pet the dog-thing's head without missing a step. The two ran in perfect synchronicity, as though they'd run together for eons.

Stellan ripped his gaze away from the gruesome pair, snapping his head back to the front moments before he ran head-first into a thick tree trunk. He threw himself to the side to a cacophony of dog-thing laughter behind him. His feet tried to slip from beneath him, and he jinked and juked like a dancer having a convulsion, banging his elbow against the trunk in the process.

He cried out and slowed, wanting more than anything to stop, to lie down and rest, to give up the insane chase. An exhausted sob escaped his lips, and though he felt like crying—felt like he *was* already crying—no tears wet his cheeks. Glancing back, he slowed further, his steps becoming hesitant, but before he could stop, a monstrous dog-thing sprinted toward him, mouth open, slobbering a gruesome, viscous liquid that sizzled and popped when it struck the ground. With a start, Stellan realized the thing had no eyes and terror provided the energy to sprint.

He ran on, ignoring the pain in his feet, the yipping things behind him, the cramping in his sides. He ran because he had to.

4

Mason Harper stood in his grandmother's flower bed, sheltered by the shadows dropped by the eaves of her house, and watched. He knew the brat would come out soon. The Lady in the Lake had said as much, and she was always right.

She'd given him a task, and he was bound and determined to do it right. Her rewards were…

He shook his head, banishing the thought of rewards as something stirred in his belly. The last thing he wanted was a hard-on.

Next door, the screen door opened and closed with almost no sound. Mason held his breath, leaning even farther back into the shadows. Just as Mason's lungs began to burn, Greg Canton crossed the gravel road and slipped into the woods.

Mason lounged against the side of his grandmother's house. He had a few more minutes to wait, then the fun would begin.

5

With a full belly, Tom slid behind the wheel of his cruiser. A belch lurked far down in his guts, but he couldn't coax it out into the open. He reached in the glove box for the roll of Tums and made a face at the horrible chemically induced fruit flavor.

In his rearview mirror, he saw John Morton back out of his parking spot and flip his headlights. With a merry little beep, the Cottonwood Vale police car turned out onto the highway.

Tom drew a deep breath and let it gust out of him. Sometimes, his job rested on his shoulders like an insufferable weight bearing down on him, grinding him to dust. Usually, he felt that way when the case wasn't going well—and, no question about it, the Stellan Stensgaard case wasn't going well at all.

He cranked his cruiser to life and threw it in reverse, but then sat there with his foot on the brake and his hand on the gear selector. Not for the first time, Tom entertained the idea of retirement. Not for the first time, he looked up in his rearview mirror and sneered at himself for what he considered weakness.

Tom backed out of the parking lot and put Jenny's Diner in his rearview mirror. He considered going home, making an early night of it—the Lord knew he had gotten little sleep in the past couple of days—but he would only lie there in bed, staring at the darkened ceiling, mind going approximately ten million miles an hour.

He turned onto Lake Circle, his tires squealing a bit as he took the turn a mite too fast. Tom shrugged. *Won't hurt to take a little patrol—a little extra protection for the residents of Lake Genosgwa.*

It wasn't late, but he and John had gotten to reminiscing and laughing about times long past, and the time had gotten away from them. He glanced down at his Seiko. He thought about calling home, but since it was after ten, chances were his wife was already asleep. Janet understood that with a case such as this, she may not see him for days—and although that made him feel guilty, it was what it was.

He drove at a slow pace, high beams on, searchlight stabbing into the forest on the side of the road opposite the lake. He cruised down the asphalt road, right above an idle, the powerful eight-cylinder engine in his cruiser throbbing.

Not surprisingly, no one was out walking, and most of the lake houses down the ridge on his left were buttoned up tight, though lights blazed inside the homes and in the yards. Tom nodded to himself—it would be hard for someone who was up to no good to sneak around down there by the lake.

He turned his attention to the forest, his eyes trailing the bright white beam from the spotlight. It splashed across the trees and underbrush, stabbing into the dark spaces between them.

Unlike in movies or television, it wasn't stimulating. No boogeymen leaped out of the dark shadows to threaten him. No mysterious misty white lights guided him deeper into the forest.

I don't know what I'm expecting to see, Tom thought. *What the hell, it's better to be out here doing something than lying in bed or sitting in my office…waiting.*

He fed the iron beast under his hood a little more of the go juice, and the tires ate more ground. Tom alternated his gaze between the darkness deep in the forest and the road ahead.

He drew a deep breath, and the tension in his neck and shoulders eased out of him. He let his head fall back against the headrest, and his jaw opened wide, cracking with the force of his yawn. The chief blinked and shook his head to wake himself up.

He never saw the thing bolt from the forest and smash through his passenger window. Snarling and snapping as a wild animal on the attack would, the thing hung half-in and half-out of the car, saliva spinning in the air between them.

Tom slammed both feet on the brake pedal, and the car slewed to the side, sliding toward the edge of the road, the edge of the ridge, and the ten-foot drop to the shore of Lake Genosgwa. He ripped his gaze away from the snarling thing hanging in his passenger window and fought the car, wrenching the steering wheel to the left. His training kicked in, and he peeled his feet away from the brakes, goosing the gas pedal only enough to break the slide, then braking with less force.

As the car came to a stop, Tom turned toward the wild thing. It had the shape of a dog—at least in the torso and head—but it was as if their forms had been created by a surrealist. Nothing seemed right about the thing's shape, but with the size of a large breed working dog—a German Shepherd or a Rottweiler—and with large fangs glinting in the moonlight, the snarling beast represented a mortal threat. His mind turned to his service weapon—a Smith & Wesson Model 28 chambered for .357 Magnum rounds. He'd taken some good-natured ribbing in the last few years about his refusal to "modernize" and switch to a semiauto, but he was glad he hadn't at that moment. A 9mm slug would have pissed off the thing hanging in his window, nothing more.

Tom slid his shoulders to rest against the driver's side door while unsnapping the leather strap that secured his Magnum. He eased the pistol from his holster and leveled it at the thing that had smashed his passenger window all to hell.

The misshapen thing stopped its frantic attempts to pull itself into the front seat and hung there staring at Tom…except Tom realized the creature had no eyes in its head. It didn't even have *eye sockets*, only smooth bone covered by black fur. "Well, fuck," Tom muttered.

The dog-thing cocked its head to the side almost as if it could understand the sentiment.

Tom cocked his Smith & Wesson, and for a moment, it was as if the world had stopped. The dog-thing switched its attention back and forth between Tom's face and the huge pistol he leveled at its head.

The tableau shattered as something smashed into the rear passenger quarter panel of the car, pushing the vehicle closer to the ridge. Tom glanced out the back window. The impacts had buckled the quarter panel upward as though struck by another vehicle, but other than that, nothing.

He returned his attention to the dog-thing hanging in his passenger window, and he would have sworn on a stack that the thing *smiled* at him. One of the dog-thing's deformed ears swiveled toward the back of the cruiser, and its human-like paws pushed its bulk back out the window.

"Yes, do that," Tom said. "I don't take pleasure in killing dogs, even if they are misshapen mutant bastards such as the likes of you."

The dog-thing cocked its head, then made the creepiest sound Tom had ever heard—a cross between laughter and a train derailing. The thing slid away from the window, and Tom breathed a sigh of relief.

He lay the Magnum on the seat next to him, resting his hand on it, but lightly, as he tried to calm his racing pulse. The road ahead of him was clear, but with the damage to the rear of the car, he didn't know if the cruiser was drivable. He shook his head—already doubting his memory of the thing that had smashed through his window. Tom lay his hand on the door release, but the memory of that dog-thing was still too fresh.

He swiveled the spotlight until it lit up the woods across from his passenger window. A row of the mutant dog-things sat as still as if carved from marble, the posture of each matching the stance of every other dog-thing at the edge of the tree-line. Tom snapped the Smith & Wesson into firing position, and he leveled the gun at one of the things.

As if they'd been awaiting that cue, the entire row of dog-things charged at the side of his cruiser, coming on in eerie silence—no howls, no barking, only the sound of the footfalls. Tom squeezed off a shot, the report of the Magnum sounding akin to a demolition charge in the tight confines of the cab, and then another. Two of the dog-things stumbled and fell, but the others came on as if they understood he had only four rounds left.

Panic *demanded* he open his door, that he *get out* of the car, that he *run*, but the rational part of him knew that would only lead to one thing. He'd seen the results of a big bastard of a shepherd mauling a man, and the last thing Tom Walton wanted was a mauling by ten or more of the beasts charging the car.

As if they'd practiced the maneuver, each dog-thing in the pack slammed into the passenger side of his cruiser at the same instant, rocking it on its springs at an alarming angle. Tom had no targets, nothing to shoot at, not even the two beasts he'd already shot. The things remained silent, and worse yet, stayed out of sight.

The cruiser slid to the left, toward the ridge and the ten-foot drop. He flung the Magnum on the seat next to him, and Tom smashed the gas pedal to the floor. The rear tires screeched, but the car didn't leap forward, didn't race away from the pack of dog-things. It felt as though they held the cruiser in place somehow—and, as if the car had no traction at all, he slid toward the edge at a faster rate.

Tom glanced out his window—all that was visible was empty air. He released the gas pedal and braced himself as the car tipped over the edge and plunged down the ridge. The driver's side tires caught on something and the cruiser flipped over, barrel rolling down the steep incline.

The car came to rest against a lake house. Blood poured down Tom's face, and his vision had doubled. *Must've hit my head*, he thought at the speed of sludge. His left shoulder flared with sharp, burning pain, and Tom gasped.

The front door of the lake house banged open, and someone stepped into the beams of his headlights. *Shouldn't be out there.* His hand scrabbled against the seat next to him, searching for his service weapon, but not finding it.

"Tom? Tom Walton?" asked Will Seeger peering through the windshield. The man turned his head toward his open front door. "Better call 911, Alison!" he called. "Police Chief's had an accident."

Tom's gaze darted toward the ridge, sure he'd see the dog-things scampering down the incline, coming for him, coming for Will. "Inside," he said, but his voice was too weak for anyone to hear. Besides, Will was already walking around to the cruiser's passenger side—the driver's side doors were pinched against the front of his house. "No," Tom murmured. "Get back."

"What's that, Tom?" Seeger looked at the side of the cruiser, and his eyes widened. "Dang, Tom, what happened to your car?"

Tom's gaze flicked back and forth along the ridge, searching for the mutant freaks that had attacked him, but of them, there was no sign.

6

Joe stood right inside his bedroom door, his posture rigid, his ear pressed to the crack he opened between the door and the jamb. He'd heard Greg call out and had come awake at once.

He was almost sure his grandson had yelled something about not letting someone do something, but he wasn't sure whether he was still asleep when he'd heard that The old Marine waited in the dark, waited for what would happen next. He would die for his grandson—and smiling—if only he could keep the boy from harm.

If that's what it takes, then that's what it takes.

The idea didn't scare him, nor did his dedication and willingness to pay that price. He had been prepared to pay that price since he was a young man—since he'd become a Marine.

In the other room, fabric rustled, as if Greg had discarded his blanket and was pulling on his clothes. Joe got dressed and slipped his feet into sturdy boots meant for action—all without making a sound. The M1 was back in its secret hiding place, but he intended to get it if he had time.

He almost missed it. The door to the porch snicked shut *almost* silently.

Joe slipped into the living room, his eyes roving across the tableau shown by the bay window. Greg was on the path that led down to the dock, standing there staring at the moon on the lake, maybe. Joe let his gaze twitch toward the center of the lake, toward the movement out there.

Greg's little red kayak seemed to motor toward the center of the lake with no visible signs of propulsion. *Against* the wind, moving fast enough to leave a wake. Joe shook his head and hurried into the pantry.

When he came out holding the M1, Greg was gone. Panic bit him, and Joe danced from side to side behind the plate-glass window, his gaze streaking back and forth across the small yard, zipping to the end of the dock, searching the water. *Greg won't swim after that kayak—not after the experience he had out in the middle of the lake.*

He couldn't see Greg anywhere—which meant only one thing.

Joe left the house, letting the door slide shut in silence behind him. He turned toward the back of the house, toward the gravel road and the woods beyond, and slipped down to the corner. He peeked around the edge of the house in time to see Greg slip into the woods. "Greg!" he called.

Greg dashed into the woods without looking back.

"What in the hell?" Slinging the M1 over his shoulder, Joe sprinted across the gravel road, trying to keep Greg within sight. Greg's legs were much shorter than his, but Greg was eleven, and Joe was seventy-three. Even so, he should've been able to catch him.

"Greg! Come back!" he called. That Greg had heard him wasn't in question—he saw the telltale twitch in the boy's shoulders at the sound of his name. *What the hell is he getting up to*? Joe kept on his trail, trying to increase his speed. "Greg!"

Greg kept darting looks over his shoulder, but he wouldn't meet Joe's gaze.

"What are you doing, Greg?"

"Go back!" Greg's voice sounded flat amidst all the moss-covered trees. "Don't let her get you!"

Joe faltered a step, confused by Greg's words, by the emotion in the boy's voice. He looked around, but they were alone in the woods. He kept on, following Greg as fast as his old legs would carry him.

When Greg sobbed, Joe was close enough to hear it.

7

Stellan could no longer think, could no longer plan the best route around the trees and roots that all seemed to reach for him. Branches slapped against his face leaving streaks of blood and hooked his clothing. Brambles stabbed at him. He felt it all, but at the same time, he was numb from head to toe.

His breath shrieked from him, sounding almost as he imagined a jet airplane might. He wobbled from side to side as he ran, and the things that chased him closed in. Some ran to his left and right a few yards away, and others nipped at his heels or licked the bottoms of his feet.

Somehow, he found the strength to keep running. He lifted his feet, he put them down, lifted them, put them down, up, down. He ran and ran and ran.

But it was no use. The things that chased him were tenacious and determined.

Say now, sport. You're not giving up already, are you?

Stellan didn't—couldn't—speak. He had no more energy for actions that did nothing to keep him in front of the pack of demon dogs on his heels.

Champ, it's been fun, but I think you're as close to done as a boy can get this side of the grave.

Stellan wanted to shake his head, wanted to deny the voice speaking in his mind—the voice of his imaginary friend, but could lie to himself no longer. He tried to dredge up more energy, even glancing back, trying to scare himself into running faster, but it was no use. Stellan was spent, lifting his feet just enough to shift them forward, arms and hands flopping at his sides as if boneless.

When he stumbled, the pack of dog-things swarmed him. In the distance, a basso laugh like that of a demon in a horror movie rang through the trees.

It was the last thing Stellan Stensgaard ever heard.

8

Gary Dennis jolted alert as he saw the Canton boy jog across the gravel road. His hand was on the door handle when Joe Canton sprinted through the gravel after his grandson, slinging an M1 carbine across his back as he did so.

Gary got out of the car in a hurry, his other hand on his service weapon. He watched Joe run a few steps. "Dammit!" he grumbled and leaned inside the car to grab the microphone. He told the dispatcher he was out of the car and going after Joe in the woods. Joe *and* Greg.

He ran to catch Joe's trail. He had to sprint to keep him in sight, and even then, he was hard-pressed to stay with him. Joe might be an old guy, but he could move when he wanted to.

The forest had turned spooky. The mist had settled amongst the boughs of the trees, blocking the direct moonlight, and casting an unearthly pall over everything. Things seemed to lurch at him from the corner of his eyes, but Gary kept his gaze on Joe's back.

Ahead, Joe called after his grandson, and his grandson answered back, but Gary couldn't make out the words. For a moment, he thought he saw a dark figure chasing the boy on a path parallel to Joe's, and he opened his mouth to yell a warning but stumbled over a tree root and fell headlong into the underbrush. When he regained his feet and searched for the dark figure, Gary found nothing. *Trick of the darkness, a shadow or something*, he thought and started running, sprinting to make up lost distance.

They ran for what seemed a long time, but given his own age and state of health, Gary knew it couldn't have been more than ten or fifteen minutes. They weren't far into the depths of the forest, but far enough that the only sounds that reached Gary were the thudding of his footfalls, the thumping of his overworked heart, and the strange whistling of his breath through his throat. *Too old for this*, he thought. But he imagined Joe running in these woods alone, maybe confronting a madman, and he found the strength to go on.

Ahead of him, Joe shouted something at Greg and snapped the M1 carbine to his shoulder. *Bam-bam-bam*! The reports ripped through the early-morning silence. Gary's already fast pulse accelerated, and he jerked his service weapon out of his holster. His breath rasped in and out, in and out, and his footfalls thundered on the forest loam beneath him. His pulse raged in his temples, and his vision seemed to throb in synchronous rhythm.

Moments before he reached Joe's position, the old Marine yelled, "Greg, no!" Joe sprinted ahead, leaving Gary behind once more. With grim determination, Gary increased his pace, ignoring the telltale tunneling of his vision. He opened his mouth and panted, exchanging hot, used air for sweet, cool night air. His respirations sounded off—arrhythmic and harsh—but Gary ignored that, too, forcing one step after the next. He grunted as a deep stitch flared in his left side, but he refused to slow his sprint.

Then everything went black.

Chapter 6

2007

I

I have to risk it, thought LaBouche as he sat in the branches of a mulberry bush next to the Oneka Falls Town Hall parking lot. *I have to talk to Chaz without the safety net of an in-between. What Scott and his damn friends have been up to…that information is too important to trust to someone as worthless as Sally McBride.* Instead, he'd told McBride to call Chaz and tell him there was an emergency that needed his attention.

Dawn broke in the east, and dew glistened on his ridiculous yellow plumage. Meeting with Chaz in his current form—from a place of weakness, rather than a vantage of strength—was a significant risk, with little probability of a matching reward. At best, Chaz would take what he said at face value but stop listening to his suggestions about what they should do—he would assume complete leadership. At worst, Chaz would seize the opportunity to send him packing once and for all.

But still, the threat from Scott and his merry band was too high. If they had extracted certain information from that weakling in the north, there was no telling what they could do. *If they know about the Passage…*

But that didn't bear consideration. If they knew, there was nothing he could do, one way or the other.

Chaz's car screeched into the parking lot, roared to the door, and slid to a halt. Chaz threw the door open and lurched out of the car, his head snapping first one way and then the next. "Where's the goddamn emergency, Fuck-it-up? If this is some kind of prank…"

It's no prank, Chaz, sent LaBouche.

Chaz's head snapped around, and he sank into a defensive posture. "LaBouche? Is that you?"

Yes. Who else?

"Where are you? Come out and speak face-to-face."

That…that wouldn't be prudent. But what I have to tell you is of the utmost importance. The humans who killed Herlequin…they're not content with their crime.

Chaz glanced around in the brightening early morning. *What? Why don't we go inside? You can explain it all to me in there.*

I'll stay where I am for the moment. But, listen to me, Chaz. One of the humans is my old partner…Scott Lewis. He's a New York State Trooper. Another is the one we feared existed…the one who's been hunting and killing demons for a decade.

That old myth? Chaz scoffed and made a dismissive gesture with his hand. *Look, LaBouche, I'm going inside. Coffee. Plus, I feel like an idiot, standing out here in the parking lot and having a conversation with someone I can't see. I don't understand your need for secrecy.*

Brigitta…

Yes? What about Brigitta?

He didn't want to elaborate. He didn't want to tell Chaz about his shameful condition.

Chaz sighed. *Look, if you want to talk, I'll be in my office. It's too chilly out here for this silliness.* He turned toward the town hall, unlocked the front door, and went inside.

If he could have slumped his shoulders, LaBouche would have. Instead, he swooped down through the town hall before the door could slide closed.

Chaz stood next to the reception desk, watching the door. He erupted into roaring laughter, raising a hand to point at LaBouche.

If he could have blushed, LaBouche would have. *I know*, he sent.

"Isn't this *special*! Did Herlequin assign you that form, or was it Brigitta?" He gave LaBouche an appraising glance and smiled. *Brigitta.*

LaBouche bobbed his head in the closest approximation to a nod he could muster.

"What did you do?" asked Chaz before dissolving into laughter again. "I'm trying to imagine what you must have done to piss her off this much. I can't come up with anything."

Look, Chaz, the humans—

"No, tell me what you did. I have to know. The curiosity is killing me."

It's not important! But these humans have—

Chaz flapped one of his big scaled and clawed hands—it looked extraordinarily silly to LaBouche. "I will deal with the humans, LaBouche. What kind of threat can they possibly represent? They were aware of Herlequin because he victimized them and let them live. I've established a rule against such behavior going forward. 'Kill your food when you're done playing with it.'"

They've kidnapped one of the weaker demons living to the north. Scotty and his friends interrogated him in his own dungeon. They—

"What did they hope to learn? Why would they take such a risk? Plus, you assume that they know there are more demons in the world than Herlequin."

Certainly, they know about Brigitta. And don't you think they suspect you?

"Me? Why would they suspect me?"

If he could have sighed, LaBouche would have. *You don't think your behavior surrounding Play Time would have raised the eyebrows of your police chief? It would have concerned Scott I can promise you. It would've raised suspicions. You were foolish, you—*

"Enough!" roared Chaz. "That will be enough. I am your sovereign, LaBouche, and you *will* treat me with respect."

We are partners, Chaz. That was the deal.

Chaz worked his face into a moue. "That was before I understood about your…*disability*. You are not fit to rule us, LaBouche. Not even as my partner."

You are reneging on our deal?

Chaz sniffed. "A deal made under false pretenses is not binding."

We need not decide this now. Right now, we need to—

"I'll decide what we need to do, LaBouche. You will carry out *my* orders."

If you believe I'm going to roll over and—

Behind him, the glass doors leading to the parking lot creaked open. "Ah, Fuck-it-up. How appropriate that you would join us at this moment."

LaBouche took off and flew in a little circle. Sally McBride stood in the open door, mouth agape, eyes wide open. Her pale pink skin had bleached even paler.

"Mr. Welsh, I—"

"No, Fuck-it-up. We are no longer friends. Not after I've learned of your complicity in this scam." Chaz took a step forward and swatted at LaBouche but missed. "*On your knees*!" he roared at McBride.

If he could have fought him, LaBouche would have, but he couldn't, so he took the coward's path and ducked out the open door, leaving McBride to face Chaz's wrath alone.

2

Mason Harper walked to the end of his weathered and deteriorating dock, an ice-cold Bud in one hand, and an unfiltered Camel dangling from the corner of his mouth. He glanced at the Canton's lake house, and a smile stretched his lips at the memory of what had happened there. They had abandoned the house after that summer back in '86.

After his grandmother passed away—with a little help from Mason—and he'd inherited her cottage next door, he'd winterized it and moved in, and the house had served him well as a year-round base of operations. He brought a lot of "friends" back there, and the memories of his exploits in the cottage stretched his smile.

After that summer in 1986, things had changed. The atmosphere around the lake was different, as though something was missing. And something *had* been missing…the Lady in the Lake. Oh, she dropped by for visits from time to time—especially when he was entertaining—but he'd missed her full-time presence.

He turned and stared out at the still water, at the reflection of the setting sun dancing in the center of the lake, and his expression flattened into the blank mask he showed the outside world. Something tickled at the back of his mind, a memory—a *feeling.*

A slow smile dislodged his mask. *She's back*, he thought with excitement burbling in his veins. He didn't know how he knew it, but know it, he did.

With a wide grin on his face, he turned back to his cottage. He had a mess to clean up inside, but his smile didn't dim at the prospect of hours of tedious work.

Brigitta—the Lady in the Lake as the locals call her–is back!

3

Anger thrummed through LaBouche's diminutive form. His ridiculous bright yellow wings beat against the air, but it wasn't as satisfying as using thickly muscled arms to beat against someone's weak flesh, and it didn't do much to ease his mood. The shame of it…the humiliation of being trapped in the body of a magpie, of having to run from battle *as a magpie* was almost more than his mind could bear.

But now I have something. I've got a bargaining chip, and I can make that foul bitch change me back.

He flew and flew, high in the air out of the reach of pesky things such as shotgun pellets and bullets, out of the reach of earthbound demons. LaBouche had an idea of where she would be. He imagined he knew where Brigitta would go to lick her wounds.

Lake Genosgwa.

He wasn't sure what her deal was there, but she had some sort of gig running with the locals—a prebuilt legend that fed her. Perhaps not her preferred food, but fear sustained them all. *It would work in a pinch.*

Plus, none of Scott's asshole friends know anything about it. No, I'm sure. That's where the foul bitch will be—no doubt buried in mud at the bottom of the lake. Soaking, sulking.

Anger boiled in his blood—not only at the indignities inflicted on him but because Brigitta was now their leader. *As if she deserves to be anything other than a slave*!

He imagined the others whining and sniveling in her presence…and even he would have to play that part. The idea of it turned his stomach, but if he made a move against her in their present circumstances, the others would come down on him hard. They might even be able to send him back…

And he didn't want to go back. None of them wanted to go back. *Ever.*

No, it took far too long to break free of— LaBouche cut that line of reasoning off in a hurry. It wasn't safe to even *think* of them. Even thinking of their collective name might alert them to his thoughts, might call one of them…and more than anything in any of the worlds, LaBouche wanted to fly under their collective radar.

He shook his tiny head and tumbled in the wind for a moment. *Dammit! It's too hard to remember all the stupid rules of aerodynamic flight.*

LaBouche wasn't known for subtlety. He preferred brutality. *Can't play this that way, more's the pity. No, now it's time to be subtle, tactical…strategic.* Despite his preference for direct action, LaBouche was a master tactician. Few among his kind could match his strategic planning, his trickery, or his deceit.

I should be the one to lead! he raged. *Because she has Herlequin's blood—that's the only reason the others will look to her. But she will set that bastard Chaz Welsh straight in a heartbeat.* The thought warmed LaBouche and smoothed his hackles. *I wish it were possible to confront her, to challenge her…but they wouldn't let it be a fair fight.* And he couldn't fight them all, not all at once.

Not to mention the fact that if he killed them all, there would be no one left to rule.

Lake Genosgwa opened beneath him—a dark black smear against an otherwise lush green tapestry.

LaBouche folded his wings and pointed his stupid little beak at the surface of the lake, way out in the middle.

He streaked toward the lake, his feathers ruffling like mad as the wind tore at his plummeting body. He didn't give one second's thought to the impact of the water at the speed with which he fell. What did it matter? It's not as if it could kill him. Not really.

LaBouche impacted the surface of Genosgwa Lake with a bone-snapping crunch, but the pain was brief, inconsequential. Magpie bodies weren't suited to swimming, but he did the best he could, pushing himself deeper and deeper into the black maw of the lake. He could almost sense her, could almost hear her muttering, sobbing. *How can she be so weak? Herlequin always said she was his daughter, but no daughter of his would act this way.*

He gave up on swimming and willed his body to sink. The restriction Brigitta had imposed on him rankled more than ever. That she would do this to him over the feelings of a mere human filled him with murderous rage.

Get it together. She will see that in you if you're not careful. He tried to twist his mind away from what she had done to him, but it was hard…after all, he was a *magpie.*

The deeper he sank, the blacker the water became, and the blacker the water became, the colder it got. His lungs felt as if they would burst at any moment, and the tiny, weak body that trapped him struggled to stay alive.

The flesh of this world is stupid, LaBouche thought, not for the first time.

From beneath him came a raw, pain-filled shriek that seemed to boil the water around him and sent him tumbling with the force of the screech. *She* was down there and had sensed him.

At last.

She ascended from the depths like a torpedo launched from a submarine. A column of bubbles exploded in her wake and as the shriek grew louder and louder, the surrounding water heated up.

He wasn't able to make out any words in the garbled nonsense she was flinging into the water, but he *could* sense the emotion: burning hatred, the pain of a raw wound, frustration, and hidden beneath it all, *fear*.

You're right to fear me, he thought at the torpedo-like shape streaking through the water at him. *You should fear all of us now. But I am not your enemy, Brigitta. I bring you news.*

News? Her mental voice was abrasive, painful to receive.

Indeed. You need friends, now, Brigitta. The others will watch you, assessing you, probing for weakness. You can't afford to hide out here in the mud and detritus of the lake. You can't afford this moment of self-indulgent grief.

HE WAS MY FATHER!

Yes, as he always said. He said the same about your sisters, however, and one of the others may find it easier to manipulate one of them than serve under you. I'll repeat it: you can't afford this self-indulgent grief.

She shrieked in the water, and he felt small membranes inside his skull rupture with the force of her agony. Suspended in the dark water, LaBouche rolled his eyes.

Beyond all that, beyond the others and their petty manipulations, their petty desires for the throne, there are things you need to know. Things that threaten all of us.

Her rate of ascent halved and halved again. Brigitta's grief quieted, and she flopped on her side, lying in the water as if on a mattress. Her eyes were closed, but LaBouche had the distinct sense she was watching him closely.

Your father's murderers—they are making plans, taking steps, making preparations. We are not free of them. Worse, they've learned things…

Brigitta sat up and opened her eyes. They were as black as the depths of the lake below her. *Tell me*, she thought at him.

He told her what he knew.

They will risk a direct confrontation with so many of us? Hard to believe, Brigitta mused. She drifted closer to him.

What choice do they have, Your Highness?

But there are only five humans, and they are so, so easy to manipulate.

LaBouche squeezed his tiny eyes shut. The humans had a saying: "the eyes are the windows of the soul," and though most of them didn't understand it, it was true. He didn't want Brigitta peering into his mind, looking past what he wanted her to see, glimpsing his true motives and beliefs. *Excellency, they are new to their powers. And yet they fooled us, beat us at our own game. Even with their poor understanding of what they can do, they killed Herlequin.*

She came toward him swiftly until he floated in the water inches from her nose. Her black eyes twirled with intense emotion, bored into him as if she could dissect him with her eyes alone.

Your Majesty, we've had our differences. But none of those differences were serious for my part. Petty, yes. Disrespectful, perhaps. But—

Perhaps? Perhaps? Her mental voice sliced through him with the ease a sharp knife would have, a burning agony in its wake.

I've never been good with limits, Brigitta. With controlling my sense of humor. You know this of me, is it not true?

That seemed to mollify her, and she floated away, turning her back. *What do you suggest?*

We should kill them. The humans and any of the others who don't bend the knee. Let the deaths be swift, merciless. Let the others quake with fear, but we won't tip our hand to the humans. We will get them all at once, and we will feed. We will feast on their every thought, their every fear, every pain they may suffer.

Brigitta examined him, one eyebrow arched, her eyes again the color of spring. *I knew you were vicious, LaBouche, but I didn't think you were this...determinedly vicious.*

There is much I have kept hidden, Your Excellency. I did not want the others to discover my nature lest they use it against me somehow. Your father knew, however. I hid nothing from Herlequin.

She treated him to a half-lidded stare, but he sensed no malice in it, merely an assessing intelligence. *Perhaps LaBouche, you may be of service to me.*

If I had my own form, I would bow to you. He held his breath, not daring to hope.

Even underwater, her laughter tinkled like the sound of glass bells. She tilted her head to the side and nodded.

4

Chaz left the Oneka Falls Town Hall feeling somewhat better. Rage still burned in his heart, anger at LaBouche. He needed what the others needed: discipline, and someone to rule with a firm hand. Otherwise, everything would fall to chaos.

Brigitta is the heir apparent…but does that mean anything when the heir apparent isn't apparent?

He shook his head and slid behind the wheel of his Monaco Blue BMW 750. *Where is she*? *Has she abandoned us*? He threw the car in reverse and backed out of his parking space. If he were honest, he'd have to admit he believed she would have come for him already.

He shrugged and turned left on Main Street, intending to have an early morning drive through the country. He wanted to open up the 750's engine, to hear it roar, to bask in the magnificent V8's metallic symphony. As he drove, he let his gaze wander back and forth across the road.

If she doesn't want the responsibilities of leadership…

In a way, it was unbelievable what they'd been able to do with the town. The latest headcount showed that they outnumbered the humans living in the town by almost three to one. That would make keeping control over the place more manageable, but what he couldn't figure out, was how no one else noticed. Nobody from the county government, no one from county law enforcement, and no one from the state government or law enforcement agencies… It was almost as if everyone outside of the town were a willing participant in the ruse.

He crossed out of the city limits at one hundred and eight miles an hour. Other drivers saw him coming and got out of his way.

As they should.

As the scenery changed from that of the town to the surrounding countryside, Chaz rolled down the windows. "*Fuck you, LaBouche*!" he screamed. He screamed the words, again and again, shouting as loud as he could. It was a trick he'd learned to handle the stress of dealing with humans without killing them, and it seemed it worked on the burden of dealing with other demons when he couldn't kill them out of hand. The car was hurtling along at a gnat's tooth past one hundred and sixty miles an hour, the wind roared through the cabin of the vehicle, and Chaz's voice competed with it as he bellowed his mantra.

He almost lost control of the vehicle when a delicate hand reached from the backseat to tap him on the shoulder. The car slewed, first to the left and then to the right, Chaz's monstrous hands dancing on the steering wheel as he fought for control. The sound of shrieking tires filled the cabin. "*Fuck*!" he cried as the car slid to a halt with its right front tire on the edge of the ditch.

A bell-like laugh came from the backseat. "I don't think so," said Brigitta. "I'm in mourning."

Chaz sat still, hands on the steering wheel, his arms still braced for impact. The only part of him that moved was his eyes—they went to the side mirror, and next to the rearview mirror. Breath rushed in and out, making a chuffing noise akin to that of a slowly accelerating steam engine.

"No greeting? No weak explanation of why you usurped my throne?"

Chaz shook himself like a dog expelling water from its coat. "Sorry, Your Highness. My brain is still functioning in a state of mild panic."

"Be glad I didn't bring LaBouche with me."

Chaz couldn't stop the sneer from distending his features.

"Tell me this, Chaz: will you two alphas be able to put aside your petty competitions and serve me in all things?" She leaned forward, her eyelids narrowing, her gaze boring into his in the rearview mirror. "If I can only have one of you in my service, my choice will disappoint you."

"Yes, Excellency. There's room for both of us." It was possible LaBouche had already been in contact with her…what did that mean she knew? His mind raced, posing one question, then the next, and another and another after that. He had no answers, though. Not to any of them.

She leaned back into the luxurious backseat. "Good," she purred. "You will maintain things in Oneka Falls. No, scratch that, you will secure things here. Without your lackadaisical mismanagement of things, my father would still be alive." Her voice had risen in both pitch and volume until it distorted her words.

"Yes, Highness. What shall I do?"

"Secure our holdings," she hissed.

"I can do that."

"You'd better."

Before Chaz could reply, she disappeared with a popping noise. He shook his head and allowed the shakes to come. He had no doubt Brigitta could make good on her veiled threat to send him back. He had no doubt she *would* if he allowed it to come to that.

She hadn't mentioned it more than the once, but Chaz knew Brigitta—when it suited her, she'd punish him for what he'd done. *For what LaBouche* tricked *me into doing*! *I have to tell her about his complicity*! He shook his head. That was a stupid thought. At best, Brigitta wouldn't care, and at worst, she would praise LaBouche for his manipulation and damn Chaz for his weakness. *It would serve me better to do everything that she asks of me, to make myself indispensable to her rule.*

But how do I secure a town such as Oneka Falls? With slow deliberation, Chaz put the car in drive and turned around. *Whatever I'm going to do, I'd better get to it.* He shook his head, remembering Red Bortha. *Who can I recruit to fill that old bastard's shoes*?

It was a problem. Few demons in the population of Oneka Falls were old. Fewer still had any real power. The urge to compete with others was too strong. Powerful demons stayed far away from one another, meeting only infrequently, and only when necessary. Chaz and Red had gotten around all that, somehow. Their time spent in Oneka Falls had allowed them to become friends of a sort.

Who can I trust? *Who is* left *to trust*?

BOOK TWO:
BLACK SWAN

Chapter 1

1986

I

"Greg!" yelled Joe at his grandson's retreating back. The boy was crying—sobbing—but Greg only shook his head at his grandfather's entreaties and kept running. He didn't even look back.

A strange mist settled above Joe's head, almost hiding the branches of the trees. It diffused the moonlight, making the surrounding area seem darker, almost malevolent, while adding a layer of brightness above.

Greg's head pivoted back and forth as if he were looking for something—or maybe someone. Joe didn't follow his gaze. He kept his eyes focused on Greg's back, but he didn't yell for the boy to stop any longer. He couldn't fix whatever drove his grandson to run from him that way.

Plus, his wind had gotten sparse.

They ran on and on, moving deeper and deeper into the woods that surrounded Lake Genosgwa. Joe's booted feet thudded on the soil, and his arms ached with the weight of the M1. Despite his growing fatigue, he pushed himself on—faster and faster.

Something flickered at the edges of Joe's sight. Something black, but a darker black than the gloom that surrounded them. He ripped his gaze away from his grandson's retreating form without breaking stride, but what he saw…the *thing* running parallel to his course made him stumble and almost fall.

It was unlike anything he'd ever seen before—a shadowy humanoid form, swathed in darkness, with hints of human features, but at the same time, the thing seemed…*inhuman*. It floated an inch above the ground, disappearing and reappearing with recurring pops. Its feet never impacted the forest loam, despite its moving legs.

So that's why there were no footprints! Joe thought. He stopped running, planted his feet, and raised the M1 carbine to his shoulder in one fluid movement. "Greg! Get down!" He aimed at the black thing but checked his fire. He darted a glance at Greg, who was still running despite his shouts. "Dammit!" Joe muttered.

He needed to be sure no stray rounds hit his grandson, but the need to shoot at the thing chasing Greg mounted until drawing breath grew difficult. Joe doubled his speed, running flat out through the woods, not seeing the blurred detritus of the forest in his path. He leaped over fallen branches, slid through piles of rotting vegetation, and skipped past gnarled roots—all on automatic.

When the urge to *do something* grew too strong, Joe slammed to a stop, raised the M1 and shouted, "Greg!

Get down now!" Without waiting to see if his grandson complied, Joe sighted on the black thing in the forest and fired three shots in rapid succession. The rifle's reports filled the woods, and all three rounds slammed into the thing chasing Greg. Splatters of something thick and black flew to the ground surrounding the creature. It shrieked in the high pitch of a woman but sounded more angry than hurt. Greg darted a glance over his shoulder and slowed to a stop.

"Greg, no!" Joe yelled, waving at Greg to continue running, to get away.

The black thing snapped its head to face Joe and glared at him.

Is that… That's a woman! What's she covered in, mud? What's she supposed to be? The creature from the Black Lagoon? Her eyes were as green as the meadow in springtime, but as he watched, they dimmed and grew dark, menacing. She screamed at him, and the sound was unlike anything Joe had ever heard, eliciting a running shudder up and down his spine.

Whatever she pretended to be, she was after Greg, and that, Joe wouldn't abide. He fired again and again as he tracked the running woman with the barrel of his rifle. Each shot flew true, and each shot sent what looked like black mud splattering to the ground and brush surrounding her, but she didn't hesitate, didn't slow.

"Greg! Greg!" Joe shouted. *Hits to the body aren't cutting it, Marine!* He drew a bead on the woman's head, leading her about a foot, and he took a deep breath and exhaled it all but didn't draw more. He tried to calm himself, to still his racing heartbeat, and he tried to stand loose, relaxed, remembering his marksmanship training. Joe timed his shot for a narrow instant between beats of his heart and pulled the trigger. Time turned sluggish, and Joe imagined he could almost see the bullet inching through the space separating him from his grandson's tormentor.

Her head snapped to the side, and finally, she stumbled.

"Stung you there, you bitch!" shouted Joe. *Why hasn't she fallen? I must've winged her.* He fired again, still aiming at the woman's head, and that round rocked her head to the side for the second time. She whirled to face him, and Joe could distinguish her features at last. Despite the mud or whatever covered her, she had a beautiful face—almost elfin features in perfect proportions.

She opened her mouth and screamed, her eyes boring into Joe's.

A cold, analytical part of his mind had kept track—only three rounds remained in the magazine. He couldn't remember whether he'd picked up a spare magazine and shoved it into his back pocket as he'd always done when he rehearsed retrieving the weapon. His memory of the events leading up to the chase through the woods had hazed, had misted over as surely as the early morning sky above his head.

The woman froze, glowering at Joe. Her head hunched forward, and her arms hung straight at her sides, ending in fists. Fists with long, age-yellowed, broken and cracked fingernails. In the woods surrounding them, something popped like corn in a popper.

Joe still held the M1 to his shoulder, his finger still on its trigger. He began to take up the trigger's slack when something slammed into him from the darkness at his back. The M1 fired wild, sending a bullet racing off through the trees. Joe stumbled forward, fighting to remain on his feet, his left arm flailing for balance.

Something else hit him from the side, and he got a vague impression of black fur and flashing fangs. *Dogs*? The third weight slammed into him, and he fell, losing the rifle in the confusion. He landed amidst the knobby roots of a tree, and his breath *whooshed* out of him all at once. He flipped to his back, drawing his knees up to protect his groin and belly, ready to fend off the dogs that had knocked him to the ground.

There was nothing there.

Joe rolled to his knees, his head rotating back and forth, scouring the woods for any sign of his four-legged attackers. He darted a glance toward where the woman had last stood, but she too had disappeared into thin air. Greg had put quite a distance between them and ran still.

Sweeping up the M1, Joe resumed his chase, but this time he kept his eyes moving and his head on a swivel. He searched every shadow, every dark tree trunk, but it was as if the woman covered in black had disappeared.

2

By the time the ambulance arrived, Tom Walton had gathered his wits, due to the ministrations of Alison Seeger. He was out of the car, leaning against the quarter panel and sipping a cup of Alison's coffee.

"I still don't understand how your car ended up down here, Chief," said Alison. "Listening to heavy metal on patrol again?"

"Don't pester the man, Alison," said Will.

Will's son-in-law—Tom couldn't remember his name, despite having met him twice—grunted and smirked in the background. Tom didn't much cotton to the man, and he thought he'd caught Will shooting a dirty look at the man, so it seemed unanimous. "No, no. It's all right, Will," said Tom. "I don't much understand how I got down here either." The last thing in the world

Tom would admit to was being pushed over the edge of the ridge by a pack of eyeless dogs.

If that's even what happened... He'd hit his head as the car slid down the steep incline, and he'd spent significant energy trying to convince himself that had caused his strange memories.

"Well, whatever the reason, I'm just glad you're not hurt worse than you are." Alison smiled at him, but the concerned expression in her eyes didn't change.

"You and Janet, both. And me, of course." He waved to his bloody face. "This looks worse than it is, I think."

"I don't imagine you've been sleeping much, have you?" asked Will. "First, the body, and now this mess with the little boy up the road." Will shook his head, an expression of sadness stealing over him.

"Yeah, you could say that." Tom watched the ambulance driver try and fail to navigate the steep driveway that led from the ridge to Will's garage. "I better get up there, before they end up down here parked next to me."

"I'll walk you up," said Will.

Tom nodded and started walking, holding his hand up to stop the ambulance from any further attempts.

Will fell in step beside him and cleared his throat. "I hope you know, Tom, that there won't be any shenanigans about the damages. The town is good for it, and I trust you to make sure everything gets taken care of."

Tom looked at him askance and nodded. "Absolutely, Will. I apologize again for the inconvenience."

"It's nothing." Will made a shooing gesture with his left hand. "I welcome the interruption."

Walton glanced over his shoulder as Alison, Sammy, and Sammy's husband went inside the house. "I don't remember your son-in-law's name, Will."

"Chris Stanton." Will grimaced and belched. "Excuse me."

"I take it you don't care for Mr. Stanton?"

"A guy could say that," said Will in a gruff voice. "He rubs me wrong."

"Same here," said Tom. "He seems… No, never mind."

Will glanced at him with a sour smile on his lips. "Nothing you say about Chris will offend me, Tom. Hell, if you think he's an asshole, it will only heighten my estimation of your intelligence."

Tom shook his head and winced at the lightning bolt of pain the movement caused in his neck. "I shouldn't have said anything."

"But you did, and now I'm curious. To tell the truth, Tom, I'd appreciate hearing your thoughts on the man. I have my suspicions, and a second opinion would ease my mind."

They walked in silence for a few steps before Tom nodded. "Okay. Chris strikes me as someone untrustworthy. I get a feeling off him, a feeling I usually get off skells."

"Skells?"

Tom shrugged. "Yeah, you know. Suspects. Criminals."

Will's eyelids narrowed, his lips curled down in the deepest frown Tom could remember seeing, and the muscles of his face hardened. "Yeah. Me, too, I guess."

As they neared the ambulance, the EMTs jumped out of it and took roughly thirty-seven ginormous cases of equipment and a gurney out of the back. One of them came toward Tom carrying a neck brace.

"Will doesn't need a neck brace," said Tom. "He wasn't even in the accident."

"Ha-ha," said the EMT. "This is for you, Chief, and you know it."

Tom held up both hands, palms toward the EMT. "The chief doesn't need a neck brace, either. All I need for you to do is close up this cut in my scalp."

"No, Chief. Let us run you in to the emergency room. Get you checked out by a doctor."

"I don't have time for that, gentlemen. I'm on a case I can't make heads or tails of, and on top of that, I'm not hurt. Anyone can see that."

Shaking their heads, the EMTs led him toward the back of the ambulance and made him sit on the rear step while they dressed his wound. Will stood close by, and his gaze kept straying toward the lake house.

"Will," said Tom in a soft, but implacable, voice.

Will met his direct gaze with a frank expression before arching his eyebrows.

"Is there something…something I should know?"

Will grunted a harsh laugh that held little humor. Again, his gaze drifted to the front of the lake house. "I'll say this, Tom. If I ever call you out here about that son of a bitch, I'd recommend you get here in a hurry." He turned to meet Tom's gaze. "That or send a meat wagon."

One of the EMTs shot a glance at Will but said nothing.

"Well, now, Will, that doesn't go a long way toward making me understand the whole story."

Will shook his head and lifted his shoulders. "I don't know anything, Tom."

"But you suspect."

It wasn't a question, but Will answered him anyway. "Yes, and you can guess what I suspect."

Tom nodded. "You *call me,* Will, if your suspicions pan out. Don't do anything…"

Will flapped his hand in the same shooing gesture he made before. "When the boys finish torturing you, I'll give you a ride to the station."

"I'd appreciate it," said Tom, but his probing gaze never left Will's face. "But I'll have that promise from you, Will."

Will turned to face him. "Tom..."

Tom raised his hand to interrupt. "No, Will. You're too good a man to spend your life in an orange jumpsuit over a bastard such as that."

Will shrugged. "You understand, Tom," he murmured. "You've got daughters of your own."

"I do, Will. I understand, but *you call me.* Before you do anything."

Will cleared his throat and nodded.

"Not good enough, Will. Make the oath."

Will stared at him for the space of a few breaths. "Yeah, okay. I promise." Despite his reluctance to make the pledge, his tone was one of relief—as Tom had expected.

"Have you... Have you had any trouble with dogs running wild around here?" Tom asked.

Will started. "Dogs? No, not that I've heard about, anyway." He glanced up at the ridge. "Why do you ask?"

"No reason," said Tom. "We had Leland out earlier today. We came across...a strange set of tracks—tracks such as a pack of wild dogs might make."

Again, Will looked up at the ridge. "In the woods, I expect."

"Exactly." Tom shrugged. "It wouldn't hurt to keep your eyes open."

Will nodded without turning from the ridge.

"It wouldn't hurt to keep a shotgun handy, either," Tom murmured.

Will shot a sharp glance his way before returning his gaze to the ridge.

3

"Stephen! Stephen, wake up!"

He rolled over, groaning and opening his eyelids a slit. Stephen expected to see predawn light, but it was as dark as a tomb in the room of his parents' lake house he shared with his wife. "What's the matter, Mary?"

"He's gone, Stephen!"

"Who? Greg?"

"Of *course* I mean Greg! Who else would you think I meant?"

Stephen sat up and rubbed his burning eyes. "Are you sure he's not in the bathroom?"

"Not unless he's invisible!"

Stephen slung back the bedclothes and stood, wincing at the sour taste in his mouth. "Okay, okay. I'll go look." He paused a moment to pull on a pair of jeans and flip-flops.

Out in the living room, Greg's blankets lay puddled on the floor next to the couch, but his clothes were gone. Stephen glanced out the big bay window but saw only the darkness of the lake's black water and darker pre-dawn sky. He turned, his gaze zipping around the kitchen and settling on the door to the pantry. In five long strides, he was there, staring into the deep pantry, at the open gun safe at the far end, and his stomach sank toward his ankles. He raced to his parents' bedroom door and knocked.

"Mmmph."

"Mom, it's Stephen. Is Dad with you?" For a moment, Stephen was sure he would hear his father's voice, sure that Greg had found a way into the gun safe and was out somewhere playing with the rifle. It was an irrational fear. Number one, because Greg knew better, and number two, because gun safes were built to withstand the best efforts of eleven-year-old boys.

"What? Is… Stephen? Where's your father?"

"Dammit! Greg's gone, Dad's gone, and the gun safe is standing open!"

For the space of two breaths, his mother didn't answer. "I'll call Tom Walton," she said in an icy calm voice. "You go find them both."

"I will!"

"Stephen!" called Elizabet.

"What, Mom?"

"Take the shotgun. Shells are on the top shelf."

"Will do!" Stephen turned and ran three steps before his mother called out again.

"And check the porch before you go far!"

"Will do," he called over his shoulder. Twenty seconds later, Stephen stepped out onto the back porch, shotgun in hand, his front pockets stuffed full of 12-gauge shells. Mary stood behind him, holding a flashlight and breathing hard.

Together, they swept the yard, finding nothing and no one. They turned toward the rear of the house and stepped to the middle of the gravel lane. To their right sat one of Genosgwa's police cars. Across the road from them sat the Canton and the Harper garages, though both looked buttoned up tight.

"Go to the cop car," whispered Mary.

With a curt nod, Stephen turned and jogged to the car. The driver side window was open, the car was empty. "That's weird," he muttered.

Bam-bam-bam! The three shots thundered deep in the forest.

"Stephen!" Mary gasped.

A few moments later, more gunfire sounded.

"Let's go!"

Stephen shook his head and put his hand on Mary's shoulder. "Give me the flashlight. You go back inside with Mom."

"What? No!"

He put his hand on the flashlight but only rested it there. "Mary, I don't have time to argue. Go inside and stay with Mom." He stared at her a moment before tightening his grip on the flashlight. She allowed him to take it from her but stood gazing back at him. "*Go*!"

Without waiting to see if she complied, Stephen turned away, slipping the flashlight to his armpit and thumbing shotgun shells into the loading tube. He racked the slide and ran into the forest, holding the shotgun in front of him, gripping both the flashlight and the shotgun's fore-end in his left hand.

As he left the lights of the houses and cottages on the lakeshore behind, the woods closed in around him, like the tightening grip of a giant. More gunfire sounded ahead, and he increased his pace.

Stephen ran into the darkness, if not without fear, then without letting his fear slow him. He had the shotgun, and that was a comfort, but the night pressed in on him, leering at him like a drunken carnival clown.

The flashlight was less than useless, its sickly yellow beam bouncing with each running step, pointed at the mist more often than not. He clicked it off and shoved it in his back pocket without missing a step.

As much as the gunfire had scared him, the utter silence that replaced it scared him more. "Dad! Greg!" he cried into the darkness.

No one answered.

4

As soon as Greg's mother returned to the Canton house, Mason stepped out of the shadows. Stephen Canton stared into the darkness of the woods, oblivious to anything else, and Mason smirked at his back. He had things to do, people to meet.

He waited for Mr. Canton to run off into the forest, then Mason turned and ran alongside the gravel lane toward the asphalt road at its end. The Lady in the Lake wanted him to show two of her friends where the Cantons spent their summers.

Mason had no idea why they needed him to guide them up the dead-end road, but he didn't much care, either. *She* wanted him to lead them and lead them he would.

5

Gary came to slowly. He lay on his side, his arms splayed, and his legs laced over one another. His neck ached, as did his back. For a moment, he had no memory of where he was, no idea why he lay on the ground out in the middle of the woods. But as he sat up, it came back to him—seeing Joe Canton race across the road with his M1, following his grandson deeper into the woods; the gunshots, the calls for Greg to stop.

He pushed himself to his feet, looking around for his pistol. He remembered having drawn it and it wasn't in his holster. *Must have dropped the damn thing when I passed out.* But he didn't see it, not anywhere. *That's bad,* he thought, and as soon as he finished thinking it, a derisive voice spoke in his mind, *You think*?

He slid his Maglite out of his belt and turned it on, spending a few minutes walking a widening search pattern, spiraling out from the point where he'd fallen, but he couldn't find the gun. He'd lost Joe, he'd lost Greg, and Gary Dennis had lost his service weapon.

Worse yet, the mist had settled lower, obscuring the higher branches of the trees, and the surrounding woods had darkened. Turning on the Maglite had squashed his night vision, and a curtain of darkness enveloped him outside the light cast by the flashlight. He could no longer tell from which direction he'd come into the woods.

It was as if he'd fallen through reality into an unfamiliar, evil forest, blindfolded and then spun around to destroy his sense of direction.

He swept the beam of the Maglite back and forth, looking for either his pistol or tracks made by the Cantons. His frustration mounted, and his pulse accelerated. *Better get a grip, son. Don't want to pass out twice in one night, after all.*

Gary jogged a hundred yards before stopping and repeating the search for Joe or Greg's trail. He turned to his right and ran another hundred yards—knowing what he was doing was stupid, knowing his actions would most likely lead to him getting more and more lost, but doing it anyway. Joe Canton was a fine man, and Gary counted him as a close friend.

After zigzagging through the woods for ten minutes, Gary stopped and rested, bent at the waist, his hands on his knees, while he took huge, deep breaths. His Maglite shined up at the layer of fog, but it still illuminated the surrounding area up to about ten paces away. Outside of that circle, however, it seemed as though the woods had gotten darker—as if someone had drawn black curtains over what little light the pre-dawn sky had for him. "Well, fuck," muttered Gary.

As he straightened, an all-too-familiar noise chilled his blood—the low growl of an angry dog. He played the flashlight in a wide arc around him but could see nothing—no eyes reflecting the light back at him, no shadowy forms twining between the tree trunks. After a moment, another growl joined the first.

By instinct, or maybe muscle memory, Gary flipped the Maglite to his left hand as his right hand slapped on his hip—on his empty holster. "Well, fuck," said Gary again, but this time he said it with more passion.

The growling came from his left and a little behind him. Gary turned in that direction, the beam of his Maglite dabbing into the darkness that swathed the woods as would the timid brush of a novice painter on his first canvas. He expected to see eyes shining red in the flashlight's beam, but again the beam illuminated nothing.

Another dog began to growl, and it was behind him, despite his turn to face them. It was as if the dogs were approaching him one by one instead of in a pack. He shook his head and spun around but saw only more darkness. He picked the direction from which no growls sounded and sprinted away.

The moment he began to run, the growling evaporated into playful yips and barks. *If only I had my pistol*! But he didn't, and part of him thought it was awfully convenient for the dogs that he didn't.

He ran, his chest hitching every time he drew a breath, and purple spots danced before his eyes. Gary stayed ahead of the dogs, but he was sure they were chasing him. He knew better than to run from the dogs, that it would only trigger their instincts to run him down, but he didn't want to face a pack of feral dogs barehanded.

Something howled in the distance before him, and he shifted his path to the left to avoid it. He ran on, pulse thundering in his ears, pain developing in his left side. The flashlight grew heavier with each step he took, and he shifted it to his right hand as his left hand began to ache.

Well, fuck! He knew what the signs were. *Can't keep running...I'm not an eighteen-year-old and haven't been for thirty-nine years, but I don't dare stop. Heart attack will stop me, though. It'll stop me dead.*

As if they knew his plight, the dogs behind him began to howl and bark as though celebrating a victory. Answering howls came from ahead of Gary, and again he wearily turned and continued his plodding run.

He'd lost his sense of direction. *Am I running in circles*? *That could be how they're getting in front of me.* Even as he entertained the idea, though, he knew it wasn't true. No, each new howl, each new bark, only underscored that more and more dogs were joining the chase.

He ran and ran, growing dizzier and dizzier with each step, his thundering pulse racing, pounding through his veins, his blood pressure thumping in his neck and temples. His breath rasped, and his side ached and burned as if someone had stuck him with a hot ten-inch blade.

The dogs—or whatever variety of four-legged bastards they were—closed on his heels. Their footfalls drummed behind him, a rhythmic accompaniment to his own sliding, shuffling steps. He shined the Maglite in a wide arc in front of him as he ran, his left hand pressed into his side over his rib cage.

His cheeks felt hot, sweaty, but he was cold—as cold as if he were already dead. He shook his head to clear such thoughts, and as he did, the flashlight danced over a black-furred form for half a second before the creature leaped behind a tree. "Dogs!" he shrieked in a watery, weak voice. "Just dogs." What he'd seen was the size of a large German Shepherd, though with the black fur and mahogany markings of a Rottweiler. *If I have to fight a bunch of those bastards at once, well…it's been a good life. But they don't seem to want to fight… They want something else… But what*?

He lurched forward, his feet clumsy, his lips numb, but even so, he thought he might survive the night if he were lucky and smart. He slowed his pace, ready to spring forward if he was wrong, but the dogs behind him seemed happy in the chase at whatever pace he set and didn't close the distance between them. Bleary-eyed, nauseous, and faint, Gary Dennis stopped running.

As when he had first encountered them, the dogs stayed outside the circle of light cast from his Maglite and growled. Gary lurched against a tree, resting his cheek against the rough bark, gasping like a fish on the shore. He tried to still his racing heart, tried to will the ache in his side away.

The dogs quit growling but paced back and forth at the edge of the light. He shook his head, wondering what sort of canine game they were playing. *Do they know that if they push me, I will die*? *Do they only want to extend their game*?

Gary put his back to the rough tree trunk and sank into a squat, but the second his butt touched the ground, the growling began on all sides. He pushed himself back up the tree trunk, and the noise stopped. "Well, fuck," Gary said with a sigh. "I guess you bastards are content to let me catch my breath but not rest."

A single yip answered him from the darkness.

6

Will Seeger dropped Tom off in the police department parking lot. He sported a white bandage at the hairline on his forehead, and since the adrenaline was wearing off, his hands shook, his neck ached, and the cut on his scalp burned. He pushed through the door, hoping for a cup of hot coffee.

"Tom! There's trouble at the Canton house," said Shelley Myers, the night dispatcher.

Walton waved at her. "It's okay, Gary's there."

But the dispatcher shook her head. "He radioed in and said he was out of the car, going into the woods to help. Then, Elizabet Can—"

"Slow down, Shelley. Who went into the forest? Who did Gary follow?"

"Joe Canton and his grandson, Greg. Gary said he saw them run into the trees, and Elizabet Canton just called to say that her son, Stephen, has also gone after them—both armed."

"Get me the keys to a car!" Walton turned and walked to the hall that led to the armory. "And call in everyone! Tell them to roll toward those woods!"

Shelley nodded and ran back to the dispatch room.

Tom opened a reinforced steel door and pushed into the armory. A rack of pistols adorned one wall, and beneath it rested a rack of tactical shotguns. Tom stepped to the other side of the room and removed the bar securing the assault rifles.

Genosgwa's police department had seven officers—counting Gary Dennis—under his command. Tom grabbed a box of loaded magazines and removed three AR-15s from the locked rack on one wall of the armory and put them on the maintenance table near the door. On the other side of the room, he unlocked the rack of Remington 870 tactical shotguns and withdrew three, adding them to the rifles. He grabbed two boxes of double-aught buckshot and added them to the box of magazines. He put the box of ammunition in the hall, then grabbed the rifles and shotguns, leaning them against the wall in the hallway. After locking the armory door, he walked back to the lobby with the shotguns under one arm and the AR-15's under the other. "Shelley!" he called.

She came on the run, her eyes widening as she took in the sight of him laden down with weapons. "Yes, Chief?"

"Box of ammunition in the hall, can you grab it?"

Myers nodded and slid the keys to one of the dayshift cars across the wooden countertop that served as the reception desk. "You get the car open, and I'll bring that box."

Tom grabbed the keys and used his foot to open the door. He loaded the weapons into the trunk. As he finished, Shelley staggered out the door, straining to carry the box of heavy ammunition. He took it from her and put it in the trunk. "Tell everyone to meet me at Gary's car."

"Yes sir, Chief."

Tom slid behind the wheel and fired up the engine. He flipped on the lights and siren, backed out, and raced toward Lake Genosgwa.

7

"Dad! For God's sake, cry out!" Panic surged through Stephen's mind, and adrenaline surged in his blood. He hadn't heard a thing since the last burst of gunfire—the forest seemed to absorb all sound, to suck it up greedily like a parched man drinking cool water.

Stephen slowed to a stop and turned in a circle, no longer sure which direction led back to the lake house, no longer sure if he'd been running in a straight line or in a circle. His eyes had adapted to the darkness—not that it helped all that much... The black blanket that surrounded him seemed impossible to penetrate. He had almost completed a full circle when he saw it.

Stephen hunched and peered into the black maw of the forest, searching for the glint he'd seen a moment before. He walked forward, squinting, but the glint didn't repeat itself.

He straightened up, a grimace twisting the muscles of his face. *It's my mind playing tricks on me again. How am I ever going to find Dad and Greg*?

"Well, fuck. I guess you bastards are content to let me catch my breath but not rest," someone said.

The voice sounded familiar to Stephen, but he couldn't place it. It wasn't his dad's voice, but even so, he started toward it. A yip sounded as if in answer to the man's speech, and Stephen paused. It sounded like the yip of a large, playful dog, but the man's words belied play. "Who's there?" he called.

"It's Gary Dennis. Who's that?"

After suppressing a sigh of relief, Stephen straightened and walked on.

"But be careful, there are dogs in the dark out there."

"Dogs?" Stephen asked. He pulled the flashlight out of his back pocket and flicked it on, shining it in a wide arc in front of him. At the extreme edge of the light's ability to penetrate the darkness, something reflected the light back at him. "Is that you?"

"Yes. Is that Joe's son?"

"It is, Gary. Stephen Canton. I'm armed. Shotgun. Don't freak out when you see it."

"Son, that's music to my ears. Maybe we can scare this pack of dogs off."

Stephen picked up his pace. "Have you seen my father? My son?"

Dennis let a sigh gust out of him. "I followed Joe into the woods and stayed with them for a bit, but I…" He sighed again. "I had an…incident, and I lost him. I… I think I'm lost."

"Crap. I'm all turned around, too. I heard gunfire." He stepped into a small clearing and approached Officer Dennis where he leaned against a tree trunk on the opposite side.

"Yeah, I did, too. It was right before I… Look, I passed out right after I heard three shots from your dad's carbine. I haven't heard a thing since then—except for these damn dogs."

Stephen shined his flashlight at the edges of the glade, but he could see nothing beyond the first row of trees. "Dogs? I don't hear anything."

Gary Dennis cocked his head to the side as if listening. "There's a pack of them in these woods," he said. "They chased me for a while, but it didn't seem as if they wanted to catch me. It was as though they were herding me, maybe."

Stephen couldn't help but chuckle. "A pack of sheepdogs chased you?"

Gary's eyes flashed with irritation for a moment, but then a rueful grin painted his face. "I'll admit it sounds a mite silly, but when they were chasing me, it didn't *feel* silly."

Stephen lifted his shoulders and let them drop, careful not to point the shotgun in Gary's direction. "Well, they seem to have gone back into hiding now."

Gary nodded but seemed uneasy. "Could be." His gaze came to rest on the shotgun. "In any case, I'm glad you've got the shotgun." He gestured at his empty holster. "When I blacked out, I was holding my pistol. When I came to…" He shook his head.

"Was it around here?" Stephen turned another circle, again shining his flashlight on the ground at the edges of the glade.

"No," Gary sighed. He pushed himself away from the tree and moved to stand at Stephen's side. "I'm afraid I have no idea where I was when I passed out. I got turned around after I came to, and when the dogs were chasing me, I ran randomly, turning when they got in front of me." He shrugged.

"I'm not sure how I can catch up to—"

"I think we'd better address our own issue, first. If we can get back to the road, I can radio for more support. We can get old Leland Chambers out here with his dogs, and he—"

"I can't leave them out here! Not with some psycho that's after my boy!"

"Stephen, I understand how you feel, but we're not doing anyone any good wandering around in the darkness. We need help to search these woods. We need more eyes, more bodies." He gestured at Stephen's weak flashlight. "We need better light. We need something to mark our trail."

Stephen shook his head. "You can go back, but I have to—"

"No, Stephen. Hear sense! You're not helping them stumbling around lost in the dark, putting yourself in danger." Gary lay his hand on Stephen's shoulder. "Look, I count your father as a good friend. Good enough that I may know his mind on this. He wouldn't want you out here alone, stumbling around in the dark with a wild pack of dogs lurking in the shadows."

Again, Stephen shook his head, but this time he voiced no objection.

"Your dad was a Marine—*thinks* like a Marine still. He can handle himself in these woods. And he's got his M1. He can protect your grandson while we go for help."

Stephen met his gaze for the space of three breaths, then hung his head. "I hope you know the direction out of here, because I sure don't."

"We'll have to figure that one out together."

8

Greg's thigh muscles burned. He hadn't heard Grandpa Joe call out in a long time. He didn't know if his grandpa still followed behind him, but that was what Greg wanted—for him to turn back so Greg could lead the Lady in the Lake away from his family.

That shows courage on your part, champ. Guts. If you keep this up, we can save your family from otherwise inevitable heartbreak.

Greg kept running. "Tell me where to go."

You're doing fine, sport. Just keep running, keep leading that old Lady in the Lake farther into the woods. Keep on keeping on, in other words.

"I'll reach the other end of this little chunk of woods soon. The road is ahead."

I don't think so.

"I've been coming to Grandma and Grandpa's lake house for a long time. I know these woods pretty well."

Harsh, abrasive laughter filled his head, making the inside of his skull itch. *Oh, do you? Pardon me. My mistake.*

"Well, I *have*. I've played in these woods for years. There's not that much of them separating Grandpa's gravel road and the hardtop that goes around the lake."

Ah, but are you so sure that the woods you're in now are the same woods that you played in for "all those years?" Does everything look the same?

Greg glanced around at his surroundings—*really* looked—for the first time. *I don't know what you're going on about—it's just trees.*

Are they the same *trees?*

"How would I know?"

You are making my point for me, kiddo. And that is the question: how would *you know? It's dark, and you're running—barely looking at your surroundings, mostly focused on your feet. You might be anywhere, sport.*

Greg shook his head as he ran. "No, I couldn't. I ran across the gravel road into the woods, so those are the woods I'm in. I haven't come across the paved road—Lake Circle—or any of the other gravel roads. That means I'm in the woods across from Grandma and Grandpa's house.

Oh, excuse me. I must be mistaken. AGAIN.

Greg suppressed a sigh. "I really don't understand what you're talking about. How could I be anywhere else?"

You're the one with all the answers, sport.

"It just doesn't make sense."

It makes perfect sense to me. But, never mind all that for now, you've got bigger problems. Look behind you.

Greg threw a quick glance over his shoulder and gasped. Behind him ran the Lady in the Lake, dressed in shimmery black mud. As his gaze met her eyes, her irises blazed crimson, and bloody tears squeezed from the corners of her eyes. But at the same time, she looked happy, excited. "What do you want?" he shouted at her.

Her only response was an evil grin that exposed sharp fangs. She raised a finger and pointed ahead of him.

Greg looked forward, and a little yelp escaped him. A row of big dogs sat in a line blocking his path. Except they were unlike any dogs he'd ever seen. Their ears would have looked more at home on a bat or a reptile. Their legs ended in what looked more like human hands than a dog's paws. And their eyes—

What eyes, champ? They don't have eyes.

Greg veered to his left, pouring on as much speed as he could—unsure of which scared him more, the Lady in the Lake or the dog-things. His invisible friend chuckled inside his mind.

9

Mason slowed to a jog and then to a walk. Lake Circle was just ahead, but no cars sat parked alongside the road, and no people stood waiting. He was a little later than the Lady in the Lake had wanted him to be, but the Cantons had been slow, and there was nothing he could do about that. She would understand.

He stopped walking and peered into the dark woods to either side of the gravel lane. Thomas Hill Road was a dead end, so he had to be in the right place. Mason stood for a moment, shifting his weight from foot to foot, glancing over his shoulder every now and again. He wasn't sure what to do next, so he did what he always did when he was uncertain: nothing.

He squatted and snaked a dry twig out of the grass on the side of the road and peeled the bark from it, creating a small pile between his feet. After a few minutes, he rocked back onto his butt and kicked his feet out.

The summer had been…*wonderful.* The Lady in the Lake had opened his eyes to so many things, so many pleasures. He still couldn't understand why a beautiful woman would want to have anything to do with him, but his father had always told him never to look a gift horse in the mouth.

Not that Mason knew what that meant. It sounded stupid.

"Hey there, boy," rasped a voice from the darkness.

Mason scrambled to his feet, peering around him. "Who's there?" A nasty chuckle answered him, but he thought it came from the woods on his side of the road.

He peered into the darkness, the partly stripped stick forgotten in his hand.

He gasped as a pair of eyes glowed red from the trees.

A bald man stepped from the shadows farther down the road. "Don't mind him, kid."

Mason tore his gaze away from the glowing red eyes and turned toward the man. "Are you…"

"Show us where they live." The bald man motioned toward the woods. "Come on out. There's no sense having a snack when we're about to have a complete meal."

Another man stepped from the woods, younger, with a full head of black hair. He snapped his tongue against his teeth. "That's hardly the point, Red."

"Did the Lady in the Lake send you?" asked Mason.

The one called Red nodded, but the other one just laughed.

"Come on, kid. Take us to the house," said Red.

Mason lifted his chin. "The Cantons live back this way." He began retracing his steps up the gravel lane. "What are you two going to do?"

"None of your business!" snapped the black-haired man.

"Chaz, that's not very nice."

Chaz shrugged.

"We both have tasks," said Red. "One of us will stay at the house, the other will venture into the woods."

"And me? What do I do?"

"Brig—" began Chaz.

"The Lady in the Lake has another job for you, kid," said Red. "You are to help whoever goes into the woods."

"Okay." Mason looked down, surprised to find he still carried the denuded stick. He let it fall from his fingers. *I hope Chaz stays at the house.*

Behind him, Chaz laughed.

It was as though he could read Mason's thoughts. *But that's crazy.*

Chaz laughed again, and it was a low, mocking laugh.

Chapter 2

2007

I

Scott, Mike, Benny, Shannon, and Toby sat in a large corner booth toward the back of the restaurant. Hartman's corporeal existence rotted away in the medical school's industrial digester, but the afternoon's activities still weighed on the group. Scott kept stealing glances at Toby when he thought Toby wasn't paying attention.

But Toby was paying attention, and he leaned toward the state trooper. "What is it?"

"What?" A blush crept up Scott's cheeks.

"Why do you keep looking at me, Scott? Is there something you want to ask me?"

Scott's gaze drifted away from Toby's. "No, it's nothing."

Toby smiled crookedly. "Let me guess. You're wondering how many I have on my list."

Scott's blush deepened, but he nodded while avoiding everyone's gaze.

"But you know they're just..." Benny stole a quick glance at the students sitting around them and hunched forward. "Demons," he whispered.

"Yes, I understand that. But thanks for pointing it out, Benny."

Benny sat back as if Scott had chewed him out, and Shannon draped her arm around his shoulders, pulling him close.

Toby watched the exchange with solemn detachment. "But still, your instincts—your *cop* instincts—demand you find out, that you *investigate* my methods."

It hadn't been a question, but Scott nodded anyway.

"I've been at this a while. I've developed certain…let's call them 'best practices.'"

"Best practices? You make it sound like it's…"

"An industry? A profession?"

Scott nodded.

"What you don't understand, Scott, is that hunting these demons down and ending their miserable lives on this planet *is* my profession. Teaching college? That's my *cover*. My habits have kept me alive."

"Still, it sounds so…so *clinical*. So detached, as if you can do this with no emotional impact."

Toby leaned back in the padded booth, a sly grin on his face. "I wouldn't be much good at it if I let it get to me." He waved his hand toward the world outside the booth. "But I understand where you're coming from. Listen to me, Scott, and this is important: the world you think you live in is not the *real* world. In the real world, demons live amongst us, and they're feeding on us.

Feeding on our children—" Toby snapped his jaws shut, but it was too late.

Scott leaned toward him, his eyes blazing. "You don't need to remind me of that!"

Toby grimaced and raised his hands in supplication. "Sorry about that, Scott. I wasn't thinking." Scott tilted his head to the side but refused to meet Toby's gaze. "But my point is the place where you're coming from, the mindset that leads you to wonder about me, to wonder if I would have been a serial killer or something like it if I didn't have the capacity to see and hunt demons, it's the mindset you developed *before* you understood what the real world was. You've got to move past it."

"Do you really think I would have *tortured*—"

Mike gestured as if he were patting the empty air into the tabletop.

Scott nodded and went on at a reduced volume. "I just spent the afternoon *dealing* with our friend, Hartman. Do you believe I haven't moved past it?"

Toby inclined his head. "I believe you are starting to."

"And how could you not?" asked Shannon.

Scott shifted his gaze from Toby to Shannon and nodded at her.

"But I'll tell you anyway, Scott. I'm not a sociopath, and I would recognize it if I were. But what I am, is a soldier, and like any good soldier, I compartmentalize my emotions. I can't let them get in the way of what I must do."

Scott tilted his head to the side and relaxed, lifting one shoulder and letting it drop.

A small grin played on Toby's lips. "But still, you want a count of how many?"

Scott repeated his one-shouldered shrug.

Toby chuckled and looked around the table, his gaze coming to rest on Mike's face. "Before you brought Oneka Falls to my attention, I had a list of four people I know are demons. In addition to that, there were thirteen that were *probably* demons, and perhaps twice that number that I still needed to check out. And before you ask, not everyone I check out goes on my list as a demon."

Scott put his hands on the table, fingers spread. "Forty-three people?"

Toby shook his head. "Twenty-six people, thirteen probable demons, and four *confirmed* demons."

"But what I don't understand, Toby, is that if you can tell just by looking at them, how can you not know if those thirteen are demons?"

Toby chuckled. "I'm only one man, Mike. Surveillance takes time, and so does maintaining a fictional life as a cover." He shrugged, smiling. "I just haven't found the time to go lay eyeballs on them."

"It's too bad you can't teach someone else how to spot them."

Toby bobbed his head in agreement. "Yeah. I'm wondering…" He closed his eyes and pressed his lips into a tight line. "I keep thinking the three of us can't be the only ones who have ever escaped from a demonic attack." When he opened his eyes, he turned his gaze on Benny.

Benny inclined his head, the movement slow and deliberate. "Your 'food for thought' question."

"What?" asked Mike.

"I asked Benny to consider something. A question. Whether others like you and Scott exist out there, and if there are, how we can go about finding them."

"And?" asked Scott.

Benny lifted his shoulders and snorted. "It's only been a few days. I'm not a supercomputer that you can just feed a punch card into and—"

"Computers aren't programmed with punch cards anymore, Benny," said Mike with a smile.

"Whatever. I'm not a computer. And I don't have a special, mystical grasp on truth with a capital T. Mike's comment emphasizes one of my limitations. I've been in an insane asylum since I was eleven, guys."

"Well, what about the other thing?" asked Scott, leaning forward and staring at Benny.

"What other thing, Scott?"

"Can Toby teach his…his ability to others?"

Benny tilted his head back, his affect going flat, his lips pressed into a thin line. He looked away from the table, gazing through the smoked glass windows of the restaurant. "Why is it you all expect me to have all the answers?"

Toby lifted one shoulder and let it drop the way Scott had before lifting one corner of his mouth. "Because so far, you always have. Plus, you said Mike didn't have a superpower because you hadn't decided what he needed yet. Remember?"

"Joke! It was a joke." Benny closed his eyes and pinched the bridge of his nose. "I can almost see it; I can almost see what Toby's doing. But only *almost*."

"Can you see what I do?" asked Shannon with a note of excitement in her voice. "If I can teach all of you how to do this thing, our lives will get much easier."

"No, it's the same." Benny heaved a sigh. "And anyway, even if I *can* see what you're doing, that doesn't mean I'll be able to *explain* what you're doing. And even if I figured out how to explain it perfectly, it doesn't mean anybody else could do it."

"Then we're back to recruiting," said Mike. "But how do we do that without sounding like a pack of crazy people?"

"No, there's something more important we need to figure out."

All eyes at the table turned toward Scott.

"Weapons. Firearms are a waste of time; we've seen that again and again. At best, they are a distraction. We need weapons that are *effective* against these fuckers." He gazed intently at Toby. "We need more of your tranquilizer rifles."

"Yeah," said Toby. He picked up his napkin and began to shred it into little pieces, building a small mound in front of him. "About that…"

"Yeah, I get it," said Scott with a sour grin. "It's not exactly legal."

"It's not that… To have mine made, I had to go to a lot of bad places on the Internet. Websites that are distasteful at best. Skinhead websites. Torture websites. Rape and rough sex websites. When I found the guy that made mine, he contacted me and wouldn't even give me his name. I called him 'Q' after the guy in the James Bond movies." Toby shook his head. "I'm not even sure if the contact information I have for the guy is still valid. And he thought I was a serial killer. I'm sure of it. Who knows if he'd make another?"

Scott lifted both hands, palms up. "Only one way to find out."

Toby returned his gaze without expression. "That's true, but that doesn't address the heightening tolerance to M99 the demons are exhibiting."

"Maybe we can kill two birds with one stone," said Mike. "Is there anything else we can use instead of the M99?"

"There are other tranquilizers and ridiculously strong opioids—say carfentanil—we could try." Toby drummed the fingers of his left hand on the table. "My concern is this: *why* are they developing a tolerance to M99? I'd never shot Hartman full of it before, and yet he took as much M99 as a much stronger demon would have."

"Your concern is that even if we switch to something like carfentanil, they will just develop a tolerance?" asked Benny.

Toby grinned and shot him with his finger gun.

Scott grunted and pursed his lips. "But we can't go on with one effective weapon. Look what almost happened at Hartman's place…if Shannon hadn't been there…"

"That's an excellent point," said Toby.

"Okay, forget tranquilizers, then." Mike leaned forward, his gaze boring into Toby's. "What about that stuff you had in the canisters? That stuff we used to burn Herlequin. Wouldn't that work?"

"Chlorine trifluoride? Sure, that would work. It would work to burn the demon up, it would work to burn the room the demon is in up, and it would work to burn down an entire city block if we let it."

"But we used a slew of it in the middle of the woods…"

Toby grinned and spread his hands. "I'd planned to use it for a controlled burn of Herlequin's corpse if we needed it. I'd never planned to shoot those canisters with the shotgun." He cocked his head to the side. "You both saw what happened, how incendiary the stuff is. Would you want to use it in any enclosed space? Would you want to use it in any place you were trapped inside?"

Both men shook their heads.

"Something else, then?" asked Shannon.

"Acid!" said Benny in a voice that would've sounded natural coming from an excited eleven-year-old. "We can get a bunch of those big squirt guns, you know, the kind with the pump thing that shoots the stream so far. We—"

"The range on those things is terrible," said Mike.

"Would they even stand up to acid? Aren't they made of plastic?" asked Shannon. She shuddered and pulled a face. "Imagine if it *leaked*!"

"We might come up with something to solve those problems, and acid would be an effective weapon against demons, considering it would pull them apart at the molecular level," said Toby in a thoughtful voice. "Still, the range…"

"Not to mention accuracy issues," said Scott.

"What about paintballs?" asked Mike.

"You have the same range and accuracy issues, I think." Scott pursed his lips and stroked his chin.

"I don't know about that, Scott. We could always rifle the barrels if we can't find something already rifled. And I think they have a special paintball you can buy that rotates on its own. Something to check into, anyway."

"Okay, so if we can overcome the issues with paintballs, what would we use? If we put acid in them, they might break as we're running around fighting. They might end up doing more damage to us than the demons. If we use the chlorine triwhatsit, we've got the same issue as Toby has already mentioned."

"There are other things we could do with the paintball, though," said Toby. "If we made our own paintballs, lots of options are doable. Chemicals that on their own aren't that bad but when mixed create lethal poisonous gasses."

"Lethal to demons? Wouldn't it also be lethal to anyone else nearby?"

"Okay, so what about using two things that combine into a very potent acid or base—a mobile industrial digester."

"I don't understand why we have to make our own paintballs," said Benny.

"We would make paintballs that had two distinct chambers. Unbroken, the chambers would keep the two substances apart, but once the paintball hit something and broke open, it would splash both compounds all over whatever you hit, and they would combine, doing whatever their chemical nature demanded." Toby leaned back like a man sated by an extravagant meal. "I like this idea. It's got possibilities."

"I'm sure we can find out how to make paintballs," said Mike. "And if we can't, I'm sure Scott could flash his badge and find out whatever information we need." He turned to the trooper and raised his eyebrows.

"I'm sure I can find out, but I doubt it's even a secret. We can find it on the Internet."

"I'm sure it's something simple—a gelatin thickener, perhaps," said Toby. He had a faraway look in his eye and directed his gaze out the wall of windows next to their booth. "In fact, I bet I can get a recipe from one of the chemists here—oh shit!" He rocked forward, staring out the window.

"Did you just remember something?" asked Benny.

"We've got to get out of here! *Now*!"

Scott twisted around and craned his neck to see out the window behind him. "What is it?"

Keeping his hand out of the sight of anyone outside the booth, Toby pointed out the window. "There's a demon coming this way."

"He might have nothing to do with us," said Shannon in a wistful tone.

A grimace of intense concentration settled on Benny's features for a moment, and he squeezed his eyes shut. When he opened them, his gaze locked on Toby's face. "No. He's got everything to do with us."

"But how would he know where we are?" asked Shannon.

"Everybody get moving!" snapped Toby. "My tranquilizer rifle is back at the apartment!"

Mike glanced at Scott and treated him to a terse nod. They were both armed with pistols. "Scott and I can slow him down."

Toby shook his head. "Not without collateral damage. Not without him getting to one of you. No, it's time to run, and it's time to run now!"

2

Dan Delo strode across the small square of green grass nestled between buildings on the university campus. LaBouche himself had given him his mission, and he'd given instructions on where to go, but as Dan looked around, he didn't see the people that LaBouche had ordered him to find. The people LaBouche wanted dead.

Each building faced the square with a glass wall, doors set in their middles. They had signs above the doors—The Cosmic Cheeseburger, All Green Grazing, No Soup For You, and, even stranger to Delo, The Lamb and The Lion. Dan could make no sense from the names—well, except for the cosmic cheeseburger one. He supposed the others were restaurants, and perhaps the names said something to the young people attending the university—maybe they gave clues as to what sort of food they sold.

Not that it mattered. In a moment, one of the places would be a mess of shattered glass, splintered wood, broken bodies, and blood. Lots of blood.

Dan longed to stretch his great wings. Keeping them pulled in tight to his body all the time irritated him, which might have explained his horrible temper and the tendency to dismember his victims while they were still alive. Or not.

Thick muscles—what the humans called a bodybuilder physique—rippled beneath his purple scales—scales so dark many mistook them for obsidian. A shade lighter, his leathery wings almost doubled his height and made him appear even bulkier. Around his head, his scales had fused into a protective helmet of a kind, with spikes and horns sticking out like the ball of a morning star.

He'd tried to make his human visage unintimidating—he appeared as a rail-thin geek, not a muscle in sight, with slicked-back hair and wire-rimmed glasses. Very few people paid attention to him—not until it was far too late.

It wasn't the guise he preferred wearing, but LaBouche had been specific about that. He hadn't wanted to take any chances that one of the humans might have recognized him after seeing him in Oneka Falls.

As it was, he had to rein in his temper almost every fifteen seconds as young humans brushed against him or stepped on his feet or pushed him to the side. He wanted to lash out, to rake his majestic silver claws down the side of a perfect face, or to bite a chunk out of a muscled athlete's shoulder.

But he did none of those things.

With razor-sharp focus, he peered through the tinted glass front of The Cosmic Cheeseburger. Inside more pathetic young humans sat, drinking one of their foul concoctions, or eating the flesh of bovines stacked in bread.

He rolled his shoulders, trying to ease the tension out of his back and neck, trying to keep himself loose and ready for the destruction he was about to wreak on the unwitting humans in one of the four eateries. He didn't see the five people for whom LaBouche had given him images, and he stopped short outside the door to the restaurant.

"Move your ass, geekster."

Someone shoved him to the side, and without thinking, Dan lashed out, swatting the young man to the ground. The student lay there, bleeding and spitting his teeth out onto the concrete. The demon shrugged and turned away.

He strode toward the restaurant called All Green Grazing, ignoring the high-pitched whining from behind him. He applied his intense focus on the humans sitting inside, but again, his search was fruitless.

As he turned to approach the building with the No Soup For You sign emblazoned above the door, a hand fell on his shoulder and pulled him around.

"Who the fuck do you think you are, chummy?" demanded the young man who'd grabbed him. "You can't punch someone and think it's okay to walk away!"

"My mistake," said Dan Delo. He took half a step forward, planted his hand in the center of the athletic man's chest and pushed him hard. The man screamed as his feet left the ground and he flew backward, landing in a heap next to the other bleeding student. Dan glared at the surrounding students, meeting their gazes with hostility and open hatred. "Anyone else have complaints?" he asked. No one replied, and he went on with his search.

After he'd searched all four restaurants and found nothing, his blood boiled, and his hands itched to take his frustration out on a human, but LaBouche had been specific: he wasn't to draw attention to himself.

With one last glare at the students who stood frozen and silent, staring at him, Dan Delo turned on his heel and left the square. As soon as he rounded the corner of the closest building, he dispensed with the fiction of walking, spread his wings, and soared into the sky.

3

Toby led them through the tunnels that ran underneath the school. The tunnels allowed easy travel between buildings in the winter, when snow covered the ground, and were open to all. But almost no one used them in the warmer months, and the five of them ran into no one.

He led them up the stairs to the building that contained the office of Doctor Drew Reid—the persona he had created to shield himself from scrutiny during the years he'd been alone, during the years he'd been stalking and killing demons. As they came up from the basement, he glanced out through the lobby and saw another demon lounging outside.

The waiting demon was a weird, a demon that walked on two legs, but that had four arms—two longer arms and two shorter that grew from below her armpits. She had dark, wispy wings as if created from black mist. Her malachite eyes glowed in the afternoon sun, and she had two large tusks that grew from her lower jaw sticking out of her lips. Her tusks and fangs were burnt gold—the color of fallow fields in the fall.

With a grimace, Toby turned on his heel and ushered the others back down into the tunnels. "Another demon is standing guard up there," he said.

"Is there another place we can exit the tunnels?"

"Sure. These tunnels go to every building on campus."

"That must've made it easy to get bodies to the medical school," said Scott.

Toby's only reply was a grunt.

After a short walk, he brought them to a flight of steps that led to the mechanical room of the College of Engineering. "I've been here twice in the entire time I've taught at this school, so no one would expect us to come out here."

"You hope," said Mike.

"Yes, I hope."

"Should we take a moment and discuss why and how these demons found us?" asked Shannon.

"I'd rather do that when we're safe."

Benny crossed his arms. "Nowhere is safe in a world populated with demons who can hide behind a human mask."

"*Relatively* safe." Toby led them up the steps, and before opening the emergency door that led outside from the mechanical room, he disabled the alarm.

They stepped out into the noon-time sun, squinting as their eyes adjusted to the light. Toby looked in all directions before nodding. "Looks like we're clear," he said.

"Where can we go? Your apartment?" asked Scott. "If they found us here…"

"It's the safest place," said Toby with a shrug. "Plus, we can walk there. And we won't know if they are watching the place without taking a look."

"Why not take the cars?" asked Shannon.

"We just ran into a demon guarding my building. I think it will be best to leave the cars for a while since they can trace them back to us."

Feigning nonchalance they didn't feel, the five walked across the parking lot that separated the campus from the woods that enclosed it. Toby kept his head on a swivel but saw no other demons.

They took the path students had made between the apartment complex and the campus. It exited the woods in the back of the apartment complex, and there, Toby called a halt. With a low whistle, he began pointing out demons that lounged at the pool, bent over a car with its hood up, sweeping the stairs, even one running a lawnmower.

Scott stepped up beside him. "And now, we can't even use the tranquilizer rifle."

Toby's frown was a grim one. "It seems not. A demon followed one of you." Toby bit off the next sentence instead of saying it. He'd been living in that apartment for years, killing demons at will, and none of them had sussed him out.

"We killed more than a common demon in their ranks when we burned Herlequin," said Benny in a soft voice. "We killed their king; we've got to expect them to—"

Toby chopped his hand through the air, not wanting to discuss it. "We need to find somewhere else."

"Find somewhere else? We need to *hide*. We have no weapons, no way to fight these things." Mike ran his hands through his hair, then let them drop. "Toby, what are we going to do?"

It was a good question. Unfortunately, Toby was out of ideas.

4

"And your name, sir?"

Mason flashed his best smile at the effeminate little man. "Don Daba. I made a reservation earlier this morning on your website."

"I see. One moment, please." The man behind the counter typed his name into the reservation computer. "Ah, here it is. One adult, staying for five days?" He lifted his gaze from the computer and arched one eyebrow at Mason.

"Yeah, about that. I might have to stay longer, or something might come up that calls me away."

The little man frowned and returned his gaze to the computer. He tapped a few more keys and smiled. "That shouldn't be a problem—at least, as of now. We are nowhere near capacity for next weekend, but you may want to check back during the week. Better yet, once you know for certain, let us know if you wish to extend your reservation. If you want to leave early, it may necessitate a penalty."

Mason nodded, curling one hand into a tight fist. He very much wanted to punch the hotel clerk right in the face. There was no reason, not really. He sometimes took an instant dislike to a person. "Excuse me for asking, but have you ever modeled?"

The clerk jerked his head back, frowning. "Modeled? For a magazine?"

Mason chuckled and rested one forearm on the marble countertop. "Well, I meant for an artist. I think you'd make a great subject."

"Artist?" The clerk looked him up and down in a frank, appraising way. "Do you mean for a painter?"

"Something like that." Mason fought to keep his smile pleasant.

The clerk gazed into his eyes for a moment. "Why no," he murmured. "I've never done that."

"You should think about it. Your face has such fine lines." Mason allowed his gaze to crawl down the man's form. "Your body, too. It would be exciting to work on you."

"Work *on* me?"

Mason chuckled and thumped the counter with his knuckles. "Figure of speech."

The clerk tilted his head to the side. "You paint?"

"Something like that." Mason glanced out the twin glass doors of the hotel. Outside, the sun shone brightly on the downtown street. "I'm here in Rochester for work, but if I have time, and you are available…"

The clerk smiled and nodded once.

Mason allowed his smile to show his genuine pleasure—though the enjoyment came from something other than what the clerk suspected.

5

With a guttural roar, LaBouche sprang to his feet, muscles rippling. He backhanded Dan Delo with all his strength, breaking a spine off his head, and the purple demon reeled away, arms and wings flapping to regain his balance. "What do you mean you didn't find them?" screamed LaBouche. "How could you miss them? And why are you here? Why aren't you still on the campus looking for them, you pompous idiot?"

With one hand caressing the broken spine, Delo glared at him with burning hatred. "You said I'd find them in the restaurant! There were *four* restaurants!"

LaBouche scoffed and took a menacing step forward.

"*And they weren't in any of them*!" Dan Delo stepped forward, spreading his wings wide behind him. "It's not my fault—"

"Not your fault? *Not your fault*! Well, whose fault is it?"

"LaBouche, you're not being fair! You put such constraints on me—"

Growling, LaBouche advanced on the younger demon, his chartreuse alligator eyes glinting with fury. He smiled his best smile—the one that showed every one of his teeth in his full, V-shaped mouth. "Yes. You're right, of course. I put unfair constraints on you.

Constraints such as: don't let anyone know your true nature, catch the people I sent you to catch, keep your temper, and do what I ask. How silly of me." LaBouche stopped his advance when he was almost nose to nose with the other demon. "This will *not* make Brigitta happy. More to your sadness, it does not make *me* happy." He snapped his teeth in Dan Delo's face, then grinned his most sinister smile—again showing the multitude of his teeth.

To his credit, Dan Delo didn't flinch—if he had LaBouche would not have stayed his hand. The purple demon stood statue-still, however, his gaze resting on LaBouche's face.

Behind LaBouche, the door opened.

"Ah, there you are, LaBouche," said Brigitta. She took a few steps into the room before slowing to a halt. "And who is this?"

"He is beneath you, Excellency. We were…discussing his recent failures." LaBouche stepped to the side and slapped Dan Delo on the back of the head, and the purple demon fell to his knees.

"I see," said Brigitta. "Shall I leave you to it?"

"No, Your Majesty. Your needs are far more important." He glared down at Dan Delo. "Leave us, swine. I'll deal with you later."

Brigitta watched the winged demon leave the room, his gaze averted, his shoulders slumped. When the door closed, she turned to LaBouche and grinned. "It always strikes me funny when one of the winged ones slumps. They look so silly."

"That they do, Your Highness."

She tilted her head to the side and blinked at him. "That doesn't suit you, you know. That false deference. I'd rather you be yourself."

LaBouche nodded once. "As you wish. I merely wanted to express my respect for you."

Brigitta laughed and slapped his shoulder without any force. "You mean you merely wished to avoid being turned into a magpie again."

LaBouche deployed the smile he had worked very hard to cultivate. He hoped she didn't see through it. "You're right, of course."

Brigitta tsked. "It's too bad you didn't enjoy it. You made such a *cute* bird."

LaBouche somehow held onto the smile, keeping it plastered on his face until the urge to scream became an almost physical necessity. He nodded, using it as an excuse to avert his gaze from hers.

"And how goes the hunt? The hunt for the so-called hunters?"

LaBouche let the smile fade, a grimace taking its place. "That was the matter I was discussing with Dan Delo. He failed his assignment."

"And the others?"

LaBouche crossed his arms and pursed his lips. "The campus team thought they saw him inside his building—where he keeps an office. Where Scott and I interviewed him for the first time. But if it was them, they didn't emerge. And since that time, no one has seen them on campus. The team at his apartment complex..." He put his hands behind his back.

"Buck up, LaBouche. Often, these things take more time than we expect. Your efforts will yield fruit."

He raised a hand, holding it out toward the door that Dan Delo had used. "That idiot may have tipped our hand."

Brigitta laughed her bell-like laugh and patted him on the shoulder. "It's no matter, LaBouche. I have every confidence that you will catch up to them. My only concern is that your soldiers may not understand how disappointed I will be if they kill any one of the five hunters. Have you explained it to them?" Her expression had turned dire as she spoke.

LaBouche nodded, his expression grave. "I explained that if they killed any of the humans, the demon responsible should prepare for the short trip home. Which would happen *after* you had punished them."

Her menacing expression faded, and she treated him to one of her friendliest smiles.

It made LaBouche uneasy. He wasn't used to Brigitta treating him with such...warmth, such friendliness. *It's not as if she wants something from me*, he thought. *She already has everything I can offer her. And more…unless…* But no. That couldn't be. He was too far beneath her, and no matter how she acted, he didn't believe she actually enjoyed his company.

"Well, it seems that you have everything in hand. I only wanted to drop by and see if you needed anything."

"Uh, no…I think I…have everything I need." He tried to keep his speculations off his face.

She nodded and hit him with a thousand-watt smile. "Good, good. If you discover you need something that is not available, send one of the winged ones. You know where I'll be."

"Uh, yes, I will. Thank you."

She patted him on the shoulder, then, much to his discomfort, stood there, staring at him as if he were a strange bug.

"And Chaz? Are things progressing in Oneka Falls?"

Brigitta inclined her head, and her smile lost a degree of warmth. "Things are in hand, LaBouche. Recall your promise to me—recall that you said you could work with him without rancor."

LaBouche nodded. "Of course. I've never excelled at small talk."

She grinned at him crookedly and arched one eyebrow. "No, you haven't."

6

They rented cabins at a place called the Agincourt Resort. The resort lay far to the south, almost to the Pennsylvania border, in the town of Granite. The Allegheny State Park encapsulated the village on three sides—the town's main claim to fame.

The cabins weren't much—little two-bedroom affairs, with a small kitchenette and a single standard living room between the two bedrooms—but they were clean, and they allowed Scott to book rooms under aliases once he showed them his NYSP badge. A round table had been crammed into the kitchenette of the cabin Toby shared with Benny and Shannon, but it only had four chairs, so Mike had brought a spare chair from the cabin he and Scott shared, and the five of them sat around it.

"We need to get moving, to *do* something productive," said Scott. "We should at least *try* making a few dozen paintballs—then we'll know if that idea will work or not."

"You don't say? I couldn't tell you thought so; you've only repeated it forty or fifty times," said Shannon, smiling to take any sting out of her words.

"He makes a good point, though," said Toby. "I'm not used to sitting around doing nothing. What are we going to do? While away the time reading magazines and playing checkers?"

Mike yawned and stretched, his back crackling. "I don't know, it's relaxing not having to be anywhere or do anything."

"We can't afford to just sit around doing nothing," said Benny. We can't just sit here hiding. Every day we do this, the demons get to dig themselves in, to lay traps. Plus, who knows how many they are killing?"

Mike grimaced, and Scott blew out his cheeks.

"Gosh, Benny, don't sugar-coat it." Toby shifted in his seat, draping one arm over the ladder-backed chair. He grinned at his childhood friend and then glanced at Scott and raised his eyebrows. "Are you still against loading the paintballs with chlorine gas?"

Compressing his lips into a thin line, Scott raised one shoulder and let it fall. "It's too much of a risk. What do we do when it's windy? What about collateral casualties when we miss?"

"Listen, guys, I've been thinking," said Benny. "And Scott's right about the poison gas angle, Toby. You settled on using M99 because it has the required effect: unconsciousness of the demon. Somehow, we've gone from incapacitating the demons for…*processing* back at the university to trying to kill them with a single paintball. But that won't work anyway. Didn't you say that the only way to kill them and make them stay dead is to separate their blood from their body and dispose of both?"

Toby nodded. "True."

Benny leaned forward, elbows on the table. "Then why try to kill them with poison gas? All we need to do is replace the darts and the tranquilizer gun. What could we load into the paintballs to knock a demon out?"

"The darts were just convenience. M99 worked because I could get it from veterinary supply houses." Toby turned his head to the side and gazed up at the ceiling. "The Russians used Kolokol-1 as an incapacitating agent in 2002, and it's also a derivative of fentanyl, same as carfentanil. I suppose if they can aerosolize Kolokol-1, we could do the same with carfentanil, though it might be a bit harder to get our hands on enough."

"You can't aerosolize M99?" asked Benny.

Shannon giggled and flipped her hair over her shoulder. "Why do men always make everything complicated?"

"What do you mean?" asked Benny and crossed his arms.

"It's our nature," said Toby. "I guess you have a simpler solution?"

Shannon bumped Benny with her elbow and winked at him. "Haven't you ever read product warnings? We don't need fancy opiates or tranquilizers, or anything as complicated as that. All we need is bleach and acetone—mixing them produces chloroform."

"She's right," said Mike. "Why didn't either of you two geniuses come up with that?"

"We were busy coming up with everything else. Now, all we need are paintball guns and a recipe for paintballs. I bet we can get both at a store that sells paintball gear." Toby stretched and scooted his chair back from the table. "Let's go."

"Do you think we're far enough away from Oneka Falls that going out will be safe?" asked Mike.

"Yes, I do, but I also thought my apartment was safe. From now on, Shannon will have to mask us."

Shannon's expression grew solemn. "There's only one of me."

Toby extended his hand toward Benny. "Loverboy can help you."

"I suppose so, but I'm not sure… I mean, it requires a lot of concentration."

"You can handle it, Shan," said Mike.

"I hope you're right. I'm not so sure."

"To make it easier, in the beginning, just three of us will go. You and Benny, and whoever else needs to be out there. For the paintball guns, maybe Scott should go."

Scott held up his hands. "I'd be happy to get out of this place, but you have more experience with things driven by carbon dioxide. All of my experience relates to lead propelled by gunpowder."

"The principles are the same," said Toby. "And your cabin fever is a little more pronounced than mine."

"You don't have to twist my arm," said Scott with a small grin.

7

"It's the lighting," said Mason as he led the hotel clerk down an alley behind the hotel.

"The lighting? These alleys will be full of shadows."

"*Exactly*. It's the play between light and dark that I want to capture." He flashed a reassuring smile at the small man.

"I thought..." The clerk shook his head and looked at his feet. "It was silly."

Mason chuckled and rested his hand on the small man's shoulder. "No, it wasn't silly," he whispered. "But after we finish here..."

The clerk looked up, and a smile stretched from ear to ear. He never saw the scalpel in Mason's hand.

Not until it was too late.

8

"How could you let it come to this, Fuck-it-up? How could you let him manipulate me into this corner?" A backhanded blow punctuated each question, each blow staggering her in a different direction.

Her ears rang from the assault, and she blinked in silence, trying to clear her mind. She sank to one knee and bowed her head, hoping that, at least, her posture would make her more difficult to bat around like a rag doll. "But I told you his plans, my lord."

"Did you? Did you really, Fuck-it-up?"

He didn't hit her again, but he loomed over her like a cat playing with prey trapped between its front paws. She tried to block her fear—or at least block radiating her terror to him—but she knew such an act wouldn't fool an alpha such as Chaz for long. She nodded but didn't lift her gaze from the floor.

Chaz scoffed and blew a raspberry. "What good are you, McBride? What use do you have? Why shouldn't I just send you home?"

Raw fear of being sent back blossomed within her like a runaway chain reaction, and Sally didn't waste any effort trying to conceal it. "Don't do that, my lord! I…I told you everything! He tricked me, too."

“Oh, get up off your knees! You are even annoying when you grovel, Sally. Have some self-respect.”

Sally watched his feet as he turned and walked away. *It could be a trap*, she thought. *He might just be waiting for me to stand up so he can knock me down again.*

“Get up!”

His office chair creaked as he sank into it, and Sally let a sigh of relief hiss through her teeth. Moving with great care, Sally pushed up from her squat and rolled her head, trying to loosen the abused muscles in her shoulders and neck.

“Yes, yes! I’m such a mean boss, I get it. I’m a bastard, okay?”

Sally kept her eyes averted. “It’s nothing, my lord. I should be better. I should serve you better.”

“Says the parrot. For Chrissake, McBride.” He drummed his talons on the pad resting on his desktop. “Plant it, Sally.” He waved at the two visitor chairs across his desk with his other hand.

Sally’s gaze ping-ponged between the two available chairs, but she made no move toward either of them.

“Sit!” Chaz roared.

Sally jumped, and with her body on autopilot, she swooped toward the closest chair. She sat facing Chaz, unable to stop her hands from fiddling with the fabric upholstery of the chair.

Chaz's eyes narrowed as he watched her hands twiddle and dance. His expression soured into a grimace. "Do you know what, Fuck-it-up?"

She opened her mouth to speak but found her mouth too dry. She settled for shaking her head.

"As much of a pain in the ass as he was, sometimes I miss Red Bortha." A small, nervous-looking smile settled on his lips. "Isn't that strange? One alpha missing another?"

"Not so strange," Sally whispered.

"What was that?" asked Chaz, throwing one hand behind the mound of flesh that protected his ear hole, the small smile morphing into a grimace.

"I said it's not so strange, my lord. You two were…friends."

Chaz bellowed laughter, his head thrown back, and one hand on his belly. "Friends!" he gasped between gales of laughter.

Sally squirmed in her chair as the big demon laughed.

"Alphas don't make *friends* with one another," said Chaz. "At best, they can develop a working relationship—such as the one I shared with Red. I found him to be…reliable and less irritating than most."

"Yes, my lord."

"And that brings me to my reason for summoning you. Brigitta has given me a task—several if you want to know the truth. I will need help. Help such as what Red provided me before those assholes sent him home."

"Yes, my lord."

"Yes, my lord. Yes, my lord," Chaz sneered. "What's the matter with you, McBride? Why are you this way?"

Because if I were any other way, you'd no doubt beat me to death, she thought. "How shall I be, my lord?" Her voice lacked any emotion, and her eyes drifted to the middle of his desk—safe from his probing glare.

Chaz curled his lip and spun his chair to the side, presumably so he didn't have to look at her. "I need you to do me a service."

"No sooner named than started."

"As I said, I will need help to complete the tasks Brigitta requires in the time that she allows. I need another Red. I need…"

"Yes, Lord?"

"I need you to find him. Not Red, of course, we both know where he is. I need you to find me other demons *like* Red Bortha, someone I can work with without having to fight all the time. That means no alphas, but yet the demons need to be powerful, smart."

"Do you have…"

"Do I have a list of candidates?" Chaz shook his head. "No. Perhaps one of the new arrivals." He looked at her with a sly expression on his face. "Perhaps the silver-skinned one or someone with similar…qualifications. Do you know her?"

Sally shook her head once and stood. "I haven't met her, but I will look into it. And others."

"Now."

"Yes, my lord."

"One more thing, McBride. Once you've found a few candidates, I want you to approach them the same way you approached me for LaBouche, but you will not offer them a partnership."

Sally walked to the door, turned, and curtsied—which felt silly, as she was in slacks and tennis shoes. "Of course not, my lord."

Chaz nodded to her and waved her away.

Sally exited his office, pulling the door closed behind her. Once outside, she breathed a sigh of relief.

9

Scott had chosen professional paintball guns for them all—ones that included custom electronics to enable full automatic fire and polished two-piece barrels rifled for extended range and accuracy. After the practice sessions using regular paintballs Scott had insisted on, they all felt more comfortable with the weapons, if not confident in their abilities.

And Toby had been right, the store owner had given Scott a recipe to create his own paintballs—and it was *easy*. Mike had prepared molds while Benny and Shannon had cooked up the goop that would harden into the shells. When the paintball forms had set up, they'd used syringes to fill the two hemispherical chambers separated by a wall of the shell material with bleach and acetone, then they sealed the holes with a drop of superglue.

The homemade paintballs broke just as they should, and the two chemicals mixed without a hitch, producing gaseous chloroform. Better yet, the paintballs were easy to use, and all it took to go from semiauto to automatic fire was a flick of a switch—as long as the batteries held a charge.

Scott tested each of them with their paintball guns, shooting at paper targets deep in the Allegheny State Park, far from known hiking trails and pronounced them "fair to middling." Afterward, they gathered in Toby, Benny, and Shannon's cabin, their spirits higher than they had been in days.

"We need a *real* test next."

"What, on an animal or something?" asked Benny.

Scott shook his head and chuckled. "No, Benny. We need to test them on a demon—one that won't kill us."

He turned his gaze on Toby. "Do you know of any that may fit the bill?"

Toby nodded slowly. "Yeah, I do. I have a story that needs verification, and if she's a demon, we can test our guns on her."

"That sounds ominous," said Mike.

"What do you mean 'a story?'" asked Scott at the same time.

Toby tilted his head to the left and lifted that shoulder. "Where do you think I get all my names, all my potential demons?"

Scott tapped his foot. "I'm sure I don't know, Toby."

"A few years ago, I set up a website for people to talk about paranormal events. On it, I built a forum so people could tell me their ghost stories." Toby turned his gaze on each one of them in turn, his expression solemn. "You'd be surprised how many ghost stories have a demon behind them."

"I wouldn't," said Benny.

"Maybe not, Benny. But—"

"Wait a minute, just wait a minute. You're the one behind all those nuts that picket all the Catholic churches?"

Toby waved it away. "People get all caught up in it. Blame the Internet, if you need something to blame. I never posted a call for anyone to picket anywhere. If they get together on a forum somewhere, I bear no responsibility for that."

Grinning, Mike made a shooing gesture at Toby. "My, my, a *real* celebrity…"

Toby grinned back. "And autographs are only fifty dollars."

"Would I get a discount? I mean, I know someone high up in the organization."

"Uh, could we get back to business?" asked Scott.

Still grinning, Mike waved them on.

"Did all of…*them*…come from tips, from ghost stories?"

"No. A few have just been happenstance. Others got on my radar either through the media or from law enforcement bulletins. Like the stories about Abaddon. Things like that."

"Serial killers?" asked Mike.

Scott flashed a sour smile. "Easy place for them to hide. Behind the persona of a serial killer—it *is* what they are."

Mike shrugged. "I'm surprised they haven't called you in on that investigation."

Scott's shoulders lifted and fell, and the gesture seemed to contain infinite sadness. "I would be working on it right now if LaBouche hadn't…"

Benny cleared his throat.

"Tell us about this lady you mentioned before," said Shannon.

"There's not much to tell. She appears to be an old lady, but one who has been old for thirty years or more. On top of that, she lives out away from town—way out in the country and separated from her neighbors by a good bit. No one ever sees her in town buying groceries, and—"

"Someone might bring her groceries to her." Scott rubbed his temples, hunched forward and head bent to obscure his face.

"Or she shops in a different town. That's not evidence that she's a demon," said Mike.

Toby twirled a finger through it all. "True on all counts, but it's still worth checking out. The legend has it that people disappear into her basement on Halloween. Dogs go crazy in her presence. Yaddy."

"And you find these…*reports* helpful?"

"Ninety-nine percent of them are garbage. But that one percent… Bill Hartman was a one-percenter."

"What does it matter?" asked Shannon. "What does it matter where Toby gets his names? They are the names of *demons*."

"Then let's go check her out," said Benny. "It's the only way we will ever know if the story is correct or not."

"It's a long drive—three hours from here. Or more."

Scott looked around the cabin. "It's better than sitting here—even if she is just an eccentric old lady. When should we go?"

"I vote right freaking now," said Shannon with a grin. "Besides, I'm hungry, and I'm tired of eating the crap we have here."

"You heard her," said Benny, pushing his chair back. "Last one in the car has to sit between Scott and Mike!" With that, he turned and bolted through the door.

Shannon turned a bemused gaze on the others. "Sometimes I think he's still eleven."

"Sometimes he still is," said Toby without a hint of a smile.

10

With Mike driving their rented Lincoln, it had only taken them an hour and a half to make the drive from the Agincourt to the turn off one of the myriad roads that connected Route 104 and Lake Road. Everything was in line with the story from Toby's website.

"I'm still not sure about this, Toby," said Shannon.

"It will be fine. Benny will be right here to help you."

Benny bumped his shoulder into hers. "Yeah, right next to you."

"I know." Shannon's fingers tried to tie themselves in knots. "It's just that I've never done this…"

"You've never created a disguise for someone so far away, but you have done this. It's *okay* if it's not perfect, Shan. This is a test run, remember?" Toby put his hand on the door handle and popped it open. "Get the trunk, Mike."

"But if it slips…if I fail…you'll be exposed. I don't… What if it goes wrong and I can't keep you disguised? What if she sees through it? What do I do then?"

Toby flashed a lopsided grin at her and lifted one shoulder. "Then do whatever you did at Hartman's house. It seemed to work."

Shannon wagged her head side to side. She grabbed Benny's hand and squeezed. "You can't go anywhere, Benny. No getting distracted, either."

"How can I avoid distraction with a woman like you sitting next to me?"

Mike snorted and looked at Benny in the rearview mirror. "Smooth, Benny, real smooth. But the time for schmoopy ended when we got in the car."

Benny looked at him in the rearview mirror and cocked his head. "I—"

"It's game time, people! Cut the bullshit!" snapped Scott.

An awkward silence followed, only broken when Mike burst out laughing. Scott glared at him, and Mike held up his hands in supplication. “Sorry, sorry. But really, Scott? Game time?”

Scott leaned across him to flip open the glove box and punch the button that released the trunk. Without another word, he opened his door and got out, slamming it shut after him and walking around to the rear of the car.

“Touchy,” muttered Mike.

“It’s only been a few days, Mike,” said Shannon. “Given what he’s been through, he’s handling it well.”

“Yeah, I guess.”

Toby slid out of the back seat and joined Scott at the rear of the car. He reached inside and picked up his paintball gun and a kidney-shaped magazine full of their special paintballs. “If this doesn’t work…”

Scott reached into the trunk and pulled out Mike’s Remington 870 and began thumbing shells into the ammunition tube. “I’ve got you, Toby. If it doesn’t work out, Mike and I will come on the run. We’ve got the rifled barrels, so we’ve got extended range, and we’ve got plenty of slugs. It’s not ideal, as you pointed out, and I wish we had your fancy tranquilizer gun as backup, but if the paintballs don’t work, Mike and I will put her down with the shotguns. Or at least keep her busy enough for you to escape.” Scott leaned to the side and peered through the rear window of the Lincoln. “Do you think she can handle it?”

Toby smiled with one side of his mouth and rubbed a hand through his hair. "Probably."

"And you feel comfortable risking your life on 'probably?'" He arched an eyebrow.

Toby made a show of examining his weapon. "Seems like we are all risking a lot on probabilities and chances." He scuffed his foot in the gravel alongside the road. "Anyway, what other options are there?"

"We could try the frontal assault. I still say—"

Toby chopped air with his hand. "No, that's plan B. We need to know if Shannon can do this or not. We need to know if these paintballs work and if we can make the paintball guns deliver. This demon is *weak*, Scott. Or senile. Or both." He shrugged. "It's better to fail against one such as her than one such as Brigitta."

Scott's only answer was a grunt. He rapped his knuckles on the rear quarter panel of the car. "Get a move on, Mike!"

From inside the car, Mike grumbled something, but he popped his door open just the same and slid out. Scott tossed the loaded shotgun to him and began loading the one issued him by the NYSP.

Toby walked to the open rear door of the car and leaned inside. "Are you two ready?"

Shannon took a deep breath and let it trickle out. A look of concentration settled across her features, and Benny's eyes glazed over.

"I'm making…you into a…teenaged girl," said Shannon in a breathless, halting voice.

"Swell. At least make me cute. And I'm talking prom queen cute."

Shannon giggled. "Toby as a cute 16-year-old girl, coming up."

Toby chuckled and turned away from the car. "Everyone ready?"

"As we'll ever be," said Mike.

"One sec," muttered Shannon. She leaned forward in the seat and stared at Toby for the space of three breaths. "Okay. Poof, you're a prom queen, but without a prom dress circa 1976. I put you in modern clothes. Get busy."

"You made me Sissy Spacek? I hope you left the pig's blood out of the image." Toby arched an eyebrow at her, a wry grin dancing on his lips.

"Sissy Spacek? The actress? Pig's blood?" murmured Benny.

"Movie reference, Benny," said Shannon. She pointed at the house. "Go, Toby. This isn't as easy as it looks."

Toby nodded and turned toward the dirt road that led up to the house. The house sat on top of a hill, with a cleared space around it such that it had a good view of the road in both directions. He tried to climb the slope as he imagined a teenage girl would.

He was about halfway between the road and the house when the screen door creaked open and banged shut again. Toby lifted his gaze toward the house and plastered a fake smile on his face. The owner of the house was a demon, no doubt about it.

She stood about five and a half feet tall but had the blockish body of a Russian powerlifter—barrel-chested, chunky legs, long arms. Her skin was gray and thick like an elephant's but giving off a vague impression of tree bark. Her breasts were large and pendulous, and her belly was thick and round.

The demon's face was elongated, its bone structure out of scale with the rest of her. Her jaw was long and drooped down over her chest, giving her a perpetually shocked, open-mouthed expression, while gravity appeared to have stretched her cheekbones and ocular cavities such that her eye sockets were no longer almond-shaped, but elongated vertical ovals.

Toby couldn't see any details around her eyes or her mouth; what appeared to be black smudges or thick black smoke, obscured both parts of her face. "Great," he muttered.

The demon had German Shepherd ears, and they swiveled toward him as he spoke. "Who's there?" she asked in a querulous voice. "Whoever you are, I need nothing you have to sell. I won't buy anything."

Toby fought to keep a smile plastered on his face, wishing he could judge where she was looking—either at him or down at the road toward where they had parked the car. "I'm not selling anything, ma'am."

"Then why are you here? Who gave you permission to come onto my property?"

Toby gestured at the road behind him with his left hand, but in a vague, distracted way, keeping his right hand—and his paintball gun—hidden behind his back, just in case she could see through the illusion. "My car…" He continued walking, fighting the urge to glance back at the trees edging the road and hiding the rented Lincoln. He knew Mike and Scott were working their way through those trees, getting to the edges of the property and getting a better vantage on the demon.

"Stop!" the demon roared in a commanding voice. "I don't want visitors!"

That's strange, thought Toby. *Here I am, a helpless teenage girl—she should be salivating at the thought, not trying to drive me away.* Toby kept climbing the hill, acting as if he hadn't heard the demon's command. "My car is…broken. The doohickey came loose again. I can't…" Toby kept putting one foot in front of the other, shaking his head as if frustrated. "May I please borrow your phone?"

The demon lifted her too-long arms over her head and shook her fists at the sky. "Do I look as though I have a phone, missy? Do I look as though I care about your doohickeys and your car? Get out of here!"

Toby paused and lifted his gaze to meet the demon's. He plastered a woe-begotten expression on his face, then looked behind him at the road. "But there's no other house close. And no one comes out this way, not very often. I haven't seen a single other car since mine quit." He started walking again, holding the demon's gaze with his own.

"Your problem! I didn't invite you here. I don't care if there's no one else to help you. Leave! Leave now!"

Toby shook his head and pretended to sniff as if he were crying. "But…but I *need your help*!" he wailed. He was almost at the top of the small hill, virtually in the demon's front yard.

"I'm warning you! Stay away from me!"

*Can she see through it? Can she see through Shannon's illusion? Why is she…*scared? Toby slowed but kept his feet moving, trying to act like a confused teenager. He shot a glance behind him, back at the road, then turned back to face the demon once more. "Please help me."

"*Are you deaf, girly*?" screeched the demon. She took a threatening step toward Toby, raising her hands and hooking her fingers into claws, the visible parts of her face drawn into a mask of rage…and something else.

Fear? What else could provoke that display? Toby stopped and turned toward the woods on the opposite edge of the property. His eyes scanned the length of the trees, looking for Scott or Mike, but he saw nothing and no one.

He turned back to the troll-like demon. "Please!" He lifted his free hand, palm up as if entreating the beast to help. "My cell phone has no service. I can't… The car won't start."

The demon rumbled deep in her chest and took two rapid steps toward Toby. "I warned you, girly! Didn't I just?"

"I need your help!"

With a throaty roar, the demon charged toward Toby across the small front yard, her arms raised above her head and twisted to rake her thick fingernails across Toby's face. Without hesitation, Toby turned and sprinted away from the troll, moving away from the loose gravel of her drive.

He dove and rolled into the long grass at the top of the hill, coming to rest on one knee and bringing the paintball gun up as he did so. *Here goes nothing*, he thought and pulled the trigger. He set the gun for semiautomatic fire and watched the paintball arc away from him and slam into the demon's chest between her breasts.

She stumbled to a halt, swatting at the broken paintball casing. The acetone and bleach combined in an exothermic reaction, boiling into a gas that she inhaled. She pulled her head back and sneezed.

Toby fired, again and again, both paintballs zipping from the barrel of his gun to the troll's torso. Neither paintball went where he had aimed, but they hit nonetheless and added more chloroform gas to the breathing space around the demon.

"*What is this? How dare you come here and—*"

Toby flicked the switch that changed the paintball gun from semiautomatic fire to full automatic and squeezed the trigger for half a second. Four paintballs arced away from him, each following their own wobbling, off-kilter trajectory, but each one finding a part of the demon's body. With each new hit, the beast jerked, as if she expected more pain.

No, these aren't bullets. A savage grin distended Toby's face.

"Who *are* you?" The demon slowed and dropped her arms as if their weight had become too much for her to support. "Why are you doing this?"

Toby's answer was a one-second burst from the paintball gun. This time the last few rounds cut through the air over her shoulders and slapped into the trees at the edge of the drive. *Short bursts it is,* he thought. *Unless there's a bunch of them.*

The demon swatted at the spots where the acetone and bleach boiled, as if no more than a human woman slapping at bug bites. The troll staggered another step, then stopped. She turned her face toward Toby. "Are you… Are you the one? The *hunter*?" Her voice degenerated into a fearful whine.

Toby didn't answer but stood, holding the paintball gun loosely.

She flicked her fingers at him. "Why can't I see you? You are no teenage girl…I sniffed that out right from the start. And I smelled the thing—the *not-gun*—you keep shooting me with."

"Not being able to see who's attacking you is a bitch, isn't it?" Toby said. Maintaining distance, Toby walked around the troll-like demon. He glanced at the house, worried there might be other demons inside, but it was quiet, dead.

"When I…first heard about you…I stopped… Why have you…come…for me? I abstained…" The demon teetered forward and had to take a quick step to stop herself from falling on her face. "What is…" She flicked one of the wet spots on her flesh." What is…this…junk?"

"Chloroform," Toby said with a shrug. "Who else is in the house?"

"The house?" slurred the demon. She turned her head ponderously toward the porch. "I've been hiding…hoping you…would…pass me…by—" Her jaw snapped shut, and the demon fell forward, landing on her face.

"That was easy," said Toby. Even so, he leveled the paintball gun at the facedown demon and fired three short bursts at the area around her head. Wisps of gas danced around her.

"Is she out?" called Scott from the woods behind him.

"I don't know yet. But the chloroform seems to work."

Scott grunted from his hiding place.

"Keep an eye on her, Scott. I'm going to check out the house."

"You should let Mike and I do that," said Scott. We *are* trained for it, you know."

"Good enough," said Toby with a shrug. He squatted, holding the paintball gun across his knees, and watched the demon for telltale signs that she was playing dead.

Mike and Scott emerged from the woods, each slinging a shotgun over their shoulders and readying their own paintball guns. They met on the porch, and without a word, Scott kicked the door in, and they both charged through.

Toby fired a few more rounds, hitting the troll-like demon in the head. She didn't move, didn't even twitch. He fished the small walkie-talkie out of his back pocket and keyed its mic. "Bring the car up, Shannon. Good job, by the way."

"Benny said she could smell you."

"That's what she said. We'll work on it."

Down the hill, the Lincoln's V-8 rumbled to life, and its tires crunched gravel. From behind him came the sounds of Mike and Scott clearing the house, banging doors, up-ended furniture crashing to the floor. Toby shook his head and grinned.

"We're back in business," he said to the unconscious demon.

Chapter 3

1986

I

In the distance, Greg cried out, and though Joe tried to run faster, he'd reached his maximum. For the first time in his adult life, Joe felt unequal to the task before him. For the first time in his adult life, he felt lost—unsure of which direction to go, unsure what to do next.

He shook his head and tried to focus on getting to Greg. *He's all that matters,* he thought. *I've got to protect Greg.*

In the darkness ahead, a humanoid figure loomed. Joe slid to a stop, raised his rifle, and fired. He hadn't taken the time to control his breath or calm his pulse, so had to settle for a center of mass shot. But the round went high, clipping the woman in the shoulder and spinning her to the side.

The shriek of rage rang into the night.

"No! No, Grandpa!"

It was Greg's voice, and he was close by the sound of it. Joe shifted the rifle to high port. "Greg, where are you?"

"Go back, Grandpa! Don't let her get you!"

Joe shook his head. "Greg, she's not after me, she's after you! Stop running and come to the sound of my voice."

"Grandpa..."

The boy sounded exhausted, out of breath. The woman in black took a step toward Joe, and he snubbed the rifle butt to his shoulder once more and leaned into it a little. "Don't do it, lady!" He didn't understand how the woman was still moving. He couldn't have missed all those shots, and the likelihood that all those .308 rounds had hit her and not caused lethal damage was close to zero. But there was no denying the fact that she was still up and functioning—in truth, she didn't seem injured at all. *What the hell is going on here*?

The crazy woman came on, walking straight at him, as bold as she pleased. Joe squeezed off the two remaining rounds in the magazine, grimacing as her torso twitched from side to side with each impact. He ejected the magazine, trading it for the full magazine in his back pocket. He released the bolt and brought the rifle back up to firing position. The entire maneuver had taken mere seconds, but the black-swathed woman had vanished again. She'd disappeared without a sound.

Again.

"Where are you, Greg?" he shouted.

Greg didn't answer, but ahead dogs growled in warning.

2

Tom Walton passed the string of Genosgwa police cars and pulled in behind Gary Dennis's cruiser, then slammed the car into park. *This night is turning into a clusterfuck of epic proportions*! He got out of the car and opened the trunk, waving at the other officers to join him.

Tom took an AR-15 for himself and three of the magazines he'd loaded. He slipped two of them into his back pockets and rammed the other into the rifle. "There are six magazines for each AR, boys, but don't load yourself down with ammunition. I'm taking sixty rounds, and I figure that's enough to stop a small invasion, let alone this crackpot after the kids. If you end up with a shotgun, take a pocketful of extra shells."

Tom stepped away from the cruiser and walked toward the woods. Each AR-15 had a flashlight attached under the foregrip, and Tom switched his on, playing the beam across the trees closest to the road. One by one, the other officers joined him, and when they were all gathered together, Tom said, "We don't know much, but we know this: Gary Dennis, Joe Canton, and Stephen Canton all went into these woods tonight, following little Greg Canton. We don't know for sure that anyone else is in the woods, but each of those three men carried firearms. That means each of us needs to be hyper-alert and hyper-careful. I don't want any friendly fire incidents, men." He shook his head, plastering a mournful expression on his face. "The paperwork is such bullshit on that stuff." That earned him a chuckle from a few of the men.

"What's the plan, Chief?"

"The plan? The plan is simple. We line up about five yards apart, and we search every blessed inch of these goddamn woods. Stay within eyesight of each other *at all times.* The first one of you that breaks that rule earns both an ass-kicking and a month's worth of shifts on your least favorite schedule. Everyone clear on that?" When they all gave him a nod, Tom nodded back. "Good. We're going to maintain trigger discipline, and these firearms will stay on safe until I say different. Defend yourselves but make sure you are *defending* yourself if you fire." He stared into each man's face in turn, getting a nod from each officer before he moved on.

"Chief Walton? Is that you?" called Elizabet Canton from the kitchen door of her lake house.

"Yes, ma'am, it is, but I'm a mite busy at the moment. We are about to search these woods for your menfolk, so you'll pardon me if I don't take the time to speak to you right now."

"Well, okay, Chief. I expect you to update me before you leave."

"Of course." With that, Tom turned toward the woods then shot glances at the men on each side of him and stepped into the chilly darkness. The moon shone down on them, lighting up the surrounding forest, and they hardly needed their flashlights.

After twenty-five minutes, they emerged from the woods on the thin strip of grass bordering the shoulder of Lake Circle. They hadn't seen a thing—no boy, none of the men, no madman. Tom stood for a moment, not moving, just staring at the trees across the road. The forest on that side of the road was thicker, darker, and less well-traveled than the woods on the shore side of Lake Circle. "Gary wouldn't cross the road," Tom muttered.

"No, sir, he wouldn't do that," said Pete Martin. "I've only known him for three months, but that's enough time to get to know Gary pretty well. I guess if he were hot on the trail of someone…"

Without looking at him, Tom inclined his head and then turned back toward the woods they had just traipsed through. "Gather around, it's time for a palaver." He waited a few moments for his officers to gather in a circle. "Did any of you see anything at all? Broken branches or disturbed underbrush? Anything you discounted?"

Each of the officers shook his head.

"Now, that just doesn't make sense, does it? If it were just Greg and Stephen Canton, I could come to buy that they may have crossed this ribbon of blacktop, but Joe Canton? Gary Dennis?" Tom shook his head.

"What if they were chasing someone?" asked Martin.

"Or being chased," said Michael Arnold, the evening shift commander and senior officer.

Tom dropped his chin toward his chest. "Yeah. I guess that's a possibility, isn't it? But Gary would've radioed Shelly. Updated his position, at least."

"Maybe his handheld couldn't get a clear signal."

"That could be, Michael. Do we turn back and search these woods again, or do we cross this road and go on?"

Arnold shook his head and eyed the dark woods across the road. "It would be better to get Leland Chambers out here with his dogs than for the seven of us to head into those woods. We are too few, and that section of woods is too big."

Tom agreed with him and treated him to a terse nod. "We're going back through these woods toward the cars. This time, let's spread out more—say ten yards separation."

Tom led his men back into the woods, and at first, it seemed everything was the same as their first trip through the woods.

"I've got tracks here, Chief," said Mike. The trail he'd found turned out to be four sets of tracks—a set sized for an eleven-year-old boy, and three sets of adult footprints.

"Well, that makes things easier, doesn't it?" said Tom. "Good eyes, Arnold."

They followed the trail farther into the woods and, as if they'd crossed an invisible boundary, lost the sounds of the lake lapping against the shore and lost the moonlight behind a ceiling of mist. The forest seemed darker, and their flashlights seemed less effective. After another hundred paces, the tracks disappeared—as Stellan Stensgaard's footprints had on the other side of the lake.

Tom called a halt and motioned for his men to gather around. *This makes little sense. How can the tracks just…disappear as if they'd never existed*?

Tom turned and retraced his steps until he was out from under the mist. Once there, he turned back to his officers, but he could barely see them in the darkness. He didn't care for the feeling in his stomach, like a mild electric shock causing his guts to twitch and jerk.

Something was very wrong, but Tom had no idea what it was.

3

"Come away from the window, dear," said Elizabet. "There's nothing to see."

Mary nodded but didn't move away from the window. The muscles in her back and neck had snarled and locked so hard they felt like iron—as if she would never relax again. Elizabet was right, however, there *was* nothing outside to see. Only the black of night, the woods across the road, and seven abandoned cop cars.

"Come now, dear. Come rest. Tom and his men are very good at what they do. They will let us know as soon as there's anything to know."

Again, Mary lifted her chin and let it drop, this time accompanying the gesture with a gust of breath. *This is so frustrating*! She closed her eyes, praying silently that Stephen would find their son and bring him home whole. Mary opened her eyes, and when she did, something flickered at the edge of the trees across the gravel road.

She stared at the space where she'd seen the movement, but the flicker did not repeat. Mary forced herself to relax, forced her tense, rock-hard muscles to relax, and stepped away from the window. "I know you're right, Elizabet. I just can't help it."

Elizabet looked up at her with a compassionate expression on her face. She patted the sofa next to her with one hand and waved at the cup of tea resting on the coffee table with the other. "Come sit. The tea will make you feel better, I promise."

Whiskey might, but tea? Despite her thoughts, Mary walked over to the couch and sat. She picked up the teacup and sipped at the contents. *Chamomile. That figures.* Despite her worry, despite how tense she was, fatigue dragged at her. She opened her mouth with a jaw-cracking yawn.

"Why not nap, if you can, dear?"

Mary shook her head and looked at her mother-in-law askance. "I could never sleep."

"Try, dear. You'll do no one any good if you wear yourself out."

Mary uncoiled from the couch and paced the length of the room. Each time she neared the window that gave her a view of the woods across the gravel road from the house, she stared at it, hoping to see Greg, hoping to see Stephen, but each glance was a disappointment. "I have to do something, Elizabet! I can't just—"

"I understand, but there's nothing—"

"Don't say there's nothing I can do!" Elizabet snapped her mouth shut with an audible click and averted her gaze, but not before a flash of hurt splashed in her eyes. "Oh, forgive me, Elizabet. I'm not myself."

"There's nothing to forgive, dear. The stress of this…"

Mary spun about to pace in the other direction. When she reached the window, she peered out once more, expecting further disappointment.

Instead, the figure outside terrified her, and she screamed. Elizabet bolted to her feet, her hands covering her open mouth.

And then Mary laughed. "I'm sorry, Elizabet. For a moment, I thought…" Mary looked out the window again. "There's a man out there."

"One of the policemen—"

"No. Maybe he's a neighbor, but he looks to be about Joe's age. He looks too skeezy to be a cop."

"Oh?" Elizabet came to stand at her side and followed Mary's gaze, then shook her head.

"Do you recognize him?"

"Never seen him before in my life."

Ice descended Mary's spine. "Elizabet," she said in a placid tone. "Did you remember to lock the door after you spoke with the police chief?"

Elizabet turned to face her, her expression one of confusion tinged with fear. "Why, I…" She glanced toward the kitchen. "Why, I don't recall."

Mary didn't want to turn away from the man standing in the middle of the gravel lane, as if her gaze alone held him frozen. "Please go check."

Elizabet glanced out the window. "You don't think—"

"It's best to be on the safe side, isn't it?" She patted Elizabet on the shoulder. "Please go check any doors that may be unlocked."

Elizabet turned and nodded once as her husband was wont to do. "Of course, dear. I'll see to it."

As the older woman left her side, the old man turned his face to glare at Mary. There was something about him…something about his eyes that filled her with a nauseating fear. As emaciated as any anorexic, white hair floated around the man's head like a man's hat on a boy's head. He wore an old work shirt, with dark splotches down its front, as if he had stained it with both his lunch and his dinner. An old pair of chinos and a scuffed pair of black work boots completed his ensemble. He flashed a half-grin at Mary, but his eyes were cold, hard pebbles that seemed to bore into her. He wrinkled his nose as if they were sharing a pleasant moment while jerking his chin to the left, and at the same time, Mary heard a clicking noise—a noise a bird might make.

For a moment, Mary glimpsed what she had seen when she'd screamed moments before—a tall man, with black, shriveled skin like that of an undead thing in a horror movie. His skin hung from his frame as clothing three sizes too big would; his clawed hands rested on his hips. She opened her mouth to scream once more, but the man lifted a hand and shook his index finger at her as a schoolteacher might at an errant child, and the scream caught in her throat. Then, he flashed a broad smile, showing all his age-yellowed teeth, and the sight of it made Mary wish for blindness.

"Well, I'm glad you suggested I check. Someone left the kitchen door unlocked," said Elizabet from the other room. "I've locked it, so that old man can just move on down the road."

Mary's mouth hung open; her lips stretched in a silent scream. He brought his finger to his lips, shushing her. Once more, the man showed her his teeth in a ghastly smile and then winked, and then he was just an old man again. She squeezed her eyes shut, willing the man to disappear.

When she next opened her eyes, he had, and Mary breathed a sigh of relief. Her heart raced, and her stomach knotted.

"Why, Mary, dear," said Elizabet as she walked through the room toward the porch that hung on the back of the lake house, "you look as if you've seen a ghost!"

Mary twisted her head from side to side but kept her gaze centered on the window. "I'm…I'm not sure what I saw."

"Well, what's our chary man doing now?" Elizabet called.

"He's… he disappeared."

"Oh, he's gone. Which direction did he go? The Andersons down at the end of the lane might have their parents in to visit."

Mary shook her head. "No, I don't think that man has any business here."

"Well, what makes you say that, dear?"

Mary opened her mouth, but the sound of glass shattering and wood splintering preempted her. A moment later, Elizabet's scream reverberated through the house.

4

Red Bortha stood behind a thick tree trunk in the small yard between the Canton's lake house and the shore of Lake Genosgwa. The new arrival, the one calling himself Chaz Welsh, crouched in the flowerbeds next to the porch door, and the boy Brigitta had sent to "guide" them crouched near the side of the house, looking glum. If things were going according to plan, Herlequin had begun creating a stir on the other side of the house.

To Red, it seemed like a lot of effort for a meal, especially since food was there for the taking in any inner-city—no muss, no fuss. Then again, Herlequin had refined tastes, and perhaps that made it worthwhile. In any case, Herlequin was the strongest of them, and that gave him the right to dictate how things would go.

He tilted his head to peer around the tree trunk at the new arrival. *I never knew him on the other side. Never even heard of him*, Red thought. The demon didn't act as the youngsters did, but other than that, Red couldn't guess his age, his power. That Herlequin had selected him for the evening's festivities lent weight to his credibility.

Welsh had scaled skin and clawed digits, but no wings—not that any wings known to demonkind could have lifted his bulk into the air. His size rivaled the biggest of their kind—thick muscles, heavy bone structure, long limbs, and big hands and feet. *It would be interesting to fight him*, Red thought. *Perhaps I can imagine a…slight, an insult.*

As if he could read Red's mind, Welsh turned his eyes away from the door and sought Red's gaze. A smirk rested on his lips with the ease of an expression he wore often. Red narrowed his eyes and gave the other demon a slight nod of approval.

"Well, what makes you say that, dear?" The words came from just inside the door between the porch and the house and the smirk on Chaz's face stretched to become an evil grin. The big demon bounded up the steps, ripped the screen door from its hinges, and then charged the door into the house like a linebacker plugging a hole on Sunday afternoon.

Well, that settles that. Herlequin had commanded that only one of them deal with the two women inside the house. He wanted the other one in the woods across the street, as there were interlopers to deal with.

That was okay with Red. Women screamed too much, and the sound of it grated on his nerves. *Good riddance,* he thought and turned to shuffle through the side yard toward the gravel road, taking the boy by the arm as he passed him.

5

Greg skidded around the tree, keeping himself upright by pure luck, arms splayed apart, one hand fighting for purchase on the tree's bark, the other waving about as the bronco riders on television did. His gaze danced across the small glade, searching for any dog-things that might lurk behind the trunks on the opposite side. His breath ripped in and out of his chest, and each time he gasped for air, his throat made a coughing sound like the one Gollum made in *The Lord of the Rings.*

They weren't barking or howling, at least, and in the absence of the constant din, Greg could think. *Where do I go? How do I fix it?*

His invisible friend's harsh cackle filled his mind. *Oh, boyo, you do amuse me at times.*

"What?" gasped Greg.

Wasn't I clear before we started? Didn't I say that if you didn't lead her away, horrible things would happen? Did you listen?

Yes! I did everything you said! Why won't you help me? In the distance, his grandfather shouted his name.

His invisible friend's irritation scoured his mind as if someone were rooting around inside his skull with a Brillo pad. *Perhaps that is why.*

What? I told him to go home, I can't control him! It's not my fault!

Ah, sport. Does it matter if it is your fault or not? He's still here, and I warned *you what would result. No, your cause is beyond my help, now.*

"No!" shouted Greg, loud enough to hurt his throat. "No, I won't let you!"

In answer, the creepy dog-things howled from the dark forest around him.

"You make her stop!"

Well, kiddo, I'll tell you, I don't think you're in any position to give me commands. And what makes you think I control this situation, anyway?

It was a good question, and one that Greg didn't have a decent answer for, but he knew it was true, nonetheless. His so-called "invisible friend" was not the same thing as it had been in Florida. There were too many differences, too much bad advice, and too many suggestions that Greg, himself, would never consider, let alone do.

Ah, are we no longer friends, Greg? Have you turned against me?

No, I—

I can sometimes hear your thoughts, boyo. There's no sense lying.

I'm not lying! I haven't turned against you!

*Then why do I get the sense that you are...*plotting *something? Why do you hide your thoughts from me?*

I... I didn't even know I could do that. You are part of my imagination, aren't you?

Not for the first time when asked a question he didn't want to answer, Greg's invisible friend went silent.

Behind Greg, the pitter-patter of not-so-little feet sounded.

6

To Gary, it seemed the night would never end, that they would never make their way out of the woods, that

Stephen would never stop grumbling behind him. He'd taken the lead, not out of any sense of bravery or entitlement to command, but because Stephen was so reluctant to leave without his son and father that he had plodded along at the speed of a snail. At least leading, Gary could set the pace.

These woods aren't that big. We should've been able to walk out of here in under ten minutes. Gary shook his head, glancing both to the left and to the right, searching for something—*anything*—familiar. He hated to admit that he'd gotten lost in a chunk of woods that wasn't bigger than three acres. *A fella can walk edge to edge in these woods in ten minutes.*

"Hey! Over here!"

The owner of that voice was not Greg Canton—at least it didn't sound that way—but it *was* a boy. Gary stole a glance at Stephen over his shoulder, arching his eyebrows. Stephen lifted his shoulders and let them drop, shaking his head. The unfamiliar voice bothered Gary, but he couldn't put his finger on why.

"This way, you two idiots! You're walking in circles, you know that?"

"Who's there?" Gary called.

"Just follow the sound of my voice!" The voice had become that of an adult male.

Stephen stepped up beside him. "Tom Walton?"

Gary cast a scathing glance at the younger man. "Think I wouldn't recognize Tom's voice?"

Stephen's only answer was to hitch his shoulders up and let them fall.

"Are you coming? I'm not going to stand here all night."

"Whoever he is, we don't need to worry about him," said Gary, tapping the stock of Stephen's shotgun.

Stephen shrugged again and held the shotgun out to Gary. "You're the cop."

With a gruff nod of his head, Gary accepted the weapon, checked to make sure a shell was chambered and put his thumb on the safety. "Right. Stay behind me, Stephen."

Stephen's shoulders went up and down once more.

It irritated Gary, though it shouldn't have. The man was having one hell of an evening, and if Gary hadn't been so worried about his health and everything else on top of it, he would've handled that better. "Don't worry, Stephen. We're almost out. We'll get the rest of the police force out here in two shakes, and we'll scour these woods."

Stephen lifted his chin and looked Gary in the eye. "We better get to it."

"Right." Without another word, Gary turned on his heel and walked in the voice's direction. "Hey! Keep talking!"

"Finally! I thought I would have to leave you two!"

"This is Gary Dennis, GPD. Who's there?"

"Well, hi, Gary. Hurry, will you? You're almost here."

"Squirrely, ain't he?" muttered Gary to himself. Behind him, he heard the now-familiar rustle of Stephen's clothes as he shrugged.

7

After getting the two idiots on a path out of the woods, Red skimmed through the trees in eerie silence, hanging in the air like a wraith, enjoying the low-hanging mist, the darkness. The boy Brigitta had sent to help him lagged in his wake, smashing through the underbrush with as much noise as a bull would've created. Brigitta was up ahead, terrifying the child and dealing with the old man. Herlequin's other daughters split their time between driving the child away from everyone else and harrying the ailing cop and the child's father.

That was fine with Red. His skills went another direction, anyway. Besides, playing with a group of grown men was more his style. He would gain far more sustenance from the seven men tromping around in confusion than he would from a single boy and his grandfather—and truth be told, Red got the feeling the old man didn't fear much.

Red's specialized senses told him the position of every human in the woods. He grinned with all three of his mouths and circled wide around Brigitta's playground, leading Mason Harper to where Brigitta wanted him to be.

8

Tom Walton stepped back under the ceiling of mist, feeling as lost as he had ever felt in his life. None of it made any sense, not unless the rap he'd taken to his noggin had done more damage than he had imagined. He stepped up next to Michael Arnold. "What do you think?"

Arnold looked at him sidelong and drew a deep breath before shaking his head. "It's the damnedest thing, Tom. These tracks make no fucking sense."

Tom let his head droop forward until his chin almost rested against his chest. "And where has our trail gone? We just came through this section of woods not twenty minutes ago."

Michael removed his wide-brimmed hat and ran a hand over his bald head. "I'm glad you mentioned that, Tom. I was beginning to think…"

"Ayup. You didn't even smash your head into anything earlier tonight."

Arnold examined the strange mist hovering over their heads. "And what is that happy horseshit? You ever seen mist act that-a way?"

"Never in my life." Tom shook his head. "I'm of a mind that this trip into the woods was a terrible idea."

Shrill laughter rang through the surrounding woods, high-pitched and awful.

"What in the hell was that?" asked Pete Martin in a breathless voice.

"Hold it together, Officer!" snapped Arnold.

Tom's skin crawled as the trees absorbed the echoes of the eerie laughter. He couldn't decide which was worse, that nerve-grating *yuk-yuk-yuk*, or the absolute silence that followed. *Don't care for this one bit,* he thought. He looked at his men, and they all returned his gaze, waiting for him to decide what they should do. "Listen up, whoever is out there, I'm Tom Walton, chief of Genosgwa's Police Department. I'm out here on official business, and we are armed. This is not the time to play jokes. Come out!"

No one answered him, and the utter silence of the woods around them put Tom's nerves even further on edge. He had that hinky feeling in his guts again as if eyes tracked his every move. Eyes of men with evil intent.

"Where is the boy?" he called.

As before, there was no answer, but far away, Tom imagined he could hear dogs howling and barking. He glanced at Michael Arnold and lifted an eyebrow.

"Ayup," the man whispered.

From behind them, something roared, sending ice down Tom's spine like an express elevator. It sounded the same as the African lion in the Rochester zoo. "Circle!" Tom snapped. His men gathered in a circle, their backs to one another, each man facing out. "Safeties off." As he thumbed his own safety off, six clicks sounded around him.

9

As the dog-things came up behind him, Greg sprinted across the glade. There was no moonlight, of course. The mist obscured all that. As he re-entered the woods on the other side of the clearing, a hand reached out and grabbed him, jerking him to the side and almost off his feet. A little yelp of fear escaped Greg's lips.

Joe Canton turned his grandson to face him and put one finger to his lips. Using the same finger, he pointed at the surrounding darkness. In his other hand, he held the scary-looking rifle, its butt resting on his hip, its barrel pointing up at the mist. “Now, don’t you worry about that,” whispered Joe. He lifted his gaze from his grandson and scanned the darkness surrounding them but saw nothing. He pulled the boy close and gave him a hard hug. “Ayup. I don’t understand what you were thinking, Greggy, but I’m here now. Whatever is happening, I’ll sort it out.” The boy burst into tears, surprising Joe into silence. “Now, now, Greggy. What’s wrong?”

Greg sobbed louder. “Oh, Grandpa! Now, it’s all screwed up! I can’t stop her! She’s going to—”

“Hey, now. It’s okay, Greg. I’ve got you, and if anyone thinks they will get to you without one hell of a fight, well, they ain’t got the sense God gave a grasshopper.” He patted the boy on the shoulder. “Don’t you worry.” Canton swiveled his head from side to side, scanning the darkness for threats.

“Grandpa! You have to listen. You have to!”

“We don’t have much time, Greg. Whoever that woman is—”

“The Lady in the Lake!”

“What, now? The Lady in the Lake? Greg, put that out of your mind. That fat cow should’ve never mentioned it to you.”

"No, Grandpa. I already knew. I already knew all about her. She was the one who grabbed the kayak!"

"Greggy, it's just a *story*. A bit of fun, nothing more."

Greg rocked his head back and forth. "No! Grandpa, she's real. She's…she's a zombie or something, and she lives at the bottom of the lake. She's after me! She's…she's mad because I—"

"Greg, don't carry on so!"

"—hit her with the kayak paddle. My invisible friend says she—"

In the distance, someone moved through the underbrush. He gripped Greg's shoulder and squeezed it twice. "Later," he muttered. His grandson shook his head, but Joe squeezed his shoulder again. "Listen, Greg. This is important. Chances are, I'll have to shoot this noisemaker here, and I can't do that unless you're safe. That means you've got to follow a couple of rules. You listening?"

Greg nodded, but his gaze kept tripping away to scan the woods.

"Okay, listen good. I need you behind me, I need your hand gripping my belt. You stay close to me; you don't let go of my belt. Deal?"

"Yes, Grandpa. But I have to tell you something."

"No time for that now, Greg." He took his grandson's hand and put it on his belt over the pocket where he kept his wallet. "You hold on right there, Greg. If something is coming up behind us, give me a tug. Okay?"

Greg nodded, looking miserable.

"Give her a try."

Moving mechanically, Greg tugged on his grandfather's belt twice in rapid succession. "Grandpa, the Lady in the Lake, she's trying to keep us from leaving tomorrow. She's the one out here—"

"I've seen the lady dressed in black, Greg. It's just a woman playing tricks. Now, no more of this. I've got to concentrate on getting us out of here, and you've got to concentrate on staying behind me, on keeping up." Joe treated his grandson to a stern glance. "And from now on, Greg, no more of this running off when I call you. Do you understand me?"

With a sigh, Greg nodded, his gaze straying to the darkness once more.

Joe set off at a brisk pace, moving in the opposite direction from where he'd last heard the dogs braying at the moon—or whatever they were howling at. He hadn't seen the woman in black for a while, and he hoped he would see no more of her that night.

10

"Elizabet?" Mary ripped her gaze from the now-empty window, staring toward the back of the house, toward the porch door. "Elizabet!"

Her mother-in-law's shrieking died, and a wet gurgling replaced it.

She took two mincing steps toward the porch, but then threw a glance over her shoulder and out the window. The decaying man had returned, this time baring his tusk-like fangs in an evil grin. "Go away!" Mary shouted. The man threw back his head and shrieked laughter at the moon.

From the hall leading back to the porch came the sounds of feeding time at the zoo. Mary forced her legs through two more steps in that direction and tried to force the image of the man with the decaying skin from her mind. "Elizabet?" she whispered.

A harsh growl answered her—again, something she would have expected at the zoo during feeding time. *Could it be an animal? A bear, perhaps?* She thought Joe had mentioned bears when he spoke about walking in the woods, but she couldn't remember.

Her gaze danced toward the pantry, toward the gun safe hidden behind its shelves. She didn't remember if

Stephen had closed it. Almost as if her body were moving on its own, she took a step in that direction.

From the hall that led to the porch, Elizabet gasped and released a long, ragged breath. It sounded as if she were trying to speak, trying to call for help, and Mary forced her feet to move toward the bestial grunting. Fear vibrated through her nerves, and her fingers shook with it. Her throat had gone dry—as dry as it had ever been in her memory—and it hurt to swallow. Summoning even a hint of saliva hurt and burned deep in her throat.

Elizabet grunted as if she were trying to lift something beyond her strength, and a ragged, shrieking variant of laughter followed it.

Mary's mind painted the picture in her head—Elizabet pinched to the floor by a huge bear, her mother-in-law trying to push the bear away while the bear threw his head from side to side, batting her hands away. *Stop standing here doing nothing, you silly bitch*! Do *something*! But still, Mary stood there like a lump of clay, her gaze bouncing back and forth between the hallway and the pantry.

No plans or ideas sprang to mind, as if her mind had gone on vacation and forgotten to notify her. If a bear were mauling Elizabet, there was nothing she could do, though she remembered news stories about people banging pots together to scare them away. *Try that*!

Her paralysis broke, and Mary dashed around the breakfast bar that separated the living room from the kitchen. Her goal hung over the stove—the pot rack—but as she ran, she threw a glance into the pantry. The lights still blazed inside, and the door which hid the safe stood thrown back, but the gun safe was closed, or nearly so.

Reaching above her head, Mary grabbed a large saucepan and one of Elizabet's prized cast-iron skillets. She began to beat the skillet with the pot before she even turned back toward the hall. With another short glance at the pantry, Mary dashed toward the porch door, hammering the skillet as she ran.

The noise was horrible, akin to an ongoing auto accident, and to it, Mary added her own shouts of "Go away!" and "Get off her!" The horrible sounds from the hall continued, but Elizabet made little—if any—contribution to them. *If she dies because I dithered here, unable to figure out what to do, Stephen will never forgive me*!

She rounded the corner into the hall and froze in her tracks, holding the saucepan in the air as if ready to hammer the skillet once more. Her jaw dropped open as she saw the thing crouching over Elizabet.

A pool of sickening gore—a mixture of blood and other bodily fluids—spread beneath her mother-in-law. Elizabet's head was thrown back as if she'd been looking for Mary, looking for help that hadn't come in time. Her expression was one of terror, shock, and immense pain. Her eyelids had peeled back, showing the sclera all the way around her irises. A single drop of blood rested in the inner corner of her left eye.

Mary's head tracked upward, and when her gaze met the inhuman all-red eyes of the thing crouching over her mother-in-law, her grip loosened and both the saucepan and the skillet clattered to the floor. The thing opposite her smirked and then winked one scaly eyelid. *Some kind of… Is it real? Can it be what it looks like? Or have I gone insane?*

The thing was huge—seven feet tall if it was an inch, and his shoulders stretched as wide as two professional football players standing shoulder to shoulder. Immense muscles rippled beneath its mother-of-pearl scaled skin. Razor-sharp talons tipped its thick, horrible fingers, and they made a clicking noise as the thing waggled its fingers at her.

Mary stood frozen, mouth agape, urine running down her left leg as the thing approached her. It walked through the gore, stepping on Elizabet's excoriated torso. As it came on, it waggled its fingers and drew her attention to its groin—*his* groin.

Mary averted her gaze, but it was too late. She knew the thing intended to rape her. *Run! Don't just stand here like a stupid cow*! She glowered at her own feet, but they seemed glued to the floor.

She raised her head and looked at the thing's face, and the expressions—a mix of greed, lust, and carnal satisfaction—she saw there turned her fear of the monster into outright terror.

"*Run…*" gasped Elizabet, her breath rattling in her chest as she tried to speak. Mary turned and sprinted for the kitchen.

Chapter 4

2007

I

Shannon pulled the car up the driveway and parked next to the demon's body. Benny popped the trunk from the little switch in the glove box, and they both got out.

Benny whistled, his eyes on the demon. "She's a looker!"

Shannon cleared her throat and gave Benny the stink eye.

"It's all clear inside," said Scott from the open front door of the troll's house.

Sitting in the front lawn with the unconscious body of the demon, Toby grunted, then bobbed his head. "I figured it'd be empty, given what she said."

"And what was it she said?" asked Benny, stealing a glance at Shannon, a stricken expression on his face.

"Dude, she's kidding." Mike came outside to stand on the rickety front porch. "We need to get you subtitles or something."

Benny grinned and pointed at Mike. "Gotcha!"

"What did she say, Toby?" asked Scott.

"She said she'd 'stopped,' and by that, I assume she meant she'd stopped feeding, stopped hunting humans." With a casual grace, Toby rose to his feet and fired two more chloroform-balls at the demon's face. "We can't take her back to the university."

"Why would she have stopped?"

Toby glanced at the house. "Does this place have a big basement?"

Scott nodded.

"It's about as big as the footprint of the ground floor," said Mike. "Why?"

"No university means no industrial digester. That means we need another way of disposing of the flesh."

"Why would she have stopped?" repeated Scott.

Toby hitched his shoulders skyward and let them drop. "She asked me if I was the…how did she put it? *Hunter*. She asked if I was the hunter, then she said all the business about how she stopped and asked why I had come for her."

"Hmmm. You've got a reputation with the ladies, Toby." Shannon threw a wink in Toby's direction before walking over and kicking one of the demon's feet. "Should we wake her up and interrogate her? She might be more amenable than Hartman was. She hasn't seen me—I could pretend to be a Brigitta-clone again."

Toby shook his head. "No, it's not worth the risk. If we learned anything from Hartman, it's that these demons are more likely to lie to us than give us any useful information, and at any moment, everything can go south." Toby shook his head once more. "No, if you ask me, our days of trying to interrogate these things are finished. Besides, we've got Benny."

"But, Toby, it wasn't Hartman that brought all those demons down on us," said Scott. He jumped down from the porch, eschewing the stairs. "That was LaBouche, and you know it."

"Yes, but what did we really learn from Bill Hartman?"

"We learned about the Passage. We learned about the first one to cross to…well, to come here." Shannon crossed her arms over her breasts.

"Yeah, but is any of that true?" said Mike.

"It's obvious by his escape that Hartman could've gotten out of those chains at any time, and yet he pretended otherwise. Why? Was it to sow disinformation? Did he see through your disguise? Or, as this one did, did he smell that you were human? We don't know the answers to those questions. But he might have known. And if he knew, that means everything that he told you was also part of his act."

Shannon pressed her lips into a thin line and shook her head. "No, he *believed* me."

"Maybe it only *appeared* he believed you." Scott walked toward the car. "Come on, Shannon, we've got to go shopping." He turned his gaze to Toby. "What is it you need to get rid of this hunk of rotten meat?"

"The industrial digester works by pressurizing sodium hydroxide, then heating it. We won't be able to pressurize anything, not without making a huge vessel like the industrial digester and then rigging up a compressor or something." Toby tilted his head to the side. "No, let's go old school. We'll need a big cast-iron tub, lye, and a big heat source. Or we could use fifty-gallon drums, but we need to boil the lye, or it will take forever."

Scott looked down the length of the Lincoln. "I don't see how we'll get a cast-iron tub in this thing. We could get a fifty-gallon drum in the back seat."

Toby's expression soured. "If we use a drum, it'll mean dismembering her."

"No, I've got an idea," said Mike. "Get two barrels, then go to one of the box stores for the lye, and while you're there pick up an angle grinder with cutting wheels and a cheap welder with the accessories that go with it."

Toby turned to face him and arched his eyebrows.

"Have you ever seen one of those big mobile barbecues? The kind made from barrels? They cut off the ends and weld the couple of them together."

Toby cracked a smile, and his eyes twinkled. "That's thinking with your dipstick, Jimmy."

"Jimmy? Why did you call Mike—"

"It's from a commercial, Benny. Don't worry about it."

Benny drew a deep breath and blew it out in exasperation. “Maybe I do need subtitles.”

“Come on, Benny-bear,” said Shannon. “Go shopping with Scott and me.”

“*Benny-bear*?” said Toby before laughing.

Benny winced but said, “Don’t be jealous, Toby.”

Mike shook his head, looking down to hide his grin. “Don’t worry, *Benny-bear*, we are not jealous of that nickname.”

With a sigh, Benny turned and got in the car.

“Come on, Toby. I’ll help you get this big thing down into the basement.”

“Okay.” Toby bent to grab the troll-demon’s arms but then straightened. “Get something to catch all the blood.” He looked down at the demon. “Something big.”

“Roger,” said Scott, sliding behind the wheel of the Lincoln.

“Are we going to go back to the hotel?” asked Shannon.

Toby shrugged. “Any reason not to?”

“We could use this,” said Shannon with a glance at the demon’s house. “Would they ever expect it? Us, living in the demon's house?”

“It would be cheaper, Toby,” said Mike. He swept his arm toward the vista. “Plus, it’s defensible as hell.”

“Not a bad idea,” said Toby. “We’ll just have to be careful.” He held up an index finger as would a father lecturing a group of children. "We'll have to make sure no one follows us. That no one sees us come here. Otherwise, it will be for nothing."

2

Dan Delo grumbled as he ascended into the overcast sky. LaBouche had given him *errands* to run. Errands!

He's gone soft in the head! The old bastard has lost his mind if he thinks I will sit still for this.

As he spiraled toward the bruise-colored clouds, he happened to glance down. Below him, a child stood in the center of Neibolt Street, pointing up at him. Cursing himself for his stupidity, Dan Delo created a mask of invisibility.

I've got to calm down. Dan Delo wagged his head back and forth, grimacing at his mistake. *LaBouche has me so pissed I'll get myself sent back.*

He dropped his left wingtip and swept through the sky, racing the wind and the rain toward Lake Ontario and the five demons living there that LaBouche had commanded he speak to.

3

"One problem with being way out here in the boonies is that there's no way to get good Internet access," said Toby over dinner.

"Eww. Porn," said Shannon with a grin.

Toby rolled his eyes and shooed her away.

"Why do you need Internet access?" asked Mike.

"There's a lot of information out there. There're a lot of things I can do, can check on, with Internet access. Plus, there's the whole issue of money."

"Money?" asked Scott.

"Yeah, money. I have plenty—enough to support all of us—but it's not liquid. I'll need to free it up."

"But can't your Internet activity be traced?" asked Mike.

"And why do we need you to support us?" asked Scott. "I've got a job, remember? One I want to get back to."

"I remember, and I'll bet LaBouche remembers, too. You can't go back, Scott. Not until—"

"I can't go back? No, that's not part of the bargain. I *love* my job. I enjoy putting assholes like Abaddon in jail."

"And I've got an interview with them coming up," said Mike.

Toby folded his arms across his chest. "How do you think my apartment got blown? Why were all those demons at the university? Why is it I went for ten years with no one finding me, and now demons are all over my shit? Isn't it possible that LaBouche followed one of you? He is a bird, for Christ's sake."

Scott nodded, his expression resting in agreeable lines. "And a little one. Even if he is bright yellow."

"*Exactly*. So how do you expect to go back to work? How do any of you expect to go back to your normal lives, when there's a chance that LaBouche knows all about them?"

Shannon frowned at him.

"And don't pretend I'm the bad guy."

"So, you blame us for losing your safe spots?" Shannon arched her eyebrow and tilted her head to the side. "You hold that against us?"

"No, of *course* I don't."

Shannon inclined her head toward him and stared him in the eye.

"Okay, okay. I admit to being irked, but I'm not holding it against any of you." Toby spread his arms wide and then put his hands face down on the table on either side of his plate. "Herlequin ruled the demons here. He was their monarch, their *king*. When we killed him, we declared war—at least that's how they will see it."

"Why? You've been killing them for years, right?"

"True, and they've *never come after me*. But now they are. They're coming after each of us. If you think nothing will change, I'm sorry to tell you you're wrong. Everything has changed."

"I can take more bereavement leave, but leaves are finite, Toby. I'll have to go back sooner or later." Scott leaned forward and rested his chin in the palm of his hand.

"The key phrase is *sooner or later*, Scott. How long that period lasts depends on how well we can take this war to the demons."

"Couldn't I just go with Scott and keep him disguised?" asked Shannon.

"All day? How would he explain your presence? Plus, how can he walk around as a trooper while disguised as someone else?"

"Toby, stop being dense," said Benny. "That's my role."

"I wouldn't need to go with him all day. All we need to do is disguise him until he's inside the building and when we pick him up at night."

Toby tapped the edge of his index finger against his front teeth. "Risky. I'd need to go along—to make sure LaBouche, or some other demon, wasn't there watching, just waiting for Scott to arrive. We'd have to—"

"Why would it matter?" asked Benny.

"Good job picking up your role again." Toby grinned to take out the sting. "Look at it this way: Scott's walking through the hall at the barracks, heading for the parking lot to leave, and poof! He no longer looks like Scott, but the demon twenty feet behind him saw the change and *knows* it's Scott. All he has to do is follow the man who no longer looks as Scott should." Toby frowned. "But none of that matters, anyway. Scott's job isn't to sit in an office. He works outside the barracks most of the time, and we're right back to Shannon tagging along all day."

"Oh," muttered Benny. "That's a good point."

"I'm glad you agree."

Scott pursed his lips. "I can extend my bereavement leave, but I'm not making any promises past that. I'm not ready to give up being a cop, Toby." He leaned back in his chair, and it creaked with the shifting of his weight. "I'm not ready to throw away my seventeen-year career."

Toby combed his fingers through his hair and tapped his foot. "Well, I guess it will have to do. Do me a favor, though, huh?"

With a shrug, Scott bobbed his head. "What?"

"Let me know before you go back to work so I can get the hell out of here."

Shannon slumped forward and rested her forehead on the table in front of her plate. "Oh, don't be that way, Toby," she groaned.

"We're in this together," said Mike. "Mostly, because of you, Toby."

Toby shrugged and shook his head, looking at Scott through narrowed eyelids. "I'm not pissy, Shannon. And, yes, I brought you all into this, Mike. My point is, *I don't want to die at the hands of a demon.* I appreciate Scott's position, I really do, but again, I don't want to die."

"Toby, I'm sure we can work something out," said Benny in a slow and methodical manner. "We will not go behind your back."

Toby looked at each of them coming to rest with his gaze on Benny's face. "You and Shannon know what is at risk as much as I do. You've been through it." He shook his head and bared his teeth at the memory of his ordeal in the Thousand Acre Wood. "I started all of this—the tracking and killing of these demons—without knowing why I was doing it. It was... It was a compulsion, I guess. Something in my subconscious that remembered what happened back then. Before I regained my memories, I might've been able to walk away from this, but now, I can't. Someone has to drive these evil motherfuckers away. Someone has to send them back to Hell." Again, his gaze bounced between each of them, and again, it came to rest on Benny. "If they kill us all sitting around this table because we've been stupid, there is no one else, and they will go on terrorizing kids, raping and torturing people, all of it. I'm not willing to risk that for Scott's career."

"We don't know that we're the only people aware of their existence, Toby," said Mike. "There may be others out there, as you said yourself back in the restaurant."

Toby nodded. "I hope there are, and I hope we can find them, *teach* them. But let's be honest, the events that brought all of us together were serendipitous. If Scott and LaBouche hadn't come and told me about Oneka Falls, I would've never gone there. I had no reason to." He held up a hand to forestall Benny's interruption. "Sure, sure. I might have tracked a demon there and found the nest on my own, but Benny wouldn't have been there. Mike may have no longer been there, and without the two of you to goose my memory into gear, I may never have remembered my childhood. I might've gone on believing I was Benny Cartwright hiding behind alias after alias. And more to the point, we wouldn't have fought Red Bortha together. Herlequin would still be alive. I couldn't have killed him on my own."

The room was silent for the space of five breaths after Toby finished, each member of the cabal lost in their own thoughts for the moment. Then Scott leaned forward and cleared his throat. "I get it," he said. "You've made your point, Toby, and for now rest assured I'm not going to be going back to work. But—"

"We need to make it work," finished Benny. "Scott is valuable to us, not only because he's good with his weapons, but *because* he's a New York State Trooper."

Toby slumped back in his chair and grinned. "Yes." He inclined his head toward Scott. "We'll try to figure it out, Scott. I have no idea how, but we will try." He glanced at his watch. "Time to go check the *pozole*." He pushed himself away from the table, his chair scraping across the unfinished pine floor.

"*Pozole*?"

Toby grinned. "Yeah. I got the idea for our digester down there in the basement from a news story on the drug cartels. *Pozole* is the name of the traditional Mexican stew. It's what the cartels call it when they dissolve bodies this way."

"Eww, gross!" Shannon turned her face away, grimacing.

4

Dan Delo spiraled in toward the house on the hill. His last chat hadn't gone well, and his ego still stung from the reproach served by the demon he'd just left. *Idiot believes he can sit the war out. Idiot thinks LaBouche will stand for that.*

He shook his head and cupped his wings to slow his descent. Dan landed on the hill in front of the house, his thick thigh muscles taking the shock of landing in stride. He glowered at the home, his glowing azure eyes bouncing from window to window, checking to see if he was being observed.

Satisfied he wasn't, he dropped his cloak of invisibility and adopted his standard human visage. The house had seen better days: dressed in peeling paint, warped siding, rotting steps leading up to the rotting porch. He detested when demons let things go; it showed a distinct lack of confidence, of belief in the superiority of demonkind.

"Why would LaBouche want a sad sack like this?" he muttered as he climbed the steps. A tread cracked beneath his weight, and his foot sank through the rotten wood. "Damn lazy asshole!"

"Well, that's not very nice, is it?"

Delo's head snapped up, his gaze bouncing between curtained windows. "Who's there?" Either boredom or the shock of his foot going through the step had erased the name of the demon he was there to check in on.

"That's a little rude, fella. You've come to visit me, not the other way around. You're on *my* porch."

A strange odor drifted to his nostrils on a puff of wind. Dan couldn't place it, but it disturbed him, made him wary. "My name is Dan Delo," he said, plastering a smile on the face of his visage. "Your cousin, Lee LaBouche, sent me around to check on you." His gaze tracked to every shadow, every place someone might hide.

Nothing. He swallowed and wrinkled his nose at the scent in the air.

"That old bastard LaBouche sent you, did he? How is that yellow-scaled monkey?"

Delo nodded and hunched his shoulders, unfurling his wings in case he needed a rapid getaway. Not that he feared the human hunters, but they had trapped Herlequin after all. "Show yourself."

"No, I'm more comfortable where I am. What does LaBouche want?" The aroma on the air was strange, partially sweet, partially sickening. It carried an air of decay about it but held the bouquet of fresh blood.

"Ah, you smell her. Does the fragrance delight you?" The voice contained a note of mockery that set Dan Delo's nerves on edge. The owner of the voice laughed. "She was quite enjoyable. She put up a grand fight. Had you been but a few minutes earlier, I would have shared." When Delo didn't reply, the voice said, "Come now, demon. There's no need to be so tense."

Dan adopted a loose posture but didn't relax. "Will you not come out?"

The silence stretched for the space of a few breaths, then the door opened, exposing a darkened maw of a foyer. "I shan't, but you are welcome to come inside."

Delo eyed the darkness but didn't move. *Could be a trap*, he thought. But he was almost sure that he spoke to another of his kind rather than one of the tricksy human hunters.

"Come now, there's no reason to fear. I don't bite." Raucous laughter sounded inside the house. "At least that's what I told her right before I bit her."

He stood silent, his glowing azure eyes focused on the darkness.

Inside the house, the demon sighed. "Is that it, then? Has LaBouche instructed you to give me a message?"

Dan Delo straightened, trying to seem even more massive than he was. He was not considered an alpha—not *yet*—despite his apparent traits that supported the idea. "LaBouche gives me no instructions. I am here as a favor."

A snide chuckle sounded from within the darkness. "Oh, I'm sure."

Delo bristled and dropped his visage. "Look upon me, then, and disrespect me at your hazard."

The demon inside made no answer.

"That's better!" Delo spat. "LaBouche commands you—*commands*, mind you—to return to Oneka Falls.

Once there, you will report to Chaz Welsh in the Oneka Falls Town Hall, who will command you further."

Again, the demon inside the house had no response.

"Indicate that you've heard me."

"Oh, I heard you."

"Then my duty here is done. Disrespect me further, and I will show you no mercy."

"Yes…I see."

Dan Delo stared into the darkness, trying to decide if the demon were mocking him without response. He narrowed his eyes but still couldn't penetrate the darkness. He whirled, jumped from the steps into the air, and flew away.

5

Mike found a spot in the front parking lot of the Ontario County Public Library and shifted the Lincoln into park. "Your destination, sir," he said, putting on his best snooty butler-voice.

"Why thank you, James," Toby said with a grin before turning to Shannon. "Are you ready?"

"I wish you'd let Benny come with us."

"You need to develop confidence in your ability. You can't do that if Benny is always around to backstop you."

Shannon nodded but didn't appear convinced. "Yeah, I know. And to answer your question, I'm ready, and so are you."

"Good. Just two friends going to the library, right?"

"Two friends who share no common features with Toby or Shannon."

"Good enough." They each opened their door and got out. Toby stepped to the driver's side window. "Remember to come on the run as I won't be calling for help to test the walkie-talkie."

Mike rolled his eyes. "Go on, Mr. Bossy-pants."

Wearing a faint grin, Toby walked around the front of the car and met Shannon on the sidewalk. "Remember, Shan, if there're demons inside, I'll tell you, but they won't be able to see through your illusions. Not any more than any of the other demons could."

"And the scent? What if that doesn't work?"

Toby twitched his shoulders and flashed a grin at her. "If it doesn't work, it doesn't. We'll cross that bridge if we ever come to it. Come on, though, let's stop wasting time in the parking lot. I've got me an Internet to find the end of."

Shannon waved him forward with a sweep of her hand. "Lead on, Macduff."

"It's Burton."

"Har, har," said Shannon with a long-suffering air.

Inside the library, the aromas typical to libraries everywhere assaulted them—dust, old books, and old carpet—but there was something else, too. Something not identifiable, something that hid underneath the other odors.

"Can I help you?" asked the librarian behind the check-out desk. Her name tag read "Connie Parsons."

"Yes, my friend here thinks he needs to get on the Internet. Do you have access?" Shannon put on her best smile.

"Oh, of course. This *is* 2007." Connie smiled back at Shannon. "Our desktops are right over here."

Toby and Shannon followed the librarian through the racks of periodicals and past empty worktables to a bank of cubicles along the far wall. In each cubicle sat an old Macintosh.

"We only have Macs. I hope they will do."

"Anything with a web browser is fine, Connie," said Toby with a small grin.

"Well then, there you are." Connie patted Shannon on the forearm. "I hope you don't mind me saying, but you two make such a cute couple."

Shannon blushed but bobbed her head and dimpled. "Thank you."

Toby seemed not to have noticed, and he pulled out the cubicle's only chair and sank into it. The librarian tsked and pulled over a chair from the neighboring cubicle and offered it to Shannon before returning to the main desk near the front doors.

By the time Toby had woken the machine up and started a web browser, it had already bored Shannon. She let her eyes wander around the library, examining the art that festooned the walls, and counting the stacks that led to the back of the building.

An old man stared at them from across the room, and Shannon offered him a polite smile. The man didn't smile back, and Shannon looked away. She continued to scan the items in the library, and every time her gaze passed the old man, he was staring at them. "Toby," she said.

"Hmmm? Almost done."

"There's a man over there. He's staring at us."

"Well, you are gorgeous," said Toby in an offhand manner as if everyone knew it were true.

Shannon blushed to the roots of her hair. "Thanks," she said in a small voice. "He's staring, but not as a man stares at a woman. More like how a man stares at a cheeseburger."

"Cheeseburger?" said Toby. "I'm almost done, Shan."

Shannon hummed to herself and tried to steal glances at the man, but his intense stare lingered on her. "Toby," she said again.

"Still watching?"

"Yes. Still *staring* at us."

Toby stretched and yawned, and as he did so, he gazed at the old man for a moment. "Ah," he said.

"What? Ah, what?"

Toby clicked a few more buttons. "He's a demon."

"Can he… You don't think he can see through my—"

"No, he's hunting. Hungry."

"You can tell all that with one quick glance? How?"

Toby shrugged and closed the browser. "All done. And how? I've been doing this for ten years. Hunting demons, tracking them as they hunt their prey. He's lost to the hunt right now. Lost in the expectation of what's to come. He can't think of anything else, and he stopped trying to act human. That's why he's staring the way he is."

"Oh."

Toby stood and pushed his chair in under the cubicle's desk. "Let's go. Try to act casual. Don't let on that we know anything," he whispered as she stood.

She nodded once but couldn't resist stealing another glance at the demon pretending to be an old man. "Is he…"

Toby put his hand on the small of her back and pushed her gently toward the door. "He's one of the weirds. You should be glad that you can't see them, old-parchment-like skin, extra arms, hooves. But we don't want him following us, so shake a leg, Shan."

They walked toward the door, and the librarian looked up and smiled. "My, aren't you efficient?"

Toby flashed a grin at her but didn't stop to chat.

"Are you two new to the area?" Connie stepped out from behind her desk.

With a sigh he tried to mask with a fake cough, Toby stopped and turned so he could see both the librarian and the demon. "Yes, we're from the Southern Tier. We moved here a week ago."

The librarian smiled. "Oh, isn't that nice? Tell me, have you decided on a church?"

"No, not yet."

"Well, in that case, I'd like to invite you to my church. I attend the Methodist Church up by the lake. It's exquisite and relaxing. Plus, we are more open than some other faiths."

Shannon tilted her head to the side, a confused grin on her lips. "More open?"

The librarian blushed a little and lifted her shoulders in a self-conscious way. "I hope you don't mind, but I saw neither of you is wearing wedding rings. It would bother no one at my church. That's all I'm saying."

"Oh," said Shannon.

"It's an antiquated notion in today's society, and people your age don't much cotton to the idea, but some in this town would look down on you for living together without being married." The woman's blush deepened.

"Listen to me, prattling on like an old hen. The invitation's open any time."

"And we thank you for it, Connie," said Toby. He rested his hand on Shannon's arm. "We do need to run, though."

The librarian smiled, and Shannon thought she looked a little hurt, but the old man had gotten up from his table and was walking toward the doors. "It was sweet of you, Ms. Parsons," said Shannon. "Have a good evening."

As they turned toward the door, the librarian said, "A good evening to you."

They pushed out into the dusk of the coming evening. "Let's get to the car, quick!" said Toby and set off walking fast. After a few steps, he glanced upward and stopped dead in his tracks and threw a glance over his shoulder, then back into the sky. "Oh, shit," he muttered.

"What is it?"

"*Run*!" Toby grabbed her arm and sprinted toward the car.

6

Dan Delo peered down in the gloaming as the old demon came out of the building. Two humans stood on the sidewalk, and the ancient beast by the doors stared at them. Chances were, the old one belonged to the group of demons LaBouche had sent him to find, and Delo began to spiral in for a landing in the grass next to the building.

The hunt had enraptured the demon below—a sure sign he'd outlived his usefulness to the others, despite what LaBouche might think—but the tableau unfolding below him had a strange feel. The humans stood close together, muscles tensed as if they knew about the old one stalking them. One of them surveyed the sky, and his eyes locked on Dan Delo. He said something to the female, and both ran toward the parking lot.

The hunter! he thought. A wide smile stretched across Delo's face as he tucked his wings and plummeted toward the earth.

7

Chaz stood in the large single room allocated to the Oneka Falls Police Department. He grinned at the demon he'd appointed as the chief of police—the new one with the silver skin—and picked up one of the department's new HK 417's that had just arrived. "And these are automatics?"

The new chief who called herself Nicole Conrau, nodded, sending shimmers of light dancing across her sable hair. “Full auto, chambered in 7.62 x 51 NATO—as you instructed, my lord.”

“No need for such formalities between us, Nicole—or is it Nicky? You’ve done well.” He flashed a wide smile at her. “Call me Chaz.”

The demoness smiled, stretching her lips between the two golden tusks that grew from her lower jaw and extended past her lips. Her skin was a silvery shimmer—like liquid mercury—and she had beautiful malachite eyes. Black wisps made up the insubstantial wings sprouting from her back, but Chaz thought her most attractive feature was the extra pair of arms. A touch smaller than the arms sprouting from her shoulders, the secondary arms seemed…dainty. “Are you sure? I wouldn’t want to assume,” she said. “And I prefer Nicole.”

“Yes,” Chaz crooned. “I don’t see any need for formality between us. Tell me, Nicole, have you taken a mate in this realm?”

Nicole’s smile stretched, and she blinked at him like a young schoolgirl at her first real love. “Why, Chaz, I think you’re flirting with me.”

Chaz beamed back at her and set the HK 417 back in its crate before offering her his arm. “Shall we find surroundings that are…more conducive to our…*needs*?"

Nicole wrinkled her nose at him and winked. "Before our first date? The very idea!" Chaz's smile faded, but before it disappeared, Nicole chuckled low in her throat and nestled close to him, pressing her breasts into the thick muscles of his arms. "Don't give up so easily, Chaz. It takes all the fun out of playing hard to get." She growled deep in her throat, and her vermillion tongue snaked out from between her lips. She licked his neck over his carotid artery, and Chaz shivered.

"Definitely no need for formalities," he whispered in a husky voice.

"I should say not," she crooned in his ear. "Otherwise, the evening might not be as fun."

8

By the time Toby and Shannon reached the car, Mike had the trunk lid open and was holding out a paintball gun for each of them. Toby skidded around the back corner of the vehicle, grabbed his weapon, and twisted to face the two demons advancing toward them. Shannon took her gun, staring wide-eyed at Mike. He bent over the trunk and pulled out both a tactical shotgun and his own paintball gun. "I take it both that innocuous-looking fellow who just appeared out of thin air and the old man are demons?"

"Yes," said Toby. "Old man is hungry. The innocuous-looking one, as you call him, is a giant purple flyer who seems to have just been passing by and dropped in for a quick bite."

"Had to bring *two* of them, didn't you? One demon doesn't satisfy you anymore, does it?"

Toby grunted. "Keep your groups tight, we don't want to put any civilians to sleep. If you use full auto, keep it to one-second bursts, the accuracy goes all to hell after that."

"Why don't we just run?" Shannon asked with a tremor in her voice.

"Because the big one can fly."

"As fast as a car?"

Toby ignored the question and advanced to the edge of the grass, bringing the paintball gun up as he went. He targeted the closer of the two demons—the big purple demon who had dropped out of the sky—and squeezed off a single shot. The paintball arched toward him and exploded on the demon's left shoulder.

The demon turned his head and sniffed, then wrinkled his nose and flapped his wings without taking flight. He tilted his head to the side and glared at Toby through eyes that glowed with dark blue light.

The older demon charged forward, dropping forward to run with a quadrupedal gait, hands curled into fists protected by bone-like pads across the front knuckles. His skin was a pale cream color and stretched tight over his frame, giving the impression that it would rip if he bent his joints too far. He was a weird—he had a tiny extra arm that hung from his chest, a nub of a tail, and his legs terminated in broad yellow hooves.

Toby swiveled at the hip, flicked the switch that enabled automatic fire, and sent a short burst at the oncoming demon. As he did so, the massive purple beast narrowed his eyes and watched. Three paintballs arced from the barrel of Toby's gun and splattered across the cream-colored demon's head and shoulders.

Intent on sating his hunger, engrossed in bringing his prey down, the old demon ignored the exothermic chemical reaction and the resultant chloroform gas. The big purple monster, however, didn't. He turned to face the cream demon and flapped his massive wings a few times, creating a stiff breeze.

Mike came up on the other side of the car and dropped the shotgun at his feet. Shannon came to the other side of Toby and snapped a shot at the purple demon.

The purple demon growled deep in his throat and flapped his wings again.

"What's he doing?" asked Mike.

"It's strange..." Toby shifted his aim to the wing of the demon and fired a long burst of paintballs at him. The beast made a peculiar noise—a cross between a frustrated dog's whine and the scream of someone dying in a chemical fire—and flapped his wings hard enough that his feet came off the ground.

"Is he—"

"He's blowing the gas away with his wings!" shouted Toby.

Mike aimed at the advancing pale-skinned demon and fired a short burst. The flying beast again twisted toward the other fiend and sent a breeze flowing past the old one, carrying the chloroform away.

"We can't keep letting him do that!" said Shannon.

The cream-colored demon was almost on top of them, and Toby took a step away from Shannon. "I'm going to open up on the old guy, when I say, both of you open up on the other one." Toby shifted his aim to the older demon and fired a one-second burst, then another. The purple demon flapped his wings, and Toby shouted, "Now!"

Mike and Shannon both fired at the winged demon, Mike, in short, controlled bursts, and Shannon just holding the trigger back spraying the area around the demon's feet.

The demon squawked and turned to clear the area in front of him. As he did, Toby fired three short bursts at the oncoming demon. The older beast made no noises—other than the pounding of his hooves and hands on the grass—he still didn't seem to notice the danger from the paintballs.

"Avoid the paintballs, you fool!" snapped the winged demon.

"No, keep ignoring them," said Mike.

"Keep firing at the grape," said Toby. "Keep him busy."

The big demon's azure gaze snapped to Toby, and he sneered. "Are you the hunter?" He shifted his head toward Mike and Shannon. "Are you the ones who murdered Herlequin?"

The library doors opened with a squeak, and Connie Parsons stepped out. "What's going on out here?" Her eyes widened as she saw Toby, Shannon, and Mike standing there pointing paintball guns at the demons—who looked human to her. "What are you three doing?"

"Everything's okay, Ms. Parsons!" called Shannon. "Go back inside, please."

"Forget her! Keep firing!"

The old demon skidded to a halt and peered over his shoulder. He swung his head pendulously between the librarian and Shannon, his nostrils quivering as he sniffed the air. With a grunt, he turned and thundered toward the librarian.

"Mike!" shouted Toby. "Pull out the stops!"

Mike tossed the paintball gun on the hood of the car, stooped, and scooped up the tactical shotgun. He advanced, bumping a round into the chamber, then leveled the scattergun at the big purple demon and fired. The slug took the fiend in his gut, and he doubled over in midair, screaming with rage and pain. He dropped to the ground, still doubled over, hands around his middle.

"Shan, with me!" Toby sprinted away from the car, moving at an angle to change his line of fire and avoid the librarian. Shannon followed, a look of determination spreading across her face.

Toby slid to a stop on one knee, raised the paintball gun, and took careful aim. He fired two quick, single shots and grimaced as the second shot went wide, striking the sidewalk near the librarian.

With a shriek like a malfunctioning jet engine, the big purple demon whirled with his wings extended to create a gust of wind. He hopped in the air, flapped his wings, and swooped at Mike. After two quick blasts with the shotgun, Mike dove to the side, missing being eviscerated by the talons on the demon's feet by a breath and a prayer. The demon skidded in the grass, digging furrows with his claws.

"Need help here!"

Toby waved Shannon ahead. "Stay on the old bastard, I'll help Mike." He peeled away, paintball gun spitting a stream of chloroform-balls at the purple demon's back.

"What do I do?" shouted Shannon.

"Keep shooting it!" snapped Toby over his shoulder. He continued throwing unrelenting fire at the demon's back and wings, and the beast spun to face him with a roar. "Get clear, Mike!"

"I will crush you!" the winged demon screeched. "All of you!"

Toby darted behind an evergreen, stopped, whirled around, and ran back out the same side from which he'd entered. The demon's gaze had gone to the other side of the evergreen, and Toby had a moment to fire at him unobserved.

Mike picked himself up and took a moment to transfer shotgun shells from his front pocket to the loading tube. With that accomplished, he raised the shotgun and fired—this time at the demon's wings. Slugs three-quarters of an inch in diameter punched holes through the leathery skin of the demon's wings, and with each one, the demon screeched at ear-splitting volume.

The big demon sprinted and flapped his wings, leaping into the air with his last step. He gained altitude, darting glances at Mike as he beat his wings with fury.

Toby shifted his attention to the older demon and shouted, "Mike! Shannon needs help!"

Backed into the corner where the building made an L shape, the demon stood before her, menacing her.

Shannon had lost her paintball gun and had both hands up in front of her face.

"Do your thing, Shan!" shouted Mike.

Toby shook his head but didn't waste his breath shouting that with the demon looking straight at her, her thing wouldn't help. He sprinted to close the distance, and when he was close enough, he pulled the trigger and held it, firing a stream of paintballs at the demon's back, trying to keep the paintballs from straying too far off target.

The cream-colored demon stepped back, tilting his head in confusion. He turned in a half-circle and spotted Toby. Without another glance at Shannon, he left her standing in the corner, dropped to all fours, and charged Toby.

With the thing coming straight at him, Toby flipped the selector switch to semiauto, took careful aim, and pulled the trigger three times. The rounds slammed into the demon's face, one impacting his cheekbone under his left eye, another smashing into his lips, and the third hitting him in the forehead. The demon shrieked and shifted to a bipedal gait, reaching for Toby with his arms.

Toby jinked to the side and fired point-blank as the demon raced by him. The ancient imp staggered a step, and then turned like a drunken sailor, his eyes glassy, and his mouth hanging open.

Mike shot him in the back, the shotgun's report booming in the early evening air. The demon staggered forward a step, then fell face down in the grass. "Where's the other one, Toby? The flyer?"

Toby spun in a circle, scanning the sky above them, but of the purple demon, there was no sign. "Gone, for now." He turned to Shannon. "You okay, Shannon?"

Shannon inclined her head and walked to where the demon had batted her paintball gun into the bushes. "I played dead again."

"Good thinking, Shan," said Mike.

"I wish I was more useful in a fight." Shannon lifted her shoulders and let them drop with an exhausted sigh, then she bent and retrieved her weapon.

"You saved the librarian. I call that useful," said Toby.

Shannon shrugged again but wouldn't meet his gaze.

"Speaking of the librarian," said Mike, nodding toward the library's doors.

Toby followed his gaze. The librarian was standing just inside the glass doors, a cordless phone pressed to her ear. Her eyes were wide as she looked back and forth between the three of them, and then at the demon lying on the ground. "Don't have to be psychic to know she's calling the police."

"Nope."

Shannon sighed. "Should I talk to her?"

"No use. Let's get out of here." Toby turned toward the parking lot.

"What about this one?" asked Mike, kicking the demon's foot.

Toby made a dismissive gesture with one hand. "It's his lucky day. We don't have time to get him loaded into the car." As he walked by, he fired a stream of chloroform-loaded paintballs into the demon's back. "Besides, I wouldn't want to risk driving around with him when we might get pulled over and questioned. Come on, let's get a move on."

They loaded their weapons back into the trunk of the car, and Mike slid into the driver's seat once more. He started the Lincoln, backed out of the parking lot, and threw the car in drive.

"Shan, can you disguise the car, please?" asked Toby. "Anything is fine, as long as it doesn't look like this car."

Shannon nodded.

Mike turned left onto Ridge Road, then he took an immediate right onto a worn macadam road that connected Ridge to Route 104 by way of the ball field parking lot. He continued turning at random, weaving their way through the small industrial area north of the town.

"Was one of them lying in wait for us?" asked Mike.

"I don't think so. The purple bastard seemed to be just passing by."

"Awesome. Just our luck."

"You betcha."

"Was that one from inside on your list?"

In the back seat, Toby shook his head, then reclined against the seat's headrest. "I thought the troll was the only one in the area."

"And instead, there were two… How likely is that?" asked Shannon.

"Not very."

"Do you think they know where we are?"

"No. If they did, they would have attacked us at the house."

As they passed Casey Park, Mike flipped on the headlights. "So, was it just a coincidence?"

Toby opened his mouth to answer, but before he could, Shannon screamed and threw her hands up in front of her face. A colossal tree slammed into the road in front of them, and Mike locked up the brakes.

Chapter 5

1986

I

Red moved through the woods surrounding the circle of cops, moving silently, saliva drooling out of all three grinning mouths. His three tentacles waved about him and above his head as if governed by minds of their own, but Red tingled with excitement and didn't care how he might look. Besides, who could observe him out there in the woods? The kid, and, based on the thoughts flitting through the kid's mind, the kid thought the display was cool.

The cops chattered in a tizzy—like monkeys—as Red kept circling around them and making different animal noises from different directions. The darkness made him almost invisible, even if he hadn't blurred the humans' minds so they wouldn't perceive him.

The men held guns before them, pointing them into the darkness as if mere firearms ensured their safety. Then again, they didn't know they'd stepped into Herlequin's domain, and none of them knew they faced one of his strongest guardsmen. Red wanted to shout laughter in their faces.

Red whirled for a few steps, clapping his tentacle-tipped talons above his head. He allowed the humans to hear the sound, delighting in their fight-or-flight responses. One of the younger men raised his weapon to his shoulder.

"Not until *I* say so, Martin!" The words rang with the practiced ease of one used to authority.

Red grinned as he watched the man in charge. Herlequin had sent his daughters after the man on the other side of the lake, and they'd pushed him down the embankment. The men were off limits—Herlequin's orders—but that didn't mean Red couldn't fuck with them. "No, not until *I* say so," he said in a waspish voice.

"Who said that?" asked the young man with the rifle at his shoulder—Martin. "Show yourself!"

The demon twisted through the trees, strumming a staccato beat with his talons on the tree trunks as he passed. He allowed the men to see the chips of wood arcing through the air but nothing else.

Herlequin had learned his lesson in Oneka Falls—no wanton killing of adults, especially adults of the law enforcement persuasion. The king extended this rule to demons *and* to their familiars.

Red had explicit orders: drive the adults out of the woods—out of *Herlequin's* forest, which didn't always match the copse that humans thought they walked through—*before* they stumbled into Brigitta's prey.

Sated, but repressing a sigh, Red began to drive the cops from the woods using their fear of the dark as his stick. When it was time, he sent Brigitta's boy running ahead as his carrot.

2

"Do you see that?" asked Stephen.

"See what?"

Despite being behind Officer Dennis, Stephen pointed at the mist above their heads. "The mist. It's thinning."

Dennis twisted his face skyward and paused for a moment. He turned and looked behind them, examining the low-hanging mist. "I'll be damned," he muttered and turned to the front. He picked up the pace. "Lights ahead, unless my mind's playing tricks on me."

By the time the mist dissipated to clear air, the two men were running flat out, leaping over brush and fallen limbs as they went. Once again, the sound of the lake lapping on the shore reached them on the wind. Once again, moonlight filtered through the boughs of the trees above their heads and reflected off the windshields of the police cars parked along the side of the road.

"Tom's already here," said Dennis with an air of approval. "No moss grows under his behind, I'll tell you that for nothing."

Stephen stopped at the edge of the gravel road and looked in both directions. "Yeah, but where are they?"

Gary opened his mouth to answer, but before he spoke, a spine-tingling shriek split the night air. Before the sound even died, Stephen was sprinting through the gravel, running toward his parents' lake house. Gary clutched the shotgun in his grip and rushed after him.

Stephen rounded the side of the house and ran full tilt into the door that led into the kitchen. He slammed into it with a booming crash, stumbling back, almost falling—and would have if Gary hadn't steadied him. "I left that unlocked!" he said, then started as a horrendous banging started in the kitchen.

"What the hell's that?" asked Dennis.

Without answering, Stephen sprinted around the back of the house, and Gary followed.

"Let me go in first!" shouted Dennis. Stephen didn't reply, and Gary wasn't even sure the man heard him in his panic. The horrendous banging continued for a moment longer but stopped with a clatter.

The screen door lay on the lawn—ripped off its hinges and flung away. Stephen didn't even pause before leaping the three steps leading up into the porch and barreling toward the house.

"Stephen! Let me—" He gave up as Mary Canton screamed from within the house. If it had been his wife, he wouldn't have stopped, either.

3

Mary sprinted toward the kitchen, cursing herself for a coward—for leaving Elizabet at the beast's mercy. She slammed her hip into the corner of the breakfast bar, and wretched pain leaped up and down her spine. She slipped as she tried to turn the corner to the pantry, and the thing behind her cackled.

"Where are you going?" the thing grated. "Don't you want to hang out? Dinner and a flick before we get down to business?"

Mary shoved herself to her feet without looking at the thing chasing her and threw herself toward the pantry door.

"Oh, a pantry. How humorous. I like to keep my food in the pantry, too. Mind if I borrow yours?" The thing boomed with laughter.

Mary only had one thought on her mind—the gun safe door. *Dear God, let the safe be unlocked*! She shouldered the hidden door out of the way and grabbed the handle of the gun safe. She pulled with all her might, expecting resistance, expecting the door to be as massive as it appeared.

The thick metal door was not heavy, though her prayer was answered. She almost fell as the door swung open. A light came on as the door swung open, illuminating the interior. Inside, a hunting rifle with a scope stood in a rack, and a big nickel-plated revolver hung in a holster attached to the back of the door. The pistol looked similar to the ones all the cops carried on the TV shows. Relief sang in her veins as she reached for the gun, praying Joe kept it loaded.

"My, that hidden door thing…that's quite creative. You must give me the name of your contractor."

The voice came from right behind her, the beast's breath tickling her ear. Mary's blood froze, and her muscles locked tight. The beast's large hand came to rest on her shoulder, its sharp talons slicing through her blouse.

"Doesn't that hidden door smack you as creative?" he crooned.

As much as she wanted to, as hard as she tried to make her hand grasp the butt of the pistol, she didn't even twitch. None of her muscles would do anything—she just stood frozen as the thing hooked her blouse with a long talon.

"We won't need that toy on the back of the door. I brought one of my own—well, I suppose that's a lie. I didn't have a choice to bring it or not. It's attached to me, you see. Right here, between my legs. That's enough gun for both of us, don't you agree?"

Her breath caught in her throat, and her thoughts froze in her mind, shaking in the beast's grip; waiting for the creature to do whatever it was going to do was the best she could do. Her eyes, though, they moved just fine. Her gaze danced back and forth from her right hand to the butt of the pistol, as if her insistent gaze would force her hands.

"I've got to say, miss. I prefer the silent type. I enjoy women who play hard to catch, but you're well and caught, yes? Don't you think it's a little rude to ignore everything I say?"

"*Get away from her, you bastard*!"

Her heart lurched in her chest. *Stephen*! she thought. *He's come to save me*! But even as the thought rolled through her mind, some sadistic part of her brain replayed the memory of the demon, and she despaired. There was nothing on God's green earth that Stephen could do against such a creature.

The demon's hand left her shoulder, and her blouse disappeared with it. "Oh, now look what you've made me do! Now I've ripped her shirt." The thing laughed, sounding every bit like a plane crashing into concrete. "Nice tits, lady."

"I said, get away from her!" shouted Stephen.

"Take this damn thing, Stephen! Get down, Mrs. Canton!"

Who else is here? *And why should I duck*? That last voice was unfamiliar to Mary, but even if she'd known it, her mind slugged along at the speed of half-frozen corn syrup; her gaze stuck to the butt of the Magnum as if glued to the thing.

"Mary, get down!" shouted Stephen.

She heard the tiniest of clicks—as if someone had thrown a switch—and she realized what her husband wanted her to do. She threw herself forward, letting her knees go weak as she did so, reaching for the butt of the huge Magnum as she fell. Her fingers scrabbled along the leather holster's edge, but she missed the pistol by a country mile.

Ka-BLAM! The report of the shotgun thundered in the enclosed space of the pantry, and Mary couldn't help herself: she screamed.

4

Stephen racked the slide of the shotgun, ejecting the spent shell and hammering a fresh one in its place. The noise made by cycling a round into a pump shotgun should have sent fear shivering through the nervous system of anyone on the receiving end of it, but the colossal beast at the other end of the pantry didn't even twitch at the sound.

The…*the thing*…standing between him and his wife had been turning to face him when he fired. The gargantuan scaled monster had to hunch his head to avoid the pantry ceiling, and as the shotgun pellets slammed into his side, he had straightened, punching his head straight through the sheetrock ceiling and bellowing at the impact of the almost point-blank shotgun blast.

With a grunt, the creature stooped to pull his head out of the ceiling, glaring at Stephen with eyes that bore no other color but red. Those eyes…they seemed to glow in the pantry's gloom, and without quite deciding to do it, Stephen fired a second time.

"Stop it!" the thing roared at him. The demon lifted his scaled arms to the sides, smashing through the shelves of canned and dried goods as if they were nothing more than papier-mache.

Stephen cycled the shotgun, sending another smoking casing flying into the living room. "Get away from her!"

The scaled creature cackled—a harsh, barking sound—and drew his expression into a smirk. "The only way I can get away from her is to walk out of the pantry… Straight…through…you!" As he said the last word, the demon lunged forward, long talon-tipped arms stretching toward Stephen.

"Good God!" shouted Gary Dennis. "Good God!"

Stephen lurched away, backpedaling into the kitchen as fast as his feet could move. He pulled the trigger a third time, and the pellets slammed into the demon's chest—affecting the thing about as much as if he'd flung spitballs in the demon's path.

"You've made a mistake, friend," said the demon in a bored-sounding voice. "You've brought a gun to a claw fight, and you know what they say about that."

Stephen's rump slammed into the counter, and his left foot slipped forward just as he pulled the trigger a fourth time. The double-aught buckshot punched a hole in his mother's ceiling. *That won't please Mom.* Along with the thought came the fleeting image of his mother lying in a pool of her own blood on the floor, her skin lying around her like so much forgotten confetti.

The demon burst through the door to the pantry, peeling the door and the door frame right out of the wall with his shoulders. He brandished his claws—his four-inch-long claws. He smiled at Stephen crookedly and tipped him a wink. "Is your dance card full, sweetie?"

Stephen worked the pump of the shotgun, searching his mind in a panic, trying to recall how many rounds he fired, and how many shells the damn gun held. Gary Dennis was backing away into the living room, his hand going to his holster, again and again, pulling up empty air as if he were a robot with a programming problem.

The demon ignored Gary, giving every ounce of his attention to Stephen. "Your toy is no good against me, son. You might as well turn it on yourself as shoot me with it again." Despite his words, a greenish-black ichor oozed from each pellet wound.

Stephen brought the shotgun to his shoulder and aimed it at the thing's face. "Maybe," he said. "I bet it hurts like a son of a bitch, though. Should we check to see if your eyes are immune to shotgun pellets?"

The scaled beast didn't slow his inexorable advance, and instead, he flashed a lopsided grin at Stephen. "Do what you want—it won't change a thing. In a few minutes, I'll go back inside that pantry and have my way with your wife." The thing shrugged. "You won't be alive to see it." A slow grin spread across the demon's features. He lifted an index finger, pointing it straight up in the classic Eureka pose. "Ah, I've just had an idea! What if you *were* still alive? Would you enjoy that? Would seeing how she reacts turn you on? I could leave you alive...broken spine, say." He glanced to the side, fixing Gary Dennis with a cold glance. "Of course, I'll have to kill *you*. If you're still here when I'm done with him, that is." He hooked a monstrous thumb at Stephen.

Stephen's aim faltered, the barrel of the shotgun wavering back and forth. "You leave her alone," he whispered. "If you have to kill someone, kill me, but leave her alone."

"My friend, Red, was right. When the begging starts, everything gets oh-so-much more interesting!" The titanic demon leered at Stephen, bending at the waist to lean forward, and winking at him in the way whores wink at potential customers.

5

Mary sat dazed on the floor of the pantry, a warm sticky fluid running down the side of her face. For a moment, she didn't recognize the pantry, didn't recall the events that had led to her slamming headfirst into the gun safe. As it came back, her hands began to shake.

The pantry was a wreck; splintered wood, ruptured sacks of food, and burst cans littered the floor. The rampaging demon had turned the shelves into kindling and toothpicks, and a hole the size of a basketball hoop had appeared in the ceiling.

She heard the thing threatening her husband, pinning him against the corner of the countertop between the sink and the prep space. She tried to stand, but her shaky knees gave out, and she thumped against the gun safe.

The gun safe! She got to her hands and knees and turned like a dog chasing her tail. Her heart sank as she saw that the gun safe had closed during the fracas. *They should have told me the code*! Out of desperation, she grabbed the door's handle and pulled, almost falling over once more as it swung open with ease. Relief swept over her like a wave of warm water.

Using the door to do it, Mary pulled herself up and stood swaying for a moment getting her balance. She grabbed the Magnum and pulled it out of its holster, surprised at how much she liked the weight of it in her hand.

"My friend, Red, was right. When the begging starts, everything gets oh-so-much more interesting!" the beast said.

Mary turned, forcing herself to go slow and avoid falling. The thing leered toward her husband but did nothing else, seeming to enjoy dragging things out. She looked down at the pistol in her hands. *I have no clue what I'm doing with this thing.* Joe's warning about novices hurting the ones they loved instead of the person threatening them again flashed through her mind. Her gaze tracked back up to the demon's back.

He raised his titanic arm until the claws gouged the ceiling, sending a shower of white dust earthward.

Mary stumbled out of the pantry, holding the heavy pistol in one shaking hand. The tip of the barrel wavered back and forth, sometimes centered on the demon's broad back, but often—*too often*—straying past him to either side. She didn't know what else to do, though, and she had to do something before the thing gutted Stephen.

Mary raised her other hand and gripped her wrist as she'd seen them do on the cop shows. She squeezed her eyes shut and jerked at the trigger.

Nothing happened. *Safety*? she thought.

"Give it to me!"

Mary turned her head, feeling as though she couldn't move her head fast enough. Gary Dennis stood at the edge of the living room, both hands out, palms up, as if imploring her to do something. He waved all ten of his fingers. Mary looked at the big pistol in her hands and tossed it to Officer Dennis.

He caught it with both hands, and with the dexterity of one who has practiced something a million times, spun the pistol on the flat of his hand until the grip rested in his palm, then extended it at the demon. He held the gun with both hands—instead of grabbing one wrist—his left hand cupped, fingers wrapping around the fingers of his right. His knees were bent a little, and he leaned forward at the waist.

Examining his posture, shame flashed through Mary like a four-alarm fire. Without warning, the mammoth, nickel-plated pistol roared.

6

Stephen followed the bright arc of the pistol as Mary threw it to Gary. Dennis snapped into a two-handed firing position and squeezed the trigger. The round took the demon high in the side of his head, exploding out the other side with more greenish-black blood splattering the wall and ceiling.

The demon snapped his head to the side, turning the gaping golf-ball-sized exit wound in his skull toward Stephen and glaring at Gary. Stephen steadied the shotgun and began to take up the slack of the trigger.

As if the demon could see out of the hole in the side of his head, he grabbed the barrel of the shotgun and with a rough jerk, snatched it out of Stephen's hands. Still glaring at Gary, he bent the scattergun in half before putting it back in Stephen's hands.

Gary fired again, and again, his aim was true. The demon staggered back, another .357 round snatching his head back. Gary thumbed the hammer back, the mechanism clicking in the silence that followed the deafening report of the pistol.

"*Don't do that again*!" roared the demon. "*I'll make you pay if you do*!"

Gary's only reply was another chunk of lead from the big gun's barrel and its accompanying clangor.

The demon shoved Mary headlong into the pantry as if an afterthought before launching himself at Gary with a roar.

Gary stood his ground, thumbing back the hammer and squeezing off one round after another as the demon approached. His cheeks quivered, but his stance was rock solid.

A low rumble issued from the demon's throat as he advanced with deliberation. His hands clenched and released with each step. He reached Gary in four giant-sized steps.

Gary thumbed back the hammer and pulled the trigger again, but instead of the deafening roar and another slug impacting the demon, there was only a harsh click. Without missing a beat, Gary reversed the pistol, holding it by the smoking barrel, and hammered at the demon with it.

The demon batted the pistol away, turning Gary ninety degrees with the force of the blow. With his other hand, the scaled beast jabbed his claws into Gary's chest, then raked them downward. Gary screamed and tried to pull away, but the demon was too quick, grabbing Gary by the throat with his other hand.

With a glance at Mary, Stephen charged at the demon, sprinting from the kitchen dredging as much speed from his muscles as possible. He had no plan, no idea what to do to defeat the beast standing in his parents' living room, just knowing he couldn't stand by and watch the demon butcher Gary.

"No, you fool!" shouted Gary. "Get away! Get *her* away!"

Stephen hesitated, glancing over his shoulder at the pantry. He slid to a stop and turned on his heel, ducking into the pantry.

7

Chaz Welsh glanced over his shoulder as Stephen ducked into the pantry. When he turned back to face the cop, his face bore a wicked grin. "You and me, now, sweetheart. You should have left when I gave you the chance."

"I've been a cop for twenty-three years. You don't scare me."

Chaz laughed. "Yes, I do."

The cop swung at him then, making a wide arc with his fist, throwing his hip and shoulder forward, putting all his weight behind the blow.

Still laughing, Chaz caught his haymaker in one hand and squeezed. With a popcorn clatter, the bones in Gary's hand shattered and his finger joints disintegrated.

The cop screamed, and the demon laughed harder. "Delicious," he said between bellows.

The cop struggled against him, trying to pull his shattered hand out of his grip. With a shrug, Chaz opened his hand and grinned as the policeman flew backward, slamming into the couch and flipping over it. Chaz leaped over the couch and landed on him. He extended the claws of his feet, digging them into the man's abdomen. "Now, let's have us some fun!"

8

Stephen slid into the pantry, his eyes wide, his face as pale as Mary had ever seen it. She lay on the floor, with a long piece of splintered wood impaling her left side. Blood slicked the floor beneath her, and she felt faint. It had become harder and harder to draw breath with each passing moment.

"Mary!"

With a numb, enervated hand, Mary pointed at the gun safe. There was still a hunting rifle in it, and who knew what other weapons Joe had tucked away.

Her husband's gaze darted from her face to the gun safe but came back to her face. He shook his head. "Guns don't seem to do much good. We have to get out of here.

Gary is…" He snapped his mouth shut and shook his head harder.

In the other room, Gary Dennis screamed.

Stephen kneeled beside her. "He's buying us time to get away," he choked out. "Can you stand?"

"We can't get away…he's too fast, too…" She ran out of breath and gasped another into her beleaguered lungs.

"He's busy with Gary. Here," said Stephen as he threaded his arm under her shoulders and knees. He grunted as he stood, and his knees popped with a sound Mary associated with deboning a chicken.

"Rifle," she whispered.

Stephen looked down at her and smiled. "I can't get both. You're more important." He took two steps toward the kitchen. "Besides, if the shotgun and a .357 Magnum can't bring him down, Dad's little .243 deer rifle won't do a thing."

He had to turn her to the side to carry her out of the pantry door, but luckily it was wider after the demon had plowed through it. Stephen didn't even glance at the living room, instead went straight to the side door. "I've got to put your feet down, Mary. Try to stand." He matched actions to his words, and she gasped as her legs took her weight. He unlocked the door and threw it open. "Can you help me? Can you walk to the car?" He pressed the keys to their rental car into her hand.

Mary nodded but didn't believe she could walk, not even a step. Behind them, the demon roared, and Gary emitted a long, grating screech that wound down to the rattle of the dead and gone.

"Gotta move, now, Mare," said Stephen with a sad smile. With gentle firmness, Stephen pushed her out the door and closed it in her face. The lock snicked closed as he bolted it from the inside.

"No! Stephen, no!" she shouted.

Something slammed into the door, rattling the entire wall of the house and cracking the windows over the kitchen sink. Through the door, Stephen groaned.

9

Joe Canton had always felt at home in the woods. He'd never gotten lost, and no animal had ever threatened him.

But that was before.

He slipped through the woods without making a sound, avoiding the underbrush, avoiding dry twigs, with Greg hanging onto his belt all the while. He held his M1 carbine at high port, ready to bring it to bear at a moment's notice.

Joe hadn't seen the woman in the black outfit since he'd shot at her the last time, but things *were* moving in the woods. At one point, the sound of a lion roaring whispered at him on the wind—and if that wasn't proof dementia was setting in, Joe didn't know what was.

Greg tugged on his belt, and Joe stopped. He turned toward his grandson. "What is it, Greg?" he asked, his gaze bouncing back and forth between the trees behind them. "Did you hear something?"

"She will kill them," said Greg in a listless, spiritless voice.

"Who, Greg?"

"The Lady in the Lake, Grandpa. I ran away because she was going to kill one of you to keep us from leaving. I didn't stop, didn't listen to you, because *he* told me it would be too late if you caught up to me. He's…he's so different up here… I…I don't want to be his friend anymore."

Joe eyed his grandson with concern. What the boy had been through in the past week was enough to cause anyone to go a little off-kilter, let alone a sensitive eleven-year-old. "Don't worry, Greg. No one's going to hurt anyone, not tonight. Who is it that you don't like anymore?" Joe's mind ran in circles, suggesting each child who came to visit on the same shore as his lake house and then rejecting them. His mind settled on

Mason Harper, and though he couldn't explain the feeling, he believed that was who Greg meant.

"My…my invisible friend! In Florida, he was funny, he told me jokes. But up here…up here he's been nasty, mean. He's the one who said the Lady in the Lake would kill one of you unless I left, unless I ran away into the woods. He's the one that tried to…" Greg looked at the M1, and his cheeks burned with shame. "He said I had to make you go away, or it would be too late to save anyone at the house."

Joe squatted, awkwardly holding the rifle away from them both. He looked up into his grandson's scared eyes. "Greg, I'm going to ask you something, and I want you to give me an honest answer. No beating around the bush, okay?"

Greg nodded.

"This invisible friend… How does he… How do you talk to him?"

Greg lifted a hand and tapped his temple with it. "Inside my head. Sometimes I talk to him out loud, but he always talks to me inside my head."

Joe took a deep breath, dread piling up inside him. "And does he tell you to do things often? Things you don't want to do?"

Greg's face scrunched up into an expression of annoyance. "That's just it. In Florida, he never told me to do anything. He never did much of anything back home, he just said funny things. But up here…"

"Up here it's different. *He's* different."

"Yes. He tells me to do things all the time, and if I don't want to do them, he calls me names or says I'm a brat or something like that."

Joe rested his hand on his grandson's shoulder. "Now, this part is important, Greg. Do you still only hear him inside your head? Even up here, when he's telling you to do things."

Greg bobbed his head, looking miserable and exhausted.

Joe didn't know what to say. He didn't know much about mental health or psychiatry or any of that nonsense, but it sounded as if his grandson might've developed a problem that was beyond him. "Can you tell him to go away?"

Greg looked down as if he could sense his grandfather's unease and shrugged.

"Well, you think on it while I get us back home."

The boy raised his head, his expression grave, his eyes haunted. "When we get back…I think they'll—" Greg burst into tears.

10

Mary grabbed the doorknob and rattled it with all her strength. "Stephen!"

"Run, Mary!" On the other side of the door, her husband screamed.

"Oh, yes! Please run, Mary!" bellowed the demon. "I'll be out in two shakes, dearie."

Through the door, Mary heard a sickening crunch, followed by a ripping sound. The window above the sink exploded outward as if someone had thrown something through it, and Mary's gaze tracked that direction.

The narrow concrete path that led from the kitchen door circled around toward the porch and connected with the wider cement walk that led down to the dock. Lying in the center of that narrow path, was a head.

Mary didn't want to go look, she didn't want to see who it was, but she *needed* to. She stepped closer to the gruesome thing, resting her hand against the side of the house for support.

Inside the house, the scaled beast shrieked laughter through the open window. "Are you sure you should do that, Mary?" he asked. "Are you sure you want to know who that head belonged to?"

She glanced through the broken window. The demon stood on the other side of the breakfast bar, leaning forward and resting his elbows on the countertop. Human blood coated his claws, his hands, but his own wounds had closed over as if they'd never happened.

She turned her attention back to the gruesome thing lying at her feet. The head rested face down, and she had to nudge the bloody thing with her foot. Her breath gusted out of her, and she felt a pang of insane guilt at the level of relief that coursed through her.

It wasn't Stephen. The head belonged to the cop…to Gary Dennis.

11

Stephen slumped against the door, pain throbbing in his limbs. A goose egg grew to epic proportions on the back of his head, and the muscles in his neck were alive with burning, electric pain.

The demon leaned against the breakfast bar, resting his elbows on it. His face twisted with a huge grin, and his solid-red eyes glinted with amusement.

He glanced into the living room, a sick dread filling him. The furniture lay upended, and Gary's legs extended from beneath the couch. Blood coated everything and pooled beneath Gary's body.

Too much blood, he thought. *Sorry, Gary.*

Gritting his teeth, Stephen levered his legs underneath him and pushed himself up against the kitchen door. The demon stared at him for a moment but then turned his attention back to the kitchen window as if Stephen offered no threat. He swept the area with his gaze, looking for a weapon, something that might hurt the hulking demon.

Or at least keep his attention.

I've got to buy enough time for Mary to get away. She should be at the car by now.

12

Mary's gaze bounced from the severed head at her feet through the kitchen window at the demon watching her. "What *are* you?" she asked in a tone that demanded an answer.

The huge mother-of-pearl beast lifted his massive shoulders and let them drop, a smile stretching on its lips. He glanced to the right, toward the kitchen door, and then turned back to her. "What do I look like?"

"A horror movie," Mary hissed.

The demon tilted his head back and laughed. "I enjoy your movies. Have you seen *The Exorcist*? It was hilarious."

She shook her head. "Is my husband dead?" Her voice sounded lifeless, flat, even to her.

The demon's scaled lips stretched wide, exposing multiple rows of fangs the color of rotten teeth. "That pansy? You deserve better, Mare. But, to answer your question, no." The beast turned his gaze to the right again. "In fact, he's regained his feet and seems to be looking for a weapon. He's a little slow on the uptake, isn't he?"

"If you let him live, I won't run away." The words hurt her to say, but she meant each and every one of them.

"Mary! No! Get away! Think of Greg!"

The demon inclined his head. "Yeah, Mary. Listen to your husband. Go ahead. *Run.*" He winked at her lasciviously. "Have I mentioned I adore foreplay?"

As Mary looked on, Stephen charged the immense creature, swinging a broom as he came.

13

The broomstick cracked across the demon's head and splintered into three fragments. Stephen's arms vibrated to the point of pain.

The thing turned its head and looked Stephen in the eye. "Wouldn't you rather be sitting against the door minding your own business? I'm trying to pick up your wife."

The piece of the broom Stephen still held was about twenty inches long and ended in a ragged point. Stephen reversed his grip on it, holding the thing point-down like a long dagger. He stepped close to the big demon, raised his arm, and plunged the broken broom handle downward with all his strength.

The demon did nothing, and the point of the handle skittered across the scales that lined his back. The scaled beast sighed as if Stephen was the stupidest, most irritating asshole he'd ever met.

"Guns don't seem to slow me down, so you thought you'd try a broomstick?" The demon rolled his eyes. "You are about four shades of stupid, aren't you?"

Stephen brought his hand up as fast as he could and plunged the broken broomstick into the demon's eye. Thick yellow goop burst from his eye socket, and when it touched the wooden weapon, sent tendrils of black smoke curling toward the ceiling. The viscous liquid glopped down the handle toward his hand, and Stephen jerked away, leaving the broom handle quivering in the demon's face.

"Do you know what? You've just crossed the line from being a minor amusement to a big pain in the ass. Do you have any idea how long it takes for an eye to regrow?" He reached up and took the broom handle between two fingers in a curiously tender way, as if he might crush it to dust by accident, and pulled it out. He slung the thing away, and with the same motion slapped Stephen with the force of an out-of-control tractor-trailer.

Stephen's feet left the ground, and he flew across the room to slam into the refrigerator. It dazed him, and he slid to the ground, woozy and fighting a losing battle to remain conscious. The last thing he thought was that he hoped Mary had started running at last.

14

"What the hell?" hissed Pete Martin.

Tom Walton snapped his hand up for silence. A small, shadow-shrouded figure stepped out of the gloom and moved toward them, staggering as if exhausted. "Who's that? Greg Canton, is that you?"

"Nuh-no, I'm Mason Harper. My grandma lives next door to the Cantons." The boy shuffled forward, darting a glance over his shoulder. "You have to help me! Get me out of here!"

"And why's that, son?" asked Arnold, shining his flashlight on the kid.

For a moment, the boy's expression seemed crafty to Tom, but sweat covered his dirty face—add that to the unreliable lighting, and he might have only been fearful. The boy had skinned his knees on a tree root somewhere in the darkness, and a torn T-shirt hung from his shoulder. "What are you doing out here, Mason?"

A wailing, squalling noise screeched from the darkness and sent shivers down Tom's spine. As the sound faded into an eerie silence, he leaned close to Michael Arnold. "What is that? Sound effects?" he whispered.

The effect on the boy was pronounced. He shuddered and took three running steps to the group of cops, his face crumpling in abject terror. "Get me out! Get me out of here!" he whispered again and again.

"I wish to God I knew, Chief." Arnold shuddered. "I don't mind telling you that I'm not sure if the silence or the noises bug me more."

Tom wagged his head. Their flashlights seemed worse than worthless, unable to penetrate the gloom. Anger and frustration bubbled in his blood. *We're worthless out here… Can't do a goddamn thing*! He stepped away from the others, ignoring Arnold's warning hand on his shoulder. Something rumbled deep in the woods, like a giant dog issuing a warning growl. "You can take your bullshit sound effects and go choke on them," Tom muttered. He turned back to his officers, his face set into grim lines. "We aren't doing much good out here, men. We can't track anything in this darkness. Hell, we can't even track *ourselves.*" He dropped a hand to rest on Mason's shoulder. "We haven't found the boy we're looking for, but we *have* found a boy in trouble. We're getting out of here. Now."

"But what about the—"

Tom made a chopping gesture through the air. "We're not helping the Cantons, are we? Running around like a pack of fools while a psychotic asshole gets his jollies trying to freak us out. I can't make heads or tails of these woods tonight, and I don't think any of you can either. If anyone has any other ideas, now would be the time to bring them up." He looked at each man in the face, pausing a moment to give the man a chance to speak.

No one did.

"All right then. We're getting out of here. Follow me." Tom turned in the direction he thought would take them back to the Canton's lake house and set off at a brisk pace.

After he'd taken twenty steps, and his officers had fallen in behind him, an eerie male voice rang out in the woods. "Wrong way, dumbass," the voice said.

"Why don't you come out here and show me, then?" Tom shouted. "I won't arrest you; I promise."

In answer, the man stalking them laughed.

Tom didn't turn away from his chosen direction. He used every trick of woodcraft that he knew to keep himself from walking circles. It was hard without using the sky as a guide. After a few minutes, he slowed to a stop, peering into the darkness on all four sides.

"Mister, we're going the wrong way," said Mason. "We have to go that way." The boy gestured over his shoulder.

Tom squinted at him and cocked his head to the side. "You're Maven Harper's grandson, right? You said you live next door to the Cantons?"

"In the summer."

Tom darted a glance in the direction he'd been leading them and frowned.

"It's this way, Officer," said Mason, pointing behind them.

"How can you tell?"

Mason shrugged. "It seems…*right*."

Tom shook his head, then lifted a hand and let it drop. "Well, I'm all turned around in this soup. Can you lead us out?"

Mason hooked a thumb over his shoulder. "This way." He turned and walked away, pausing after a moment to beckon the group of officers.

With a shrug, Tom followed him.

After they'd walked for ten minutes, the mist began to dissipate in the boughs of the trees, and starlight peeked through. Another few minutes' walk brought them out from under the fog. Tom called a halt and turned, staring into the murk behind them.

"It seems…*darker*…maybe more menacing," said Arnold.

Tom looked at him askance before shaking his head. Arnold was not a man given to flights of fancy, nor was he easily frightened, but fright lingered in the man's expression. "I can't explain it, Michael."

Arnold hitched his shoulders and offered a timid smile. "Who said you gotta know all the answers?"

Tom grunted, then turned and led them out of the woods. Moonlight reflected off the black asphalt surface of Lake Circle. As he stepped from the woods, Walton threw a wary glance over his shoulder. He couldn't shake the feeling that whatever it was back there in the woods, it had led them—*herded them*—out of the woods. Tom rested the butt of his AR-15 on his hip and used his other hand to rub his eyes. At least he was beginning to understand *how* things may have happened in Oneka Falls seven years before.

"What do we do now, Chief?" asked Arnold.

"Hell if I know," Tom muttered.

"Can you…" began Mason. "Can you walk me home?" He peered at the dark woods on the side of the road. "I'm…" He lifted one shoulder and let it drop. "I'm scared."

"Me too, son," said Tom. "Me, too."

Chapter 6

2007

I

Sally McBride sat behind the reception desk in the Oneka Falls Town Hall and fumed. The new one, that Nicole Conrau, came through giving orders like she owned the place. *Who does she think she is*? Sally thought. *She's a youngster, and she has only just arrived to boot*. She grimaced and scratched at the underside of the desk—over the years, she'd cut a groove in the wood during times of stress. *Someone should teach her a lesson.*

Sally slid her keyboard in front of her and began the Internet search Nicole had demanded. *But everyone knows how she's "earning" her position, everyone knows Chaz gave it to her because he wanted to fuck her… I can't blame the youngster, but Chaz…he should know better.*

She seethed in silence, completing the tasks Nicole wanted in the order she'd asked for. *Asked for*? *Commanded*! *I should rip her ears off*! *And why does she want this stupid shit, anyway*? *This information is a thing for accountants*! *How the hell am I supposed to make heads or tails of this bullshit*?

But to understand her assignment was to find the information *and* summarize. Sally's understanding of the Internet showed little promise, let alone her ability to parse the results her searches returned. *And why does this finance crap matter? It isn't as if any of this banking information leads anywhere*!

Money flowed from one account to another, stocks bounced from one brokerage house to another, then they were sold, sometimes repurchased at once. None of what she looked at made sense. Not to Sally.

2

The phone rang in his ear while Mason fidgeted with his little bag of tricks. He'd developed the habit over the years, unpacking the black leather doctor's clutch, then shining his blades before repacking them, sometimes over and over to while away the time. He'd found things went smoother if he kept his mind distracted from the urges he felt.

"Welsh," grated a voice on the other end of the line.

"Hi, Chaz. It's Mason." He repacked his bag, taking extra care not to smudge his polished blades.

The call rumbled as Chaz covered the speaker on his end for a moment. "Yeah, what do you have for me?"

"Not much. I haven't been able to find the people you want."

The line hissed and popped for a moment. “Then, why call?”

Mason heaved a breath, then let it whistle out.

“Stop that!” snapped Chaz. “You know I hate that.”

“Sorry. It’s a habit, and sometimes old habits are the hardest to break.” He began to take each of blades out of the clutch again. First, the big knives, then moving down toward the scalpels.

“And so? I’m busy over here, Mace.”

“Yeah, sorry.” He hummed to himself for a moment, organizing his thoughts and putting the blades out of his mind. “I’ve got one of my feelings.”

“Oh?”

To Mason’s ears, Chaz sounded half-there, distracted. “Chaz.”

Chaz heaved a sigh. “Yeah? I’m busy, Mason.”

“There’s something wrong here. The people you want aren’t in Rochester.”

“You can’t know that, Mason. It’s a big city, and the hunter is resourceful.”

Mason wrinkled his nose. “He’s not so resourceful that he can make five people disappear. Remember, Chaz, you and Red spent a lot of time teaching me how to track prey. Am I good at it?”

“Yes,” said Chaz without pause. “The best I’ve ever seen in a human.”

“Right. They aren’t here.”

"But where else could they be?"

Mason shook his head and stood. He walked from the bed of his hotel room to the big windows that overlooked Rochester's downtown district. "My gut says they are somewhere to the east."

"Gut, huh?"

Mason shrugged but said nothing.

"And you've checked—"

"I've checked everything, Chaz. I've seen the demons LaBouche set to guard his apartment, but they didn't see me. I've cruised the campus. I've been by the trooper's house." He drew a breath and whistled with the exhalation. "They aren't here."

"Fuck," said Chaz. "Okay. Would it do any good to hang out? Maybe wait for them to come back?"

Mason grimaced and turned back to the bed, his eyes dancing over the shiny blades arrayed on its cover. "There's been…a complication."

Chaz bellowed laughter. "What was her name?"

"I…" Mason shook his head. "I didn't catch it."

"All right," said Chaz, still chuckling. "Pack and go, then. Call me when you get home. I'll pop over later if that's okay with you."

"Roger that," said Mason as he packed his knives away.

3

Mike cursed, and the tires shrieked as the car slid toward the massive tree lying across the road. The scent of smoking rubber burned the back of their throats for a split second before they slammed into the tree with enough force to lift the rear of the car into the air. Mike and Shannon crashed against their seat belts, and Toby jolted forward into the back of the front bench seat, and the air exploded out of his lungs.

A dark, winged figure streaked down from the night sky and kicked the rear quarter panel opposite Toby with both taloned feet. The passenger side back tire came off the ground, and the back of the car careened toward the ditch next to the road. Toby flew across the back seat and slammed into the rear door.

Before he could recover, the window set into the door above him shattered, and a large purple hand reached in to grab him by the shirt. The demon jerked Toby through the window and threw him across the ditch into the parking lot of Casey Park. He landed hard and felt something in his shoulder pop. He skidded across the gravel lot, sharp-edged rocks digging into his skin. The demon slammed his claws into the roof of the car and pulled, leaving behind ten strips of peeled metal. Shannon screamed, and Toby pushed himself up, but dizziness overcame him, and he again fell into the sharp stones.

The trunk popped, and the driver's side door came open at almost the same moment. The demon cackled and leaped over the car to land next to the driver's side door. He grabbed Mike by the hair and slung him to the ground. The demon lifted one of his feet and stomped downward, but Mike rolled out of the way, scrambling on his hands and knees toward the ditch.

With a groan, Toby pushed himself into a seated position using the arm that didn't hurt. His vision swam, and his ears rang, but the demon wouldn't care about either—he would come for Toby, and most likely after he'd killed Mike and Shannon. He rolled to his knees, then pushed himself to his feet and staggered toward the open trunk.

Shannon's door opened, and though the demon peered in her direction, he snapped his attention back to Mike as he strode toward him with purpose. Though he looked, Toby couldn't tell if Shannon had gotten out of the car—if she was out, she squatted below the level of the windows. *Good girl*, Toby thought. Lurching and staggering like a zombie, Toby crossed the parking lot and navigated the ditch. The big purplish-black demon hadn't noticed him yet, and that fact gave Toby a measure of hope.

Mike was playing cat and mouse with the winged demon, first juking toward the ditch, then hurling himself behind the fallen tree. He was unarmed, and given the demon's size and agility, Mike wouldn't be able to keep away from him for long.

As Toby climbed out of the ditch, Shannon duck walked around the rear of the car and reached into the open trunk, and he moved to join her at his best speed. The demon had been smart back at the library, beating his wings to blow the chloroform gas away. *If only I had my tranquilizer gun*! Toby thought.

He reached the car and withdrew the shotgun. He put his lips next to Shannon's ear and said, "Take two paintball guns; give one to Mike."

"What are you going to do, Toby?"

Toby lifted the shoulder that didn't hurt and dropped it. "What I can."

"Give me the shotgun. You're hurt, and I'm not."

Toby shuffled back a step or two. "You've never used it."

"It doesn't look harder than one of these," she said, lifting a second paintball gun out of the trunk. "You take one to Mike."

Toby shook his head and staggered back toward the parking lot. Using the pump shotgun would be a problem. His right arm had gone pins and needles from the shoulder down, and he couldn't lift it past his waist.

Holding the foregrip with his left hand, Toby dropped the stock of the shotgun and jerked it up, letting momentum work the slide. He turned toward the demon. "Hey!" he shouted. Mike darted a glance in his direction and dove behind the tree, going prone.

The demon turned toward Toby, grinning wide and exposing myriad sharp fangs. "I haven't forgotten you," he said in a singsong voice. "Don't you worry, Dan Delo never forgets a face…or a debt."

Toby grasped the shotgun's stock with his right hand and fired from the hip.

Dan Delo shrieked as the slug ripped through his right thigh, slinging gore in its wake. He staggered, but with a shriek of pure rage, put his head down and charged at Toby.

After using the weight and momentum of the shotgun to rack the slide once more, Toby fired from the hip again. This time, the slug hit the demon in the shoulder and spun him one hundred and eighty degrees. Toby dropped the butt of the shotgun and pumped another slug into the chamber. He took a few steps forward, then grabbed the stock and fired again.

Dan Delo shrieked as the slug hit him in the small of the back, shoving him across the road toward the car. With a screech of pain, he flapped his great wings and ascended into the sky.

Toby worked the slide again, but since his right hand refused to go higher than his waist, aiming at the flying demon was pointless. Instead, he made for the last place he'd seen Shannon—the trunk of the Lincoln. As he ran, he felt the wind of Dan Delo's passage above his head and ducked, escaping the demon's claws by fractions of an inch.

He slid around the back of the car, almost crashing into Mike and Shannon, who squatted near the back tire. He thrust the shotgun at Mike. "I think my shoulder's dislocated."

Mike took the shotgun and handed over his paintball gun. "How do we handle him?"

Toby bared his teeth in an ugly grimace—half pain, half frustration. "If he's aware of the paintballs, he just flaps his stupid fucking wings and blows the gas away. We distracted him before by shooting the other demon, but now…"

"I'll just have to distract him with this." Mike gestured with the shotgun; his lips pressed into a thin line. "You and Shannon pepper him with the chloroform."

Toby frowned. "I'm not sure that's enough, Mike."

In the air above them, Dan Delo screamed, and the wind of his passage buffeted the car.

"Guess we'll find out," said Mike. He sprinted away from the car like a track star at the beginning of a race.

"Mike!" Toby hissed. "Dammit!" He fumbled with the paintball gun in his left hand. "I suck with this hand, Shan. You hit him in the face, I'll try to keep him off balance."

"I..." Shannon rocked her head back and forth. "Toby...I'm...I'm no good at this. You have to do it."

"Shannon, I *can't*. I can't lift my right arm past my waist, I can't be effective that way. I'll set this on full auto, and just do my best to keep the thing busy fanning away chloroform. You can do it; you *must* do it."

Shannon swallowed hard, looking at the paintball gun in her lap as if it were an alien thing. She shook her head once and stood.

Down the road, Mike fired the shotgun—the booming report answered by an earsplitting scream from the sky. Mike racked the slide of the shotgun, then dove to the left, rolling at the edge of the road. He came up in a squat, the stock of the gun already at his shoulder, and fired again.

Dan Delo howled and fell from the sky, landing on his side, blood and brains leaking from a massive hole in the side of his head. He lay there twitching, then his limbs flopped on the macadam like epileptic snakes.

"Yes! Mike, you got him!" shouted Shannon, holding her fists above her head. She sprinted toward the demon.

"Shannon, no!" shouted Toby, but she either didn't hear him or ignored him. He ran after her but was too far away and too slow to catch her.

As Shannon approached him, the big purple demon cackled and sprang to his feet. He whirled to face her, his wings extended, and the claw on the end of one of his wings slashed her. The force of the blow sent her reeling away.

Mike straightened and sprinted toward the fight, dropping the shotgun as he got close. He lowered his shoulder and slammed into the demon, his arms encircling Delo's waist. He drove forward, straining to wrench the beast off his feet, and succeeded only in lifting one leg.

Dan Delo looked down and cackled with glee. He lifted an arm high above his head and then brought it down elbow first into the back of Mike's neck. The sound of the impact was sickening, and Mike flopped to the ground at the demon's feet. The demon glowered and sent the shotgun skittering away into the ditch.

Delo turned his gaze on Toby and leered at him. "And now, *mighty hunter*, it's time for you to pay your debt."

Toby skidded to a halt, and sprayed paintballs at the purple demon, firing in one continuous stream. *If nothing else, I might put Mike and Shannon to sleep so they won't have to suffer.*

Dan Delo cocked his head, listening intently. His face bunched, and he snarled at Toby. "Your payment will have to wait, but I will take a small advance." He looked down at the man lying at his feet and lifted one foot. Then his gaze returned to Toby's, and he stomped on Mike, claws of his feet extended.

In the distance, Toby heard what had caught the demon's attention—sirens.

4

LaBouche read the note from Sally once more, then crumpled the paper into a ball, squeezing it in his fist. *The gall! We are in a war for our very existence, and the demon securing our base goes courting*! He turned and stomped out of his impromptu command center. He wanted more than anything to take the news to Brigitta, but she'd made it clear that he and Chaz had to work together.

They needed Chaz focused—focused on defending Oneka Falls, on securing their base of power. *Why can't that dumb asshole just do as he's told*? Now, LaBouche would have to take the time to travel to Oneka Falls and speak to him. Time that he should spend planning, setting traps, and gathering the demons who had moved away.

Preparing for the coming war, in other words.

5

The purple demon ground his foot into Mike's upper back and then transferred his full weight to that foot. He launched himself into the air, and with an evil laugh, flew away.

Toby rushed toward Mike. "Shannon!"

A groan came from the ditch on the side of the road.

"Shannon! I need you! Mike's hurt!"

Another groan sounded, but she raised her head. "Mike?"

"He's down, Dan Delo stomped on him, elbowed him in the neck." Toby dropped the paintball gun and slid on his knees to Mike's side.

"Are those…are those sirens?" asked Shannon, sounding like she'd had three too many Manhattans.

"Are you okay, Shannon?" Toby tore his eyes from the mess that was Mike's upper back in time to watch her stand, stagger to the left, and fall again. "Shit!" he muttered. He ripped his shirt off, wincing at the pain in his shoulder as he wrenched his arm out of the sleeve.

Mike's wounds were severe—he was bleeding profusely—and the first thing Toby needed to do was to get the bleeding under control. He pressed his shirt over the wounds, then looked toward Shannon.

She was standing again, but in the fragile-looking way of drunks everywhere, her hands held out for balance. She glanced at him, widened her eyes once as if to clear them, then climbed out of the ditch and onto the road. "Tell me what to do."

She slurred as she spoke, and that worried Toby. "Shannon, where are you hurt?" He darted a glance at her, watching her approach. She weaved a strange path between the edge of the road and where he stood.

"Sirens," said Shannon. "Getting closer."

"Shannon, I need you to go through the car. Get all our weapons, get anything that might point to one of us. Mike rented the car, so there'll be a record of it, but there's nothing we can do about that. Get everything else."

"You don't need my help with Mike?"

"I do, but we don't have time for both. Get going; get the car cleaned out."

"I can't carry everything."

Toby gave her a terse nod. "Multiple trips. Hide stuff in the woods."

She stood swaying for a moment, her eyes on the back of Mike's head. "Is he—" she choked.

"No, not if I can help it. Remember, I went to medical school, though I haven't worked on a live person since residency. Still, anatomy is anatomy." He glanced up at her diamond tears glittering in the moonlight. "Go, Shan. I won't let him die."

She turned—a little too quickly—and staggered sideways for a moment. She straightened and moved toward the car, leaving Toby to return his full attention to trying to stem the flow of Mike's blood.

The sirens grew louder, and Toby lifted his head to gaze down the length of the road—back toward Route 104. There were no spinning red and blue lights, yet, and that was a good thing.

"Unnh," groaned Mike. His muscles tensed, and he drew his arms to his sides as if he were about to do a push-up.

"Lie still, you're wounded."

Mike didn't move, and he relaxed his arms. "Demon…" he whispered.

"Gone." Toby glanced toward Shannon as she emerged from the woods and weaved her way back to the car. "Mike, we'll have to abandon the car. Cops are on the way, and…"

"And they can't catch us here." Each time Mike spoke, his voice was stronger.

"Yes, that's it."

"That'll be the county, first. Is this Monroe? Can't remember."

Toby shook his head even though Mike was face down and couldn't see him. "No, it's Wayne County."

"Don't know anybody at the Wayne County Sheriff's Department. Once they check out the scene…they'll call the troopers, for sure. Can't leave anything in the car—"

"I've got Shannon seeing to that, Mike. Don't worry."

"I'm not."

You should be, Toby thought, noting the amount of blood that had saturated the T-shirt pressed to Mike's back. *It* should *worry you that you may never walk again.* Mike had moved his arms, and that was a good thing given the blow to the back of his neck, but Dan Delo was huge and looked heavy—and he had stomped on Mike's spine. "Mike," said Toby with forced casualness. "Can you feel your feet?"

Mike chuckled. "Deftly handled, Doctor Pathologist. But, yes, I can feel my feet. Pins and needles, but there."

"Good. That's good, Mike." Toby glanced up at the intersection on 104 and grimaced at the red and blue spinners reflecting off the signs and buildings on each corner of the intersection. "But I can't risk moving you."

"I figured as much, Toby. You and Shannon get out of here."

"We're not leaving you, Mike," said Shannon from behind Toby.

Toby frowned down at Mike's back. "Did you get everything out of the car, Shan?" said Toby in a hushed voice.

"Yes, everything I could find. It's all in a pile about twenty feet from the tree line."

"My shotgun," said Mike. "In the ditch. And you have to, Shannon. We can't risk Toby getting caught. Or you."

"Or *you*, dumbass," said Shannon but without anger in her voice.

"Can't help that," said Mike. "Anyway, I know all the tricks. Take my wallet, Toby."

"But you rented the car—"

"Yeah, I did, but that'll take a little time to sort out. I've got amnesia," he said in a wry tone. "Can't remember who I am or why I'm here. All I remember is the gang of thugs that attacked the car when I stopped because of the fallen tree."

Toby stole a glance at the car, at the caved-in quarter panel, the strips of shredded metal on the roof, the broken glass. *It could work, at least for a day or two.* He looked at Shannon and nodded. "Shannon, are you with it enough to do your thing?"

Shannon stared him in the eye for a few seconds, then inclined her head.

"Can you make me invisible? Can you make a group of people overlook me?"

"I've never tried that, and I've never tried to deceive an entire group. I have no clue if—"

"We've got to chance it. I don't want to leave Mike until the ambulance arrives."

"I'll be fine, Toby. You two get going."

"While I respect your medical opinion, Doctor Richards, I'll stay right here." Toby grinned up at Shannon. "You go stand with the stuff, Shan. Try your best, that's all we've ever asked of you."

"But Mike will recover? Fully recover?"

Toby peered at the end of the road and frowned at the two police cars racing toward them. "I think so. Go on now, Shannon. Before they're close enough to catch sight of you."

"Or you," said Mike.

Shannon glanced at oncoming vehicles before returning her gaze to Toby. "You *think* so?"

"I'll be fine, Shannon. Scout's honor," said Mike.

Toby gazed steadily back at her, then bobbed his head. "If they see me, they see me, Shannon. You don't come out of the woods, not for anything. Someone has to get away to tell the others what happened. Dan Delo will come back—he'll bring others up here."

"But—"

"Shannon, there's no time. Get going!" said Mike.

Shannon shook her head and turned toward the woods. "I don't like it." When neither man answered her, she walked into the woods.

"You should go, too, Toby. I'll be fine."

"I think so, too, Mike, but I'm staying right here until I'm *sure*. Who knows how long it will take for an ambulance to get out here?" The sirens were almost on top of them, and Toby knew without looking that the Sheriff's Deputies were close. "Make sure they call for an ambulance right away."

"They will."

"And don't let them take you to Rochester General. Tell them you want to go to Strong or Highland."

The police cars made a V, blocking the road, lights and sirens going. Both deputies got out of their vehicles and left the front doors open. One rushed forward, gun drawn, to check around the car, the other came toward Mike. Toby sat statue-still, trying to breathe without making a sound.

"Sir?" the deputy asked, shouting over the noise of the sirens. "Are you conscious?"

"Yes, Deputy. Are they still here?"

"Who, sir?"

"The...the men who did this. There were three—no four of them. *Maybe* four... They...they attacked me."

"Anything, Stan?"

"Is that my name?" asked Mike, adding a slur to the words.

Don't lay it on so thick, Mike. Don't overdo it.

"What?" asked the deputy. "What did you say?"

"You…called me 'Stan.'"

The deputy shook his head. "No, sir, I was talking to the other deputy. He's near the vehicle. Is the car yours?"

"I… remember…a tree in the road? It's all so hazy."

The deputy squatted next to Mike and tilted his head to the side. "Whose shirt is this?"

Oh, shit! Toby thought. *I should have had Shannon make it invisible, too.*

"Shirt? It's my shirt," said Mike.

"No, I mean the one on your back. The one sopping up the blood." The deputy hooked the blood-soaked shirt with his pen and lifted it. Toby jerked his hands back just in time, wincing at the pain that erupted in his shoulder with the sudden movement.

"Must've passed out. Is there a bus coming?"

"Bus?" The deputy squinted down at Mike. "Are you on the job?"

Mike was silent for a few seconds. "I… I… I can't remember."

"What's your name?" The deputy rocked back on his heels and let the shirt fall back to cover Mike's wounds.

"It's the damnedest thing… It's…it's as if it's on the tip of my tongue. I can almost remember…"

"Did you hit your head in the accident?"

"Accident?"

"Don't worry, sir. The ambulance is on its way. Should be here any minute now."

"Good. I…"

"Did one of the men try to help you? Is that who owns this shirt?"

"I really don't know, Deputy."

The deputy sighed. "That's okay. You said there were four of them? Can you describe them?"

"I'm not sure. They attacked me when I got out of the car, but it's all so hazy."

The other deputy approached. "That car is beat to hell, and not just from the accident. Looks as though somebody took after the roof with an axe."

At the intersection with Route 104, the buildings and signs again glowed with spinning lights as the ambulance turned onto the road and sped toward them.

6

LaBouche pushed his way through the glass door of the Oneka Falls Town Hall hard enough that it slammed against the wall. He had his state trooper badge looped through his belt for the benefit of any humans still working there, but he didn't plan on any playacting. He walked right up to the reception desk. "Where?" he asked Sally McBride.

Sally flashed him a sour grin. "They took a long dinner."

With a covert glance around, LaBouche hissed, "They don't eat—at least not like that."

"*Of course they don't!*" Sally snapped. "They're off somewhere, *fucking*."

The acid in her voice surprised LaBouche. *Can she be jealous? How can she be jealous if Chaz is giving his affections to another? After all the abuse, all the degradation he has heaped on her?* He stared at her, his gaze zipping from her eyes to the set of her shoulders, to the corner of her mouth, to the way her ears lay flat back against her head. *She is!* LaBouche smeared a fake smile on his lips while resting the tips of his fingers on his chin. "He has treated you horribly, Sally," he said with a hint of humor in his voice.

Sally frowned but nodded.

LaBouche rested his elbows on the reception counter and leaned toward her. "You're not jealous, are you?"

She jerked her head back as if he had spit in her face and opened her mouth to speak.

"Because if you are, I must conclude that you are stark, raving mad."

Tears glimmered in her eyes as she crossed her arms over her chest.

LaBouche snorted and curled his lip. “That’s why things are the way they are, Sally. That’s why you’ll never rise above your current position.”

“I can’t help it,” she wailed. “I *hate* Chaz, but… I don’t… I don’t want her to have him!”

LaBouche’s grin broadened, and he lifted his arms, palms pointed toward the ceiling. “The heart wants what it wants, Sally.”

She glared at him through her tears but had nothing more to say.

He lay one hand on the counter and drummed his fingers. “Where would they go? Chaz’s house?”

“Well, I wouldn’t know!” snapped Sally.

LaBouche’s smile didn’t fade, not one millimeter. “Of course you would, Sally.”

Sally looked down at the surface of her desk and then away toward the far corner of the room. “Shannon Bertram’s apartment.”

“The woman with the hunters? That’s brash, even for Chaz.”

Sally lifted her round shoulders and let them drop, setting her fat breasts and belly jiggling. “It’s close,” she said sourly. “It’s just across the street.”

“Ah. Convenience has its advantages. Where?”

Sally didn’t answer, she seemed lost in thought.

LaBouche leaned across the counter and snapped his fingers in her face, and she startled. "I asked you: 'where.'" All of his previous jocularity had faded, and his voice had gone as cold as an arctic wind.

"Out the door, turn left, straight across at the traffic light, through the parking lot, up the stairs on the side of the building, the door at the top." She turned to glare at him. "Happy?"

LaBouche straightened and narrowed his eyelids at her. "You'll want to watch yourself, McBride. I know you're upset, and I'm making allowances, but I'll have your respect."

Sally flapped her pink, pudgy hand at him. "Whatever. Get out and take your threats with you."

LaBouche glared at her for the space of ten breaths, neither one of them moving or looking away. Finally, he spun on his heel and pushed out into the fresh night air, slamming the glass door so hard it cracked.

7

Dan Delo circled the smashed car, far too high to be in danger of being shot by the hunters. His wing ached in the cold air, but the membrane would heal, given time and adequate sustenance. Below him, the cops traipsed back and forth between the hunters' car and the knot of EMTs around the one he'd stomped on.

The woman was in the woods, no doubt hiding, but the other one… The other one had disappeared. Even so, he wanted to watch where the woman would go. On the other hand, it might be fun to stop her from going anywhere.

He wondered if that old idiot at the library had gotten away. Part of his intent in attacking the car was to check the trunk—something he hadn't had time to do. He had watched the woman take their weapons out of the trunk, but the angle had been wrong, and he hadn't been able to see if the old demon was back there. If that ancient demon was in the trunk and woke up now…well, Dan would have to go to his aid, proscription against attacking cops or no.

The EMTs loaded the ambulance and departed in a cacophony of sirens and engine noise. The two cops walked around, shining their flashlights on the ground, picking up spent shotgun shells and trying to figure out what the broken paintball shells were. Dan Delo circled lower and focused his ears on the two men.

"What do you think, Stan?" asked one.

Stan sighed and kicked the remains of the paintball into the ditch. "Drug deal gone bad? I'll be damned if I know, Guy."

“Nah. What kind of idiot would it take to do a drug deal in the middle of a well-traveled road? Plus, you saw the guy. Clean-cut, decent shape…and he called the ambulance a ‘bus.’ I bet you dinner the guy’s on the job.”

“You think? Maybe he’s undercover. DEA or something such as that. Maybe that’s why he caught the beating.”

Guy straightened and stared at Stan as if he lost his mind. “No one going undercover in the drug trade would dress this way. He looks more like a police chief than a drug dealer.”

Stan bowed his head. “Let’s check what they’ve got in the trunk, then. I bet it’s drugs.”

Guy scoffed and strode toward the wrecked Lincoln. “Key’s in the ignition, you said?”

“Yeah.” Stan walked over to stand at the trunk. “I mean, think about it, Guy. A large American-made four-door, a guy traveling alone… Suspicious, right?”

Guy shook his head and leaned inside the car, retrieving the keys. “Stan, those guidelines were for Interstate traffic. Does this look like an Interstate?”

“No, but everybody has to get off the Interstate sometime.”

Guy didn’t respond but walked to the back of the car and opened the trunk. It was empty. “I guess you owe me dinner, Stan.”

When Dan turned his attention back to the woods, the woman had disappeared. Again. He searched for her from the air, but it was as if she had turned invisible. With frustration pounding in his temple with the rhythm of his pulse, Delo turned south and began the long flight toward Oneka Falls.

8

Mason sighed as he switched off the ignition of his van—what his co-workers at the freight company called "his serial killer van." The thought made him smile as it always did. Sometimes, the best place to hide was in plain sight.

He had the van "outfitted for camping," though he detested camping. It featured a metal-framed single bed along one wall of the rear compartment of the truck. He'd installed curtains to cover the back windows—blackout curtains, to boot—so nothing would disturb him when he was "trying to sleep out in the woods." Those were the changes he talked about—the other changes were nobody's business…unless they wanted the "special tour."

He glanced in the extended rearview mirror. The bed—and its current occupant—was reflected there. She sat scrunched up against the metal screen headboard, eyes wide as she stared back at him. A gag kept her teeth apart, but more to make her uncomfortable than to keep her quiet—one of his modifications to the van that he didn't share with anyone was the studio-quality sound dampening. His guest could scream her head off, and no one would be the wiser unless he had the windows open. He tipped her a wink and opened his door.

She struggled against her bonds, but with tempered steel handcuffs and the quarter-inch-thick leather cuffs around her ankles, she couldn't get away. She would leave when *he* said, and in the condition he dictated.

He drew a deep breath and whistled through his teeth as he exhaled. "Don't worry," he said. "I'll be right back."

As he locked the door to his garage, he chuckled. He loved that part of the game. He'd leave her in the van for a few hours—or maybe more, depending on how the mood struck him—getting her out when he wanted. In the meantime, she'd jump at every sound, every vision her brain conjured out of the dark.

Mason couldn't draw sustenance from her fear like his friends could, but he fed on them, nonetheless.

9

Shannon kept the cloak of invisibility over them until they stood beside the strip mall half a mile east of the intersection of 104 and the road where Dan Delo had attacked their car. The strip mall contained a Chinese restaurant that was still open, and in the darkness next to the building, she changed her illusion, so they no longer looked like they'd been in a war, and so Toby was wearing a shirt again. "Toby, how long until the car gets here?"

"An hour or two, yet. Rental car companies never deliver at the time they say they will."

Shannon sighed and put a hand over her eyes. She was still dizzy from the blow of the demon's wingtip, and the cut across her forehead burned. "I don't know how long I can keep this going."

"Let's go inside," said Toby. "At least you can sit down and rest."

Wearily, Shannon nodded and followed him through the door.

10

"They should be back by now," said Benny from where he stood near the door. He twitched the curtains aside and peered out the narrow window to the side of the door.

Scott nodded but said nothing.

Benny rounded on him, his expression an angry one. "How can you just sit there?"

Scott lifted an eyebrow. "Is there anything we can do? I don't remember having a second car."

Benny scoffed and turned back to stare out the window, watching for headlights on the road beyond. "Something's wrong, Scott. I'm telling you. I can feel it."

"You can feel it, or you can *feel* it?"

"I'm not sure how to answer that, Scott."

"What I mean is: do you *believe* something is wrong, or do you *know* something is wrong because of your gift?"

Benny scoffed again and chopped his left hand through the air.

"That's what I thought," said Scott. "Benny, I've been through situations like this a million times. Stakeouts, waiting for drug buys with an undercover, whatever. Man, you've got to put away the stress and learn to wait. Your mind will play tricks on you—you'll imagine everything that could go wrong—but none of that means anything." Scott chuckled. "One time I—"

"I'm not in the mood for war stories, Scott. This is different, and you know it."

Scott held up his hands in supplication. "Okay. I was just trying to help."

"I… I think one of them has been hurt. I…"

Scott got to his feet and walked over to stand next to Benny. "Go on."

"Maybe…" Benny bowed his head and swiped at the hair hanging down in his face. "What if…they were ambushed?"

"And the paintball guns didn't work?"

Benny shook his head and waved the question away. "I don't have details!"

"Okay. Tell me what to do."

Benny stole a quick peek at him, his face drawn into sheepish lines. "I don't know, Scott."

Scott cocked his head to the side. "Which one is hurt? Don't think about it, just say the first name that pops into your mind."

"Mike."

Scott pursed his lips. He'd expected Benny to name Shannon as the one hurt. Mike was the last one who should get hurt. He had the training and the experience, and that should've allowed him to avoid injury. "Well, if it's true, it's true. There's nothing we can do about it from here."

"Can't you call them? Call Toby?"

Scott pulled his cell phone out of his pocket and tossed it to Benny. "No service way out here."

Benny looked at the phone as if it were an alien artifact, then he tossed the device back. "I can't stand waiting!"

Scott understood the sentiment. "Waiting's the hardest part, Benny. I was trying to tell you that earlier."

Benny nodded absently and looked out the window.

II

LaBouche kicked the Bertrand woman's door hard enough to pop it off its hinges and send it walking across the small kitchen where it slammed into the oven before it fell. He entered the tiny apartment with a grimace on his face and his hands tucked into fists. "Hey, dumbass! Where are you?"

The rustling of fabric on fabric and a muted whisper came from the closed door on the other side of the small family area. LaBouche crossed the family room in three giant strides and kicked that door off its hinges, too.

He glimpsed silvery skin and black mist streaking into the bathroom before the door slammed shut. Welsh lay on the bed, sound asleep and snoring.

LaBouche grabbed him by one mother-of-pearl scaled ankle and pulled. Welsh squawked as his butt hit the floor, then he thrashed as the rest of him came off the bed.

"What… Who…" he muttered. His eyes came to rest on LaBouche's face and cleared. "How dare you!" He jerked his foot back, but LaBouche's grip was too firm.

"How dare I?" LaBouche punctuated the question with a savage jerk of Welsh's ankle. "How dare I? I'll tell you how I dare: I'm busy doing Brigitta's will, and you are here with a silver-skinned *whore* acting like a couple of…of kids!" He flung Chaz's ankle to the side and drew his leg back to deliver a kick.

The bathroom door slammed open, impaling its knob in the wall, and Nicole Conrau stepped out, wrapped in a towel. She glared at LaBouche, then shifted her gaze to Chaz. "Are you going to let him insult me this way?"

Chaz growled deep in his throat and sprang to his feet, his all-red eyes glaring at LaBouche. "Get out of here while I'm still of a mind to let you," he grated.

LaBouche smiled, but his expression was ugly. "How I've waited for you to threaten me since Brigitta gave me my true form back. Oh, I've watched you, Chaz. I've seen you strutting around as if you're a Bantam cock, and I've waited for a reason to deal with you."

Chaz grinned, showing his fangs. "And now you've got it. So, what will you do, LaBouche? Run back to Brigitta?"

"I think I'll—" In mid-sentence, LaBouche sprang, baring his own shark-like teeth and throwing his arms wide. He slammed into Welsh and wrapped his arms around the demon's torso. With a savage twisting lift, he swept Chaz off his feet once again and drove him through the bedroom wall to the floor in the living room. Furniture splintered beneath them as the two rolled and fought.

Nicole Conrau came to stand in the bedroom door, observing the fight with a small smile on her face.

12

As the clock ticked away toward midnight, Toby piloted the rented Cadillac down the freeway at eighty miles an hour. Scott sat next to him, staring out the side window, and Shannon and Benny sat in the back seat murmuring to one another. As Toby flicked his turn signal on and cut across the lanes for the off-ramp that would take them to Strong Memorial Hospital, Benny bolted up straight.

"No!" he said.

Toby looked at him in the rearview mirror. "No? What's up, Benny?"

"Don't get off here," said Benny, as he stared out the windshield. "We can't go to the hospital yet."

"No?" repeated Toby.

"No," said Benny firmly.

"Okay, then where?" asked Scott.

"Airport."

Toby shook his head. "Why, Benny? There's nothing there but parking lots, a few cops, and a lot of security."

Benny shook his head. "We need to go to the airport." He snuck a peek at Shannon. "Now."

Toby watched his face for a few moments—something which made Benny nervous since they were still barreling down the highway at eighty miles an hour—then he grinned and bobbed his head. "Okay, Benny. To the airport, we go."

"Good," said Benny.

"Can you give us a hint?" asked Scott.

Benny shook his head and slumped against the back seat as if the conversation exhausted him. Shannon lay her head against his shoulder and closed her eyes.

Toby glanced at Scott and shrugged.

13

Mike awoke in a hospital bed, and for a moment, had no memory of what had happened. His back ached like never before, and he was as sore as the time he'd flipped his car in a drunken stupor. His mouth tasted foul—as if a combination of asphalt, chalk dust, and bat guano coated the inside of his mouth. An IV dripped a clear liquid into his arm, and he tried to reach for it with his other hand, but the handcuff stopped him.

Outside his room, the hospital whispered the muted tones of hospital night shifts everywhere—not quiet, but not as loud as during daylight hours. Mike figured there was a police officer stationed outside of his door.

"Hey!" he called. There was no answer, so Mike felt around in the bed until he found the button that would call the nurse. He pressed the button and waited.

And waited.

Then, he waited some more.

When the nurse finally arrived, anger thrummed in the back of his mind. "What do you need?" she asked.

"Water would be nice."

She looked at him for a moment, then pointed with her pen at a water pitcher on the bed table.

Mike pressed his lips together to keep from shouting at her, and rattled the handcuffs against the bed rails, instead.

Her eyes widened, but then she nodded. “Let me get you a cup.” She poured water from the Styrofoam pitcher into a large plastic cup with a built-in straw. She held it for him, and Mike took a long drink.

“What time is it?” he asked her when he finished drinking.

“It’s a little after midnight.”

“Why am I handcuffed?” He rattled the handcuffs against the bed rail again.

The nurse shrugged, glancing over her shoulder. “Your chart says a detective wants to ask you a couple of questions. Something about your accident.”

Mike grimaced and rattled the handcuff chain again. “And is the detective waiting somewhere?”

The nurse shook her head. “No, we are to call when you awaken.”

Mike looked up at her. “Well, I’m awake. I don’t much care for being in handcuffs so go call whoever you have to call and get these damn things off of me.”

The nurse deployed her professional smile—the one that said Mike was being an asshole—and turned and left him alone once more.

He knew what the detectives would ask him—questions about his identity, about Toby, about what had happened in Oneka Falls—and he didn't want to answer them. He pulled against the handcuffs again, testing the limits of the chains.

Even if his pocket held his key, there was no way he could reach the locks.

Chapter 7

1986

I

Stephen groaned and cracked his eyes open. The demon—or whatever it was—had left. The place was a wreck, splinters of wood and shelving, the pantry door, slivers of glass—and blood…blood everywhere.

Stephen pushed himself up and groaned a second time as the world began to spin. His head ached as if someone had put it in an industrial vise and squeezed. He put his hand on the back of his head to explore the damage and felt the massive lump, as well as a long, bleeding gash just below the crown of his head.

"Gary?" he called, hoping the man was only unconscious but knowing deep down a person couldn't lose that much blood and survive. "Mary? Mom?"

No one answered him. He crawled to the base of the breakfast bar and pulled himself to his feet. The world spun harder, and for a moment, he didn't know whether he was going to puke or pass out.

He puked.

Trying to pull himself together, Stephen walked to the shattered window above the sink and looked out into the darkness. Gary Dennis's head lay in the middle of the concrete path outside the window. "Oh, Gary. I'm sorry."

He turned, and using the counter for support, he walked around the edges of the kitchen and made his way into the living room. He grabbed one of the throw blankets from the floor, and after shifting the upended sofa off him, covered Gary's body.

The living room looked as if the wildest riot in history had taken place in it. Gary died trying to give them a chance to get away, just as Stephen tried to sacrifice himself so that Mary had a chance at escaping. "I hope you did, Mare."

He threaded his way through the destruction and stopped at the opening of the hall that led to the porch. In his mind's eye, his mother's figure—*her body*—blazed, lying in a pool of blood, the skin ripped from her torso.

He didn't want to endure the sight again.

He turned and went out the kitchen door. Dawn threatened to break across the lake, and he turned toward the gravel road at the back of the house. *Please don't be there*, he begged. *Please let that rental car be gone, and Mary with it.*

He hesitated at the back corner of the house, scared to round the corner and see for himself if Mary had gotten away. He closed his eyes, squeezing them shut until tears leaked out. Steeling himself, he walked around the corner and gasped.

The rental car sat where he'd left it, and Mary's body lay splayed on the hood, naked and bloody.

Mary hadn't gotten away. Gary's sacrifice… It had all been for nothing.

Stephen's scream echoed through the early morning air, disturbing the dawn song of the birds living around the lake. His knees gave out, and he pitched forward into the gravel, not even attempting to break his fall.

He couldn't think, couldn't process his loss beyond the raw burning horror of it, the pain. He lay there, face down in the gravel, and when he heard footsteps approaching, he didn't care, he didn't move. Stephen hoped it was the demon, coming back to finish him off.

But, of course, it wasn't.

2

Joe led Greg out of the woods as dawn cracked the night sky. Songbirds did their thing to greet the day. He looked around to regain his sense of direction. They'd come out on Thomas Hill Road, the gravel lane that connected them to Lake Circle, but down around the bend about a half a mile from the house. He'd never felt so exhausted, so run down, not even in boot camp. Not even in Korea during the war.

A ragged scream rent the predawn stillness. Joe's head snapped in the direction from which it had come, and his hand tightened around the foregrip of the M1. He didn't feel safe out in the open, standing in the middle of the road, but when he cast his gaze back at the forest behind him, he saw no other choice.

He faced his grandson and squatted before him, putting his eyes on the same level as Greg's. "I don't know what's happening up the road, but that scream… Well, it can't be good. I don't want to take you into the middle of whatever is happening, but I can't leave you here alone, can I?"

Greg shook his head in vigorous denial. "No! Stay with me, Grandpa! She can't get you if you're with me."

"Now, don't start all that again." His voice was gruff, but he pulled the boy in for a hug. "I won't leave you." But even as he said the words, his gaze drifted toward the curve and the road. Something about the scream bothered him, but Joe couldn't put his finger on what. Greg trembled against him, his thin arms looped around Joe's neck. "There, there."

"She did this, Grandpa," said Greg in funereal tones. "My invisible friend said she would, and she did! Something's…"

"Shh, now, Greggy. We don't know anything."

Greg nodded against his shoulder. "Someone's coming, Grandpa." His tone was so relaxed, so lackadaisical, that Joe almost ignored the meaning of his words.

Joe disengaged Greg's arms and stood, guiding Greg's hand back to his belt. "If we have to run, you let go, and you run as fast as you can. Mind me now, Greg."

The sound of footsteps came from the direction of Lake Circle, and Joe turned in that direction. He checked the M1, ensuring it was ready to go, and shouldered his weapon, but let it drop to his side almost at once.

Coming up the road toward them were six cops—each one armed to the teeth—led by Tom Walton and Mason Harper. "Ho there, Joe!" called the chief. "Man, I'm glad to see you. And is that Greg I see?"

Mason stepped away from the cops, his gaze burning into Greg's eyes. A small, cruel smile flirted with his lips. "Hi, Greggy," he said.

Greg stepped closer to his grandfather, his gaze on the gravel beneath his feet.

Joe wagged his head up and down once. "Ayup. He led me on a merry chase, but here we are. Tom, there's a woman—"

Tom held up his hand like a traffic cop ordering someone to stop. "We'll call in Leland Chambers and get to the bottom of whatever is going on in these woods. Don't you worry, Joe."

Joe nodded, but his worry didn't abate. "Did you hear it? From down around the bend?"

Tom shook his head.

"A scream." He hooked a thumb of his free hand over his shoulder. "I can't go check it out." He jerked his head toward Greg. "He doesn't want me to leave him."

"I'll stay with him, Mr. Canton," said Mason in a piping voice.

Joe looked down at the boy, a wrinkle forming between his eyebrows, but said nothing. Greg stepped behind him, and his hand fluttered against the small of his grandfather's back.

Tom turned toward one of his men. "Martin, you go. Double-time it!"

The officer sprinted down the road, his feet crunching in the gravel. It didn't delight Greg as much as the noise his grandfather's GTO made as it rolled through the gravel, but he liked the sound—even after a night of terror. The rest of the policemen gathered around them, the older ones nodding to Joe.

"I've got to tell you, Tom," said Joe. "I fired this tonight." He glanced at Greg, then met Tom's steady gaze. "I fired at someone. A woman dressed in black."

"Okay," said Tom with a solemn nod. "Did you hit her?"

Joe cut his gaze away. "It *seems* I did, but it didn't slow her down any. Things…" Joe waved his free hand at the woods. "Things got confused, weird… I'm not sure…"

"Ayup," said the chief with a terse nod. "We ran into a bit of that ourselves—a low hanging mist, disappearing tracks, something that…taunted us." Tom shrugged. "I'm not sure I can explain any of it, Joe."

Joe nodded once, his expression cheerless and despondent. "Do you suppose…" He twisted to glance at Greg's face, then shook his head.

"We can discuss it later," said Tom. He turned his attention to Greg. "And you, Greg? Are you okay?"

Greg peeked out and imitated his grandfather's terse nod, but avoided meeting anyone's eye.

"It's okay, son," said Tom. "You've had quite a night, too, I'll bet."

"Should we get on up to the house?" said Joe in a worried tone. "Stephen is there, but Mary and—"

"Elizabet called the station to say Stephen went into the woods after you two."

The thing that had been bothering Joe solidified in his mind. He took two steps up the road, almost without thinking about them, then stopped and took Greg's hand. "Will you stay here with Chief Walton?"

"He can stay with me," said Mason, still grinning like a cat watching a mouse.

Greg turned a horrified expression on his grandfather and took a step closer to him. "No, Grandpa!"

Joe fought for calm, but that scream… He directed his gaze at Tom and lifted his free hand then let it drop.

"Martin will be back. That or he'll radio to let us know it's safe. Give him a minute."

Joe stared toward the bend in the road, the muscles across his back tensing. He rested his hand on Greg's shoulder and gave him a little squeeze. "Hear that, Greg? Not much longer to wait."

3

Pete Martin sprinted up the gravel lane, rounding the bend at speed, compensating for the slipping gravel beneath his feet. He held his AR-15 with both hands, ready to snap it into firing position should the need arise.

The string of Genosgwa police cars stood where they'd left them, parked on the right shoulder of the gravel lane, facing toward the Canton lake house. A man lay in the center of the road, on his face and not moving.

Pete slowed, then stopped. He tightened his grip on the AR-15. "Sir?" he called. "Sir, are you injured?"

The man lying in the road didn't move, but he moaned, and Pete took a few cautious steps toward him. That's when he saw the nude woman laid out as if on display on the hood of a nondescript rental car. She was bloody, long furrows ripped along her sides, chunks of flesh missing from her trapezius muscles, one leg cocked to the side at a savage angle, as if her hip had been dislocated.

Pete took a few more steps. "Ma'am? Are you all right?" He clenched his jaw in disgust. *Of* course *she's not all right, you jackass*! *That much is obvious*. He turned his attention toward the man lying face down in the gravel. He stepped toward him and squatted to his side. He lay a hand on the man's shoulder and gave him a gentle shake. "Sir? Are you injured?"

A wail escaped the man, but still, he didn't lift his head or roll to his side.

"Sir, I need you to tell me if you're injured. Did you hurt that woman?"

The man flung himself onto his back, his eyes burning, gaze boring into Pete's face such that Pete rocked back and fell on his rear. "*You leave her alone*!" the man grated. His hands scrabbled into fists, scooping up gravel in the process. "*You stay away from her*!"

Pete's eyelids fluttered several times, his knuckles going white on the AR-15. "I'm a police officer, sir!" The man had been in a life or death struggle, that was plain—he was bloody, his clothes hung in tatters, and his eyes…his eyes were glazed and faraway, or perhaps a concussion swaddled his awareness.

Pete had never seen Joe Canton's son, at least not that he remembered, but he would bet his salary the woman on the hood of the rental car was Mary Canton. "Stephen Canton?"

The man got to his knees, one foot flat on the ground as if getting ready to start a track meet. His wild, crazy gaze bounced from feature to feature on Martin's face. "Are you a demon?" he shouted.

"No, I'm a cop. I told you. Pete Martin." Pete got his legs underneath him, in case he had to flee. "Is she…" He cut his eyes toward the body on the car. "Is that your wife, sir?"

The man hopped forward, snarling, and he flung the gravel away. "Prove it! Prove it!"

Prove I'm a cop? Pete swallowed hard. "I need you to answer my questions, sir."

The man threw back his head and screamed. "*Prove it*! *Prove it*! *Prove it, or I'll kill you, you bastard*!"

Holding the AR-15 in front of him as if it were a shield, Martin scrambled away from the man he believed was Stephen Canton. Once he was ten steps away, he released the death grip he held on the AR-15's foregrip and thumbed his radio. "Chief, this is Martin. I think we've got a problem down here."

4

As he heard the radio call, Joe kneeled and picked Greg up with a one-handed grip, holding the M1 away from his body with the other hand. He glanced at Tom, then turned and sprinted toward home.

"Grandpa! Grandpa, was that my daddy?" Greg asked in a breathless voice. "What's happened to him? What's wrong?"

Joe grunted and kept running. Behind him, Tom and the others followed.

He rounded the bend, gaze darting from the string of police cars, to Martin's back, to Stephen…Stephen crouching in the gravel, screaming at the morning sky.

In Joe's arms, Greg began to cry.

Joe skidded to a stop and flung the M1 into the grass on the side of the road. He longed to put his grandson down and go to his son, go comfort Stephen, but Greg had his arms locked around Joe's neck.

Pete Martin shot a glance over his shoulder. "Don't bring the boy any closer," the cop said, cutting his eyes toward the row of police cars. "Keep him *back*."

He was trying to communicate something to Joe without saying it outright, but Joe did not understand what it was. There was something on the hood of the lead car, but Joe couldn't tell what it was from his vantage point.

Stephen stopped screaming, and when Joe returned his gaze to his son, Stephen's gaze was on him. "Son…are you… Are you okay? Where is Mary? Where's your mother?"

At the sound of his wife's name, Stephen's eyes cut toward the rental car, and something cold and ugly uncoiled in Joe's guts. He opened his mouth to speak, but his voice failed him. His throat spasmed as he swallowed, then he tried again. "And your mother?"

Stephen's eyes cut toward the house, and then zipped back, but he wouldn't meet Joe's gaze. Instead, he stared at his knees.

Joe staggered as his knees tried to come unhinged. He squeezed his eyes shut, but nothing could deny what he'd seen in his son's face. *Elizabet is gone*. Without opening his eyes, Joe turned and faced the lake.

"What is it, Grandpa?" asked Greg in a tremulous voice. "Where's Mommy? Where's Grandma?"

Joe didn't have the words to answer, even if he had been able to control his voice, which he couldn't. Behind his closed lips, his teeth trembled, and a lump of raw, burning pain rested against the back of his throat. He hugged Greg close.

"Where are they? Where are they, Grandpa?" Greg asked, but by the cheerless nature of his tone, Joe thought he knew the answers.

"Mr. Canton, is that your son, Stephen?"

Joe opened his mouth, but still couldn't find his voice, so he settled for nodding. He heard the crunch of boots on gravel as the other officers arrived, and Tom started issuing orders.

"*Demons*!" shouted Stephen. "*Dad*! *Dad, demons*!"

Mason burst into derisive laughter.

Joe half-turned at the sound of Stephen's voice—the insanity in it, the brokenness—then turned to glare at Mason.

The kid stood on the other side of the car Pete Martin had warned them about. His eyes opened wide, and a vast grin cracked his face. "*Cool*!" His gaze locked on something on the hood of the car.

Stephen lunged to his feet, wild gaze ripping from Officer Martin to the boy from next door, his hands clenching and unclenching. "*Demons*!" he shrieked.

"Daddy! Daddy!" shouted Greg. "*What's wrong*?"

Stephen's gaze snapped to meet Joe's. "Get him away! Can't you see? They're *demons*, Dad! *Evil*! *For Chrissake gimme your gun*!"

Something inside Joe stretched and stretched until he felt sure it must snap. He longed to rush to his son, to stand by his side and calm him, but he dared not. One glance into his son's eyes told him that. Instead, he squeezed Greg tighter and took a few steps back.

Confusion flashed in Stephen's eyes for a moment, then he was in motion, sprinting toward Pete Martin with his hands curled into claws, his mouth open as if he were a wild animal about to rip the policeman's throat out with his teeth. At the last second, he flung himself away, rolling in the grass on the side of the road.

"Stephen!" Tom Walton's voice cracked like a whip. "You cut this out, right now!"

Stephen came up into a crouch, his body hunched over something. "I won't let you get her!" he shouted. "Not again! I won't let you have her!"

"Stephen! Son, I—" Joe's mouth snapped shut as he watched his son stand tall, the M1 carbine held at his waist, his finger wrapped around the trigger. "Stephen, no!"

Stephen turned his head toward Joe, his manner lackadaisical and unconcerned. "Are you one of them, too?" He asked in a matter-of-fact tone. "Are you a demon, Dad?"

"What?" Joe took a step another back, another step away from his son and the madness in his eyes. "Demon? Son, I don't understand."

For a moment, Stephen looked as young as Greg, his expression one of great sorrow and loneliness. His eyes cleared and filled with tears. "They…" He shook his head as if to deny his own thoughts. "A demon came, Dad. It…it…" Stephen slung his head back and wailed.

"Stephen, put your father's rifle down," said Tom, just as calm as you please. By his tone, he might've been at a church picnic, or having a beer down to the Legion Hall.

With his head still flung backward, Stephen laughed. "Gary Dennis is dead," he said. "The demon ripped his head off. He tried… Gary tried to give us time to get away, and I tried to give…to give…Muh-muh-muh…" His head snapped forward, and his gaze sought his father's. "Why didn't she run? Dad, why didn't she use the time to get away? I tried to keep it inside…the demon, I mean…told her to…to run, but…"

With a sinking feeling, Joe realized that something horrible had happened while he'd been in the woods. Beyond murder, beyond a physical assault…something had broken his son's mind—maybe for good. "I don't know, Son. I don't… I don't have any answers, Stephen."

Stephen's gaze drifted away from his own, but not before Joe saw his eyes empty of conscious thought, of willpower. Not before he saw something dark and ugly command them. Again, Stephen threw his head back, gazing into the heavens.

"Stephen! Look at me, Son. I've got Greg here, with me. Greg is safe, I've kept him safe all night, and I will keep him safe as long as I'm able." Joe took a step toward his son but hesitated at taking another. "Stephen, just put that old M1 back in the grass. You have no need of it."

An inarticulate howl rose in Stephen's lips, and it made the hairs on the back of Joe's neck stand up straight. Stephen's head came forward, occupied by the same empty eyes as before, and his gaze danced between the police officers, but it always came back to rest on Mason Harper, growing darker and darker. "*DEMONS*!" he shouted.

"No, Son! They are just men, just people, same as you and me. They are no threat—" Joe's jaws slammed together as Stephen turned his gaze on his father. His face contorted with insane rage, hurt, and betrayal.

"*DEMONS*!" he screamed, sending such a look of hatred at his father that Joe stepped back and averted his gaze.

"Yes, Stephen," said Tom Walton. "It does look as if demons paid you a visit. If the things you say happened, who could say whether it was a demon or a man?"

"What?" Stephen growled.

Tom sighed. "If you only knew, Stephen, of the things that happened around here in the late seventies. People said Owen Gray was a demon, but he wasn't. Not in truth. He was a sick bastard, that's all, but at the time...at the time, everyone was too close to the heinous things that he did. Same as you're too close to the events of this past night. Don't make any rash decisions, son."

Joe dared to hope that Tom's smooth, placid voice would have a calming effect on his son. He looked at Stephen, gazing into his face, but his son didn't return his regard. He still held Joe's M1, his finger still curled inside the trigger guard, but his expression had gone slack, his eyes distant.

"Why don't you let me hold that, Stephen?" asked Tom as he took a step toward the distraught man. He twitched his chin at the rental car. "There's been enough death here, don't you think? There's been enough wasted life." He stopped three paces from Stephen and held out his hands.

Stephen's mindless expression cleared. He squeezed his eyes shut, and tears tracked down both cheeks. His throat convulsed as he swallowed, and the keening wail sounded from behind his closed lips. He took his finger out of the trigger guard, but he didn't give the rifle to Tom.

"Look at her legs! It's like one of them is snapped clean off at the hip," said Mason. "*Cool!*"

In rapid succession, emotions chased each other across Stephen's face. He twisted the rifle to put the barrel underneath his chin and slipped his thumb inside the trigger guard.

"No, Stephen!" shouted Joe.

Moving with the reflexes of a much younger man, Tom threw his shoulder into Stephen's chest, knocking the rifle to the side with one arm, and driving the younger man back, both of their feet scrabbling for traction in the gravel.

Stephen bellowed and growled, and the M1 went off, its report thundering across the lake and back.

The other six men that made up the Genosgwa Police Department rushed forward, Michael Arnold wrestling the M1 away from Stephen, and the others trying to help Tom control him.

They all fell in a heap, all except for Michael Arnold who stood to the side, holding the M1.

"Get out of here!" yelled Greg, looking at Mason. "Go home!"

Mason lifted his gaze to Greg's face. "Dude, your mom got her ass kicked. You should *see* it!"

"Mason Harper!" snapped Joe without looking at him. "You get out of here while you still can." His tone oozed threat—all the anger, sadness, confusion of that long night poured into two sentences.

Mason laughed but took a step away from the car just the same. "I wonder what Elizabet looks like…"

With an inarticulate growl, Joe took a single step toward him, and Mason ran home.

5

As Joe Canton led him down the gangway to their waiting jet, the horror of the events of the summer overcame Greg for a moment. His father couldn't travel with them, not yet. Not until the doctors said he was stable, and not until the drugs had more of a chance to get him under control.

A lump formed in Greg's throat at the thought of his father, and how he ranted and raved about demons at every opportunity. No one believed Stephen, of course. No one but Greg.

No one believed Greg about the Lady in the Lake, either.

When Greg remembered his mother or grandmother, a horrible, aching pit, as black as Hell, opened within him. He didn't dare look at the darkness for long, because it seemed the darkness stared back. He had the feeling the darkness would *always* stare back at him.

That *she* would always be looking back at him.

And no doubt she will, champ.

Greg shivered as the thought—*the voice*—sounded in his mind. It felt so…oily, so diseased. Greg didn't understand how he'd ever mistaken it for his own mental voice. The voice sounded nothing like him.

It's not too late, boyo. Just slip your hand out of your Grandpa's and scramble through that door at the end of the gangway. Outside, steps lead down to the tarmac. Just sprint around the end of the building and—

Greg shook his head and squeezed his eyes shut. He didn't want to have an invisible friend any longer. He wanted the thing to leave him alone.

Ah, Greggy, that hurts my feelings. Besides, we have such fun—

His grandfather squeezed his hand and gave him a little shake. "It'll get easier, Greggy," he said. "I promise you. And in the meantime, don't you worry. I'm right here, I'm with you. We'll get through this." He gave Greg's hand another squeeze. "And before you know it, the two of us will be three, and you'll have your Daddy back, too. Ayup, we'll get through this together. The three of us."

The four *of us*!

Greg shivered at the force of the scream in his mind, but he decided not to pay any attention to the voice. Never again.

He gazed up into his grandfather's face and smiled. The smile wasn't very big, nor a happy one, but it *was* a smile.

6

He wasn't supposed to be there. His grandmother had forbidden him to set one foot on the Canton property, but what she didn't know wouldn't kill her. *At least not yet.* Mason cackled at the idea.

He glanced toward his grandmother's cottage, then to the other side of the Canton lake house. No one was watching as he ducked under the police tape and slipped into their screened porch. That he might get in serious trouble for breaking into a crime scene only heightened the pleasure he felt at his defiance.

The back door was locked, but Mason had come prepared. The big bald man—Red Bortha, he'd called himself—had come for a visit the day after their escapade in the woods. He'd brought a present—a shiny set of lock picks—and he had taught Mason the rudiments of their use.

Mason slipped the black leather case out of the back pocket of his jeans and ran the zipper open. The sound made him think of other zippers and of other visitors in the days since the murders, and an erection thundered to life behind the zipper of his jeans. He worked the lock, ignoring the sensation in the pit of his stomach and the old lock opened with a soft click. He pushed the door open, unable to contain a predatory grin.

The short hall that led from the back porch to the main living area of the Canton house was painted maroon with blood. "Elizabet," he breathed. He dropped to his knees, hoping the blood was still wet, but it had all dried. He ran his hands across it nonetheless, then sniffed his fingertips and palms. "I wish I could have been here," he murmured. "I wish I could have seen it."

There will be other nights, sport, said the voice of his invisible friend. *My daughter and I are well pleased with you.*

"Thanks," he said. "Happy to do my part."

Indeed. I've got other things for you, boyo. Give it a few days—time for things to settle a bit—and then little Candice up the shore might warrant your...attention. You know her, don't you?

"Candice Sebastian? I call her the Ice Princess because her shit don't seem to stink. Yeah, I know her."

*Ah, good. Maybe we can...*educate...*young Candice.*

Mason smiled and climbed to his feet. "Happy to help."

I knew you would be, kiddo.

Mason wrinkled his nose. "I'm not a kid."

No. No, of course, you aren't. I apologize, Mason. Habits are hard to break, and old habits are perhaps the hardest of all.

"It's okay. I don't mind 'sport' and 'boyo' and stuff like that. I just don't enjoy being called a kid."

Noted. Now, why don't you go through the kitchen and see if the police missed any of the old man's guns?

A wide grin distended Mason's cheeks, and a feverish glint shone from his eyes. "Yeah." He sucked in a deep breath and whistled as he exhaled.

Chapter 8

2007

I

"Okay, we're here, Benny," said Toby, putting the Caddy into park. "Now what?"

"Inside," said Benny. "We've got to go inside." He opened his door and dragged Shannon out.

Scott shook his head, but Toby popped open his door and got out. "Come on, Scott," he said.

"At least the terminal's a small one," said Scott. "It won't take us long to cover every square inch of the place." He climbed out of the car and closed his door. "Then can we get back to rescuing Mike from the nurses?"

"Come on, doubting Thomases," said Benny.

They followed Benny across the pick-up lanes and into the terminal. He led them upstairs and to the left wing where he stopped, staring at the people from the red-eye. Scott nudged Toby and pointed at the bank of information monitors. The arrivals screen listed the flight as originating in Orlando, Florida.

"Who are we waiting on, Benny? Mickey Mouse?" asked Scott with a smile.

Benny didn't answer, he just stared into the face of each person who came down the hallway. He'd attracted a little attention and more than a few hidden smiles, but no one seemed to be the person he wanted.

"Are you sure this is the right flight?" asked Toby. "Maybe we're on the wrong side."

Benny ignored him, taking several steps away from the group. He kept scanning the faces of the crowd, until the rush died to a trickle and then died out. Benny shook his head and turned toward Shannon. "I don't understand it."

"Well, that just makes it unanimous," said Scott.

"But I was so sure…"

"It's okay, Benny. All of us make mistakes from time to time." Shannon threaded her arm through Benny's and gave him a peck on the cheek.

Toby raised his hands to shoulder height, palms up. "So…can we head on over to the hospital now?"

With slumped shoulders, Benny nodded.

2

Toby parked the rented Cadillac in what Benny referred to as "the wart," which was nothing more than a behemoth concrete parking structure attached to the main hospital. They walked across in the covered walkway, into the lobby of the hospital that was still busy, despite the hour.

"Scott, I'll need you to flash your badge and get Mike's room number," said Toby.

Scott looked at him for a moment, but then treated him to a terse nod and walked over to the information desk.

"Toby..."

"What is it, Benny?"

"Toby, something... I feel strange."

Toby chuckled. "Benny, you *are* strange. But don't take it to heart. Who isn't in this little band of misfits?"

"Not that kind of strange, Toby." Then he turned away, his eyes scanning the room, scanning the people in the room. "No...no..."

"What kind of strange, Benny?" Toby turned an amused glance on Shannon, but Shannon wasn't paying attention to their conversation. Her gaze was glued to the doors that led out into the portico.

Scott strode back over, slipping his badge through his belt. "He's up on the fourth floor," he said. "But there's a complication, Toby..." His gaze tracked from Toby to Shannon, and then to Benny. "What's going on?"

"No idea," said Toby.

"He's here...somewhere." Benny took two aimless steps away from them, still scanning the room, still looking people in the face and then dismissing them.

"Who is here? Dammit, Benny, make sense!"

"Him," said Shannon lifting her arm to point at the double glass doors leading outside. "He's here."

Benny whirled to face her, then followed her gaze. "You're a genius, Shan!" he whispered. "It's him! Toby, that's him!"

Toby peered out the double doors as a cab pulled forward under the portico roof. A tall, very tanned man got out of the back seat and handed a few bills through the driver's side window. He pulled a small suitcase and an overnight bag out of the back and then walked around the rear of the cab. His eyes tracked across the front of the hospital, scanning upward as he leaned back to see the top floors.

"Who is that, Benny?"

"It's him!" As Benny said the words, the tall man outside dropped his gaze and stared at them.

"Him who?"

The man smiled, picked up his suitcase and bag, and entered the hospital lobby. He walked toward them, his gaze bouncing between Toby and Benny. The man stopped a few feet from them and set his luggage at his feet. He met Shannon's gaze, then Scott's, then returned his gaze to Benny's face. "I'm not crazy, am I?" he asked.

"No," said Benny. "No, you're not crazy." Benny laughed. "Trust me, I know crazy, and you're not it."

The tall man turned his gaze to Toby. "You're the one, right? The one who hunts them?"

Toby ran his hand through his hair and then down over his face. "I wish one of you would tell me what's going on."

The tall man looked at Shannon again. "You weren't there. You didn't help."

"No, you're wrong there. Both Shannon and Scott helped," said Benny as he took a step closer to the newcomer. "They had to deal with another threat—Brigitta and her pet."

The man nodded as if that made everything clear. "Who's Brigitta?"

Benny bounced on his toes like an excited eleven-year-old. "Brigitta was Herlequin's daughter."

The man turned his gaze on Benny and cocked his head to the side. "Herlequin?"

"That's difficult to explain," said Toby. "Listen, I can see that you and Benny somehow know each other, but…"

"Oh! Sorry!" The tall man blushed. "I'm Greg Canton." He held out his hand, and Toby took it.

"As if that means something to us," Scott muttered.

"I'm Toby. The one bouncing on his toes is Benny, and the beauty is Shannon. The grumpy one's named Scott."

The tall man looked at them each in turn, nodding and smiling. "Did all of you…" He wound down like a windup toy running out of spring.

"No. Shannon, Toby, and I did, though."

"Did what?" asked Scott.

"Survive the woods," said Greg. "You survived being chased by the Lady in the Lake."

Benny shook his head. "No, we survived Herlequin's game."

"There's that name again."

"Herlequin was the one behind it all—the one who made us all run in the woods while his daughters chased us."

"This isn't the place for this discussion," said Scott, glancing surreptitiously at the security guard who was staring at Benny. "We need to get moving. We're drawing too much attention. And, Benny, try to act your age."

"We've got to, uh, pick up a friend." Benny picked up Greg's overnight bag and slung it over his shoulder. "You might as well come on up with us, meet Mike." He looked at Greg and flashed him a smile.

"Come on," said Scott. "The elevators we need are around this way."

"Uh, before we go, there's something you should know," said Greg as he bent to pick up his suitcase. "We'd better hurry. We are in danger here."

“What do you mean we're in danger?” asked Scott, taking a small step toward Greg.

“I'm not sure how to explain it…it's just that…sometimes, I get these feelings. I can sense some kind of…thing.” Greg shook his head, looking to Benny as if for help. “I can't explain this right.”

“Well, I hope you can do a better job than that,” said Scott.

“I'm sorry,” said Greg, shaking his head. “My father… The night of my mother’s murder—my mother and my grandmother—my father said he met…” Greg looked down at his feet, then glanced at Benny sheepishly. “He's insane, you see, but he's always maintained that a demon killed my mother and grandmother. Sometimes I get this feeling…a presence I can almost sense…”

“The part about the demon makes sense,” said Toby. “But your father's not insane. There are demons here. Herlequin was their king.”

“I'm not sure what that means,” said Greg, shaking his head and looking lost. “I… When you killed him, it sent a shockwave through my mind. But he—whoever he was—was always just a voice in my head. When I was a kid, I thought he was my invisible friend, and there may have been an invisible friend before he started talking to me, but that summer when…when everything happened, my invisible friend turned…nasty, sour.

That's when I first met the Lady in the Lake." Greg looked at them as if lost.

Toby cocked his head to the side. "That's a story that needs telling."

Greg looked away. "Anyway, whatever I can sense—things similar to the Lady in the Lake and the voice in my head—are headed this way."

"Demons," said Toby.

"How many?" asked Scott.

That earned another shrug from Greg. "Well, not all of them, but more than one. Only one is close, but the others are moving fast."

"Then we'd better get a move on," said Scott. "Toby, you're with me. The rest of you get back to the car, get it loaded, get it started, and be ready to move. We'll get Mike, and we might come back on the run."

Without another word, Scott turned and strode off toward the bank of elevators. Toby followed him, with a glance back at Benny and a small shrug.

Benny turned back to Greg and ducked his head. "It's a stressful time. We're not usually so…" Benny lifted his hands and let them drop.

"It's no problem," said Greg.

"Come on," said Shannon, turning back toward the passage that led to the wart. "Let's get back to the car."

3

Brigitta stepped into the ruins of what had once been a living room. She nudged a chunk of yellow-scaled flesh with her bare toe and curled her lip. "*This* is how you two alphas work together? Is this what I can expect from the two of you? You two buffoons rolling around on the carpet like a pair of children?"

LaBouche stood next to Chaz, his blood and Chaz's blood both splattered across his body. He didn't meet her gaze—he didn't want her to see the rebellion in his own. Behind him, in the hole through the wall into the bedroom, Nicole Conrau tittered like a drunken whore.

"*He* attacked *me*! It was unprovoked and unexpected. He barged in here—"

"You *will* shut your mouth!" Brigitta's voice was quiet but laced with acid. She took a step toward them, lifting her hand and slapping Chaz hard across the face. "Do not make the mistake of thinking I can't go on without you. Do not make the mistake of thinking I can't punish you in creative ways that will be as bad as sending you home."

Chaz brought a hand up to his cheek but said nothing. Again, Nicole Conrau laughed.

"Were my instructions not clear? Did I leave room for interpretation? Did I forget to express my wish that you two work together? Is there any doubt in either of your tiny brains that the times demand we put aside petty differences?" Brigitta looked around the room, her gaze dancing over the smashed furniture, the chunks of scaled flesh—both yellow and pearlescent—the splashes of blood, and she hissed with anger.

"I apologize," said LaBouche.

Brigitta's gaze snapped to his and fire danced in her eyes. "Why do you apologize? And to whom?"

"I apologize to you, Your Majesty, for my overzealousness. I should have come to you with my concerns, rather than try to solve them for myself."

Beside him, Chaz scoffed.

"And what are these...*concerns*, LaBouche?" Brigitta asked in a mild tone that fooled no one.

"A...concerned party informed me that Chaz had abandoned his work. That he and this trollop behind me had slunk off into the shadows to rut without a care in the world about the war effort. I allowed this knowledge to infuriate me, and I acted out of anger." LaBouche dropped to one knee and bowed his head. "Please forgive me, Excellency. It will not happen again."

Brigitta rested her hand on the back of LaBouche's head. "In all the time I've known you, LaBouche, how is it I never knew you could be contrite?"

"You can't be buying this, Brigitta! You can't be that simple!" snapped Chaz.

Oh, that was a mistake, thought LaBouche, smiling down at the carpet. Brigitta's hand left the back of his head. *Another slap*?

"Simple? Am I simple, Chaz?" The room fell into an algid silence. "Nicole? Am I simple?"

"No, my queen." Nicole's voice was smooth and sultry.

"Tell me, Chaz, what should I do with you? LaBouche is correct, you abandoned your duties." She turned her back and stepped away, then whirled back to face him. "You allowed Nicole to seduce you, to distract you from the tasks I had laid before you."

"But we had everything in hand! We took a moment, sure, but my work did not suffer for it. I can promise you that, Brigitta."

Mistake number two, thought LaBouche with a shiver of anticipation. He wasn't sure what punishment Brigitta would inflict, but he felt sure that Chaz was only making it worse.

"Hmmm." Brigitta put her hands behind her back and closed her eyes. When she opened them, fury danced within, and she began to pace back and forth before them. "It seems to me that you are intent on compounding your errors with excuses. With *familiarity*." She rested her hand on the back of LaBouche's head, almost a caress. "I'm beginning to see what LaBouche dislikes about your character. I'm beginning to understand LaBouche's anger."

LaBouche's smile widened for a moment, and then he gasped as pain lanced through him from the back of his skull. Brigitta snapped her hand up toward the ceiling, gouging the skin from the rear of his head in four rows.

"That doesn't lessen my anger at him, mind you. LaBouche should have come to me rather than taking matters into his own hands. Where the two of you are concerned, I cannot trust your judgments. Neither of you will attempt to correct the actions of the other."

"Yes, Your Majesty," said LaBouche.

Chaz remained silent.

Ah, the trifecta! This could be it…

"LaBouche, go get yourself cleaned up. I don't want the lesser demons seeing you in this state and making assumptions. You *will* remember this and act accordingly."

Disappointment filled him, but LaBouche stood and bowed over her hand. "As you say, my queen." Without another look at Chaz, Nicole, or Brigitta, LaBouche left the remains of Shannon Bertram's apartment.

He wanted to see what Brigitta would do to Chaz. He was halfway down the stairs to the parking lot when Chaz screamed, and LaBouche's large V-shaped mouth curled with a derisive smile.

4

Scott flashed his badge at the nurses sitting behind the counter that served as the floor's station. "Scott Lewis, New York State Police."

"What can we do for you, Trooper?" asked a sandy-haired nurse.

"We got a report of a suspicious character brought in from a traffic accident up in Ontario. They said downstairs that the guy's up here."

The nurse frowned and dropped her gaze to something on her desk. "I thought he belongs to Wayne County."

"Yeah, the accident happened up there, but we think he's a person of interest in one of our cases." Scott hooked his thumb and pointed it toward Toby. "We need to talk to him."

The nurse tilted her head to the side, still looking down at her desk. "It says here access is restricted until the detective from Wayne County questions him."

Toby sidled up to the counter and smiled. "Let me see that."

"Well, I don't know…"

"Come on, if you can't trust a trooper who can you trust?" He kept the smile going and turned up the wattage a little as the nurse looked up at him.

She grinned a little and shrugged. “I guess you’re right.” She lifted a pink square of paper from the desk and handed it to him.

Glancing down, Toby read the note, and then looked the nurse in the eyes. “Can I borrow your pen?”

The nurse’s smile faltered. “What kind of trooper goes around without a pen?”

Scott blew a breath out through puffed cheeks. “You don’t know the half of it. This guy never brings a pen, but what’s worse, he never brings any money to pay for lunch.”

“I’ll have you know that important things weigh on my mind,” Toby said, half turning to face Scott. “These small details…that’s why I have you.”

“Yeah, yeah.”

With a chuckle, the nurse handed her pen to Toby, and he wrote something on the little square of pink paper. “There,” he said, giving both the paper and the pen back to the nurse.

She read it and chuckled again. “I guess that clears everything up. Your guy is in 418.” She waved her hand down the corridor to the right. “Seventh room down on the left.”

Toby grinned wider and treated her to a wink. “Thank you…”

The nurse blushed a little, then said, “It’s Delilah. Delilah Lara.”

"Lee LaBouche," Toby said without missing a beat. Beside him, Scott stiffened but said nothing. "It's nice to meet you, Delilah."

"You, too, Lee."

Toby turned toward Scott and winked. "Why don't you talk to the skell. I'd better question Ms. Lara, here."

Scott rolled his eyes and turned away. As he walked away from the nurses' station, Toby began to roll out his patter. Scott tried to keep the smile off his face but was only partially successful. He walked down the hall, glancing at the numbers stenciled above the doors. When he reached Mike's room, he darted a glance back toward the nurses' station, but Toby had them all enthralled, telling a story and making wild arm gestures. He ducked inside the darkened room. "Mike?"

The light over the bed blinked to life. "It's about time you showed up," said Mike.

"The others had a few issues with the car."

Mike grunted and threw back the sheets. "You'll have to help me. I can't walk. My legs are like pins and needles, still."

"We've got to get you out of here, Mike, but are you sure…"

"Yeah, I am. Toby's a doctor, after all."

"A pathologist," said Scott.

Mike chuckled. "Close enough. He still went to medical school." Mike swung his legs off the bed, slapping both thighs as he did so. “I don’t think I can walk yet.”

Scott nodded. “Just a sec. There was a wheelchair outside a room up the hall.”

“Be careful, the nurse said that a deputy—”

Scott waved his hand through the air. “Yeah. Toby’s keeping the nurses distracted.” Scott ducked out and retrieved the wheelchair. He got Mike in the chair and wheeled him out of the room, heading up the hall, away from the nurses’ station. At the corner, he turned back and whistled, and then he wheeled Mike around the corner and down to the bank of elevators. “Toby will meet us at the car.”

“Yeah,” slurred Mike.

“Are you sure we should take you out of here?”

“Just the painkillers. I’m fine.” Mike’s eyes drifted closed, and his head lolled to the side. “Shannon okay?”

“Yeah. She got her bell rung is all.” The elevator doors opened, and Scott wheeled the chair into the room. “Oh, listen, Mike. We just met a strange guy down in the lobby, and Benny’s acting like he’s known him forever.” Scott shrugged. “He seems aware of what’s going on, though.”

Without opening his eyes, Mike yawned until his jaw popped. “The more, the merrier, I guess.”

Scott grunted. “What are we doing, Mike? How can we…” Scott shook his head.

Mike cracked his eyes open and glanced up at the trooper. "We are doing what we have to do, Scott."

"But…I mean, how can we fight these things? How can we expect to have an impact? If what Hartman said was true—that an uncountable number of demons remain trapped in their home realm. I mean, who cares if we killed Herlequin? Who cares if we kill LaBouche, even? There will just be other demons to replace them."

"I know it seems impossible—" Mike closed his mouth as the elevator dinged and the doors opened. Across the lobby stood two Wayne County detectives and a guy in a cheap suit.

"Do you recognize any of them?" whispered Scott.

Mike shook his head.

"Okay, play it cool, then." Standing behind the wheelchair, Scott pulled his badge out of his belt and shoved it in his pocket. He pushed the wheelchair out of the elevator and headed toward the hall that connected the lobby to the parking garage. He kept his eyes focused straight ahead and his expression neutral.

The detective standing with the two deputies looked their way, but his eyes skimmed right on past them. He muttered something to the deputies, and one of them turned and walked out through the front doors.

"I hope you have your badge," muttered Mike.

Scott didn't reply. He kept his gaze down and kept pushing.

Behind them, the elevators dinged again, and another elevator's doors slid open. The Wayne County detective's gaze meandered toward the elevators, and for a moment, Scott thought they would get away with it.

5

Shannon and Benny sat in the front seat of the rented Cadillac, and Greg lounged in the back. Shannon had the engine running, as Scott had ordered. "Where are you from, Greg?" she asked.

"I live in Florida—grew up there. My grandmother and grandfather had a lake house up here, though, and I spent a lot of summers here."

"Shannon, Toby, Mike, and I are all from a little town south of here. A town called Oneka Falls." Benny turned in place and threw his arm over the seatback. "That's where the demons live. Oneka Falls."

"Why do you call them demons?"

Benny glanced at Shannon, then returned his gaze to Greg and tilted his head to the side. "That's what they are. Demons."

"What, like in The Exorcist?"

"We've seen no evidence that they can possess people like they could in that movie. Also, they have physical bodies—at least they do here. To get rid of them, we have to drain their blood and then destroy their flesh. Once that happens, they can't come back to life." Benny shrugged. "It sends them back to Hell."

Greg said nothing, staring down at his lap.

Benny laughed. "It's not as crazy as it sounds."

"Well, I'm glad you realize it *sounds* that way."

"But you've *experienced* it. You had Herlequin in your head, and then there's whoever this Lady in the Lake is—although I'll bet you a vanilla milkshake that she's Brigitta. And whatever happened to your mother and grandmother."

"Someone murdered them. Savagely. Or something." Greg looked out the window. "And as for what happened to me, it was so long ago…and I was so young… My grandfather was with me in the woods—well, not at first, but he followed me. He shot at whoever—or whatever—chased me that night. He said it was a woman dressed in black, but…"

"But you know better." Shannon turned in the seat to face Greg. "Deep down, you understand that what happened was real, no matter what your adult brain tries to tell you."

Greg lifted his shoulder and let it drop. "But our younger selves believe so much that our adult selves discredit. Kids are given to flights of imagination and—"

Benny leaned against the seatback, his eyes boring into Greg's. "But you're *here*, Greg. You listened to that little voice in your head, that younger version of you, when it said to get on the plane. You listened when—"

"How do you know that?"

Shannon laughed and reached across the seatback to pat Greg's leg. "Haven't you figured it out?"

Greg's gaze bounced from Benny to Shannon and back again. "Figured out what?"

"Benny is our resident psychic," said Shannon, still smiling. "From what you said about Herlequin talking inside your head, I thought you were, too."

"Outside of my invisible—outside of Herlequin, I've never heard anyone else's voice in my head. I..." Greg shook his head. "I just get feelings about where these..." He shook his head again.

"Demons," said Benny. "You sense the location and movements of the demons. It's your superpower. Mine is reading minds. Toby can see them, and Shannon, she can—"

Greg sat bolt upright in the seat. "They're here! One of them is inside the hospital!"

An expression of intense concentration passed over Benny's face. "Shannon! They'll need you..."

Shannon already had her door open and was sliding out of the car. She turned back to Benny. "You two stay here but listen in, Benny. If we need you, I'll call. Open the trunk."

Benny nodded once, then opened the glove box and released the trunk.

"What's going on?" asked Greg. "We've got to get out of here! Where's she going?"

"Don't worry about Shannon, Greg. They'll never see her coming. She is going in to distract them, so Toby, Scott, and Mike can get away. Then, she'll come back, and we'll leave." Benny clapped his hands as though knocking off dust. "Easy peasy."

Greg slid toward the door. "But we can't let her go in there—"

"Greg, listen to me for a minute. I was just about to tell you that Shannon can trick their eyes. She can make them see whatever she wants. As long as she has fair warning, no demon will ever notice her."

6

Shannon grabbed one of the paintball guns out of the trunk, slammed its lid hard enough to leave finger-dents, and trotted toward the hall that connected the parking garage with the hospital. She checked the paintball gun as she ran, making sure the hopper was loaded full of their special paintballs, and that there was plenty of compressed carbon dioxide in the tank. With that done, she concentrated on the illusion she wanted to project—an old lady using a walker. An old lady without a paintball gun.

She pushed through the double doors that led to the lobby as a man in a cheap suit turned toward a Wayne County deputy and shoved his finger through the deputy's eye. The deputy squealed in pain, and the man in the cheap suit smiled.

Across the lobby, Toby stepped out of an elevator, and between him and the man in the cheap suit, Scott pushed Mike in a wheelchair.

"Demon!" shouted Toby, pointing at the man in the cheap suit. The demon spun around and laughed at Toby.

Behind the information desk, the hospital security guard was on his feet. He had the phone receiver pressed to his ear and spoke into it rapid-fire. Scott stood frozen, staring at the demon in the cheap suit.

Too late to mask them, Shannon thought, hoping Benny was listening. *There is a demon here, and they are in plain sight.*

The demon crouched, then exploded upwards, leaping across the lobby to land on the reception desk. He reached down, almost casually, and swatted the security guard across the face, leaving horrible gashes in the man's cheeks and splattering blood on the wall behind him. The phone flew away, and without even looking, the demon leaped toward Toby.

But Toby was already moving, sprinting away from the elevators in a hunched-over run like a commando—but an *unarmed* commando.

"Toby!" Shannon called. She bent and put the paintball gun on the floor, then shoved it as hard as she could in his direction.

Toby dove toward the gun, and behind him, the demon screamed in rage. Scott hesitated, glancing over his shoulder, but Toby waved him on. "Get Mike out of here, Scott!"

The demon squatted as if he were an Olympic powerlifter getting ready to deadlift, slapping his open palms against the floor as he pushed off, leaping toward Toby like a giant frog.

Fire! Shannon thought, putting as much energy behind the vision as she could. *You're leaping into fire*!

The demon squawked and kicked his legs in midair as if he were trying to push off the wall in a swimming pool, but there was nothing to push against. Toby tucked and rolled, sticking out one hand at the last second to grab at the paintball gun, but he succeeded only in sending it spinning. The demon came down behind him but landed on its side and hissed in pain. Toby pushed away as the fiend looked around in confusion, no doubt seeing flames but not feeling them.

Shannon dredged up the memory of Herlequin's demon visage—not his pure form, but the gargoyle-like thing he presented to the children as he ran them through the forest. *Why are you attacking Herlequin*? she thought at the demon. *Toby isn't here, that's Herlequin*! *Can't you see his tusks*? *His wings*?

The demon scrubbed at his eyes with the heels of his hands and rocked his head from side to side. Toby scrambled toward the paintball gun on his hands and knees, and the demon peered after him as if trying to penetrate smoke or mist with his gaze. "Muh-My lord?" Again, the beast scrubbed at his eyes.

Of course, *that's Herlequin*! *Who did you expect to be here*?

The demon squinted at Toby, then turned his head to peer around the room, as a human with lousy eyesight might. His gaze swept past Shannon once, then again, but on the third pass locked on her face. He raised a hand and pointed at her. "Trickster!" he shrieked. "Dan Delo warned me about you! I didn't believe your kind could fool my eyes." The demon drew his legs under his torso, his quadriceps bunching. He pulled his arms between his legs and put his palms flat on the floor. "I will take him your severed head as an apology. A nice gift, no?"

Benny, help! she thought as she turned and sprinted toward the door.

The Wayne County Sheriff's Deputy standing post out front stood peering into the lobby through the glass double doors that led out to the portico. After seeing Shannon's face, he drew his pistol and stepped through the doors. His eyes widened at the sight of his fellow deputy writhing on the floor with one hand over his eye, blood and gore spurting through his fingers. His gaze snapped to Shannon. "What the hell's going on here?"

See the demon! she thought at him. *Look at him, flying on his demon wings, dripping drool to the floor as he goes.* She had no idea how the evil thing looked, but that didn't matter as long as she made the deputy *think* he saw a demon straight out of a horror movie.

The deputy's eyes snapped up, tracking the demon's flight through the air. For a heartbeat, he stood frozen, mouth gaping, eyes wide, but then he lurched into action, snapping his pistol up and squeezing the trigger.

Scott reappeared from the hall that led to the parking garage, carrying one of their Remington 870 shotguns. He brought it to his shoulder and fired. "Get out of here!" he shouted.

The deputy spared him a microsecond's glance, but his aim never wavered as he tracked the demon through the air. The reports of his pistol slapped at the air three times.

Shannon ducked past Scott, sprinting for the passage to the car park. *Scott is invisible*! *You can't see Scott*! She flung the thoughts over her shoulder like mental hand grenades. The doors from the car park slammed open, and Benny was there with Greg at his side. She waved them back. Behind her, the shotgun boomed twice in rapid succession, and in its wake, the paintball gun fired on full auto.

Benny took a step into the hall. "Toby!"

Shannon slid to a halt and spun. The demon wearing the detective guise stood between Toby and Scott, holding the uniformed deputy by the neck. She took a step back toward the lobby. *He's on to me, Benny*!

He's not on to me, said Benny's voice in her mind. Benny ran past her, his face a mask of concentration.

"Benny! No!" she shouted.

The demon glanced at them and sneered. Muscles bunching, he lifted the deputy into the air and hurled him to the stone tiles lining the floor of the lobby so hard that the stone flooring exploded upward as the body hit. He turned and sprinted toward the hall to the garage, glaring at Shannon. Scott fired the shotgun again, and the slug ripped into the demon's shoulder but didn't even slow him.

The demon barreled past Benny without a glance, charging straight at Shannon with a murderous expression on his face. He loosed a guttural growl as he drew near, throwing his hands wide.

Still unable to see his actual form, her imagination provided a vision of long claws held ready to rend her flesh from her bones. She shrank back until her shoulder blades banged into the wall, then her knees buckled, and she slumped to the ground.

The demon laughed and loomed over her, lifting his hands over his head and shouting, "Boo!" like a reject from a cheap Halloween attraction. "Now, Trickster, you will pay for your crimes!"

Are you sure you have the right Shannon? she thought desperately. *It's hard to tell with so many Shannons sitting here.*

"No!" the demon yelled. "No more tricks from you!"

"How about one from me?" asked Greg. He stared at the demon with an intensity that made his hands shake. Veins and tendons stood out from his elbows to his wrists, and his cheeks burned crimson with the effort.

The demon whirled to face him, and Shannon hustled to the side, painting a duplicate image where she had been. "What tricks?" the brute demanded.

"This," hissed Benny. Cords bunched in his neck, and twin rivulets of blood ran from his nose. He hunched forward as though walking into a category five hurricane, then brought both hands up to chest height and made a pushing motion.

The demon howled and slapped at his temples with both palms. He staggered back, stepping right through the space Shannon had just vacated, stopping only when his shoulders banged into the wall.

Benny swept one hand to the side, and the demon's legs flew out from under him, dumping the thing to the tiles. Benny swept his other hand toward the ceiling, then brought it down, palm toward the floor.

The demon screeched and flattened against the unyielding floor.

The blood trickling from Benny's nose gushed as though someone had opened a spigot in his sinuses, and at the same moment, the sclera of both eyes reddened with blood.

"Benny!" Shannon cried.

He paid her no mind, shuffling closer to the writhing demon, pressing downward with both hands.

Shannon turned to Toby. "Help him!" she cried.

Scott and Toby sprinted toward the demon, but it was too late.

With a sickening crunch, the demon stopped writhing, flattened against the stone floor, and Benny collapsed.

7

Mason grinned, standing outside the door to his garage. It was very late—or very early—by the feel of the night air. He'd spent ages and ages in the dark—sometimes he thought he'd spent more time outside between midnight and dawn than he had in the daylight.

It was time to drop in on his guest—to wake her up if she'd fallen asleep—and scare the shit out of her. To that end, he wore a mask—one he'd made himself and was proud of.

He slipped inside the garage, closing the door without so much as a click from the latch. Crossing to the rear door of the van, he had to fight to keep from giggling with anticipation.

Chaz and Red had taught him tricks like this—ways to drive his victims batshit with fear, ways to make it impossible for his victims to think. They'd been incredible teachers, sharing decades—or maybe *centuries*—of knowledge with him. Red had helped him refine his artistry, and Chaz had helped him develop his brutality.

Remembering Red dredged a strange emotion from the depths of his black heart. It wasn't sadness—Mason's passions bore little resemblance to what other people talked about—but he missed the big bastard. He wished he'd see Red lounging in the corner, drinking in the fear that beat off Mason's guest in almost-palpable waves.

He shrugged and pushed thoughts of Red out of his mind. He was dead, and that was the end of it.

Mason approached the twin rear doors of the van on the balls of his feet, taking shallow breaths. He gripped the handle and put his finger on the button of his key fob—the one that would spring the locks. He took a deep breath, prolonging the moment, letting the anticipation build.

When the moment was right, he pressed the button and jerked the door open. The woman inside screamed and whirled to face him. He lurched at her, arms up above his head, fingers curled into pretend claws.

She screamed so loud Mason thought she might rip her vocal cords as she scrambled away, jerking against her restraints. The pungent aroma of ammonia and sulfur filled the van's tight confines as the woman pissed her pants.

It was one straw too far, and Mason couldn't stop the cackling laughter that bubbled up from his chest. He slammed the rear doors of the van without a word to his victim and hit the button on the key fob that would re-lock the doors, then turned and walked away.

As he passed the driver's door of the van, he stopped for a moment to admire the mask he had made from the skin of Kelley-Ann Malley's face and head.

8

“Help me!” cried Shannon as she sprinted to Benny’s face-down form.

Scott skidded to a halt; the Remington 870 centered on the demon’s head. “Is it dead?”

Toby spared a glance at the demon then stooped to check Benny’s pulse. He peered into Benny’s eyes and grunted. He gazed at Shannon and bobbed his head. “He’s out, but his pulse is steady.”

“What, that’s it?” Shannon turned Benny on his back. She gasped at the torrent of blood coming from his nostrils. “What’s wrong with him?”

Toby shrugged. “He applied too much—”

“Dammit! Is the demon dead?”

Toby turned and peered at the demon. “The question isn’t whether it’s dead, the question is will it stay dead?”

“And what’s the answer?”

Toby brought his gaze up to look Scott in the eye. “Your guess is as good as mine, Scott. We’d better clear out of here.”

“What about Benny?” asked Shannon.

“He’s fine,” said Toby. “The subjunctive hemorrhages in his eyes are the worst of it. He’s exhausted, I think.”

“You *think*?”

"Yes, Shannon. He overexerted." Toby turned and squatted next to her. "His pulse is fine. The hemorrhages in his eyes will clear in a week or so, and the nosebleed will stop."

"What if it doesn't?"

"If it doesn't stop in ten minutes, I'll pack his nose with gauze. I can do that in the car." Toby lay a hand on her shoulder. "Come on. Help me get him to the car. We need to clear out of here, even if the demon *is* all the way dead. The cops will be here soon."

"Yeah, but where can we go? Back to the troll's house?"

Toby shook his head. "Bad idea. The demons will be all over the area after tonight. We still have the rooms at the Agincourt."

Scott arched an eyebrow and glanced down at the demon. "Do we bring this one with us? Set up another…whatever you want to call it?"

"No time," said Toby. "Grab his legs, Scott." They handed their weapons to Shannon and then lifted Benny and carried him to the car.

"Wait," said Greg. "How do you destroy the bodies?"

"No time to explain," grunted Toby. "We've got to move."

Greg turned toward Shannon. "How?"

"We bleed them, then use acid to—"

"It's a base," muttered Toby.

"—destroy the remains. We burn the blood."

"Would fire destroy the body and the blood?"

"Yes, but to get it hot enough, we'd burn down the hospital. Now, leave it! We've got to clear out of here."

Greg nodded but stepped toward the demon. He held out his hands, like a man warming them over a campfire. His face contorted with effort.

"What are you doing?" asked Scott. "We have to—" His jaws snapped shut as the demon burst into a bright blue flame.

The intense heat cracked the tiles twenty feet up and down the hall, and the wall above the demon warped and the paint curled to black shreds. The fire burned bright, and in a matter of seconds, the demon's body disintegrated to a pile of white ash. As soon as Greg withdrew his hands, the fire disappeared. It didn't fade or die out, it roared with full force one moment and disappeared the next. The heat dissipated at a rapid rate, accompanied by the faint bell-like sounds of the stone tile cooling and cracking further.

"Neat trick," murmured Scott.

"Thanks," said Greg, then his eyes rolled up in his head, and he passed out.

9

As dawn broke across the water of Lake Genosgwa, Mason stretched and took another scalding shot of coffee. He'd arranged his studio—thick plastic sheets draped over everything, his instruments and materials arrayed and easy to reach, his antique exam table in the center of it all.

The memory of the woman freaking out when he visited her in the night brought a smile to his face, but the smile faded as he recalled the aroma of her urine. *Maybe I'll shower her before I begin.*

He walked out to the end of the dock, whistling tunelessly. "Are you here?" he murmured. "Are you hungry? Want breakfast?" As with most days, there was no answer, no telltale ripples from the center of the lake, no voices in his head.

Mason shrugged and turned away, downing the last of his coffee. With a stretch and a final glance out at the lake, he turned and walked back to the cottage, dropping his coffee cup off inside on his way to the garage across the gravel lane.

It's going to be a good day. Even if Brigitta isn't here.

10

Tom Walton grimaced at the visitor's entrance of Millvale State Hospital and parked his car. He sat for a moment, staring at nothing, his mind going back to what had happened in 1986.

He could understand how the events could have broken Stephen Canton—or anyone. He couldn't imagine what it must have been like to fight the madman that had killed Gary Dennis, both Elizabet and Mary Canton, and save none of them. Tom bore his own deep wounds cut by guilt's blade. He never caught the killer—hell, he'd never even been close.

The old chief shoved those thoughts out of his mind with a sniff and opened his door. He was early for morning visiting hours by at least thirty minutes, but if one of the older staffers was on duty, they might let him in early anyway.

Walton had been coming to visit Stephen every couple of months since 1986, despite the long drive. He'd seen Stephen descend deeper and deeper into madness with each passing season. He didn't disagree with Joe Canton's reasons for packing his grandson up and taking him back to Florida, but it sure hadn't done Stephen any good.

Getting out of the car, he stretched his back with a groan. He'd spent far too many hours in the front seat of a vehicle throughout his career, and he was paying for every one of them in his retirement.

He shuffled into the building via the visitors' entrance, signing in at the guard station and then taking the elevator up to the third floor—to the most secure unit with the most violent residents. The elevator opened onto a six by six foyer across from the only door—the door that led into the unit. He approached the door and pressed the buzzer, looking up into the closed-circuit camera mounted in the corner. After a moment, there was a loud buzz and a click as the door unlocked.

Tom opened the door and stepped into the visitor's room. It was empty given his timing, but as always, he detected the faint scents of disinfectant, body odor, and urine. He imagined those were the scents common to all locked psychiatric units everywhere—they'd been present in every ward he'd ever visited.

The door across from him opened and Robert Bunch stepped into the room. "Hey there, Chief! Long time no see."

"Ayup," said Tom with a smile. "Seems I've been coming on days you've had off for the past little while. How's life treating you?"

"*Comme ci, comme ca.* But I'm not quite ready to retire."

Tom crossed the big room, smiling. "I can recommend it, Robert. Oh sure, at first it seems it's a death sentence, but then the grandkids come 'round, and it all makes sense."

"I'm going to go out on a limb, Chief. Using my amazing psychic powers, I deduce that you're here to visit Stephen Canton."

"Ayup. It's been a few months, and I thought I'd see how he was getting on. Any change?"

"Not to speak of, Chief, no." Robert shook his head. "Sometimes there's no helping them."

Tom nodded but didn't meet Robert's gaze. "What he went through…"

Robert frowned at his feet. "He's been… Well, Chief, I'll just be blunt. Stephen has been on a tear for the past two or three days. He's in a manic phase and is not making much sense." He lifted his gaze to meet Tom's. "I hate that you've driven all this way for the visit you're about to have."

Walton shrugged and put on a smile. "His father was a friend."

Bunch nodded as if that said it all. "Grab a chair, and I'll go get him."

"Thanks for that, Robert. And thanks for letting me in early. I know it's against the rules."

Bunch smiled. "You served the public for a long time, and to me, Chief, that buys you a bit of special treatment."

Tom grinned and nodded his thanks, despite disagreeing with the sentiment. He found a seat amongst the plain wooden tables and their matching uncomfortable chairs, grimacing as his back sang out.

It only took a few minutes, but by the time Stephen shuffled into the room, Tom's back was a ball of hot agony.

"Chief! You've got to help me!" Stephen rushed toward him, both arms held out in front of him. "He's in danger, Chief Walton!"

"Have a seat, Stephen, and tell me about it." Tom had seen that sort of behavior before—Stephen reliving the night, or at least the days leading up to the night, when his world had ended. The night someone had murdered his wife and his mother.

With a paranoid glance over his shoulder, Stephen sank into the chair opposite Tom. "I've got to be careful, Chief. Some of the staff members are part of it. I can feel it." He turned his wide, dilated eyes on Tom. "I can't see them, not the way I could that night, but at least two of them are demons."

Tom nodded as if it all made sense. He'd heard it all before—on too many occasions to count. "Do you remember the last time we talked about the demons?"

Stephen made a frantic shushing gesture. "Keep your voice down, Chief. If they figure out I'm onto them…"

"Stephen, do you remember what we decided the last time we spoke of demons?" said Tom, but at a reduced volume.

"Sure thing, Chief." Stephen darted glances around the empty room. "Uh… Maybe you could…"

Tom arched an eyebrow. "When the demons trouble you, you are to get a piece of paper and a pencil and write down everything you can remember."

Stephen grinned and smacked his forehead with the palm of his hand. "That's right! That's…that's right. That way, you can look into it. You can find the demon that killed my Mary." As he said his deceased wife's name, Stephen's face crumpled.

"That's right, Stephen. Did you write anything down, this time?"

Stephen frowned down at the tabletop. "No. Why is it I can't remember after you leave? The demons are giving me something to make me forget. It's in the medicine. Or the orange juice."

Tom shook his head sharply. "No, Stephen. We discussed the medicine before, remember? It's good for you. It checks out, remember?"

"Right, right, right. Checked by the FDA. Or was it the DEA? Well, never mind all that, Chief." Stephen leaned forward across the table, his butt coming up out of the chair until his face was inches from Tom's. "Forget all that. This time, Chief, Greg is in real trouble. You've got to help him! He was safe. Dad took them to safety, but now he's back. He's right back in the thick of it, Tom! Can't you help him?"

This is new, thought Tom. *He's worried about his son before, but it's always been that version of Greg that existed back then, that version of his son who got lost in the woods on the night of the murders.*

Stephen turned his head to peer at the door that led to the rest of the unit. "There isn't much time, Chief. I know what you're thinking right now, but it's not true. Well, it *is* true, but it is not true right now. I mean, it *has been* true…you know, before. But right now, it's not true."

Tom bobbed his head in what he hoped was a reassuring manner. "I'll keep my eyes peeled. Can you tell me what I'm looking for, Stephen? Your son's, what, eleven?"

"No, no, no, Chief. That's how old Greg was the night the demon took my Mary and ate my mother. That was in 1986," said Stephen in the tone reserved for the very old and the very young. "He'd be thirty this year. No! Thirty-two. I can't give you a description. I haven't seen him in a long, long time. I told my dad not to bring him here."

Tom sat as still as if he were carved from stone. "Thirty-two, you say? Not eleven."

"No, not eleven. But I get why you would think that, Chief. As I said, what you're thinking was true before but not now."

"What am I thinking, Stephen?"

Stephen looked him in the eye and winked with exaggerated slowness. "You think I'm trapped on that night. You're thinking I don't understand what's really going on, that reality and Stephen Canton are quits with each other. Most of the time, that's true. I'm sure you've already figured that out, Chief. But in this case, it isn't. Greg is in danger." Stephen whirled to his feet, sending the chair skittering across the linoleum floor. "Why didn't he stay away, Tom? Why did he have to come back? He's too much like his mother!"

"How do you know he's back?" Tom spread his arms wide, palms up. "I mean, correct me if I'm wrong, Stephen, but you haven't been outside of this unit in a long time. Has Greg called you?"

Stephen waved it away. "All I can tell you is that I know, Tom. And yes, I know I'm crazy. I know I've spent the last twenty-one years in a loony bin. There's no reason for you to believe me, Chief, but you *have to anyway*. You're his only hope! You've got to find him and put him back on a plane to Florida. Make him leave, Tom. For my father's sake, get Greg the fuck out of New

York." Stephen hung his head, seeming to deflate in on himself. "Tell him…tell him to never come back here."

11

"What you do not understand, Dan Delo, is that I don't care about your excuses." He stepped close to the purple demon and shoved his V-shaped mouth into Delo's face. "I gave you a task—the recall of the demons in that part of the state—and you always have the overriding responsibility to kill these hunters when you see them." LaBouche poured his anger and disgust at Chaz's ridiculous sexual exploits into his expression. "You failed at both." He wasn't treating the demon fairly, but he couldn't be bothered to care.

Dan Delo pulled his head away, keeping his expression as close to neutral as possible. "I did what I could. They carried new weapons—they shot gas pellets, and I—"

"*And you didn't stop them*!" LaBouche bellowed. "Or did I misunderstand you? Are the hunters all dead?"

Dan shook his head, a sour expression in his eyes.

"I see. Then you must know where the hunters are hiding. Can you lead me back there?"

"How could I know that?" Delo sneered.

LaBouche's hand rocketed forward and staggered the purple demon back a step. With deliberation, LaBouche stepped forward to fill the space. "*You should have followed them*!"

"But Herlequin's rule! The police—"

"Are you unable to keep yourself from the vision of the police? You possess wings, you massive fucking oaf! You should have *flown* above them, followed the hunters who escaped your pathetic attempts to inflict harm."

Dan Delo lifted his chin but—wisely—kept his mouth shut.

"Because of you, I had to scramble. I had to send a single demon to the hospital where they took the one you injured. I sent the one embedded in the police force…and, now, *he's dead*. He's not only dead, he's *gone*, and I must send more demons up there to root around trying to pick up the trail."

"Gone?"

"*Gone*. As in 'sent back home.' All because of your incompetence!"

Dan's face writhed, and he opened his mouth several times but didn't speak.

"That's better," said LaBouche. "You fucked up. You deserve this."

With a sour expression, Dan Delo nodded. "How can I make it up to you?" he grated.

LaBouche grinned. "I've got an idea…" He put a banana-yellow hand on Dan's shoulder. "Do you know where Lake Genosgwa is?"

12

"Um, a bunch of demons… Up ahead," said Greg. He pointed through the windshield. "Up by those cabins down the road."

"Well, it was too good to last anyway," said Scott from behind the wheel of their rented Cadillac.

"That's the Agincourt Resort?" asked Greg.

Scott grunted and swung the car in a lazy half-circle across the road. He pointed the nose back the way they'd come. "How did they find us?"

"Maybe they have someone like Greg," muttered Shannon in a sleep-slurred voice. She was in the back seat along with Mike, Benny, and Toby—wedged in like sardines, but no one had expected a sixth passenger.

Scott gazed at Toby in the rearview. "What next? Any ideas?"

Toby's sigh was all the answer he needed to give.

"Pennsylvania?" asked Shannon. "We're close to the border."

Scott shook his head. “My badge buys us nothing in Pennsylvania.”

“I’ve got an idea,” said Greg.

“There might come a time when your badge buys us less than being in another state gains us,” said Toby. “But for now, I agree with you.”

“Then we could get lost in New York City for a few days,” said Shannon.

Scott wagged his head to the side. “There’s always that.”

Toby sighed. “I bet there are hundreds of demons in Manhattan alone. They can probably rent an apartment in some boroughs and never leave home while eating all they want.”

“I own a place we can go,” said Greg.

“But I could hide us until we found a place to stay. We could keep low profiles after that. Room service, take out.” She twitched her shoulders and stifled a yawn.

“Do you guys know where Lake Genosgwa is?” asked Greg. “I own a lake house there.”

“No, I don’t think the City…” Scott turned his head to look at Greg. “What did you say?”

“I own a lake house on Lake Genosgwa. The place’s been empty since 1986, but we’ve paid to keep it up. No one knows I’m in New York. No one would know if we stayed at the house. I’ve got a car, too, though I don’t know if it will start.”

"How did you come to own a house up here?" asked Toby with a trace of suspicion in his tone. "I thought you lived in Florida."

"I do. I inherited the place from my grandfather. It's where…" He choked up and shook his head.

"It's where his mother and grandmother died," said Benny in a weak voice. "We can't ask him to stay in that place."

"No, it's okay. I was planning on going down, anyway. To see the place, maybe put it up for sale." Greg wiped his eyes with both hands. "But if we need to lie low for a few days; it's the perfect place. We should stop somewhere random on the way and pick up supplies, but once we've done that, we can pull this beast into the garage and lie low in the cabin. No one will look for you at the lake."

"And you don't mind staying there?" asked Shannon.

Greg shrugged, his face wrinkled up with discomfort. "I won't know that until we arrive, but twenty-one years have passed. If it bothers me, I'll go into Genosgwa and rent a room at the hotel. You can stay at the lake house as long as you want."

Scott flicked his gaze to the rearview mirror.

"If you're sure, Greg, that would make our lives easier," said Toby.

"I'm sure."

"Won't they be able to find us there?" asked Shannon. "Eventually, I mean?"

"Maybe," said Scott with a shrug. "But the delay in finding the Agincourt leads me to believe they are finding us through mundane methods. Investigation rather than divination."

"Sure," said Toby. "I could probably find us at the Agincourt."

"I definitely would have found us," said Scott. "All it takes is time and shoe leather to find someone in a motel. Or anywhere that involves people outside of the conspiracy to hide."

"Conspiracy to hide," murmured Shannon. "I like that."

"I don't," said Scott sourly.

"Can you get us to Genosgwa?" asked Greg. "I can give you directions from the town center."

"No problem," said Scott.

13

Tom Walton shook his head for the umpteenth time as he turned off Lake Circle and onto Thomas Hill Road. He'd debated whether to take the time to check the lake house—it had stood empty for over twenty years, but first Joe and later Greg paid Preston Peters to perform quarterly maintenance. *Greg* might *have come for a visit*, he thought. *But how would Stephen know that? Maybe Greg called to tell him?*

Tom drew a deep breath and puffed out his cheeks as he blew it out. The drive back from Millvale took more than two hours, and he'd repeated these same thoughts over and over and over until he was sick with the mental argument.

His tires crunched gravel as he idled the car down the lane. Before the events in the Canton lake house occurred back in 1986, he'd always been a little jealous that Joe Canton had scraped together the beans required to buy a place on the shores of Lake Genosgwa. The gravel lane had always seemed so relaxing, but since that summer, Tom could hardly stand to spend five minutes on Thomas Hill Road.

And Greg? Wouldn't he hate the place now?

He suppressed a sigh.

What will it hurt to check? I'm already there, for Chrissake…

14

Mason grinned as he turned the key in the garage door for the third time since he'd finished his coffee. The first time, she'd shrieked after he'd ripped open the back doors of the van and flashed his toy at her—the big knife blade glinting in the early morning light. He'd had so much fun; he'd left her to stew for another hour before taking her out for a shower.

He'd left her *au naturel* after hosing her down from the spigot he'd had installed inside the garage. Oh, she hadn't liked the frigid water, but it excited *him* to see her body's reaction to it. That was what it was all about anyway—his excitement.

He closed the door behind him but didn't throw the bolt. He planned to take her over to the house this time. Mason drummed his hand against the side of the van as he walked down its length, smiling at her whimpers and panicked cries.

He'd only just laid his hand on the handle of the back door when he heard tires crunching gravel.

15

Tom idled his car down the gravel lane and pulled to a stop between Joe Canton's garage and his lake house. He sat for a moment, peering at the home, looking for signs of habitation.

There were none.

Can't let it go at that, can you?

With a sigh, Tom pulled the car to the side of the road between the Canton garage and the one now owned by that little prick Mason Harper. He shoved the gear selector to park and opened his door, groaning at the stiffness in his joints. After swinging his feet out, he sat for a moment, massaging his knees and trying to force the stiffness out. With a sigh of resignation, he stood, and as he did, a door opened behind him.

"Is that old Tom Walton I see?"

"'Old' is right," said Tom. "How are you doing, Mason?" He kept his tone light, but ever since that night in 1986, something about Mason Harper set his nerves on edge. He'd seen him around town for twenty years, but he couldn't shake the memory of the boy practically salivating over Mary Canton's broken, ravaged body.

"You've got a slew of years left on your dance card, Tom." Mason closed the door to his garage behind him and locked the deadbolt. "What brings you out?"

Tom shook his head and glanced at Joe's house. "A fool's errand given me by a mental patient."

Mason tilted his head back and looked at him with an expression Tom thought perfect for a reptile. An alligator or a Komodo dragon, maybe. "And how is Mr. Canton-the-younger?"

Tom's shoulders twitched in a quick shrug. "About the same, I guess."

Mason took a few steps closer, peering at Tom's face as if it were a book he was trying to read. "And what did the poor man want you to check out?"

Tom didn't answer. Instead, he turned toward the lake house. "Have you seen anyone poking around the place?"

"Around the Canton place?" Mason shook his head. "No, no one's been out for a few months, and the last one—the *only* one—was Preston Peters."

"Ayup. Quarterly maintenance, then."

"That would be my guess, yeah."

Tom watched Harper out of the corner of his eye. The man just stood there, staring at Tom while he thought Tom's attention was elsewhere. *Why isn't he going about his business*? Tom cleared his throat. "Well, I don't want to keep you."

"No bother. It's a nice morning for a chat."

"Ayup." Tom nodded once, as Joe Canton had been prone to do. "I guess I'll walk around the house and fulfill my promise to Stephen as long as I'm here."

"Sure, but I'm telling you: there's nothing to see."

"Oh, I know. But I *am* here…might as well make it worthwhile." He rapped his knuckles on the side of his head. "Get this old bastard to shut up and leave me alone." Mason didn't reply, but the man's gaze crawled on the back of his head. "Day off?" Tom asked, feigning nonchalance.

"Week off," Harper said with a wink. "I just got back from Rochester last night."

"Rochester, eh? What's in Rochester?"

"Inspiration."

Tom turned to face him, and as he did, he caught a fleeting glimpse of a cold, calculating expression on Mason's face. "Inspiration?"

Mason smiled, and his expression became the picture of openness, of friendliness. "Sure. I fancy myself an artist in my spare time." He waved his hand at the woods behind him. "I've got my fill of Mother Nature's inspiration right here. I take vacations in city centers to get a sense of the urban."

Tom scratched behind his ear. "A sense of the urban, huh?"

"That's it."

Tom cocked his head to the side and let his gaze settle on Mason's face. "Well, I won't keep you," he said again.

Mason met his gaze, a hint of amusement flirting with his expression, and the moment drew out. "Say, Tom. How long since you retired?"

"Seven years. Why?" asked Tom, confused by the sudden shift.

"Oh, nothing. I was just wondering. You should take up art yourself. Find a hobby."

"Ah," Tom forced a chuckle. "Granddaughters keep me plenty busy."

Mason lifted his chin. "Granddaughters. Yes. How many do you have again?"

The longer I talk to this bastard, the more he looks like a lizard, Tom thought. *Be damned if I'll speak to him about the grandkids.* He shook his head and half-turned toward the Canton lake house.

"I understand," murmured Mason. "Protect those grandbabies."

Tom grunted but turned his face back toward Mason. "Can't ever be too careful."

"Oh, no doubt, no doubt. You never know who you're chatting with. Not really. Know what I mean?" Mason laughed, but to Tom's ear, there was something off about it. "I could be this Abaddon character, after all. Wouldn't that be strange?" A smile decorated Mason's face, but it didn't reach his eyes.

Somewhere deep inside Tom, alarm bells started ringing.

16

Scott pulled off onto the shoulder, accompanied by the steady clicking of the turn signal. He glanced at Greg, who was staring at the woods on the side of the road. The man had gone as pale as death. "Anything?"

Greg startled, then laughed. "No, I don't sense any demons."

"That's a good thing, right?" asked Shannon.

"Yes," said Greg with an air of detachment. "Sometimes I wonder…"

In the back seat, Benny coughed and chuckled. "But all this *is* real, Greg. There are demons here, and you can sense them."

Greg took a deep breath. "I'm not sure whether I'd rather be as crazy as my father."

"Nah. Crazy's not all it's cracked up to be," said Benny.

"You are such a goof," said Toby.

"What did I say now?" Benny sat bolt upright and turned toward the woods. "There's something wrong!"

"What?"

Benny glared at Scott as he slapped the back of the front seat. "Go!"

"Demons?" asked Scott.

"Yes, but the human kind. Go!" Benny urged.

The back tires spit gravel and dirt as Scott mashed the accelerator to the floor.

17

Tom played it cool, but it took all of his thirty-three years of law enforcement experience to keep his poker face. "I'd laugh, son, but I don't care for that type of humor."

Mason dropped his gaze. "Sorry. I get these strange thoughts from time to time. Grandma always said I needed a governor for my mouth."

Tom grunted, his expression placid, but inside, his mind raced. *Think! Come up with something to put him at ease, then get your old ass out of here, Walton! Call the troopers when you hit Lake Circle.* He lifted a hand to scrub through his cropped hair. "That's just the grumpy coming out. Goes with getting old, I expect. Plus, driving all the hell over the state to visit Stephen always turns me into a grouch."

"I understand," breathed Mason.

"Well, I won't keep you."

"You keep saying that, Tom. What is it I should be doing?"

"What?" Tom scratched his ear. "Oh, whatever you had planned." He hunched his shoulders as if to protect his neck. "I believe I'll head out."

"Hmmm."

Mason didn't move, and his expression never changed, but the air between them seemed charged with electricity. The alarm bells ringing in Tom's mind became klaxons. He turned back to his car, but before he could open the door, Mason's hand fell on his shoulder.

"Aren't you forgetting something?"

"Eh? What's that?" Tom's pulse rate had trebled, and his voice quavered a bit.

Mason cackled, and for the first time, Tom believed the harsh sound reflected Harper's genuine amusement. "Your walk-around of the Canton place."

"Oh. Well, you convinced me it was a waste of time."

"Did I?" Mason's voice seemed stronger, more confident, and his grip tightened on Tom's shoulder.

"Sure. Who'd be out here, anyway?"

"My point," said Mason. He took a step closer, crowding Tom against the door of his car. "No one comes out here. Not anymore. Not since all that happy horseshit in 1986." He giggled and peered up and down

Thomas Hill Road. "I have the place to myself most of the time."

Tom's expression darkened, and fear tickled his belly. It wasn't a strange emotion to the former chief of police, but he hadn't felt it in seven years and didn't much care for its return. "I'll be on my way then."

A faint smile touched Mason's lips. "No, Tom. You won't." His grip on Tom's shoulder tightened to the point of causing pain.

Tom swiveled to face him. "Listen here, Mason. I don't know what I said to make you angry, and I *am* an old man, but there's a reason I've lived to this ripe old age, son." Tom leaned close, getting right up in Mason's face. "Now, take your *goddamn* hand off me!"

"A for effort, old man," murmured Mason.

"I mean it, Harper. You get your—"

Mason caught his weight as Tom slumped forward. He slid his blackjack back into his back pocket. "Two in one day," he mused. "This is going to be a *grand* day."

18

"Hurry, Scott!" Benny's voice carried a note of urgency that seemed foreign to his personality.

"What is it, Benny?" asked Shannon.

Benny shook his head in answer. “We have to save him!”

“Save who?” asked Toby.

Scott cranked the wheel, and the Caddie tried to slide out from underneath them as it hit the gravel. An expression of intense concentration settled on his features as he brought the car under control. “Where?”

“Keeping going! Around the bend!”

“That’s where my grandparents' lake house is,” murmured Greg.

19

Dan Delo flew west over the black waters of Lake Genosgwa, projecting the image of a hunting kite. It seemed like a fool’s errand, but LaBouche had insisted…again…and Dan was in no position to argue.

He landed on the ragtag dock LaBouche had told him about and scanned the houses up and down the shore before turning and scanning the lake for fishermen or swimmers. With a grunt, he adopted his innocuous visage—hyper-thin, glasses, slightly greasy hair—and walked ashore.

In the distance, a V8 engine whined and plowed through gravel. Dan paused for a moment, cocking his head to the side and listening.

20

Still smiling, Mason dragged Tom Walton into his garage. He had never gotten around to building facilities inside the cottage for keeping more than one prisoner—despite Chaz Welsh's repeated nagging that he "prepare for the possibility." Tom's heels dug twin furrows through the gravel.

His butt bumped into the locked door, and he swung Tom to the side and dropped him face-first to the ground. He turned and slid the key into the lock.

A car roared onto Thomas Hill Road, and Mason's eyes snapped toward the bend. Adrenaline flooded into his bloodstream, and Mason delighted in the sensation. He flung the door open and grabbed Walton by the armpits, dragging him inside the garage. He had no time to secure him more than that, as a big Cadillac came slewing around the bend in the road. Excitement tinged with a kernel of fear made his nerves sing, and Mason reveled in it. There wasn't much that made him feel alive anymore.

He stepped outside and closed the door.

21

"What's the matter, Benny? Who do we have to save?"

Benny shook his head, sliding forward to the edge of the rear seat and juking his head from side to side, trying to get a better view out the windshield.

"Talk to us, Benny!" snapped Scott. "Communicate!"

"It's…" Benny shook his head. "He's got Tom Walton." Without warning, Benny slumped back in the seat, thumping Shannon with his shoulder as he did so.

"Walton? The former police chief of Genosgwa?" asked Scott.

"Yes."

Scott took the bend in Thomas Hill Road too fast, and the big car slewed through the gravel, digging furrows as it slid toward the edge of the road and the old cottonwood trees beyond.

"Who's that?" asked Toby, pointing through the windshield.

"I haven't been here in—" Greg squinted and leaned forward. "It can't be," he murmured. He gasped and straightened up, lifting an arm to point at the path leading toward the lake. "Demon!"

"Christ!" snapped Scott.

"Pull over!"

22

Brigitta sat in one of Shannon Bertram's easy chairs, one leg over the arm of the chair kicking the air in a listless manner. On the ground before her, Chaz Welsh groveled and begged for mercy, but leniency had led them to that very moment, and she'd be damned before she'd compound one error with another more grievous one.

Across the room, Nicole Conrau stood, both sets of arms crossed under her breasts. Her wispy black wings made lazy circuits through the air as she watched Chaz writhe. Something about her demeanor irritated Brigitta.

"You've done well, Conrau, but it's time for you to get back to work. Go see to the weapons. Get them distributed to—" She snapped her mouth shut and sprang to her feet, gazing west.

At her feet, Chaz sighed in relief as her attention focused elsewhere, but made no other movement.

"What is it?" asked Nicole.

"Can you fly?" Brigitta demanded, motioning at the shadows of wings on Nicole's back.

Nicole nodded.

"Go across the street and take one of the new machine guns. Get to the house on Lake Genosgwa I told you about as fast as you can. I'll send backup as I find them."

Nicole sprang toward the door with another nod and a smile on her lips. She eschewed the steps and leaped over the railing instead, gliding through the air at a speed much higher than her feebly flapping mist-wings should have achieved.

"Visage!" yelled Brigitta.

Nicole lifted one of her four hands to acknowledge the command.

Brigitta turned back to Chaz Welsh and kicked him. "On your feet, lizard!"

23

Mason plastered a smile on his face and lifted a hand in greeting toward the Cadillac. He walked along the edge of the lane, wearing his "I'm so neighborly" face. All four doors of the Cadillac swung outward at almost the same moment, and the trunk lid sprang open.

A man he'd never seen before got out of the driver's side, and Mason recognized him as a cop in one glance. Behind him, a guy in bandages slid out of the car using the rear quarter panel for support, followed by another stranger. On the other side of the vehicle, a man and a woman got out—and the man was staring at Mason as if he could see through Mason's act. Mason marked the man as someone who might need special attention if the encounter went south.

Mason stopped, stunned, when the last person exited the Cadillac. Even after twenty-one years, Mason recognized him right off. "Well, hello, Greggy!" he called with a laugh.

24

The man LaBouche had sent him to speak with walked past the space between the cottage and the lake house, but he didn't so much as glance Dan Delo's way—his gaze focused on something beyond the lake house.

Dan flapped his great wings and rose straight up between the two homes. He ascended until he could see past the roof of the lake house, then hovered, watching.

25

Greg got out of the car, his gaze riveted to the man walking toward them. *It can't be,* he thought. *How can he be here right at the exact moment I arrive after twenty-one years of absence? What are the odds?*

"Well, hello, Greggy!" Mason called with a laugh.

Greg's stomach tied itself in knots. The memory of Mason looking at his mother's body and saying "Cool!" leaped unbidden to his mind. "Mason…"

"Oh, I'm honored you remember me after all these years." Mason smiled, and it appeared to be a friendly smile, but Greg didn't trust it. Not after that day in the woods.

"Let me see your hands," said Scott from the other side of the car.

Mason glanced at him, all smiles, then bent his arms at the elbow, lifting his hands to just above waist-height. "No problem, Officer." He gestured toward his cottage with his chin. "I live right over there. Mason Harper's the name. Greg can tell you."

"You live here?" asked Greg.

Mason lifted his hands, palms out, turning his easy smile back to Greg. "Sure. I inherited the place when my Gran died."

Greg felt Scott's gaze on the side of his face but didn't turn. He couldn't bring himself to let Mason out of his sight.

"What are you doing here, Greg? I never thought I'd see you back here…not after that night in '86."

For a nanosecond, a hungry—or perhaps greedy—expression showed on Mason's face, but then the mask snapped back into place. Greg crossed his arms.

"Well, whatever the reason, Preston Peters has been keeping the place in fine shape. You can move right in if that's what you want."

"Who is this guy, Greg?" asked Scott.

"He used to visit his grandmother during the summers. She lived next door." Greg shrugged. "I haven't seen him since I was eleven."

Mason watched the exchange with a small smile playing at the corners of his mouth. "Well, it was nice seeing you again, Greg, but I'm in the middle of something, so we can catch up later." He tossed a wink at Greg before turning to face Scott. "Okay if I lower my hands now, Officer? Okay if I go on with my business?"

Scott opened his mouth to answer, but before he could speak, the door to Mason's garage slammed open.

26

Nicole swooped in for a landing in the Town Hall parking lot, then swept through the lobby at a run. She rounded the corner into the Police Department and swept the HK 417 she'd assembled and oiled—the only one ready to go—off her desk. She spun and reversed her course out of the building, ignoring the questions thrown at her by her officers and Sally McBride.

In the parking lot, she turned and ran around the side of the building, where, in relative privacy, she adjusted her visage to that of a sparrow and leaped into the air, heading west at her best speed.

27

Tom Walton tumbled out of the garage, a thin trickle of blood sliding down his neck from behind his ear. "You'll have to do better than that blackjack, Mason Harper," wheezed Tom.

Mason whirled toward him, an expression of rage settling on his features like a well-worn glove. He took a single step toward the old man.

"No, you freeze right there!" snapped Scott, drawing his Glock 37. "And get your hands back up!"

Mason stopped and bent his arms at the elbows, lifting his hands out to the side. "Listen, Officer, there's been a mix-up here. Old Tom slipped and hit his head on his car. I was moving him to my van to run him in to Genosgwa and get him help when you pulled around the curve."

"That's a lie!" Tom sagged against the doorframe and touched a spot on the back of his head, wincing in pain as he did so. His fingers came away bloody. "The bastard cold-cocked me."

"Tom, listen, you *know* me. I wouldn't—"

"Save it, Harper!" snapped Tom. "I *do* know you, and truth be told, I've always thought there was something wrong with you. That woman handcuffed in the back of your van told me what that something is."

"Abaddon," murmured Scott.

Greg twisted his head to the side, staring at Scott. "What's that?"

Scott slipped his finger inside the Glock's guard and rested it on the trigger. "Everyone back off."

Mason cocked his head and turned to glance at Scott, a lopsided grin on his face. "Officer, I don't know who you believe me to be, but—"

"You freeze right there!" snapped Scott.

Mason lifted his hands to shoulder height. "Whatever you say." His expression didn't change, but his eyes hardened.

"You a cop?" asked Tom.

"Trooper. BCI," said Scott. "Is he who I think he is?"

"I'd stake my thirty-three years as a cop that he is."

Mason chuckled, but a thin line appeared between his brows. "I don't get what you two imagine you know about me, but let me assure you—"

"Shut up," said Scott. "Down on the ground."

Mason twisted his face toward Greg. "Tell them I'm harmless, Greggy. Tell your friend to back off."

But Greg wasn't looking at him. His attention was on a bird hanging in the air above his lake house.

28

Dan Delo's gaze grazed across the tableau before him. The old man in the door stared at Brigitta's pet killer, as did the man pointing a gun at him. One of the men from the car's back seat had circled around to do something in the trunk, and the woman from the library just stood there, as if she didn't know what to do. The other man from the front of the Cadillac lifted his gaze from Brigitta's pet and turned to stare at Dan. The last occupant of the car leaned against the rear, head bowed. There was something familiar about how he stood…

"You!" Dan bellowed.

29

"You!" a voice boomed from the air above them. The cop with the gun twisted his head to look, and the moment he did, Mason dropped his hands and sprinted for the woods.

"He's getting away!" screeched the woman from the Cadillac.

Mason ran between the two garages, breaking the cop's line of sight. He kept his head down, not sparing a glance at old Tom Walton. He wanted all the speed he could muster. *If I can get to the woods on the other side of Lake Circle, I'm home free,* he thought. *Tom's a known quantity. I can always come back for a visit.* Despite the circumstances, he giggled.

"No, he's not," said a voice to his right.

A voice that was far too close, almost within arm's reach.

Mason darted a glance to the right, and something thumped into his chest and broke, spilling something wet across his chest. The guy with the beard stood behind the Canton's garage holding a paintball gun and smiling at Mason. His chest felt hot—like he'd spilled his coffee on his shirt, but he didn't have time to think about it.

A paintball gun? Mason wondered. *What the hell*?

He continued to run, drawing deep breaths of air to fuel his muscles. A sudden wooziness overcame him, and his legs turned leaden. He stumbled once and recovered, but the second time he fell and couldn't get up.

30

Dan Delo darted a glance at Brigitta's pet and watched him crumple to the ground. *LaBouche said to protect this mortal at all costs. Brigitta puts stock in this…this killer of other humans, but* why *is beyond me. These others…these hunters, are they not a priority, too*?

He hesitated, flew toward the fallen human for a few wingbeats, then paused again, looking back at the Cadillac. The man leaning against the car looked around, then up at Dan Delo, an expression of confusion on his face. Dan dropped his visage, letting the man see his real features, and the man smiled.

He smiled!

With an incoherent roar, Dan Delo swooped over the house and down toward the man, feet first, talons extended. Still grinning, the man he'd stomped on up north dove into the back seat of the car, and the other man from the library stepped from behind the car, raising a shotgun.

Dan Delo veered away, but not fast enough.

The shotgun boomed, and burning pain ripped through his left side. Another cannon-like boom sounded behind him as he dove behind the lake house, and something tugged at the tender membrane of his right wing. Pain blossomed from the point of impact, and Dan Delo shrieked in both pain and fury. *Why do they always shoot at my wings*?

31

Nicole Conrau swept in from the east, skimming across the lake's wind-ruffled surface, the HK 417 held at port arms. As she neared her destination, a purple-winged demon dove behind the house, accompanied by the sound of gunfire.

Without slowing, Nicole veered to the south, staying as low as she could, angling toward the last house in the string of homes dotting the shore.

32

Tom followed Mason Harper's run with his eyes and watched the bearded man step out and shoot him with a paintball gun. Then the shotgun sounded and out of instinct, Tom ducked back inside the garage, but he moved too fast and almost fell. He leaned against the wall, eyes pressed closed, sucking in long, steady breaths, waiting for the dizziness to pass.

When he opened his eyes, a gorgeous brunette stood in the door. "Are you all right?" she asked.

Tom nodded. "Who are you?"

"You said there was another woman in here?" She glanced at Harper's van. "In the van?"

"Who are you?" Tom repeated.

"Shannon. Shannon Bertram."

The name struck Tom as familiar, but he couldn't place it. "Why do I know that name?"

"Oneka Falls," she said, walking toward the van.

Tom gasped. "One of the survivors…"

"That's right. The other two are outside."

"Who's shooting? And at what?"

Shannon shook her head. "That's hard to explain. Let's get this woman out of here."

Tom shook his head. "Van's locked up tight. I expect Mason Harper has the keys."

An expression of intense concentration flitted across Shannon's face. "Okay. They'll be here in a second."

"What do you—"

The bearded man stepped in front of the door and tossed a key fob at Shannon's back.

"Look out—" Tom began, but the woman spun before he finished and snatched the key fob out of the air as if performing a well-rehearsed carnival trick.

The van's horn blipped, and the locks *thunked* open. "You said you were a cop," said Shannon. "Do you have handcuff keys?"

"What?" asked Tom, staring at her as though she had an extra set of arms.

"Do you have a key for her handcuffs?"

Absently, Tom patted his front pockets.

33

Toby sprinted to the side of the yellow and white cabin, and Scott moved to cover the area between the two garages. "Get down, Greg!"

Greg stood in the middle of the road, staring at the roofline of his lake house, mouth hanging open. Mike slid to the other side of the car and stuck his head out. "Come on, Greg. Back here with me."

Greg turned as though in a dream and plodded back to the rear door of the car. He shook his head but dropped into the back seat.

Toby nodded to himself and ran the width of the lake house in a running crouch, his eyes bouncing between the roofline and the corner of the house. He had five more rounds in the shotgun and however many he'd shoved into his front pocket. The big purple bastard from the other night had found them somehow—*again*—and the paintballs had no effect against him. *I wish we'd thought to send Greg for the tranquilizer rifle before we left Rochester*! He grimaced. *And if wishes were fishes…*

He slowed as he approached the corner, twitching the barrel of the shotgun back and forth between the house and the trees in the yard, between the house and the lakeshore. The sun winked off something down the shoreline to the south, but Toby didn't catch what made the reflection.

A large stump stood about fifteen feet from the side of the house, and it would offer a hiding place that had a good angle on the backyard, but getting there would mean exposing himself. He stole a glance back at the car, hoping to see Greg looking his direction. Maybe the man would point out the big purple bastard's hiding place, but Greg stared straight ahead.

Shock, thought Toby. *Can't blame him, I guess.*

34

Nicole reached the last house in the line and flew into the woods that looped around its southern side. She flew at the level of the treetops, flitting and swerving between them as if she were born to it.

She stretched her senses, trying to figure out what the hell was going on, but the shotgun blasts stopped after the first two, and that big purple idiot stopped his screaming. An unnatural silence choked the woods—everything within hiding out and waiting for the next shoe to drop.

Why is Dan Delo here? Did Brigitta send him as backup? If so, how did he get here before me?

She slowed as she approached the area opposite the cottage Brigitta had sent her to find. The cottage where Brigitta's pet killer lived. She didn't descend to the ground, however. Instead, she hugged close to the boughs of a giant ash tree and peered east.

35

Mason Harper lay in the grass just beyond the two garages, Benny standing over him with a paintball gun. Scott hadn't seen him break away from the car, but after a moment, he realized Shannon had hidden Benny's movements—from Mason and from everyone else, so no one gave him away by glancing at him as he moved. Benny looked at him and bobbed his head.

Scott nodded back, content to let Benny keep the man under with the chloroform pellets, and turned toward the lake. A concrete path led from the gravel road between the houses.

He sneaked down the path, eyes dancing, trying to see everywhere at the same time. Scott held his pistol in a two-handed grip, covering the space between the houses.

He'd made it half the length of the house when someone leaped on him from the roof. The man looked like a rail-thin nerd from the IT department, but he had the strength of a powerlifter.

Scott lost his hold on his pistol, and the Glock went skidding down the concrete path toward the lake. A fist cracked into his cheek, and a red blossom of pain blinded him. Hands grabbed him by the shoulders and jerked him to the side. Scott swung blind but hit nothing.

When his vision cleared, he hung ten feet off the ground, ascending toward the thick green treetop. The "hands" that gripped his shoulder were large purple feet equipped with long black talons that pierced Scott's skin below his collarbones.

He looked away, nausea swirling in his guts from the shock and the sight of those talons punched through his skin. Toby crouched at the other corner of the house, the Remington at his shoulder, aimed at the purple demon carrying Scott to the top of the tree.

36

"Drive faster, idiot!" Chaz roared from the back seat.

Ricky Fast, the demon driving the Oneka Falls Police car that had, until recently, belonged to Mike Richards, grunted and glanced at him in the rearview mirror. "This car sucks."

Chaz rolled his eyes. "If Brigitta is unhappy with our tardiness, you can bet she will know who is to blame."

"Whoever set the police department budget over the past decade is to blame," said Ricky, but he pushed the car harder, nonetheless.

"Fine, fine. The next budget will include new vehicles...*if* there is another budget." Chaz leaned forward. "Follow what I did there, Ricky?"

Ricky grinned with half his mouth and flicked on the lights and siren, pushing the wheezing '94 Chevy Caprice up to one hundred miles an hour. "Hope the tires don't blow," he muttered.

37

Benny paced back and forth between Mason Harper's unconscious form and the door to his garage. He kept shifting the paintball gun from hand to hand, position to position, as though he weren't sure what to do with it now that Mason was out. Every few minutes, he sent a paintball into the dirt next to Harper's face to keep him unconscious.

Shannon was busy with Harper's intended victim, and the old police chief was helping her. Toby had gone around the side of the house, and Mike and Greg were hunched down in the back of the Cadillac. Benny nodded when Scott looked his way, and Scott returned the nod before heading toward the lake on the narrow concrete path.

Benny watched him for a moment, then turned to scan the woods again. Something felt…*off*…but he couldn't put his finger on what. A vague tickle lurked in the back of his mind, something he should recognize, but the memory eluded him. He turned back toward Scott just as the man who looked like an insane IT geek leaped at him from the roof. "Scott! Look out!" Benny yelled, but Scott didn't react, and then it was too late to do anything.

Benny ran three steps toward him, but something went buzzing by his head. The sense of wrongness in the woods doubled, and time seemed to slow. The gravel at the far edge of the road exploded upward, and Benny stopped dead in his tracks, looking at the divot, captivated by deja vu. He cocked his head to the side, and a burning pain lanced across his cheek, followed by another explosion of gravel and another divot.

"Benny!" shouted Greg from the Cadillac.

Benny glanced his way as he ducked to the side. Greg pointed at the woods behind Benny. He turned, and the memory came rushing back—the day Mike, Paul, and he had played commando in the woods behind his Oneka Falls home, the day Owen Gray had taken a shot at him from up in a tree. The memory rippled with the same sense of wrongness, the same vague sense of danger. His gaze zipped upward, to the boughs of the trees lining the edge of the woods.

He saw her just in time—a sable-haired woman dressed in a black leather miniskirt, a red silk top, and red stiletto pumps—impossible clothing for climbing trees. Benny threw himself to the ground, tucking and rolling as he hit. He kept moving until the Canton garage separated him from the woods. He heard two more bullets go buzzing past him as he rolled.

Shannon! I need you! he sent.

She appeared in the door of Harper's garage a moment later and made as if to come to him.

No! Stay under cover!

What is it?

He hooked his thumb toward the woods. *Woman up in a tree wearing stilettos and a leather miniskirt.*

Understanding washed over Shannon's features, followed by an expression of intense concentration. *Okay,* she sent after a moment. *You are invisible. Let's see how she likes a dose of her own medicine.*

Can you keep it going?

Shannon nodded but made no other response.

Benny got up and walked to the other side of the garage. He squatted and ducked around the corner, duck-walking toward the back of the garage. He paused, listening with all he had and scanning the trees where he'd seen the woman. She was still there, still focused on the area between the two garages, her eye pressed to the optics atop a wicked-looking assault rifle.

Benny lifted his arm and waved—wanting to make sure she couldn't see him. When she didn't respond, he sprinted to the edge of the trees, and she reacted to that, but only by turning her head and staring at the back of the garage.

Too loud, he thought. From that point on, he slowed down and moved with care, avoiding anything that would make a racket. He approached the tree she hid in and looked for a way to climb into its crown.

38

Toby approached the tree Scott and the purple demon had disappeared into and tried to climb it while keeping the shotgun ready to use. From above, came the sounds of a fight: grunting, gasping, the sound of fists on flesh. Scott didn't stand much of a chance against the muscle-bound brute that had grabbed him, and Toby knew time was short.

"Dammit!" he muttered. He wedged the Remington into the crook of a branch against the trunk and swung himself up into the tree using another branch. He climbed for a moment, then fished the shotgun up and found another place to wedge it so he could climb again.

39

Chaz worried and fretted in the back seat. Ricky Fast didn't live up to his name in Chaz's opinion. But Nicole's safety bothered him more than Brigitta's wrath—regardless of what he said to Ricky.

That's stupid, he thought. *She seduced you to get you in trouble with Brigitta, you idiot.* He recognized the truth of the thought, but… *It's been so long since I had a mate.* He shook his head, lip curled in disgust at his own weak thoughts.

"Hurry!" he snapped, slapping the seat between them. "Get me there! Get me there now!"

40

Benny climbed in silence, channeling every ninja movie he'd ever watched back in the 1980s, sneaking up on the woman in the tree. He wanted to get as close as possible for the first shot. He didn't want to risk a miss, or, worse yet, give her time to think about how to avoid going night-night.

Above him, the tree creaked as she shifted position, and he peeked upward, expecting to meet her glowering gaze, but that didn't happen. Instead, she had leaned out and peered up toward the Cadillac.

He was close—too close to miss, even with his lousy aim. He glanced down at the paintball gun and moved the lever from single-fire to full-auto, wincing at the click. Positive she must've heard and would attack him the second he looked up, Benny leaned closer to the trunk, trying to shield himself with the base of two branches.

When he looked up, she hadn't moved, hadn't shifted her gaze away from the Cadillac.

Suppressing a sigh of relief, Benny took careful aim, recalling everything Scott had told him—aim for the center of mass, keep the burst short, squeeze the trigger instead of pulling it. He raised the paintball gun above his head, and despite holding it with both hands, it wavered and twitched. He steeled himself and squeezed the trigger.

The gun spat chloroform-laden paintballs on a stream of compressed carbon dioxide. The demon above him twitched at the sound, almost leaping out of the tree, and looked down at him between her legs. The paintballs smashed into her chest and neck, shattering on impact and delivering chloroform into her face.

Her eyes blazed for a moment. Something clattered down through the branches past Benny, but he didn't dare look away. Her human features faded away, replaced by a silver-skinned demoness with four arms and black hair. She opened her mouth and hissed at him, her scarlet tongue darting at the air.

Benny thought she would kill him, and fear paralyzed him—her predatory gaze trapping him, rendering him unable to turn away from her malachite eyes. The vermillion tongue flickered out between two tusks the color of sunbaked wheat and tasted the air like a snake's would again, and Benny closed his eyes and waited for the end.

I love you, Shannon!

41

Scott bled from too many places to count. The freak he fought had too many advantages: strength, reach, *fucking wings*, and bone-like armor. He was tiring, and each swing Scott threw had the potential of taking him right off the branch on which he huddled. He lashed out at the demon, but the big purple freak leaped off the branch and hovered for a moment before diving back and slamming a forearm into Scott's torso.

I'm going to die in this damn tree if I can't get it together! he thought. Toby was beneath him, climbing up to help, but even with the two of them to fight, Scott didn't think much of their chances.

Would it be so bad to die here? The notion came out of nowhere, and for a moment, Scott didn't recognize it as his own, but it was. *My family…gone. Becky and Jenny are dead, stolen from me by Lee.* He'd thought the idea of getting revenge on LaBouche was enough, the idea of fighting back against the evil that infested Oneka Falls, but…

"Get out of here, Toby!" he cried. "Get the others away."

The purple demon laughed and swooped in to deliver another blow—one that cracked Scott's ribs.

"Hang on," grunted Toby.

"No, listen! It's okay. Get everyone else away. You don't need me! I can keep him here…"

"I'm right here, you know," grated the purple demon. "We speak and understand your pathetic language."

"Fuck off," said Scott wearily. He peered down, trying to catch Toby's eye. Something buzzed into the tree below him, and Toby flew out of the tree and crashed into the lake, the Remington spinning down to smack the shoreline. In the distance, a rifle report cracked.

The demon laughed. "So much for the cavalry. I'll let you pick, human. Would you rather a bullet rip you from this tree or to jump under your own steam?" The demon veered away from the tree, giving the shooter a clear sightline.

Something buzzed through the air next to his head, and with it came a fierce desire to live. With only a single downward glance, Scott flung himself out of the tree and into the cold water below.

42

Dan Delo watched the human fall from the tree and laughed. He turned the laugh into a victory whoop and spun in midair, his gaze searching the trees for whoever had come to his aid. After a moment he saw her, Nicole Conrau, four-armed and silver-skinned. She held one of the new rifles in two of her hands, grasping the tree for support with the other two. She pointed the gun at the Cadillac and executed the two humans sitting in the back with a stream of bullets.

Dan loosed another whoop and flew toward Nicole. She glanced his direction and waved him off. Confused, he hovered above the lake house.

Dead humans lay outside the door of a garage across the gravel road: two women—one of whom was the tricksy one from the library—an old man, and a guy with a beard holding a paintball gun lying at the base of the tree Nicole inhabited. Beyond the two garages, another human stirred and groaned. Dan Delo stared at him—he looked just as LaBouche had described him. *Brigitta's pet*, he thought. He drew his gaze upward, and for a moment, Nicole Conrau seemed frozen. Suspicions tickled the back of his mind, but the tricksy woman lay dead right in front of him.

When he looked at Nicole again, she grinned at him and pumped her fist in the air. He returned her salute. She held up a single finger and then brought the rifle to her shoulder once more and peered through its scope.

"No, no. What are you doing?" Dan murmured. He waved both hands over his head, but Nicole didn't see him.

She drew a bead on the head of Brigitta's pet killer.

"No!" he shouted, but he was too far away. *No*! he thought at her, but she either didn't receive his mental shout or ignored it. He beat his wings with all his strength and shot forward, trying to get her attention with his size, his movement, but her focus was absolute.

He was sure the shot would come before he could reach Mason Harper, but it did not. Without slowing, he grabbed the man with his feet and lifted him into the sky. He looked back once and shook his fist at Nicole's astonished face.

43

As soon as Dan Delo cleared out, Shannon let the illusions fade. Exhaustion rode her, and twin channels of blood ran from her nose. Benny stood by her side, lending her support, but even so, it was all she could do to stay on her feet.

"Would someone tell me what's going on now?" asked Tom Walton. "Have I lost my fool mind? How was that nerdy guy flying?" The memory of the strange trek through the woods tried to surface, but years of practice had enabled Tom to repress it without conscious thought.

"Better go get Toby and Scott," Shannon said. "I'm okay, now, Benny."

"I can call them."

"No, Scott seemed pretty torn up."

Benny looked at her for a few heartbeats before nodding.

"Ms. Bertram? What's going on around here?" asked Tom again.

"Chief Walton, we will explain everything, but if we do, there's no going back. And call me Shannon."

Tom stared at her, moving his jaw from side to side. "I don't understand, Shannon. Not any of this."

"I know. Do you know Mike Richards?"

"Chief Richards? From Oneka Falls? Sure, I do."

Shannon pointed at the Cadillac. "He's in the back seat, and he's hurt, but he might explain it to you better than I can. I…" She sighed and leaned against the wall. "I'm very, very tired."

Tom nodded once but didn't move. "Back in 1979…" He left the question unasked and just stood looking at her.

"Yes," Shannon said. "Back in 1979 is when all this…" She waved her hand to encompass everything they could see. "That's when all this started. The woods."

"Thousand Acre Wood?"

Shannon ducked her head and sighed.

"And Owen Gray?"

Shannon grinned a flat little smile. "He was a pawn, a distraction from the true thrust of events."

Tom took a deep breath and glanced toward the Cadillac. "I'm not sure I understand that."

"No," Shannon breathed. "The man who just went down to the lake?"

Tom nodded.

"That's Benny Cartwright. The guy with the shotgun is Toby Burton."

"Benny…" Tom put his hand out and steadied himself on the wall of the garage next to her.

"Go talk to Mike," Shannon mumbled. "We will explain as much as you want to hear, but please…I need to rest for a minute, and there's not much time."

His gaze crawled over her face, starting with her eyes, then dipping down to examine the blood flowing from her nose. "'Course," he said. He turned without another word and plodded toward the Cadillac.

Shannon sighed and leaned her head back. She let her eyes drift shut. Sleep tugged at her consciousness and fatigue toxins steeped in her blood. She slid down the wall until her butt hit the ground. She drew in a deep breath and held it.

44

Benny ran down to the beach. Toby stood dripping water on the dock and peering up the concrete path to see who was coming, but Scott lay on the ground. He lay with his feet in the water, his waist crossing the invisible line that separated the yard from the beach. His breathing rasped in his chest, and his eyes were closed, but he was alive.

"Hey, Benny," said Toby.

"Benny? What the hell, man?" asked Scott. "Why didn't you warn me about the fake shooter, the fake bullets?"

"Sorry. No time, and I wasn't with Shannon when she started, so I couldn't have told you anyway."

"No? Where the hell were you?"

Benny recounted the tale of stalking the silver four-armed demoness with the rifle. "I thought I was dead when she looked right at me, but then her eyes rolled up, and she went down through the branches. The chloroform put her down. I did it just like you told me to: center of mass, squeeze the trigger, short bursts."

Scott groaned. "Shannon could have made it appear I got shot without me jumping fifteen feet into cold water with broken ribs."

"Sorry," said Benny. "We were working against the clock."

"Yeah, it's all we seem to do these days," Scott sighed. "Help me." He held one hand straight up in the air. Toby and Benny both helped him to his feet. "Where's the purple bastard?"

"We tricked him into leaving."

Scott raised an eyebrow.

"We made him think the silver demon would kill Mason Harper, and the purple demon picked him up and flew away with him."

Scott made a face. "Tell me you're joking!"

"No. It was the only way we could think of to get the big purple bastard to leave."

"Pretty sure you just let a serial killer loose on the world," said Scott.

"But you know who he is. You can tell the State Police and—"

"That may be true, but who the hell knows where that walking steroid advertisement took him? How can we find him again?" Scott scoffed and shook his head. "How did you know Abaddon was important to Barney, anyway?"

"Barney?" asked Benny.

"It's a kids' show. Barney is a big purple dinosaur."

"Oh, I get it. Because of the purple, right?" Benny nodded to himself. "Anyway, we didn't *know* Harper was important, but before the purp—before *Barney* attacked the car, he flew toward Harper. He kept darting glances at him, and he appeared at his house…" Benny shrugged. "It just seemed to make sense. So, I scanned Barney to—"

At the sound of the racing engine, all three of them turned toward the gravel road.

45

Shannon startled awake to the sound of a roaring V8 coming up the road. *What now*? She opened her eyes to see Tom Walton and Greg Canton running toward her with Mike strung between them. Greg's eyes were wide with panic.

"Two more!" he cried. "Two more coming up the road."

Shannon waved them into the garage, then stepped out to get a better view of the bend in the road. *Who would they be looking for*? *Who should greet them*?

Toby and Benny came up the concrete path, supporting Scott between them. She held up a hand. *Stop*! she sent to Benny. *Can you tell who is coming*? *Can you read them*?

Benny motioned toward the wall of the Canton house and ducked under Scott's arm. He closed his eyes and held his hand out toward the bend in the road.

Chaz Welsh and someone calling himself Ricky Fast. They're in Mike's old cop car.

What should I show them? *How do I make them leave*?

Benny smiled. *Don't worry, Shan. I know just what to do.*

46

"Hurry!" Chaz urged.

Ricky grunted and kept his attention on the road ahead. The old Caprice wasn't happy with the gravel surface, and the car kept trying to slide off into the cottonwoods lining the lane. As they approached the bend, Mike Richards stepped into their path and raised a shotgun. "Hold on!" shouted Ricky, twisting the wheel.

"Fuck that! Get him!" roared Chaz.

The Caprice slid in the gravel, trying to spin, but Ricky held it, turning into the slide. He pointed the car right at Richards and floored it. As the car shot right through him, Ricky screamed. For a split second, Chaz knew they were in trouble, then the Caprice slammed into a tree, bounced off, and slewed across the road. It hit a downed log and rolled over with an ear-splitting crash.

When the car came to rest on its side, Chaz bunched his legs and exploded up through the door above his head. Warm blood trickled into his eye, but he ignored it.

They are here already! he thought. *Why are the humans still free? Still* alive? He peered into the trees, but nothing moved, and no sound reached his ears. For a moment, he wondered if the crash had deafened him, but then he heard it.

"Chaz!" called Mike Richards in a lilting, mocking voice. "Want to play hide and seek, you stupid son of a bitch?"

Chaz turned his head, tracking the sound. It came from the big Cadillac parked near the road ahead. He roared and charged, moving with speed his bulk and strength belied. He ran with the help of his arms, swinging them in great arcs and shifting his weight forward while both fists were on the ground in a strange, three-part gait—leg, leg, arms.

He leaped to the back of the car, blowing both rear tires and crushing the sheet metal of the trunk lid. Without pausing, he flung himself into the air, twisting to land facing the open car door. He growled and ripped the door off its hinges, throwing it away.

But the car was empty.

Confused, Chaz took a step back and turned toward the car he'd arrived in. Ricky hadn't moved yet—maybe he couldn't. Chaz turned the other way, and when he did, four or five things snapped into his chest and neck, splattering something wet across his skin. After a moment, the fluid boiled.

Instinctively, he glanced down and took a deep breath of the chloroform. More paintballs burst against his skin, and their contents flashed into chloroform. Chaz tried to wipe it away, tried to turn and run, but it was too late for either method of escape.

When he fell, he crashed into the crushed back of the Cadillac, one arm smashing the tempered rear window.

47

"How long will they be out?" asked Shannon.

"Not long. We need to get out of here," said Toby. "How long has it been since you gassed the one in the tree?"

Benny shrugged. "Um, I don't know. Everything was—"

"Yeah, I understand. We need to get out of here," Toby repeated.

"How? Chaz crushed the car?"

"Pile in with me," said Tom. "I'll get you somewhere safe."

"You don't realize what you're offering," said Toby, shaking his head.

"My grandfather kept a car here," said Greg. He pointed at the garage behind him. "In the garage. I bet it still runs."

"If I know Preston Peters, it's in tiptop shape," said Tom.

“And we have the van,” said Shannon, holding up the keys.

“Wait just a damn minute,” said Scott. “What about these demons? Can’t we…” He glanced at Tom Walton. “Can’t we take them out?”

Toby turned to Greg and raised an eyebrow.

“I can try, but…”

“He doesn’t know what he did back at the hospital,” said Benny. “He acted on instinct, and the fire thing is something new, something he doesn’t understand yet.” Benny turned toward their new friend. “It’s okay, Greg. We’ll work on it.”

“But we—”

“Toby’s right. More demons are on the way here, right now,” said Greg.

“*Demons…*” muttered Walton.

“How many? We can get set up and—”

“Pick a car and get in it,” said Toby. “Grab everything you want out of the Cadillac. We won’t see it again.”

“Where will you go?” asked Tom.

“Listen, Chief, you’ve put yourself and your family in danger,” said Mike.

“Harper won’t—”

“Not from him, though I suspect he’s the serial killer called Abaddon,” said Scott. He looked at Shannon and Benny. “Has anyone told him?”

Mike nodded. “Part of it.”

Tom shook his head. "Someone needs to tell me *all* of it."

"We will, when there's time. By opposing this Harper guy, you're putting yourself on the radar of power…forces, Chief," said Toby. "You may be in danger." He sighed and shook his head. "Your family may be at risk."

Tom Walton turned a confused gaze on Mike, then shifted it to Scott. "That sounds…"

"I know how it sounds, Chief," said Scott. "But it's the god's honest truth. I know that all too well, though I wish I didn't."

Tom stared at him while he drew five breaths. Then, he nodded once. "I'll be careful, though I think you all might be crazy."

Greg Canton put his hand on Tom's shoulder. "Chief, do you remember me?"

Tom stared at him, his gaze flicking from one part of his face to the next. "Greg? Greg Canton?"

"The very one. You trusted a Canton once, trust another one now."

Tom gazed at him for a second, then bobbed his head again. "Right. I'll take the woman from the van. She's a victim and a witness against Harper. I'll take her to the State Police barracks. Make out a report on Harper."

Scott nodded. "Good. Tell them he's Abaddon. Tell them Scott Lewis says so."

Tom looked at each of them in turn, his eyes lingering on Toby, Benny, and Shannon. "You call me when you can. I have to know what this is about. I have to know what happened in Oneka Falls…what happened here. Call when you're safe." Without waiting for a reply, he turned, got in his car, and drove away.

They got the gear from the Cadillac and split the cargo between Mason's van and Joe Canton's '65 Goat. Benny put the fancy rifle the silver demoness had brought into the van with a self-satisfied smile. Greg, Mike, and Scott piled into the GTO.

Toby stuck his head in the passenger window. "It's time to get out of New York, at least for a few weeks. I have a place in Erie where we can rest and recuperate."

"What are we going to do? Turn tail and run?" asked Scott.

"For now. Unless you have a better idea?"

Scott closed his eyes and groaned. "We can't just leave these three demons to—"

"We need time, Scott. We need to rest, to recuperate. We need better equipment, better plans. Hell, we need more help."

"I've got an idea about that," said Greg. "But I'll tell you in Erie." He twisted the key, and the cherry red GTO fired up on the first try.

Toby grinned and ran to jump in the van.

Greg pulled the car out of the garage, the GTO's tires crunching on the gravel in that way he liked. He took a long look at the lake house, then sped toward Lake Circle.

48

Chaz groaned and shook his head. For a moment, he had no memory of what had happened, but then it all came rushing back. He snapped his eyes open and rolled onto his side, then pushed himself to his feet.

At the base of an ash tree five hundred yards away, something that looked like liquid mercury reflected sunlight at him, and he staggered toward Nicole, ignoring his unreliable balance and his aching head. Behind him, Ricky Fast groaned, but Chaz ignored him, too.

The Cadillac sat where Chaz had disabled it, but the other car had left, and the bay doors of both garages stood open, the garages themselves empty. *Brigitta will be so pleased*, he thought, and his face twisted to match the sourness of the thought.

He stumbled to where Nicole lay. One of her shorter arms lay at a wretched angle, and ochre blood pooled beneath it. Her vermillion tongue extended through her lips, lying between her golden tusks as if she were tasting the air for scent. He sank to his knees next to Nicole and pulled her head into his lap, caressing her silvery skin, taking care not to jostle her arm. "Don't worry," he crooned. "I'll take care of you."

The air behind him popped, and a warm wind rushed past. "You've failed me, Chaz," said Brigitta in a tone she might have used to order eggs for breakfast.

"I'm sorry," Chaz grated.

"Not as sorry as you will be," she said in the same tone. "Did they *all* escape?"

"I… I don't know."

Brigitta scoffed and walked toward him. "And Mason? Did you at least protect him?"

Chaz could only shrug. "They had a gas gun. They tricked Ricky and me into wrecking the car, and when I got out of the car—"

Brigitta laughed, and the sound of it chilled Chaz to the core.

"I'm sorry," he said again, his throat dry.

"*Anāku atta ašāpu. Ana ṣēr ikkānû qinnu akāšu. Anāku atta ašāpu ina irkalla*!"

"No!" he cried. The sound of tearing flesh filled his ears and pain blossomed at his core. He tried to spring to his feet, tried to run, to fight, but his extremities had already died, and he flopped to the side instead.

The agony built and built until he thought he'd go insane if it lasted a moment more, but it continued on and on, ratcheting ever upward, and the release of insanity was denied him. His joints dislocated, his bones shattered, his organs liquified and began to dissolve, but worst of all, his blood burned in his veins and flames licked at his brain from the inside. He screamed and screamed, and through it all, he heard Brigitta laughing.

Then everything went black and silent, and Chaz had one moment to revel in the lack of pain, the absence of torment.

But only one.

"Welcome home, child," boomed a voice, and the pain began again.

I hope you've enjoyed this continuing tale of Oneka Falls and are dying to see what happens next. Our Lady Chaos picks up where this novel leaves off and you can find it here: https://ehv4.us/4ourladychaos.

To be among the first to know what I'm up to and when the newest book I write goes live, please join my Readers' Group by visiting https://ehv4.us/join. Or follow me on BookBub by visiting my profile page there: https://ehv4.us/bbub. Or, if you prefer to stick to

Amazon, you may follow my author page: https://ehv4.us/amausa.

If you haven't already read my *A Rational Man* series, you can view all three books on Amazon (please note that if your local Amazon marketplace supports series pages for Kindle ebooks, all three links will point to it): Book 1: Wrath Child: https://ehv4.us/4wrathchild, Book 2: Black Bags: https://ehv4.us/4blackbags, and Book 3, Devils Dance: https://ehv4.us/4devilsdance. For my complete bibliography, please visit: https://ehv4.us/bib.

Books these days succeed or fail based on the strength of their reviews. I hope you will consider leaving a review—as an independent author, I could use your help. It's easy (I promise). You can leave your review by clicking on this link: https://ehv4.us/2revth.

AUTHOR'S NOTE

Written on the completion of Wrecker:

I've said it before, and I'll no doubt say it again. Finishing a book is a heady experience, and finishing *this* book is even more so.

2019 began with a bang for me—but not a good bang. It started with soreness in my upper thigh and rapidly progressed until I was dragging my left foot instead of picking it up to walk. I thought it was a bad case of bursitis, which goes along with rheumatoid arthritis like sunshine goes with summer. My doctor worried it was something worse. Guess who was right…

My sore leg turned out to be something called avascular necrosis of the femoral head, which, besides being a killer movie title, is a fancy phrase that means: "part of your femur just died." Scary shit, right?

I was given strict instructions not to bear any weight on my left leg. I was told bearing even a fraction of my weight could lead to a total collapse of my hip. Even scarier shit, right?

Then, things got bad. I ended up in a wheelchair for about nine weeks, and they were the worst weeks of my life. I remember writing a sort-of cheery post about not giving up and keeping right on writing. Yeah. The muscle spasms started soon after that, and I'm not talking about your garden variety muscle cramps. I don't even like to think about the pain. I ended up taking the max daily dose of a very strong narcotic, a potent muscle relaxer, and the most potent anti-spasm medicine available, and for a while, none of that worked.

Neither Melissa nor I remember February, and I don't think either of us got more than two hours of contiguous sleep. I remember trying to get out of bed, into the chair, and out of our bedroom without waking her—all while fighting a scream. I scared the begeebus out of RealSig™ when I got to the living room (the scream won). That was in late January (I think) and the next thing I remember was going to a surgeon in March.

Yeah, enough of that happy horse manure. I wanted to let you know why completing this novel felt so much better than the others, and that's why. It's another victory over Petunia (my Personal Monster™). It's another sharp pointy stick in Petunia's eye.

But more than that, the balms that members of my Readers Group and Launch Team on Facebook dropped on us were incredible. I can't thank you ladies and gents enough, and I don't think you'll ever know how your comments, messages, and emails helped to keep us sane.

Written on the completion of Black Swan:

I'm sitting here grinning. I just poked Petunia (the new, wimpy name for my Personal Monster™) in the eye again by finishing the rewrite of this story twelve seconds ago. Oh, as with the demons in Oneka Falls, my Personal Monster™ hasn't given up—in fact, he's been mounting quite an offense these days. But, like Benny, Toby, and Shannon, I have help, and I am meeting new helpers every day.

I love being an author. I love creating fun adventures for you to read (except editing, which I need to start in a few minutes), and I love hearing from you.

Life as an Indie Author can be extremely exciting, but it has its share of millstones and dips in the road. I love being able to get books to you on my own terms, at my own pace. If I'd elected to go the traditional route, I'd be publishing my second novel right about now, instead of my ninth (and the tenth soon!). I'm willing to put my shoulder to the wheel for that.

I read that a famous thriller author thanked thirty-one people, plus the standard "and everyone else I forgot," who made his latest book possible. That's a lot of people working to push out a book… My camp looks comparatively empty… Let's see, there's me and the ones I owe huge thanks to: Supergirl, Jackson W. Barnett, Paul Martin, Ryan Schwarz, and…

You.

You know what? That "you" there at the end makes that *other guy's* list look tiny. Thirty-one? Pshaw! I've got *thousands* of people to thank.

So:

Thank you, dear reader!

Have you ever noticed that every generic term for people who read an author's work pales compared to King's "Constant Reader?"

There's more to come in this tale. I know a lot of the story, but Mr. Story is still around breaking things. Let's find out what happens together!

ABOUT THE AUTHOR

Erik Henry Vick is an author who happens to be disabled by an autoimmune disease (also known as his Personal Monster™). He writes to hang on to the few remaining shreds of his sanity. His current favorite genres to write are dark fantasy and horror.

He lives in Western New York with his wife, Supergirl; their son; a Rottweiler named after a god of thunder; and two extremely psychotic cats. He fights his Personal Monster™ daily with humor, pain medicine, and funny T-shirts.

Erik has a B.A. in Psychology, an M.S.C.S., and a Ph.D. in Artificial Intelligence. He has worked as a criminal investigator for a state agency, a college professor, a C.T.O. for an international software company, and a video game developer.

He'd love to hear from you on social media:

- Blog: https://erikhenryvick.com
- Twitter: https://twitter.com/BerserkErik
- Facebook: https://fb.me/erikhenryvick
- Amazon author pages:
  - USA: https://ehv4.us/amausa
  - UK: https://ehv4.us/amauk
- Goodreads Author Page: https://ehv4.us/gr
- BookBub Author Profile: http://ehv4.us/bbub

Printed in Great Britain
by Amazon

39045144R00391